Rule #8: A man is a gentleman only if he is never otherwise.

He matched her tone, seeking steadiness. "Except perhaps in a stable," he admitted.

Her lashes flickered up. "We're in a stable now."

God help him. "That we are."

"Just one kiss," she whispered. "I promise I shan't bother you about it again."

Bother? Rather, enchant, torment, torture. Her lips and eyes and silken neck and perfect breasts beckoned.

Damn the rules.

Romances by **Katharine Ashe**

How a Lady
Weds a Rogue

Katharine Ashe

Member of Washington County Publishers

AVON BOOKS
An Imprint of HarperCollins*Publishers*
10 East 53rd Street
New York, New York 10022-5299

Copyright © 2012 by Katharine Brophy Dubois
ISBN 978-0-06-203189-1
www.avonromance.com 4970 7895 10/12

First Avon Books mass market printing: October 2012

Avon Trademark Reg. U.S. Pat. Off. and in Other Countries, Marca Registrada, Hecho en U.S.A.
HarperCollins® is a registered trademark of HarperCollins Publishers.

Printed in the U.S.A.

10 9 8 7 6 5 4 3 2 1

To Atlas and Idaho, my constant writing companions.
You warm my toes. You lay softly contented in the
sun that shines through my office window as though
sunshine is all you need. You make me play when I
foolishly imagine I must only work. And you remind me
every day that love can be unconditional.
Thank you for making me a better human.

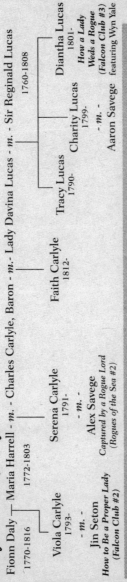

Carlyle-Lucas Family

Fionn Daly — *m.* — Maria Harrell — *m.* — Charles Carlyle, Baron — *m.* — Lady Davina Lucas — *m.* — Sir Reginald Lucas
1770-1816   1772-1803   1760-1808

Viola Carlyle
1793-
- *m.* -
Jin Seton
How to Be a Proper Lady
(Falcon Club #2)

Serena Carlyle
1791-
- *m.* -
Alex Savege
Captured by a Rogue Lord
(Rogues of the Sea #2)

Faith Carlyle
1812-

Tracy Lucas
1790-

Charity Lucas
1799-
- *m.* -
Aaron Savege

Diantha Lucas
1801-
**How a Lady
Weds a Rogue**
(Falcon Club #3)
featuring Wyn Yale

Savege Family

6th Earl of Savege — *m.* — Ellen Clemens — *m.* — Douglas Westcott, Lord Chamberlayne
1753-1810

Alex, 7th Earl of Savege, a.k.a. "Redstone"
1785-
- *m.* -
Serena Carlyle
Captured by a Rogue Lord
(Rogues of the Sea #2)

Aaron
1785-
- *m.* -
Charity Lucas

Kitty
1791-
- *m.* -
Leam, Earl of Blackwood
When a Scot Loves a Lady
(Falcon Club #1)

How a Lady
Weds a Rogue

Chapter 1

Fellow Subjects of Britain,

Scandal!

At night I lie abed, heart pounding, breaths short, and mourn England's ravagement. My soul cries and my frail feminine form aches to know that the Elite of Society to whom we all pay homage are stealing from our Kingdom to serve their profligate ways.

Stealing!

For three years now I have sought the identities of the members of the elusive Falcon Club, a gentleman's leisure establishment that regularly receives funds from the Treasury without due process in Parliament. Today I announce my greatest accomplishment in this quest: I have discovered the identity of one member. I have hired an assistant to follow this man and learn of his activities. When I possess reports that I can trust, I will convey them to you.

Until then, if you are reading this pamphlet, Mr. Peregrine, Secretary of the Falcon Club, know that I look forward to the day you and I meet face-to-face and I will tell you exactly what sort of man you truly are.

—Lady Justice

Lady Justice
In Care of Brittle & Sons, Printers
London

My dearest lady,

I am nearly breathless (as I daresay three-quarters of the men in London are now) imagining you at rest upon your cot, your breast filled with emotion, your lips trembling with feeling. I am moved by your devotion. And, like a cock released into the ring, I am roused by your eagerness to meet me in person.

But perhaps you have discovered not one of my fellow club members, but me. Perhaps I shan't be obliged to wait long for us to finally become acquainted. Perhaps my own nocturnal imaginings will soon rush from the realm of dreams into reality. I can only hope.

Increasingly yours,
Peregrine
Secretary, the Falcon Club

Peregrine,

> *Send Raven after Lady Priscilla.*
>
> —The Director

Sir,

> *I shall mince no words: You are making a mistake in this. England boasts no sharper intellect or finer natural instinct. I will send Raven after the beast, and he will go without quarrel. But with this insult you will have lost him.*
>
> Respectfully, &c.
Peregrine

Chapter 2

*M*ust . . . *get* . . . *to* . . . *the* . . . *stable*.

Somewhere in a chamber abovestairs a girl screamed.

Not a girl. A woman. Throaty voice, inebriated, a scream of pleasure. The girl's scream was in his head only. As always.

Get to the stable.

Rescue the lady.

Wyn pried his eyelids open. The parlor tilted. But he was standing. In a corner, against the wall. Nevertheless, standing. Far better situation than his host, who was lying unconscious over the threshold, bottle clutched in one hand, a woman's naked ankle clutched in the other. The remainder of the woman lay in the corridor beyond, similarly indisposed.

Wyn cast his gaze about the chamber strewn with glasses and smoke. A ruined neck cloth decorated a bookshelf, and a pair of ladies' stockings—*sans* lady—straddled the arms of a chair with suggestively vigorous intent. A snapped billiards cue protruded from a lamp top, and the butts of any number of cigars dug black holes in the carpet.

He squeezed his eyes shut. "Are we having fun yet?"

Then commenced the burning in his gut.

Ah. Awake a mere twenty seconds this time before the torture began; his most reliable nemesis had grown insistent of late. He'd no memory of eating since arriving at the country house three days earlier. Food quieted the torture in his belly. No time for that now. He'd been here too long already. If the others were in the same state as his host, he must take his leave with haste.

"Off to the races, then." Focusing on the doorway, he pushed away from the wall.

"Wha's that you say, Yale?"

Had he spoken aloud? Good God.

Carefully, so carefully, he shifted his gaze in the direction of the voice. He never hurried. Hurrying led to mistakes. Wyn Yale, agent of the Falcon Club and consummate gentleman from his sparkling boots to his neatly tied cravat, never made mistakes. He never fell. Never tripped. Never revealed a thing, not even when he could not make the sounds to pronounce his own name. Then he simply remained silent.

Pride did not drive this perfection. His father and elder brothers used to criticize him for his pride. They'd had no idea.

But apparently now he spoke aloud when he did not intend it. He was, perhaps, finally slipping. A shame. Rational precision was all he had left, after all, and of course the damned fireball that lived in his midsection.

"Wha' races?" The other guest sprawled on the divan, this one without a woman at present, perhaps due to his waistcoat soaked in wine. *Rule #3: Ladies expected a gentleman to maintain his accoutrements.* Even demireps. Wyn's great-aunt had insisted on that.

"Who's racing?" the slovenly gentleman slurred. "I'll lay ten guineas on you over any of'em. Clever son of a—"

"No race." With deliberate steps Wyn moved to the

sideboard and sloshed wine into a glass. Blinking hard to steady himself, he pivoted, carried the glass over, and curled the fellow's hand around it. Warm. Human sinew and flesh. Strange that he should notice this. But it had been an age since he'd felt another human's skin, touched another person. "Merely seeing to my horse."

The sot quaffed, dribbling wine from the corner of his mouth. "He's a pretty goer. Sell him?"

"No." Wyn had one loyal companion in addition to the burn in his gut: the sleek black thoroughbred in the stable that deserved a great deal better than him.

The man waved his hand, brushing away the refusal in that happy haze of alcohol saturation that Wyn himself had not experienced in years. Not happiness, no.

"S'just as well. Wife'd skin me alive if I spent that sort of blunt."

"Far better to spend it on drink and whores, of course," Wyn murmured, focusing on the door again. It tilted to one side, then the other.

"Din' know you had that sort of blunt either."

"Not lately, old chap." But he'd bought Galahad five years ago, before his funds ran dry.

The man slurped from the glass then again slumped into a snore. Wyn made his way over the prone bodies at the door and along the corridor. In the butler's closet he sought his coat. Had he brought a coat? The month? *September.*

He pulled his topcoat from a hook. Best to make certain it was his. He fished in the pocket for the one item he suspected only he would carry to a country bacchanalia. His fingers slipped around the knife's sheath. His pistol, of course, was still in the saddlebag. No need for a firearm at this sort of friendly gathering of wastrels. He'd brought it for the road, and because to be without it was to be a great fool.

For all his sins, he was not a great fool. Not even a minor one.

He left the house and the men and women inside locked in a revelry they all enjoyed because they knew nothing more satisfying, and made his way across the muddy drive. Within the stable all was damp straw and the musky warmth of horses. Galahad had his own stall because he deserved it, not because his temper did not allow for company; the thoroughbred was gelded, much like his master at this gathering—*temporarily*. No women while working. No drink usually either. But this assignment had called for it. Thus the horse's four eyes now. And four nostrils, and four ears.

Wyn reached for both of Galahad's muzzles, each satin black marked with a blaze. He grasped either side of the animal's face and the two heads became one. A quiet-natured fellow, Galahad did not protest.

"Can you bear her company, my friend?" Against the horse's coat, his breath was heavy with brandy. "She is very pretty, after all."

Galahad stared at him with eyes the color of earth and bumped his nose into his chest.

"You will do whatever is asked of you. We are a fine pair." He closed his eyes. "But I will soon do what I have not been asked to do. Then they will take you from me. They will take everything, but"—he dipped his voice to a whisper—"you will be all I regret losing." For a moment he stood still, the straw-littered floor bobbing beneath him. Then he set to saddling and bridling his horse.

Traveling bag slung across his haunches, Galahad followed him through the stable at his heels like a spaniel. They halted before another stall. The animal within shone like a jewel, from her tapered nose and intelligent eyes to powerful withers and silken brown coat.

Wyn bowed. "My lady, your escort has arrived." He opened the stall door.

Lady Priscilla, as prime a piece of horseflesh as could be bred, came without protest, young and light of hoof but biddable. Thus, no doubt, she had gone with Wyn's host after he won her at cards from Marquess McFee—unjustly, for she belonged to McFee's uncle, the Duke of Yarmouth.

Now the duke wanted his prized young hunter back. Who better for the job than Wyn? The crown knew that when it lifted its little finger to demand a service of Mr. Wyn Yale, penniless third son of a Welsh squire of little land and less wit, he would leap to it. And, of course, he did it because he enjoyed it. Rather, had enjoyed it. More lately he did it to keep himself in waistcoats and brandy.

But this job was different. He had not agreed to this humiliating task to please the anonymous director of the Falcon Club or the king. Not even for the sack of gold coins they would pay him. This assignment he had accepted to avenge a death.

A death for a death. One sin to cancel out another.

This time, however, he could not hide the truth of his deed from his friends—Leam Blackwood, Jin Seton, Constance Read, Colin Gray—all once fellow agents in the Falcon Club, the greatest friends a man could have. This time they would all know. This time the world would know.

The rain fell mizzling, sending mist up from the warm earth. But the sky was heavy and it would soon pour down. The filly's blanket would keep her dry. He took another blanket from the tack room and affixed it over Galahad's back.

"Now we are off to the races. As it were."

He set off along the foggy drive on foot, a lead line in either hand and hundreds of guineas worth of horseflesh following docilely behind. The gray day was still young, the walk to the village where a bottle and the Mail Coach could be found only a few miles distant. By the time he reached Yarmouth's castle two days hence, he would again be dry and suitably clad. In the meantime, to be sodden both without as well as within seemed suitable enough. Here in the middle of nowhere, in the company of none but beasts, for once he needn't even mimic perfection. And, after all, a man on his way to murder a duke ought to be allowed to enjoy the journey in whatever manner he liked.

In theory, her plan worked splendidly well.

In *theory*.

Diantha had not, of course, counted on the handsome farm boy. Thus she had not foreseen Annie's desertion. Neither had she anticipated the rain that soaked the hem of her traveling dress, or the man with the sausagelike fingers sitting in the opposite corner seat of the Mail Coach. The squalling infant in its mother's spindly arms was not an especial boon either. But at least the little bundle hadn't caused Diantha any real trouble, only a megrim the size of Devonshire, which actually had its start at the posting house when Annie gave abrupt notice with a "Best of luck to you, Miss Lucas!" thrown over her shoulder. So in truth the babe could not be blamed.

Naturally, from the comfort of Brennon Manor, Diantha could not have anticipated any of this, especially Annie's defection. Her best friend, Teresa Finch-Freeworth, adored her maid, and quite frankly Diantha had liked her too. Annie had seemed the ideal companion with whom to make her premature departure from Teresa's home under cover of propriety. Until Annie abandoned her.

Diantha pressed fingertips to temples. The megrim was worsening, but babies would cry, and she liked them quite a lot under normal circumstances. She had always dreamed of having children of her own, and Mr. H liked them. But she didn't have time to ponder that. Now she must find her mother and wrest her from the den of iniquity in which she was living.

Around the edge of her bonnet she darted a glance at Mr. Sausage Fingers. He scowled at the babe, jowls wiggling with the rough sway of the carriage.

"She is cutting her teeth, isn't she?" Diantha whispered to the mother. "My sister, Faith, cried buckets when her teeth were coming through."

"She won't stop, miss." The woman groaned softly, rocking the babe against a breast far too narrow to serve as a pillow.

"Poor dear. My mother used to rub our gums with brandy. Sometimes whiskey if Papa had already drunk up all the brandy. It is very soothing."

The woman looked skeptical and perhaps a bit scandalized. "Is it?"

"Oh, yes. Smugglers were so common on the coast, we'd no trouble finding brandy during the war." She tucked a gloved finger into the baby's hand. It latched on and the cries hiccupped. "At the next posting house, dip your finger into a cup of spirits and rub away. She will be asleep in no time." The infant's mouth opened again and out of it flew a banshee's howl. "Then drink the remainder of the cup yourself," Diantha said louder, to be heard over the din. She smiled and patted the woman's arm.

The mother's eyes softened. The babe wailed. Beneath the brim of his cap, Mr. Sausage Fingers was leering again. He had the look of a highwayman about him, if highwaymen had dirty fingernails and shifty eyes.

It was clear to Diantha now that Annie's elopement was incidental to her troubles. Men like this would populate the road all the way to Bristol and then probably the boat to Calais. The world was made of men, and some were villainous.

She knew this only vaguely, having been introduced at a young age to a nasty man named Mr. Baker to whom her mother had intended to wed her beautiful sister, Charity. Or some such thing. No one had ever told her anything in those days because she was too young *and susceptible*, they said, which meant that she was likely to get into scrapes if given rein. Now everybody was gone, so there was no one to tell her anything even though she had turned nineteen, with one exception: Teresa, whose stories were scandalously titillating and who had devised the plan for her current mission, which mustn't be thwarted even by a minor mishap like losing her traveling companion to a farm lad with large muscles in his arms. Annie had especially liked those muscles. She'd mentioned them before abandoning her, by way of justification it seemed.

Diantha hadn't any opinion of men's arms or muscles, but now she saw her plan's fatal flaw. She required a man. But not just any man. She needed a man of courage and honor who would assist her without question.

She needed a hero.

Diantha's stepsister, Serena, had often read to her stories of knights saving damsels in distress, and the Baron of Carlyle, her stepfather and a scholar, had assured her that these stories were not entirely fictional, rather based in historical fact. Heroes did exist. Now her mission was simply too perilous to undertake with only female assistance. A hero must be found.

In retrospect it all seemed quite obvious. *Of course* the plan Teresa devised had not included securing the assistance of a man. Teresa had never met a real hero. Her father barely ever looked at his women, and her brothers were most certainly not heroic; a fortnight ago all three of them had taken one look at Diantha and their eyes had gone positively feral. Since none of them had ever noticed her during her visits to Brennon Manor before, they could not be considered heroic.

Heroes cared for more than appearance. They cared about the heart.

The young mother shifted a bony hip, nudging Diantha's against the portly gentleman to her left. Intent upon his journal, he seemed not to notice. She gave him a quick glance and released a little breath of disappointment.

Too old. A hero ready to defend a lady from the likes

of highwaymen must be in the prime of his manhood. Otherwise he might not be able to wield a sword or pistol with sufficient vigor if necessary. This man had gray whiskers.

The carriage jolted. The baby bawled. The mother sobbed quietly.

"May I hold her? My sister is grown now and I miss cradling a babe in my arms." In truth, Faith had been a fidgety infant. But Diantha suspected God would forgive the fib. "Then you might have a nap before we come to the next stop."

"Oh, miss, I couldn't—"

"Of course you could. I will keep her quite safe while you rest." She tucked her arms around the infant and drew it close. Her traveling bag propped upon her lap made an excellent cushion, and she had more bosom than the babe's mother against which it could cuddle. The mother tucked the blanket around it.

"Thank you, miss. You're an angel."

"Not at all." That was the plain truth, of course.

She rocked the infant, liking its warm, heavy weight, and shifted her gaze across to the passenger whose knees nearly knocked with hers.

Not a man. Not more than thirteen and, by the look of his blackened fingertips and sallow complexion, a mine worker.

His cheeks flushed with two perfectly round red spots. He tugged on his cap. "Mum."

She smiled, and the flush spread down his rather dirty neck.

He would not do, of course. Boys could not be trusted with noble missions, even boys who went into holes in the earth every day to dig up metals for everyone else and so should be accounted heroes of a sort, if the world were quite fair about it.

That left only the man sleeping in the corner, the passenger who at the last stop had taken Annie's spot inside the coach.

The hem of his black topcoat dripped rain onto the floor around his shining black boots. His arms were crossed over his chest and a fine black silk hat dipped low over his brow. He was not a small man, rather tall and broad-shouldered, but seemed to fill the space he inhabited without undue discommodity to his fellow passengers. She could see only his hands, ungloved, and the lower half of his face.

Large, long-fingered, elegant hands, and a firm, clean-shaven jaw and nicely shaped mouth.

She blinked.

She slouched, dipped her head a bit, and peered beneath his hat brim.

Her breath caught.

She sat straight up. Beneath the soft weight of the crying swaddle, her heart pattered. She drew a steadying breath. Then another. She stole a second glance at him, longer this time.

Then she knew. In her deepest heart her final niggling doubts scattered and she knew she was meant to find her mother.

Her plan would not only work in theory. She had wished for a gentleman to assist her on her mission, and God or Providence or whoever it was that granted wishes to hopeful damsels was providing her with such a man. For if anyone could fill the role of a hero, she was certain it was this gentleman.

He was, after all, already hers.

A girl was staring at him.

It did not surprise Wyn, accustomed enough as he was to this sort of attention and not typically disturbed by it. But he'd had rather too much of it of late, although the females at the orgy he'd just left hadn't particularly resembled the girl in the coach's facing seat who now peered at him from the bluest set of wide eyes he had ever seen. Very, very blue eyes with big irises, like polished lapis lazuli, surrounded by long, dark lashes and surmounted by arched brows. Familiar eyes.

Unfamiliar girl, though. Even if he weren't half under the wagon he would remember this taking thing if he had encountered her before. The tilt of her delicate jaw, purse of her berry lips, and rampant rich chestnut curls peeking out from her bonnet were too pretty to forget. And, drunk or sober, Wyn never forgot anything, even girls who were not pretty like this one. Or men. Or villages. Or tree stumps. Or anything else. It was what made him so good at his work for the past ten years.

Her brows arched higher. "Are you finally awake, then?" she said, and he remembered her. Voices he also never forgot, especially not this voice, fresh and clear. "I thought you would never wake up," she continued without apparently requiring a response. "You know, I barely recognized you. You look absolutely terrible."

"Thank you, ma'am," he managed, without slurring of course. He would not mention that the lack of recognition had been mutual because she would certainly guess the reason for it. *Rule #4: Never bruise a lady's feelings.* A girl didn't make the sort of transformation in appearance that Miss Lucas had over the course of two years without a great deal of effort and the generous hand of Nature combined, and without being perfectly aware of the transformation herself.

Miss Lucas was not a doxy like the girls he'd gladly left behind yesterday. She was a gently bred female, the young stepsister of a lady he liked quite a lot who was married to a man who had helped him through the worst night of his life.

He rubbed thumb and forefinger into the corners of his eyes at the bridge of his nose, and looked anew.

A gently bred female . . . with a babe in her arms.

He glanced to either side of her. Neither the man to her left nor the woman to her right could remotely be considered husband or maid to this stepdaughter of a baron and sister to a baronet, never mind Wyn's slightly foggy vision. He craned his neck to his left. Neither of his seatmates suited either.

"I am traveling alone," she supplied helpfully. "Annie abandoned me for a strapping farm lad at the last stop. He was quite handsome, really, so I don't blame her. But she might have stayed until I found a replacement." She leaned forward and whispered, "I am *not* comfortable traveling alone, you see." She glanced meaningfully to the burly tradesman sharing his seat then sat back again. "But now that you are here, I am no longer alone." She smiled and a pair of dents formed in the soft cream of her cheeks.

Wyn blinked, momentarily clearing the fog. He recalled those dimples of the girl he'd met at the estate of the Earl of Savege in Devon. He did not, however, recall being unable to look away from them. But the previous posting house had only stocked gin, and the fruit of the juniper tended to muddle his senses.

Finally her words penetrated the Blue Ruin.

"Alone?" He directed his gaze at the squalling infant. It was a wonder he'd slept so profoundly. "The child's father remains at home?"

The dimples deepened. "I suppose he may. But I don't know actually, and cannot ask since her mother is sleeping and I haven't the heart to waken her." She lowered her voice. "Frankly, I am wildly curious. I cannot imagine taking to the road with an infant without assistance of some sort. Although . . ." Her brows lowered. "I mustn't throw stones, being bereft of assistance myself. Until now." Her berry lips flashed into a smile again and her vibrant gaze flickered up and down his person.

"At your service, ma'am." In the cramped quarters, in lieu of bowing, he tipped his hat.

Her smile brightened.

The fireball in his stomach danced an impatient jig. In present company he could not ask her meaning. He could not inquire of her direction, her intention, her program, or who exactly Annie was. He could not even speak her name. And he hoped dearly for her sake that she did not choose to provide him with any of this information voluntarily while sharing the coach with four strangers. But at the next posting house he would take her aside and learn what he must. Then he would return her to her family.

It was clear that Miss Lucas had run away from home. Fortunately for her, he was something of a specialist at returning runaway girls. *The* specialist in the crown's hire, the member of the Falcon Club—a small, secret organization dedicated to returning lost persons of distinction to their homes—with a special knack for corralling girls exactly like this one. Spoiled, willful, naïve, confident of their charms. Girls who could wrap people around their fingers through the sheer, mesmerizing force of their smiles.

She returned her attention to the babe in her arms. Wyn closed his eyes, sinking again into the gin lethargy, but discontent grated at him now. The filly must take second place to the girl. The Duke of Yarmouth must wait.

But there was no rush. No one would suspect anything amiss if he delayed. This assignment was obviously meant as a prelude to his mandatory retirement, a silent message that the crown no longer required his services. A final reprimand. The head agent of the Falcon Club, Viscount Colin Gray, had warned him: their director was concerned. Gray thought it was because of the brandy.

Wyn knew the truth. The director had not trusted him for five years, and it hadn't anything to do with brandy.

Now he would return Miss Lucas home, then the horse to its master, and his current existence would end in a blaze of ignominy. He folded his arms over his chest. The infant wailed. The coach bumped. Forgetful sleep came slowly.

Chapter 3

Mr. Yale awoke again only as the coach entered the posting inn's yard. He was the first to go out into the rain.

Diantha needed an enormous tea, a vigorous stretch, and then a good stroll. Her arms and shoulders ached fiercely from holding the babe.

Its mother pressed her hand. "Miss, you saved me today. You'll be in my prayers tonight."

"You would have done the same for me, I suspect." She smiled and upon wobbly knees pushed herself toward the door.

Standing by the step in the lowering light of the rainy evening, Mr. Yale offered his hand. It was perfectly silly that a tingle zigzagged about her stomach. But since she had only thrice in her life encountered a man who caused those sorts of tingles, and all three times they were him, it wasn't to be wondered at. A true hero was bound to have that sort of effect upon a lady.

She placed her gloved fingers on his palm and came

down the two steps to the drive awash in puddles, then looked up at him.

More tingles.

"Madam," he said quietly as she drew the hood of her cloak over her hair, "while I beg pardon for asking it of you, I hope you will accompany me now to the stable briefly while I see to my cattle." He gestured to a pair of horses tied to the rear of the coach. "In the absence of Annie, perhaps you will see the wisdom of not entering the inn without suitable escort." His gaze flickered to the coach's door where Mr. Sausage Fingers loomed.

"I do, sir. And I shan't mind accompanying you to the stable in the least."

"Excellent." He bowed, and now his gray eyes seemed to sparkle.

Really, his eyes were *silvery*. Black-haired and square-jawed, he was ridiculously handsome, even rather lean-cheeked as he was now. But from the first time she had seen him at a wedding at Savege Park, she had liked his silver eyes most of all. They rested upon a girl as though her every word and desire were his first concern, as though, in fact, he wished to read her mind to discover her desires rather than require her to make even the slightest effort to express them in words.

He'd done that the night of that wedding. He had read her thoughts and rescued her. He had been her hero.

He untethered the horses from the rear of the coach and drew them toward the archway leading behind the inn. A ragged little dog stood in the rain outside the stable door, watching as they passed inside.

"Look at that poor thing, all skin and bones, and favoring its forepaw. I think it is injured." She craned her neck but the stable hand pulled the door shut.

"Only a mongrel, miss."

"Someone ought to feed it. It's starving."

Mr. Yale cast her a curious glance, then turned to his task. He did not relinquish the horses into the hands of the stable hand, but saw to them himself then returned to her at the door.

"Thank you for your patience, Miss Lucas. How do you do?" He bowed so beautifully, as though he were encountering her in an elegant drawing room.

She curtsied. "Well, sir. Especially now."

"Have you luggage aboard the coach?"

"A traveling trunk and bandbox. Why?"

"Then our first order of business must be to retrieve it."

"Oh, I don't think that is necessary. The coach is bound to leave again shortly. It is only a dinner break and to change out the horses, I think."

"You will no doubt wish to dine?" He came forward and gestured her toward the door into the inn.

"I will. I am famished! I never quite realized how traveling the public coach encourages the appetite."

"Didn't you?"

"Oh, no. I hadn't planned on being so hungry at all, or I would have instructed Annie to pack a cold dinner before we left Brennon Manor." She walked before him through the door into warm air scented with roast and ale. The taprooms meandered over several attached chambers, all wood paneling and cozy crackling fires, a mix of farmers and villagers and the people from the coach clustered about the bar and at tables. Her stomach rumbled.

Mr. Yale took her cloak then pulled out for her a chair at a small table. A man wearing a starched apron appeared.

"What can I serve you, sir?"

"The lady will have whatever she desires, and I shall have a pint, an empty glass, and a bottle of Hennessy."

"Miss?"

"Whatever is best tonight, thank you." She smiled. "It smells wonderful!"

"My wife's roast and pudding, miss. Finest in the village."

"Well it isn't a very large village," she whispered when he'd left, "but no doubt I shall enjoy it. I could eat a horse at present. Not one of yours, of course. What beautiful animals you have, Mr. Yale!"

"Thank you, Miss Lucas." He did not sit. "I will return in a moment." He looked at her quite directly. "If you will remain at this table while I am gone, that would be best."

"I am so hungry, the farthest I would go is the kitchen."

He bowed and disappeared out the rear door again. She glanced at the bar where Mr. Sausage Fingers was again staring at her, then out the window at the rain.

By the time Mr. Yale returned, her food had arrived, and his drinks.

"Aren't you eating?"

"Not at this time." He poured from the bottle into a glass and drank the contents in one swallow. "But please do enjoy your dinner." He lifted his ale glass.

"Thank you." She tucked in. "It tastes even better than it smells. I barely ate a bite the entire fortnight I was at Brennon Manor, I was so excited about my journey."

"May I be so bold, Miss Lucas, as to inquire how you come to be traveling alone?"

"Teresa's maid Annie deserted me. We thought she would be terribly clever to have along, but we never expected her to decamp so swiftly, or frankly at all."

"I see. Teresa . . . ?"

"Finch-Freeworth. We attended the Bailey Academy for Young Ladies together for three years when my stepfather sent me there after the dismissal of my fourth governess. Miss Yarley, Head Mistress of the Bailey Academy, however, was splendid, so I never gave her trouble. Good heavens, this pudding is simply divine. Is the food at all posting inns so delicious?"

"Not all. As your stepfather's estate is in Devonshire, I am to understand Miss Finch-Freeworth's home, Brennon Manor, is in the North and that you have recently left there," he said without even a pause, which she liked. The night he'd rescued her at Savege Park he had also understood the entire situation with very little explanation.

"I departed quite early this morning."

"And what—" He paused. "Miss Lucas, pray forgive me for continuing to press you for details."

"Of course. Whyever not?"

He smiled slightly, the barest hint of amusement tilting up his mouth at one side. On the three occasions that he had visited Savege Park, her stepsister Serena's home, Diantha had seen him smile like that at her other stepsister, Viola, as well as at a veritable goddess, Lady Constance Read, a Scottish heiress with whom he seemed to be particular friends. But never at her, not even when he rescued her that night. Now that smile did strange things to her insides, somewhat pleasant and a bit alarming. *Warm* things.

"As I can imagine your stepfather would under normal circumstances send his carriage for you, what did he and Miss Finch-Freeworth's parents have to say of your journey undertaken by public coach?"

"Oh, they proved no hindrance. My stepfather does not know. As for Teresa's parents, Lady Finch-Freeworth is a soft woman without backbone and Sir Terrence couldn't care less what the females in his house do. I don't think he's ever noticed me, in fact."

His eyes took on a warm light that made her throat oddly tight. "I admit myself skeptical of that."

"But it's true. When we produced the letter from my stepfather, neither he nor Lady Finch-Freeworth blinked an eyelash. I did remarkably good work forging my stepfather's signature. I have a particular talent with a pen and wax, so it was quite satisfying, really."

"I daresay."

"What are you drinking?"

"Brandy. What, then, is your direction, Miss Lucas?"

"I've never seen a gentleman drink so much brandy in so few minutes, not since my father died. But my stepfather rarely drinks spirits and of course I don't know many other gentlemen, except my sisters' husbands and I suppose the curate, and naturally Mr. H. But that will change after I find my mother, go to town next month, and am introduced into society."

He set down his glass and said nothing but only looked at her with those silver eyes, carefully, it seemed. She felt studied, but not harshly. She felt *looked at*. Truly looked at. Not for her spots and fat, which she had sported in profusion until eighteen months ago, and not for her eyes, which her mother had insisted were her only fine feature. Mr. Yale seemed to look at something else. Her *insides*.

He finally said, "Who is Mr. H?"

"My future. At least that is the plan."

"I see. Then you are attempting to escape a betrothal?"

"Not at all. I will be as glad to end up with Mr. H as anybody. Or, well, perhaps not anybody. But you must know what I mean."

His slight smile came again, followed by the warmth in her midsection.

"Possibly," he only said.

The door banged open and a boy called out, "Shrewsbury Coach boarding!"

"Oh!" Diantha swiped a napkin across her mouth. "We should hurry, Mr. Yale. You must retrieve your hor—"

"Miss Lucas, do remain and finish your dinner." He did not move.

"But the coach is leaving." She stood. "There isn't time to—"

He rose to his feet and there was something shockingly intimate in the glimmer of his eyes as he looked down at her that rooted the soles of her practical traveling boots to the floor. He spoke quietly.

"Miss Lucas, it is not advisable for a lady to travel by

night on a public coach, with or without escort." His stance was so purposeful now, entirely unlike the unobtrusive man on the coach. She felt his command of the situation very oddly inside her, as she had felt his studying gaze.

"By which you mean Mr. Sausage Fingers may pose a threat to me."

"By which I mean that if you are wise you will not board another coach until the morning and instead enjoy a comfortable night's sleep here at this respectable inn."

She seemed to consider this, her brow furrowing delicately. Once more her gaze flickered up and down him, as a man might inspect a horse for purchase, and her berry lips twisted in that partial purse which was not unbecoming—rather the opposite, enhancing the bow and puffing out her lower lip.

"You cannot convince me that you would be unable to best him in a fight." She glanced at his shoulders, then his hands.

"The question is not whether I would be able to, Miss Lucas, but whether I would wish to place myself in the position of being required to."

"I see." Her gaze seemed fixed on his right hand, and a slight flush rose in her cheeks. "What have you done with your gloves, Mr. Yale?"

"I was obliged to discard them earlier today." A hedonist at the party had stubbed a burning cheroot into the palm of one of the gloves. Wyn particularly disliked that stain. "Will you sit?" He gestured to her dinner.

"I suppose I am tired and would appreciate a rest." Her brow unpleated and she turned her blue eyes upon him. "Will we hire rooms, then? I have never done so myself."

"It will be my greatest honor." He bowed.

She smiled, the dimples dipping her cheeks anew. Then her eyes widened. "Oh! My luggage!"

"I have taken the liberty of having it moved to a private chamber for you already."

"When you went out?" She blinked. "I may forgive you for not asking my permission to do so. Eventually. But I think you must have some experience traveling."

"Some." On several continents.

"So I will trust you about the folly of taking the coach at night." Her look grew sober. "But I do wish to get on with my quest as swiftly as possible." She sat, waited for him to do the same, and took up her fork again. "I haven't much time. I was only expected to be at Brennon Manor for four weeks, and two are already used up."

"Quest? Then, no scorned suitor to be avoided?"

She screwed up her brows, a look that suggested his question had lowered her opinion of his intelligence. "I already told you I am not running away from anybody. Rather, toward."

"Toward whom?"

"My mother." She peered at him closely. "Do you know about my mother?"

"Only that she does not reside in your stepfather's home and is no longer in society." And that she'd had something shadowy to do with a treasonous lord's hasty exile to the Continent years earlier. But that had been Leam's business, and at the time Wyn had his own demons to battle and little time to pursue his friends' interests.

Miss Lucas swallowed a mouthful of roast, her throat working above the unexceptionably modest neckline of her gown. It was a movement so mundane yet so enticingly feminine that he removed his attention from the sight to the bottle by his hand. The jittering thirst in his blood had relaxed with the first glass and disappeared entirely with the second. He poured a third. He never resorted to carrying a flask, but the last hour of the coach's swaying and rocking had driven his edginess unendurably high.

"She left four years ago, mere days before my fifteenth birthday." She took a sip of tea. "It had something to do with my elder sisters and my brother, Tracy, but I don't know precisely what, and everybody was glad to have her gone. She was not a nice person, if you will take my word for it."

"I shall, if you wish it."

She met his gaze for a moment, the lapis shining. "In any case, my stepfather never speaks of her now, nor does anyone else. It is as though she simply vanished into air."

"Remarkable," he murmured.

"*Isn't* it?"

It would be, perhaps, if his own history did not bear out the believability of such a thing. In over fourteen years, since the sudden death of his mother, Wyn had not seen or corresponded with his father and brothers.

"But I know she has not." Miss Lucas cut into her roast with greater force now. "When she first left, I asked after her. Papa—my stepfather—said she went off to live with relatives in the North." Her thick lashes darted up. "She has not. Or at least if she did then, she is no longer there. You see, several months ago I broke into my father's writing desk."

"How intrepid of you."

"Truly. I have done all sorts of wicked things in my life, things that made my governesses weep and pull out their hair, although not literally of course, except that once but really that was an accident. In any case, I have been troublesome, but I have never stolen anything. But she is my mother, and Papa will say nothing and frankly I am entitled to know something of her, don't you agree?"

"You must wish it quite sincerely."

"That was not an answer to my question, of course. I am not a hair-for-brains, Mr. Yale."

"I would never say so."

"And I didn't actually steal the letters. I only read them." Her slender brows cocked and a mischievous gleam flickered in the blue. "So I haven't sinned. Really."

The abrupt image of her actually sinning compelled him to reach for his glass again. "Where then is your mother?"

She set down her fork and a sweet smile slipped across her lips. "You are so refreshing to speak with, Mr. Yale. Papa never seems to know what I'm talking about and Mr. H allows me to go on and on without responding. But you are different. You seem to *know*."

Yes. He knew it would be to his advantage to put this girl on a northbound coach and wipe his hands of her as soon as possible. The innkeeper appeared by their table, saving Wyn from being obliged to willfully remove his attention once again from her pretty neck.

"My best two chambers are ready upstairs for you and your sister, sir, when you wish. Will you be taking supper, then?"

"Bring him the roast. He will be in heaven." She closed her berry lips around another forkful.

Wyn dragged his gaze away and stood. "My sister would like to retire directly. She is fatigued after the day's travel."

"But you really must eat some—"

"I will take supper in my room." He gestured her toward the stairs.

Upon the landing the innkeeper proffered him two keys. "This is for the lady's, sir, and this one is for yours there. I'll have the maid pop in to assist the lady now, and I'll send your supper up right straight."

"Thank you."

"Do thank your wife for her delicious roast and pudding, please, sir." Her smile sparkled.

The innkeeper beamed. "I'll do that, miss."

She watched after him down the hall. "I suppose it was a good idea for you to tell him I am your sister. But anyone can see we look nothing like one another." She met his gaze, her blue eyes clean and clear and without guile.

It was true. They were nothing alike, but far beyond the accidents of hair and features. She claimed to be wicked, but her face radiated honesty and goodwill. Her behavior mirrored it—taking the crying infant upon her lap for the afternoon's journey, and offering liberal praise for a simple meal. How a mother could leave such a daughter upon the threshold of womanhood, he hadn't an idea.

"Where is your mother, Miss Lucas?"

"Calais."

Intrepid, indeed. "You intend to cross the Channel after her?"

"Yes. She seems to be living with a dozen or so young women. She would have my father believe they are Catholic nuns and that she needs money to help them do handicrafts to sell at the market, which is why she wrote to him. But I am not so naïve as all that. I think she is running a school."

He measured his response. "A school?"

Her lips twisted. "No. I said that to see how you would react, and I am really quite impressed. Of course I shouldn't know about such things, but Teresa Finch-Freeworth is very helpful." She smiled, gently now. "But you would never reveal your shock over my impropriety. You are a true gentleman, Mr. Yale."

"Why hasn't your stepfather gone after her?"

"Because he does not care for her." Her gaze skittered away.

It was inconvenient. She was inconvenient, a pretty bundle of good intentions and old hurt, the latter which he could see quite plainly in her wide eyes no matter what she claimed. And now she had this indignity to bear of her mother's new profession, if it could be believed.

"Miss Lucas, I cannot allow you to continue on this journey."

Her gaze shot to him. "What?"

"I cannot—"

"No, no, I heard what you said. I am merely flabbergasted."

"I know not whether to be flattered or insulted by your surprise, ma'am."

"Oh. Of course. I beg your pardon, sir." She seemed to recall herself, and rather swiftly at that. She studied him for a moment, then released a little sigh. But she had no air of crestfallen disappointment about her, a look Wyn had seen on the faces of females often enough in his work over the past ten years. This was no doubt a game to her more than anything else. Perhaps she'd wished only to have a brief adventure and even now secretly welcomed his intervention.

"I suppose you have learned which coach will return me to my friend's house?" she asked quietly.

"It departs tomorrow at ten o'clock."

"There will be time for breakfast then. I do so dislike traveling on an empty stomach." Her voice had quieted.

"It is for the best, Miss Lucas."

She seemed thoughtful for a moment. "The public coach is uncomfortable. I might not have been able to bear it all the way to Bristol, anyway." She offered him a small sigh that lifted her breasts. "Well, then, good night, sir. Thank you for your assistance." She held out her hand, he placed the key in it, and she went inside.

Wyn returned to the taproom and the remainder of the bottle of brandy.

Diantha leaned up against the inside of her door, a peculiarly empty sensation in her stomach. Her gaze scanned the little bedchamber without interest. She had traveled so rarely, she should be charmed to bits over this turn of events: a night in a real posting house after the most scrumptious dinner possible, in the company of a true gentleman.

And now she knew where she had gone wrong again. Not her plan this time, but her notions of what a man could be.

A true gentleman could not be a hero. A true gentleman would, before all else, care for propriety and society's standards and—most importantly, *devastatingly*—a lady's welfare.

She was not a ninnyhammer, and only a ninnyhammer would fail to see that this journey was not in her welfare. She would be on the road for weeks without a proper chaperone and now not even a maid, and she would complete her travels at a French brothel. As a real gentleman, Mr. Yale had one recourse only: to escort her back to where she belonged. He could not be her hero. Not this time. On this occasion, gentleman and hero were incompatible.

She should descend to the taproom now and look about for another hero. There must be at least one among the crowd of farmers and villagers. Or she could take the next leg of her journey alone and hope to come across a hero along the road ahead.

The coach schedule affixed to the wall beside the front door had been easy enough to memorize while she was eating and explaining her quest to Mr. Yale. The Shrewsbury Coach would come through at quarter past five o'clock in the morning. She would be on it. She would find her mother and, finally, speak with her.

Diantha removed her outer garments and when the maid appeared she sent her away with a penny. Then she lay down on the soft little cot topped with the nicest quilt she'd seen and stared at the ceiling. The white paint was riddled with cracks, like her thinking on the matter of heroes.

The trouble was, it seemed to her that if any man could be a true hero, it would certainly be Mr. Yale. But perhaps there were no such paragons of epic honor and nobility in the present era. There was no such thing, after all, as the sort of love all those old stories described, the sort between a man and a woman who fell into the most sublime devotion and lived happily ever after. Both of her mother's marriages proved that to be a myth, not to mention Lady Finch-Freeworth and Sir Terrence's tepid alliance. It was true that her sister and stepsisters seemed content with their husbands, but there were a lot of money and carriages and houses involved. For pity's sake, Serena was now a countess, so of course she was happy.

But their brother, Tracy, avoided marriage, and Diantha couldn't doubt why. True love was a fiction of legends. And so too heroes must be.

She closed her eyes and tried not to think about the handsome man she would be leaving behind who was—however wonderful—only a man, after all.

Chapter 4

By eleven o'clock Wyn could nearly see the bottom of the bottle. This was not due to his excellent vision.

The taproom was still crowded, the inn the favorite local haunt of townsfolk and farm laborers celebrating the end of the harvest. Too much festivity for his tastes at present. Pushing the last of the brandy away, he pressed to his feet and wove his way through tables of boisterous men to the door to the mews. The horses must be checked. Bedding must be dry. The stall must be mucked—even by him, if need be. He'd done it plenty of times before he'd even had a horse of his own.

The night without was black, a single lamp illuminating the entrance to the stable. He crossed the pebbly drive, boots splashing, and slid open the door. He stepped inside and closed the panel, shutting out the muffled sounds of merriment in the inn and the light from the drive.

Not a yard away, a breath hitched in the darkness. A light sound, and high.

And then she cast herself at him.

She was perfectly curved where his hands met and

clasped her waist, and quivering. Her breaths came fast against his chin.

Then he did what he would not have done if he had not consumed an inch shy of the contents of a bottle of brandy in the course of three hours, or if he had employed all his senses at that moment, not only his starved sense of touch—for instance, his sense of smell, which would have told him that he did not hold a barmaid in his hands: He pulled her against him. What else did a wench intend of a man deep in his cups when she threw herself at him in the dark so close upon midnight?

She gasped and stiffened. Then she pressed her cheek to his jaw and breathed, *"Help me."*

If not for the lurching crash that sounded down the row of stalls, and the rough curse from that direction, Wyn would have behaved quite differently at this moment as well, even deep in his cups.

He did not release Miss Lucas, though every corner of his muddled mind shouted at him to do so. Instead he turned to shield her with his body, pressed her back against the wall, and whispered into her ear, "Put your arms about me and be still."

She obeyed. It took no effort to hold her and ready his stance at once. She was soft, and now that he had engaged all his senses—*God she smelled good*—and he was more accustomed to being at a ready stance than not. He drew up the hood of her cloak and his hand brushed curls silky as butter.

Heavy footsteps advanced.

"Where are you, my pretty poppy?" a thick voice slurred. "Come out like a good girl, or I'll be none too happy when I find you."

Miss Lucas's body gave a little shudder. Wyn bent his head, hiding her more fully in case the man's vision should be accustomed to the dark. He could confront him, but the tread suggested a large fellow, and Wyn was admittedly not at his best with a quart of brandy beneath his belt and no food for days.

The footsteps shuffled on the straw and came to a halt. "What's this?" A pause. "Oh, beg pardon, old chap. Just looking for my own bit of skirt, don't you know."

"Sod off, 'old chap.'" Wyn had no trouble roughening his voice. The caress of her tender earlobe across his lips had rendered his throat a desert.

The man muttered and clomped to the door, slid it open, then threw it shut behind him.

She ejected a relieved sigh and her fingers loosened their grip on his back. But Wyn did not release his captive. The brandy in his veins would not allow it. Her soft breasts pressed into his chest and her scent tangled in his murky head. With the danger passed, now he felt the woman in his arms, her warm, slight body that yielded so easily to his, so naturally. He shifted his hands, slipping them down her back, the long, graceful sweep of her spine beneath his fingertips like the rounded rocks upon the floor of a brook, and he felt woman. *Woman*, young and soft and beautiful and alive, her pulse thrumming through her trembling body.

She sucked in breath again and shifted in his hold to push him away. But he was not finished. He held her firmly, the blood rushing in his ears like wind as he curved his palm over the arc of a perfect, feminine buttock.

"Mr. *Yale*," she whispered upon a gasp. "You must *stop*."

Because even a bottle of brandy could not topple what years of training had built, he put her off and stepped back. It was no less dim in the stable, but his eyes had accommodated the dark, and he saw her. He smelled her and heard her, her light, quick breaths amidst the shiftings and snorts of the animals.

It had become something of a challenge to stand; he leaned against a stall door.

"What, pray tell, Miss Lucas"—he formed the words carefully—"are you doing in this stable?"

"Hiding from him. But he found me. Just—Just as you did." Her voice was thinner than earlier, and rushed.

"Forgive my ill manners, ma'am. At present I am somewhat—"

"Foxed."

"—indisposed."

"Teresa said men in their cups can be amorous even when they do not intend it."

He had intended it. And he wished it still. Her warmth clung to the palms of his hands and his chest, the memory of her softness upon his lips tightening his breeches.

"That beastly man was too." Her voice dipped. "He called me a *poppy*. Have you ever heard such an imbecilic thing? He looked like a gentleman, but he turned out to be *not* heroic in the least."

Wyn shook his head, jarring a fragment of clarity into it. "Miss Lucas, return to your bedchamber, lock the door, and go to sleep."

"Don't you even want to know why I am not there now?"

"I may be foxed, but I am far from stupid. I know why you are not there now."

"You know I went looking for another gentleman to assist me because you refused?"

"I know you even better, perhaps, than you know yourself." Nine girls. In ten years he had found and rescued nine runaway girls. Also two infants, one amnesiac, a pair of children sold to the mines by a twisted guardian, one former solider who'd gone a bit mad and hadn't realized he had abandoned his family, and one Scottish rebel who turned out not to be a rebel after all. But nine girls. They always assigned to him the girls. They even chuckled when they said he had a particularly good rapport with girls, as though they shared a marvelous joke. "Now go." He pulled back the door.

She went, neither defiantly nor meekly. She simply went, cutting a silhouette in the glow of lamplight from the inn that Wyn consumed with his fogged gaze, the gentle swell of her hips, the graceful taper of her shoulders. He was drunk. Too drunk not to stare and not drunk enough to be unmoved by the sight of her.

In the morning he would offer her a proper apology for his wandering hands. But now he could not. He could never lie convincingly while under the influence of brandy, and Diantha Lucas was not a girl to be lied to. Even drunk he realized that.

A sliver of sunlight sliced across Wyn's vision. Someone was scratching at the door, dragging him out of thick sleep.

He rubbed the slumber from his face and went to the door. The stable hand stood in the corridor, his brow a highway of ruts. He tugged his cap.

"Mornin', sir." His voice was far too agitated for Wyn's unsteady nerves. A bottle would cure those. But he never drank before noon. Ever. The single rule he lived by. The single rule among the many others his great aunt had bequeathed him, one of which in a thoroughly unprecedented moment of weakness he had broken the night before, and for which he would have to make amends today. Miss Lucas did not strike him as the missish short, but she was a lady, a young one at that; she might be skittish. Curiously, he could not imagine her offended. But wary now—yes.

He pressed a hand to his brow. "What is the time?"

"Near eight o'clock, sir."

Wyn's stomach tightened over the perpetual pain. Eight o'clock was far too early to feel this unsettling instability in his limbs, especially given that he'd finished a bottle of brandy only nine hours earlier.

"Is something amiss with my horses?"

"I thought you'd be wantin' to know, sir, the constable from over Winsford's been around this mornin'."

"Winsford?" His hedonistic host's country. This was not good.

"Yessir." The man nodded rapidly, his hat brim bobbing up and down. "He's been askin' after that bay filly of yours."

Exceedingly not good. "Has he?"

"He wanted to go right in that stall with her and take a look at her. But I said as the black would take a hunk out of his behind if he tried."

Despite circumstances, Wyn grinned. "He won't, you know. Galahad is as placid as a plow horse."

The fellow returned the grin. "I figured since the Lord gave me a tongue to say what I see fit, I use it as I might."

"And what do you expect to gain from this particular use of it? I don't suppose the constable is waiting at the bottom of the front stair and you will now be glad to show me the back stair for a price?"

The man's back went poker straight. "Now, see here, sir. I wasn't thinkin' to hold out my palm. I only thought as if you was goin' after the lady quick like so you can catch her, you'd better not find trouble with any nosey old constable from clean over five parishes. Why, after the way she took up that little spaniel that got its paw near chewed off at the smithy's and limpin' along like it does and she wouldn't hear no from the coachman about takin' it aboard, sayin' all the time that she'd care for it till it got well, why I figure she's the sort that needs a little carin' for herself." A flush spread across his cheeks and he pulled his cap lower. "I've a girl like that, likes to take care of everybody else and ain't got no one takin' care of her. 'Cept me now, sir, you see."

"I do." *God, no.* Damn foolishly nearsighted of him to underestimate her tenacity. Slipping, indeed. "Tell me quickly, in which coach did the lady depart and where is the constable now?"

The constable was in conference with the local law, consulting on the tricky matter of retrieving a horse stolen thirty miles away by a gentleman of means. Especially grateful on this occasion that Galahad's indisputable quality gave him the appearance of being such a gentleman, and thus recommending caution to the law, Wyn dressed swiftly.

In the stable he pressed a guinea into the groom's palm.

The man's eyes went round. "No, sir! I didn't do it on account o—"

"Take it," he said sharply. "Buy something for your girl who cares for everyone else more than herself."

He set a quick pace, considerably quicker than the Shrewsbury Coach would on the quagmired road.

The dog appeared first. Limping along the center of the road toward them, it waved its tail in uncertain greeting. Then it barked once, a high yap of pleasure. On three or so legs it leaped around, its black eyes the only discernable color in its matted coat, then turned about and raced back the way it had come.

Wyn urged his mount forward.

Veiled in misty rain, Miss Lucas stood at the side of the road beside a traveling trunk topped with a lady's bandbox.

"Do not expect me to be thrilled that you of all people have happened along," she said before he even pulled to a halt, the dog cavorting between them with little growls of pleasure.

"Good day, Miss Lucas. I hope I find you well."

"Of course you don't find me well." Her brow was tight. "But I can only expect you are happy about that."

"On the contrary, madam. I am far from happy."

He did not look happy. Despite his measured tone he looked remarkably displeased and a little dangerous atop his ebony horse and wearing all black, with a shadow of whiskers upon his jaw and his cravat tied rather hastily it seemed. Diantha had never seen him out of perfect order, which could only mean that upon discovering her missing from the inn, he had hurried after her. Which, despite the resolve she'd made to herself the moment she saw him round the bend, made her belly feel tingly again. Even a little hot, the way his hand on her behind had made her feel in the stable.

"You may help me now, if you wish." She frowned. "And I will appreciate it. But if you attempt to force me to return to my friend's house or to go home I will refuse."

"Miss Lucas, why are you standing here with your luggage?"

"Because it suits me."

He tilted his head. "This sort of stasis is unlikely to bring you closer to Calais."

"You are very clever, Mr. Yale. I'd thought before that I liked that a great deal about you. But I am coming to revise my opinion."

"Thank you." A glint shone in his gray eyes. "And I am coming to see to whom I might apply whenever I feel the need to not be complimented."

Her lips—agents of betrayal her entire life—twitched. For a moment his gaze seemed to focus upon them, and the tingles inside her turned to decidedly vibrant sparks. Her cheek had accidentally brushed his chin the night before. His whiskers had felt hard and rough. Her skin was still tender there from the scratch.

"I could not leave the dog behind, you see," she explained a bit unsteadily, though that was perfectly silly because of course a man's jaw would feel rough if one touched it in the middle of the night so many hours after he had shaved. But she could not help wondering if she touched his jaw *now* would the whiskers be even rougher. She wanted to. "But several people inside the coach with me didn't like its smell of the stable—"

"It cannot be wondered at."

"—and it would not remain in my lap when I sat on the roof. I think it is afraid of heights. Have you ever heard of anything so ridiculous, a dog afraid of heights?"

"Preposterous, really."

"You are quizzing me. But I could not strand it all alone on the road. So I was obliged to disembark prematurely. I am waiting here for the next coach."

"You will be waiting until Thursday."

She rolled her eyes. "Obviously I read the schedule at the posting inn too. I only said that to—"

"To see my reaction." A slight grin slipped across his mouth.

Who knew a gentleman's mouth could be so very . . . *intriguing*? Or that looking at it could make her feel hungry, though it was only an hour since she had eaten the snack the innkeeper's wife packed in the wee hours while trying to convince her not to leave without him. Diantha had never noticed any gentleman's mouth before. Noticing Mr. Yale's now also seemed silly.

But for a moment the night before, his mouth had touched her ear, his breath hot upon her neck, and she hadn't felt in the least bit silly. *She* had felt hot, and not just on her neck. All over. Merely recalling it now made her hot again.

"I said it to stall for time," she uttered. "I am still deciding what to do. I saw a farm a mile or so back. I am considering walking there and asking for help but I haven't perfectly worked out my plan yet."

"Ah." He looked very grave amidst the light rain that was quite like the color of his eyes. "Then let me not disturb your ponderings. Good day, ma'am." He bowed from the saddle and with an elegant tip of his black hat, started off.

She couldn't help smiling. For a man so usually elegant he was a remarkable tease. "You will not leave me here."

He did not turn around. "Are you so certain of that?"

"Entirely."

The dog loped after the horses. After a dozen yards it paused and looked back at her. Diantha's breaths shortened, a thread of panic twining up her spine.

"Mr. Yale, you may as well cease this teasing," she called. "I can see right through it."

He slowed his horse and looked around. "It devastates me that we must part company continuing to misunderstand one another, Miss Lucas." He bowed again. "But good day to you, and I wish you good fortune at the farm." He clucked to the horses and they moved off again.

She gripped her damp gloves together and wiggled her toes in her soggy boots.

"I had a plan," she shouted. "And I brought with me sufficient funds. I did not go off half-cocked on this mission. I had a plan."

He seemed to be too distant to hear her. She ground her teeth and muttered, "True gentleman, my mother's virtue." She threw back her shoulders. "All right, I apologize!" Then not quite so loudly, because frankly she could not bear the humiliation of it: "Please come back."

The black horse halted, and the other too. Mr. Yale drew them around and returned. Several yards away he dismounted, left the horses standing in the road and walked to her, the dog trailing at his heels. His attention was entirely upon her as though she were the only thing in the world, his usual manner, which of course she had liked very much until now.

He halted quite close, tall and dark and wide-shouldered, his black topcoat swirling about his taut thighs and fine boots, and very much like a man she might be afraid to encounter upon a deserted road in the rain if she did not already know him. But in fact she did *not* know him, not well, and mostly through her stepsisters. And the night before, when he touched her although he should not have, her knees had buckled. But for his strong hands holding her between the wall and his chest, she would have collapsed.

"Your plan was nonsensical." His eyes glittered. She could not believe it was anger. A true gentleman, like both her fathers, held his temper from ladies. But the spark in Mr. Yale's eyes now looked like anger. And a true gentleman did not stroke a lady's behind in a dark stable.

Her breaths stuttered. "My plan was not nonsensical."

His stare did not waver.

"All right," she admitted. "It was. Somewhat. But only insofar as it took a bit longer for you to appear on that coach than I imagined."

His brow dipped. "I beg your pardon?"

"I said, my plan was only nonsensical in that it took a bit longer for you to—"

"For me to appear. Yes. You hadn't any idea I would be on that coach yesterday."

She wiggled her brows. " 'Are you so certain of that?' "

"Mimicry does not suit you, minx. And, yes, I am quite certain, by the simple fact that *I* hadn't any idea."

"*Really?* How inconvenient for you. I always have a plan for everything."

"I am coming to see that."

"How is it that you came to be on this road without planning it?"

"I was at a house party and the entertainments wore thi—" He halted abruptly. "Naturally, that is immaterial. You did not know I would take that coach."

"No. I did not know *you* would, that is true. But I hoped to find a hero to help me. And then you appeared and you have quite the air of a hero about you, Mr. Yale. I have always thought so."

"I suppose I ought to be flattered by your words and no doubt sent to my knees by those dimples that have conveniently appeared at this moment—"

"I thought so until last night, that is."

His handsome features went still. "Miss Lucas," he said in an altered tone, "pray allow me to beg your pardon for—"

"You needn't speak of it. Men will do foolish things when they have been drinking excessively, after all." She did not want to hear him apologize for touching her. Somehow it felt wrong, especially since she wasn't without blame, seeking refuge in a stable due to her own reckless misjudgment. "And I meant, of course, that I thought you seemed heroic until you told me you would not assist me."

His broad shoulders seemed to release their rigidity. "She giveth, and again taketh away. Is this un-complimenting a habit of yours?"

"My dimples are perfectly sincere."

"I haven't the slightest doubt of it. I also haven't the slightest doubt that you are a remarkably troublesome young lady."

She blinked slowly, dark lashes fanning over lapis eyes. Then she turned about and walked to her traveling trunk. Without pretension she settled upon the trunk and folded her hands atop her lap.

"You've just sat in a puddle."

She turned her face away, confronting him with her lovely profile. "A mundane care." But the corner of her lips quivered not now from laughter.

Wyn's anger evaporated. Silence commenced, during which the only sounds were the snufflings of the horses that had sunk their noses in the grass at the side of the road, the soft whimpers of the mutt at his knee, and the increasingly steady rain. Each moment she less and less resembled the spoiled runaways he'd dealt with before. She was determination crossed with sincerity and an innocent sort of wisdom. And, before, he'd never looked upon a girl's face and wished to do her bidding. Rather, only once, and at that time he had felt that girl's anger too.

But Miss Lucas was not angry. She was merely seeking her past down a rainy road.

He wanted to see her dimples again. The need for it came upon him quite powerfully.

"Do you even have an umbrella?"

Her gaze remained averted. "That, admittedly, is one detail I failed to plan."

"Did you also fail to inquire of the coachman that left you off where exactly the next stop is?"

"I did." She twisted her lips. "Our disembarkation was rather hasty, in point of fact."

"I daresay."

Finally she cast him a glance. "Do you know where the next stop is?"

"I do. It is but a quarter mile up the highway."

Her face brightened. "You have taken this road before, then?"

"A few times." He knew this road and the roads to the west and south as well as he knew his name, and sometimes better. Leaving Gwynedd at age fifteen, he had not strayed too far afield at first, not for three years, until he finally made it to Cambridge. The highways and one-track paths, hills, and farms of the Welsh borderlands and western Shropshire all the way to his great-aunt's estate were more home to him than his father's house had ever been.

She leaped up. "Well, then, I should be on my way." She gave a glance at the traveling trunk, released a quick breath of decision, then took up her bandbox and set off.

Her boots sank into mud with each step but she seemed not to note it.

"Miss Lucas, I advise returning now to your traveling trunk and removing the valuables and any necessities before you continue on."

"I will send someone back for it when I reach the posting house." Her cloak was sodden, even her bonnet brim drooped, the errant chestnut curls that clung to her cheeks and throat making delicate dark swirls upon the cream of her skin.

He glanced down at the mongrel wagging its tail beside him and murmured, "She has no idea the danger this escapade offers her." Then more loudly: "I must insist."

She halted and turned to face him. She tilted her head. "You sound different sometimes. Just then, when you said that, you sounded . . ."

He waited.

Pale roses blossomed on her cheeks. "Like you did last night in the stable. And like you did that night at the ball for Lord and Lady Blackwood's wedding, when you rescued me."

Ah. Clearly she had an inclination toward the dramatic. He recalled the incident, of course: a frightened girl, a pack of rowdy lads no less disguised than he at the time, and some stern lecturing. Or perhaps only a stern word or two, but the lads had scattered readily enough. *Rescue* overstated the episode.

"Your valuables, if you will?" He gestured back toward her luggage.

"I wonder if that is what highwaymen say when accosting a lady on a road."

"I doubt it."

"Do you?"

"Miss Lucas."

"My valuables." She opened the trunk and repacked the

bandbox efficiently. "Will we walk?" she asked as he attached the bandbox to Galahad's saddle.

"Unless you have a magic carpet hidden in that trunk."

"If I had a magic carpet I would be in Calais already." Her eyes were troubled. But it was well after noon and the edge was pressing at his blood, his limbs unsteady again and his temper no better. So he left her to her ruminations and they walked in silence until the posting house came into view.

"This one is not very grand, is it? The inn in that village yesterday was so comfortable."

"The taproom here is no less so." Whiskey could be gotten within.

"Walking is invigorating, but truth be told I am simply . . ." Her gaze fluttered past his mouth. " . . . famished."

Drawing a slow breath, he scanned her bedraggled cloak and the muddy hem of her gown. She was an unusual girl, or perhaps despite her noble family merely a country girl accustomed to such walks. And with her cheeks flushed and brow damp from exertion, she was damnably pretty.

Inside the posting house, he went to the bar and ordered food for her, and whiskey. Across the rough-hewn taproom peopled with laborers, a single patron appeared out of place. A slim man, garbed all in brown and still wearing his rain-spattered hat, sat in the farthest corner with his back to the wall. Familiar. He'd seen this man on the road to recover Lady Priscilla.

Wyn paid for the bottle and glanced again. The man lowered his gaze.

"The Hereford and London Coach is to stop here shortly," he said when he returned to the table.

"Perfect. Will there be time to eat first?"

He withheld a smile. "Miss Lucas, you must reconsider your program. Although it astounds me after last night, I think you cannot be fully aware of the dangers of the road."

"Those are what you are here for, of course. As you were last night in that stable." Her eyes flared with a joyful sort of intention. Then, for a moment, confused awareness shadowed them. Wyn could do nothing to ease her discomfort; his hands and lips still remembered her and he was again without speech. His friends would be astonished were they to witness him now, struck silent by a pair of blue eyes and the memory of a soft feminine body pressed to his.

The barman set a plate of food before her. Her eyes twinkled. "How did you know shepherd's pie is my favorite, Mr. Yale?"

She swung so easily from thoughtful stillness to animated delight. Both attitudes made him want to haul her against him and caress considerably more than one round buttock. It was damned provoking.

"I did not," he managed to reply. "But I feared ordering the roast, as you might be disappointed by comparison."

"You are considerate. Or merely teasing. But you are not eating again." She narrowed her eyes. "Do you *only* drink?"

"When I am escorting young ladies about the countryside against my will, yes." Never, even when he was doing so voluntarily. But Diantha Lucas was not a Falcon Club assignment. She was apparently his own personal sort of torture.

She seemed to study him as she chewed. Finally she set down her fork and pushed the plate toward him. "Try some. It's excellent."

"Thank you. I will take your word for it."

"You look at least a stone lighter than the last time I saw you." She glanced at the bottle of brandy. "My father used to drink prodigiously. He rarely ate too."

"Ah. Then you and I have something in common." The words came without thought. More unprecedented behavior.

Her brows perked. "Your father too?"

"Prodigiously."

"Mine died of a stomach ulcer."

Pain tweaked Wyn's belly. "I am sorry for your loss."

"It was a dozen years ago. I was barely seven. I think my mother drove him to it." The blue of her eyes seemed to intensify. "Will you please help me, Mr. Yale? Willingly?"

"No, Miss Lucas. I will not help you willingly. I wish you to return home and find a solution to reuniting with your mother that meets with the approval of your family."

Her berry-pink mouth settled into its little thoughtful twist, supple and frankly delectable. Wyn spoke again because, confronted with that delectable mouth on a girl he had no business thinking such thoughts about, he deeply wished for another glass of whiskey. But he would not go that route again, not while she still possessed earlobes like silk, a neck like cream, and a derriere that begged to be handled. Temptation was best faced sober. He reached into his coat pocket for a cigar. "You must allow me to see you home."

"I cannot. I must continue on my way."

"Do you plan on doing so by subterfuge again?"

"Yes. I am quite certain that if you continue to press me on the matter, I will escape you again. But instead of stealing away in the middle of the night, which was inconvenient and won me a horrendous lecture from the innkeeper's wife, I will probably declare to everyone here that you have abducted me from my home and are forcing me to elope with you. I would demand to see the constable."

"Elope?" His hand stalled halfway to his mouth. "As in, abduct with nefarious designs."

"Yes."

He set down the cigar. "Miss Lucas, what actual knowledge do you have of such elopements?"

She tapped the fork tines against the plate. "Teresa has told me stories, you see."

"I am beginning to."

"In your black coat, boots, and hat you are an ideal candidate."

"My heroic status slips swiftly, it seems."

"Do you think so too?"

"I am clearly becoming the villain of this piece."

"I suppose you are."

"It would not bother me in the least." One constable being rather quite like another. "But tangling with the law will win you a swift journey home."

"Oh, I don't think so. While everyone is busy castigating you and you are busy defending yourself, I will slip away."

"However, now that I know that will be your plan, I will guard against it."

"I will devise another. You cannot win, Mr. Yale. I am determined." Her eyes glittered with a martial light, but perhaps too brittle. She was not a girl; her shapely figure and the clean lines of her lovely face made that perfectly clear. A bit too clear for the clear-headedness two drams of whiskey had now provided him. When the dimples appeared, they performed precisely the effect upon him that she intended—if, that was, she understood men. Which she probably did not, at least not to that extent, whatever Miss Finch-Freeworth had told her. On the other hand, the mother that had disappeared four years earlier was a madam, or so it seemed, although he was not quite certain the baroness's daughter entirely understood what that entailed either.

She was an innocent, a naïve innocent with rather too much bottom, too little sense, and a great deal of willful intention. The impulse that had driven her to the stable the night before proved it. But the glitter in her very blue eyes now suggested that her need was quite sincere—that this was, in fact, not at all a game to her.

Outside, the sounds of a coach and six rumbled, and the barkeep called out, "Hereford to London Coach!" over the murmur of conversations.

"You refuse to be swayed?"

She nodded. "Oh, yes."

"I cannot convince you otherwise? Perhaps to return home now and enlist the aid of your brother-in-law, the earl?"

"Certainly not. Alex despises my mother, and I could not ask that of my stepsister. Serena is a saint and loves everybody in the world except my mother."

"Why is that?"

She tilted her head. "Do you know, Mr. Yale, I believe you are trying to distract me so that I will miss my coach." She gathered her bonnet and stood up. "So I bid you good day and happy journey, although I do sincerely wish you were coming with me to aid me in my search and perform the duties of a hero. But, alas, that dream is not to be." She cast him an oddly sad smile and went to the door.

He went after her.

He grasped her elbow to stay her and bent his head, and her scent of wild sunshine caressed him. "Miss Lucas, allow me to speak plainly," he said quietly with only the slightest huskiness in his voice. "You ask me to play a role now when you will not do so yourself. You must admit that your determination and nerve do not resemble the qualities of a damsel in distress."

She seemed to stiffen. She replied in barely a whisper.

"Mr. Yale, I am not foolish. I know that what I am doing is dangerous and will win me chastisement, perhaps ruination. But . . ." Her lush lower lip quivered, although it seemed she fought to control it. "But I *must* do this. When I was fifteen my mother left me without a glance goodbye and without explanation. My stepfather, brother, and sisters are reticent to speak of her. Though I wish to pretend she does not exist, and have endeavored to do so for four years, I find I cannot. And, you see, it hurts rather more than I can bear." She lifted her gaze to him, sincere need in her lapis eyes. "It was an accident that you happened upon me. But now you must allow me to go and make my way of it, and forget you ever saw me. I give you leave to do so with good conscience."

There was nothing for it. He could not do as she bid.

"I will not allow you to go alone." He released her arm, for to touch her, he realized now, was a great mistake. "I will assist you."

The transformation that came over her face hollowed out a space in his lungs. Her hand darted to his and clasped it, her blue eyes sparkling, wide, and despite all, trusting.

"You *are* a hero. And a gentleman."

At present, Wyn knew he was neither. The old anger of vengeance fueled an impatience to be about his own mission that was all but heroic. And the heat of her touch through damp kidskin worked beneath his skin so that it required little imagination to strip the glove from those slender fingers and imagine feeling her. Once the glove went in his imagination, other feminine garments did as well. Quite swiftly. She was far too pretty, and he had been without a woman for far too long. He had not touched another's skin in far too long. Except hers, too briefly.

No, his thoughts were not in the least gentlemanly now.

Chapter 5

He drew his hand from hers. "Do you see the bar master behind me? He does not believe that you are my sister."

"Whyever not?"

"His low character, no doubt."

The dimples flashed. "That character leads him to wicked conclusions, you suspect?"

God, what had he done to deserve this? But sins would be punished, after all.

"He was reluctant to serve a girl of your appearance who enters his establishment on foot without a maid or luggage. I was obliged to convince him that it would be in his best interests."

Her lips twisted. "You crossed his palm with silver."

"In a manner of speaking." Threats worked too, and they were less expensive.

Her gaze darted about the taproom. "If I had a maid or companion, do you think he and others upon the road would draw such conclusions?"

He followed her attention to the corner where a woman

slumped against the wall in sleep. She was over middle age and garbed in drab, a knit scarf wound about her neck. Miss Lucas's brow creased in contemplation.

Wyn found himself smiling. "A plan is in the making, I imagine."

She flashed him a quick grin. "She was on the coach. We had a lovely chat before the dog and I went onto the roof. She is going to Stafford, but I believe she has lost that opportunity."

"And why do you believe this?"

"The schedule." She pointed to the placard beside the door and chuckled, a light, rippling sound of simple pleasure. "Good heavens, and you say you have traveled?" Her eyes danced.

He swallowed over the dryness in his throat and glanced at the man in brown.

"Then on to your plan, madam."

When they stood before the sleeping woman, Miss Lucas leaned down. "Ma'am? Do wake up. I believe you have missed your coach."

The sleeper's nose twitched and she opened protuberant eyes.

"I have? Well, dear me." She shrugged off her slumber and straightened her muffler. "Hello, miss. I was terribly sorry that nasty coachman put you off. The little dog wasn't so much of a trouble."

"Oh, thank you. This is Mr. Yale. We have come over to assist you."

"Have you, then? What a dear you are. Good day to you, sir." She gave him a studying perusal, her smile fading.

"But what is your plan now?" Miss Lucas asked. "Will you take the next coach to Stafford? It comes by tomorrow."

"Well, miss, they said if I weren't there by today I'd lose the position."

"Yet you seem untroubled about this," Wyn said.

"I'm not, sir. Happens all the time. Can't help myself. I drop off to sleep like that"—she snapped fingers as round as tea cakes—"and lose my positions left and right."

"She was on her way to be hired companion to an elderly lady," Miss Lucas explained. "But to allow so little time to travel seems very harsh. Will you await the next London coach?"

"I will, though I've barely a penny, seeing as how I've been out of a position for some time now, my last employer having something of a dark spirit and putting it about that I weren't fit for a lady."

Miss Lucas glanced at him and her eyes sparkled.

"Mrs. . . . ?"

"Polley, sir. Married Mr. Polley in 'ninety-two and lost him to Old Boney in 'thirteen."

"Mrs. Polley, might you be inclined to assist us now, and earn your journey back to London?"

"I would as long as the work's honest, sir." She looked between them, guardedly now.

"My sister requires a chaperone upon our journey yet sadly lacks one. We were forced to leave our previous residence in haste and hadn't time to plan. So you see we are in need of a lady such as yourself."

Her eyes slitted like cut melons. "Now see here, sir, I've not been living in a hole in the ground these past fifty-five years and I've a strong suspicion the two of you aren't related."

Miss Lucas laughed. "Oh, not at all. What's more, I am intended for Mr. H, a much less handsome gentleman who admires me immensely and will make a very good life for me. But I have a task I must accomplish before then—to rescue my mother from a Den of Iniquity—and I've set out on the road to do so. It was only by accident that I happened upon Mr. Yale, who is a particular friend of my family, and he has kindly agreed to assist me."

Mrs. Polley's demeanor did not alter. "Have you now, sir?"

"I thought it best, under the circumstances."

"So you see he is not kidnapping me or encouraging me to elope with him across the border or any such nonsense."

"No nonsense whatsoever," he murmured with that slight smile that made Diantha's belly dance.

"Not only that, but he was insisting to me only a moment ago that I must have a chaperone, and here you are stranded and without a position. It seems serendipitous."

Mrs. Polley did not now take her eyes off Mr. Yale. "Well I don't know fancy words, miss, but it does seem like a pot of good fortune that we've come across each other." She gave Diantha a careful look. "And you say this gentleman here is known to your kin?"

"Quite well known."

Mrs. Polley seemed to chew on the inside of her cheek. Diantha couldn't wait. "Then we are all for Bristol together?"

Mrs. Polley shifted her attention to her. "Den of Iniquity, you say?"

"You needn't remain in Miss Lucas's service once we reach our destination if you do not wish to be associated with it, ma'am."

Mrs. Polley stood, her double chin quite firm when brought to the height of perhaps four and a half feet. "I'll remain as long as I see fit, sir, which will be as long as you're trailing miss about the countryside here. She is a fine girl, this one." She patted Diantha's arm. "And I'll not have any fellow who claims he's friendly taking advantage of her. I'll stay until I'm certain I'm needed no longer."

"Excellent. Thank you, ma'am." He bowed.

Diantha grinned. She cast him another quick glance as Mrs. Polley gathered her belongings, but he was looking at her with very sober eyes now. Her stomach did somer-saults. When he looked at her like this, serious and still, it was again borne in upon her that she knew very little of him, and the notion came to her that the moment on the road when he'd looked dangerous might in fact have revealed the real man, the rest only a facade.

The traveling trunk was retrieved from the road and Mrs. Polley's luggage gathered, and Wyn saw the ladies into the next southerly bound coach. But before departing he had a private conversation with a quiet lad delivering sacks of grain to the stable—a tall youth whose clothing hung on his frame and who stared at the bone the mongrel was chewing with the eyes of starvation.

With grim satisfaction, Wyn approached him. He'd been at this work for a decade. He knew well how to pick his man.

A coin and very few words later, the lad was nodding in assent.

"I'll do it gladly, sir. Pa went off to fight the Frenchies and never came back, and me and Ma have been trying to keep my five brothers in shoes and porridge, without much luck. I'll take this to her"—he gestured with his palm gripped around the coin—"and start off to Dev-onshire right away. Little Joe's nearly as big as me now. He'll take care of the others while I'm gone."

"The contents of that pouch should be sufficient to hire a horse and pay for room and board along the road, William."

"Don't need but a stack of hay to sleep in, sir."

"As you wish. You may keep whatever you do not use, and I will give you the fee we agreed upon when you return. But haste is essential. And a mum lip. The letter I have given you mustn't be read by anyone but the baron, or Lord or Lady Savege, and you mustn't tell a soul of your purpose."

"Yessir. I understand, sir."

"Good man." Wyn left him then, reassured by the look of careful responsibility crossed with sheer relief in the youth's eyes. What he offered William as payment would be a windfall for the poor family. The lad would make good time to Glenhaven Hall, home of the Baron of Carlyle, Miss Lucas's stepfather. If the baron could not be found, William was to continue on to nearby Savege Park, the home of her stepsister, the Countess of Savege. If Wyn did not hear back from the baron or Serena and Alex Savege within the sennight, he would send another messenger, this time to Kitty and Leam Blackwood in London. Sister to the earl of Savege, Kitty was family to Miss Lucas too. If she were in town, she would come in an instant.

If he wrote to Constance, she would come, of course. But Wyn did not wish to see Constance before he completed his task, nor really Leam either, the man he'd spent six years of his life with wandering around the empire, working for the crown in secret.

Constance and Leam were the closest he had to family, and Jin Seton and Colin Gray to a degree. Rather, had been. With Leam's retirement from the club four years earlier, the group had changed. Their secret ring of fellowship had been broken.

But in truth, the change had begun before that for Wyn, more than a year before that, in a rainy London alleyway when he looked into the bloodless face of a scarred girl and saw his own death. When he began to lie to the people he cared for most in the world.

And now, again, a girl was trusting him. A girl who came to him of her own accord and begged him for help.

God help Diantha Lucas for seeing a hero where none stood. But some girls, he supposed, were blind that way.

Diantha didn't so much mind having been touched intimately by a gentleman. She minded not having been kissed first.

Teresa said men kissed ladies before they took greater liberties, and Diantha had given that some thought. Once before their wedding she'd seen her stepsister, Viola, and her betrothed, Mr. Seton, kiss each other quite enthusiastically when they thought no one else was looking, and her toes had positively curled in her slippers. Since Viola had come away from it with a dazed smile, and Mr. Seton with a remarkably satisfied look, Diantha supposed kissing was something to be desired rather than dreaded.

Her parents had never kissed. Her stepfather, a kind but limp and distracted sort of man, had barely ever come out of his study while her mother lived at Glenhaven Hall. Her real father had always been foxed. Like Mr. Yale in the stable. Which was perhaps why he had not kissed her before putting his hand on her behind.

He had released her swiftly, no doubt because he had not enjoyed touching her like that. How could he have enjoyed it? Just the memory of it made her squirm in shame. If she were like most girls, like the other girls at the academy, slim and delicate, perhaps he might have enjoyed it. Perhaps he would not have stopped. Perhaps he would have kissed her.

The coach rumbled over the rolling Shropshire countryside, Mrs. Polley asleep beside her. She was very amiable, although not particularly pleasant toward Mr. Yale. That couldn't be wondered at. Like kissing. Elegant London ladies probably kissed gentlemen left and right, which was no doubt why Mrs. Polley did not trust Mr. Yale, for he was most certainly an elegant London gentleman.

Lying in bed fitfully the night before, Diantha had imagined kissing him, and her whole body got hot, like when he'd held her in the dark. It was wrong of her to feel hot like that, she suspected, but she was after all the wayward, wicked daughter of a wayward, wicked woman.

She had always been wayward, from the time she was

a little girl. Her mother had said so ceaselessly. In the shadow of her beautiful, sweet elder sister, Charity, Diantha had never been of any use to her mother because of her poor looks and waywardness.

The wickedness, however, was new.

She wanted to kiss Mr. Yale.

He rode behind the coach, drawing the brown horse along as before. The little dog was with him now, but this coachman was much kinder than yesterday's and didn't mind it sitting in the carriage. Diantha had nothing to complain about. But at the coach's next stop, Mr. Yale's drawn brow alarmed her.

"You are unhappy with me for forcing you to do this," she said, walking beside him as he led his horses to a water trough. The rain had diminished and sunlight poked through unruly clouds.

"I am unhappy, but rather with myself for not foreseeing the sort of trouble we now have."

She drew in a tiny breath of relief. "We have trouble?"

"Miss Lucas," he said quietly, "in my life I have occasionally inconvenienced people in a manner which has left them eager to inconvenience me in return."

"Inconvenienced?"

"Displeased."

"But what—"

"I'm afraid I am unable to expand upon the whats and wherefores. Unfortunately, however, I am now being followed by a man who has ill intentions toward me. This, as you might imagine, could prove a hindrance to our progress."

She studied his profile. "You are concerned for my safety and Mrs. Polley's. Not for your own."

He said nothing. Her safety, of course, was the reason he now stood here beside her.

"Where are you taking this horse, Mr. Yale?" She stroked the animal's neck.

Mr. Yale turned to her, that slight smile pulling at the corner of his mouth that she wanted to kiss.

"You are an unusual young lady, Miss Lucas."

"Merely curious."

"She belongs to the Duke of Yarmouth, whose heir, Marquess McFee, lost her in a game of cards to a gentleman of uncertain honor from whom I have recently retrieved her. It is my task now to return her to her rightful owner."

The horse's coat was warm beneath her glove. "Is that what you hope to do with me in the end, imagining I will tire of my mission?"

"You are not a horse, obviously. But if you have an owner of whom I am ignorant, I wish you will inform me so that I might not be accused of theft."

"You often do not answer my questions."

"Don't I?"

She darted her gaze up. He was no longer smiling, rather intense, and the change made her belly tighten most deliciously. "How do you propose to avoid this man who is pursuing you?"

"I haven't an idea of it yet. But I will not allow you to come to harm because of my enemies."

"You have enemies? Oh, but I suppose everyone does."

His silver eyes glimmered. "Not everyone, it seems. You befriend each person you encounter. You are in fact an unusual young lady, Miss Lucas."

"And a London gentleman acting as horse courier to a duke and being followed by a man with a bad purpose while assisting a runaway lady to find her mother—what sort of man is that, Mr. Yale? A common run-of-the-mill sort?"

He offered her his slight grin then nodded toward the door of the pub. "We've a quarter hour until the coach departs again."

"I asked Mrs. Polley to purchase a cold lunch. Will you eat today, sir?"

"Will you cease pestering me about food, madam?"

"Probably not."

"Just so."

Wyn watched her move toward the door where the dog sat. As she approached it, the little mongrel's tail whipped back and forth. She paused and looked back.

"It likes you," she said.

"Rather, it likes you." As everyone did. Her smile, her sparkling eyes, and her warmth conveyed affection to every passenger aboard the coach, the coachman, even the surly posting house master at their previous stop. And aside from his desire to have his hands on her again, Wyn liked her too. He would not allow this new danger to threaten her. The man in brown that he'd seen twice now was a curiosity. If the man appeared again, he would discover his purpose.

But today's threat was a much greater concern. An old acquaintance, Duncan Eads, had appeared earlier on the road behind the coach. He had maintained his distance, but he was not a man to be discounted. Months back Wyn had caused him trouble, stealing a girl out from under the nose of Eads's employer, a man named Myles who owned a quarter of London's underworld. Drunk as an emperor at the time—a rather long episode of that—Wyn had made Eads look like a fool and angered Myles.

Eads had no doubt been sent here to finally make him pay. Wyn was of a mind to tell him to get in line.

"We should give it a name." She bent to stroke the dog's brow, pulling the fabric of her cloak tight around her behind. Wyn held his breath, entirely unable to remove his gaze from that generous curve of femininity that he'd briefly had in his hand.

"As you wish."

She offered him a quick smile and went into the pub.

He walked his horses to a grassy spot and loosened their leads to allow them to graze. The village's high street was peculiarly active; farmers' wagons laden with children and other adults, a cart, then a carriage of modest quality all passed by within minutes, and a number of people on foot. Eads did not appear, but Wyn suspected he would see him again when the time was least convenient. Perhaps on the road ahead. Eads might now be going around a long route while the coach was halted here, planning an ambush.

The coachman ambled from the pub, tipped his cap to Wyn, and the other passengers followed. Miss Lucas burst out the door.

"Mr. Yale, I have heard the most wonderful news." Her cheeks were flushed with life. She lowered her voice and pulled Mrs. Polley along. "Today the local squire has opened up his estate to all the surrounding countryside. Apparently this squire, Sir Henry, is quite well-to-do and he likes to throw enormous parties." She glanced about the street with an expectant air.

"I must be glad for Sir Henry and his guests." It explained the traffic. "But I am not entirely certain what his magnanimity has to do with you."

"Oh, not so much me, or only incidentally, but rather you. And the man following you."

He glanced at Mrs. Polley. Her lips were a line. He returned his regard to the girl whose blue eyes shone with excitement.

"Miss Lucas, may I suggest that you reboard the—"

"No. Don't you see? This is the *ideal* diversion." She grasped his arm, effectively grounding him in total, tongue-tied silence. He'd not forgotten the shape of her body or the heat of her touch from the night before, though he had spent the morning's ride trying to. Ten years as a secret agent of the crown, yet when confronted with Miss

Diantha Lucas, he was, it seemed, all youthful lust all over again. She had a fine figure. Not merely fine. She had perfect breasts, round and high and modestly concealed by her traveling gown, which did not however discourage him from imagining them naked.

"Diversion?" he managed.

"We must hide in plain sight." Her eyes danced, her berry lips curving into a smile of delight that Wyn wanted to taste. "There will be hundreds of people there, and if your . . . friend is not here now"—her gaze darted to the street—"he will not know you have gone off in another direction. We can hire a carriage and take another route. Don't you see? It is perfect."

"No." He did not see the perfection of her plan, but he was beginning to see the perfect idiocy of his own desires. "Yes."

He turned to her companion. "Mrs. Polley, I suspect you disapprove of this proposed program."

"Well, I don't see how it might not be the trick. If your nasty fellow might give this sweet lady grief, well then you've got to find a solution. And I don't see how my mistress's plan here is any worse than what you might come up with."

"If you do not board that coach and a carriage cannot be hired, Miss Lucas, we will be well stranded here when my 'friend' arrives."

She scanned his face. "You do not believe he will arrive here. Not here. You think he has gone ahead to accost you by surprise somewhere down the highway."

She was remarkable. So he laughed.

Her lips curved into a smile, like the breeze in spring. She was fresh and clear and direct, except of course with this entire escapade to find her mother. But her eyes twinkled up at him, satisfaction and excitement making the lapis glimmer in the inconstant rays of sun, and he could not deny her. *Rule #1: If a lady is kind of heart, gener-*

*ous and virtuous, a gentleman should acquiesce to her
every request; he should deny her nothing.* That, and, if
a carriage could in fact be gotten here, her plan actually
sounded better than anything he'd yet devised.

Her gaze shifted over his shoulder. "There! We mayn't
have to hire a carriage after all." She hailed a vehicle
crawling along at a snail's pace, an ancient barouche as
long as it was cavernous within, with a wizened coachman in a faded coat and pulled by a pair of horses as old
as their driver. Tucked inside were two ladies wrapped
in gauze at least a half century out of date, with hats and
parasols from another era.

Miss Lucas hurried to it. Wyn could not hear her words,
only her voice, clean and bright as always. The ladies responded to her with smiles. A frail hand gloved in old
lace stretched out and took the girl's. Then another lifted,
waving him and Mrs. Polley toward the carriage.

That was the moment Wyn first suspected that finally—
after many more than nine girls—he had met his match.

Chapter 6

"I told the Miss Blevinses that we are newlyweds."

"I gathered that."

"Well, I couldn't very well tell them we are an old married couple. I'm barely nineteen."

"You might have been a child bride."

She chuckled. Errant rays of sunshine played in the strands of chestnut hair escaping her bonnet and in her blue eyes, and for a moment she did appear quite young. *Nearly guileless*, he had believed.

Now he knew better.

"But of course we have no children, and I was not really prepared to invent them on the spot." She picked morsels of meat from the platter on the table and deposited them alternately with the dog at her feet and between her tempting lips. "Although I suppose I could have if pressed, but they might not have believed it. We are not well enough known to each other to do the sorts of things that old married couples do, like—"

"Finish each other's sentences?"

Her dimples flashed, propelling Wyn's hand back to the

punch bowl ladle. Sir Henry's butler mixed a potent, but palatable, concoction.

It wouldn't have mattered if he served white gin straight from the barrel. After sitting for two hours on chairs decorating the lawn, sipping tea while she invented story after story of charming childhood escapades—both hers *and his*—with which she regaled the Miss Blevinses, Sir Henry, and a half dozen other septuagenarians who hadn't seen a London drawing room since George II and therefore had no idea that the newly wedded Mr. and Mrs. Dyer were a complete sham—Wyn had nearly stood and declared his intention to annul her instantly. Instead he begged their host and the kind ladies who had conveyed them hither to excuse them while he and his bride strolled through the gardens.

He'd taken her directly to the refreshments.

About the lawn sloping to the sheep fields below, children played ball and tennis, their parents—farmers, villagers, and a smattering of exceedingly modest gentry—enjoying the produce of the harvest. All were happy with the break in the rain and Sir Henry's annual generosity. A fiddle buzzed a tune, and two dozen or so lads and lasses danced upon the turf, laughter mingling with shy glances—the awkward flirtations of youths and the innocent coquetry of maidens.

Wyn had no remembrances of a time like that in his life. He'd gone from boy to man in months. Weeks. He did not regret it; he had seen the world in all its marvels. Still, he turned away from the scene now and swallowed the contents of his glass.

Miss Lucas's gaze lingered on the dancers. "I don't think Mrs. Polley approves of the story I have invented."

"I suspect, rather, that she does not approve of the husband you have chosen."

"But you are a perfectly unexceptionable gentleman."

"A gentleman who has agreed to escort you across

England without benefit of a proper chaperone, family, or actual marriage license, recent or otherwise."

"Hm. But otherwise she is an ideal companion. Except for that abrupt sleeping habit, of course." She glanced across the lawn to where Mrs. Polley was sprawled upon a divan in the shade of a draping willow. Her brow creased. "I hope she is not ill."

"I have seen it before." In the East Indies years ago. "The body simply closes down, as though in sleep although it is not. She cannot control it, but it does not harm her."

Miss Lucas looked at him with her seeking eyes and took the side of her lower lip between her teeth. This time Wyn did not look away.

Finally she said, "Do you think we have lost . . . your friend?"

"For a time. But he will persist."

"You displeased him that dreadfully?"

"Rather his employer, a powerful man. We must find a carriage to convey us south by an alternate route. With haste."

"Well, I—"

"Be quiet, minx. I am thinking."

"Planning." She dropped a slice of cheese into the mutt's mouth. "Yes, I need quiet when I am inventing a plan too."

"Then now would be a good time to do so. For instance, you might invent a contingency plan for what to do with your companion should we be obliged to beat a swift retreat from this gathering if Eads appears."

"His name is Mr. Eads? Who is he?"

"A Highland Scot, and as strong as a Dover dockworker."

"Large, I guess. Mrs. Polley is too heavy for me to carry. But certainly you could do it."

He cocked a brow.

She nodded. "You could throw her over your shoulder like a true villain would, and carry her off while I run after, begging you to have mercy on her, like a real damsel in distress."

He bowed. "Your ingratitude is entirely becoming, Miss Lucas."

She burst out laughing. He offered her a mild glower.

She clamped her berry lips shut. But she seemed to bounce on the balls of her feet, as though the effort of remaining still proved too much, and her dimpled cheeks were lightly stained with pink. Wyn couldn't think with her so near. The punch had stilled the shaking in his veins, and now a comfortable, familiar languor stole through him, sheering the edge off his anxiety.

The Scot would search the highway north first. They must be careful. But for today, Wyn had nothing to fear. Except himself. She was still standing too close, and the liquor in his blood hummed.

"What would you say, Miss Lucas, if I told you that to pursue your mission we will be obliged to purloin a conveyance from one of these families enjoying Sir Henry's hospitality?"

"Purloin?" She moved closer, which had not been entirely his wish. Not entirely. "Do you mean to *steal* a carriage?"

He turned again to the punch bowl, as much to move away from her as to pour more into his cup.

"Have . . ." Her gaze flickered from the bowl to his face. "Have you done such a thing before?"

"When necessary." He leaned back against the table. "Is it now necessary, Miss Lucas? I am yours to command."

"Mrs. Dyer." Her lips slipped into a partial purse. "You should call me Mrs. Dyer in this company. In case someone hears you."

"You are a minx."

"I probably am. And you drink too much."

"I beg your pardon?"

"Why do you drink so much? Is the flavor so appealing to you?"

"Rather, it steadies my nerves." Ah. It would be the truth. It always required several glasses for him to mouth partial truths, after all. Her wide blue eyes apparently took him the remainder of the way to complete truth.

No lies with Diantha Lucas, except one. If she knew he meant to take her home, she would seek to escape him again. With Eads on his trail, and perhaps the man in brown, he could not risk further delays.

"Well, I am excessively nervous at the present," she said, squaring her graceful shoulders, "so perhaps I shall have some too."

"You do not appear excessively nervous."

"I am an excellent dissembler. Really, Mr. Dyer, that should be clear to you by now." She reached for a cup and lifted it to her lips. She sniffed and her nose wrinkled— her pert nose that sported two minute, round scars, so small they were not visible unless a man studied her quite closely, as he could not prevent himself from doing now. There were others across her brow and cheeks as well, tiny imperfections that rendered the grace of her features more touchable.

She was damnably touchable.

The musicians struck up a country dance. Her eyes, pools of azure in the glowing light of late afternoon, sought his over the rim of her cup. "Will it taste horrid?"

"You must judge for yourself."

"My stepfather and sister Charity say I should not drink spirits. I haven't before, you know. Not even wine." She glanced down into the cup then back up at him. "You are not going to tell me not to drink it?"

"That would be singularly hypocritical of me, I believe."

She sipped. She blinked, rapidly. Then she sipped again. She lowered the cup.

"It is not horrid."

He shook his head.

"It has not calmed my nerves yet."

"It requires several minutes."

She raised the cup again.

"It's warm," she said this time, her eyes widening. "Rather, *hot*." She placed her gloved hand over her throat then slid it down between her breasts. Her lashes flickered, and Wyn thought he saw something in them from earlier, when he'd taken her hand to assist her down from the coach: *primal awareness*.

Selfish fool that he was, he did not now for her sake play the hypocrite and remove the cup from her grasp. For he wished to see more of that glimmer in her eyes, more of that awareness directed at him. He wished to be, for the first time in years—rather, *ever*—thoroughly irresponsible with a girl. With a lady. This lady.

He wished what he wished every time he reached for a bottle of brandy, a glass of whiskey, a pint of ale. He wished to forget.

Diantha could not feel her lips. She could, however, *see* Mr. Yale's, despite the dark night and dim lamplight. She could not in fact manage to take her eyes off his mouth. His *intriguing* mouth. His mouth that looked so absolutely delicious.

De. Lish. Os. Mouth.

But it was too far away now. His mouth. And the rest of him. *Far* too far away. He had gone to the other side of the drive. She recalled him telling her quite firmly that she must under no circumstances follow him. And she had not. She was *very* good and remained *precisely* where he left her leaning up against the back of Sir Henry's carriage house at the edge of a row of mightily tall black trees.

But she *wanted* to follow him. She wanted to be wherever he was. She wanted . . . *Oh*, she *wanted* . . .

She opened her eyes, uncrossing them. He was standing before her. The lamplight rimmed about him.

"You look like you are wearing a crown." She squinted. "Are you a prince, Mr. Yale?"

"Yes. From now on you may address me as Your Royal Highness."

She placed her palm upon his chest. "I thought so. I thought perhaps you were a prince. But then you are *far* above my station. I am merely a baronet's sister. Not sufficiently grand to dance with you."

"There will be no dancing tonight in any case, so you needn't worry over it."

"*That* is a relief. Good heavens, this is remarkably fine fabric!" She stroked her fingertips across the silk of his waistcoat.

"Only the best for my wedding night." His voice sounded hoarse.

"*Wedding* night?" She snapped her hand away and somehow *his* hand was around her shoulder then, which was a good thing because in his grasp she swayed gently into the stable wall instead of into air. She regained her footing. "Have you gotten *married* today?"

"Yes, Mrs. Dyer." He released her. "To you, according to everyone you spoke to this evening."

"Oh." She felt her lips curve into a smile. Feeling! But now her nose was numb. "That *is* a relief. Because I ex-*press*-ly wished to—to—" She pawed at the air and her hand landed again on his chest. "—to *touch* you." She sighed. "If you were married I should *not*, of course."

"Even if I were not married, you should not." His hand came around her wrist, large and warm, and then *her* hand was again dangling at her side, not touching any part of him, which really was a *royal* disappointment. She frowned at her fingers, then up at him and his intriguing mouth. His *delicious*-looking mouth.

"Mrs. Polley has not yet awoken," he said with that mouth, and she blinked to keep it in focus. "We must wait for her to rouse before we set off. If we awaken her abruptly, she might be startled and alert others, though it seems that Sir Henry's servants and remaining guests are either abed or too cup-shot to notice."

"Oh, yes. She might believe she was being abducted and scream. *I* would."

"I doubt it. You would be more likely to quash your abductor over the head with whatever came to hand and grab the ribbons yourself."

"I don't suppose you will let me drive. Papa never lets me drive, though I am *quite* a fine whip as ladies go. Good *heavens*, that sounded remarkably petulant, I think."

"It is to be expected. And no, minx, I will not allow you to drive. Not in this condition."

"What condition?" She sucked in a great lungful of air and shook her head. "Mr. Yale, Mr. Yale. I am in *no* condition for anything but *one* thing."

"What is that?" His voice smiled. She *adored* the way his voice smiled, because it revealed so much. It told her he thought she was amusing, and perhaps even a pleasure to be with. Gentlemen did not feel that way about her. Oh, everybody *else* did, but that was only because she *liked* them, and people *liked* to be liked, of course. But young gentlemen did not notice her. *Handsome* men did not notice her. Rather the opposite. She was the spotty little fat girl that no one wanted to dance with unless it was to taunt and mock her and pull her hair and ribbons and pinch her until she wept.

Except *him*. *He* had danced with her, with her spots and puffy cheeks and all.

"I am in the *perfect* condition, Mr. Yale, for you to put your hands on me." She closed her eyes and let the night air filter over her lips and eyelids and—

She was hot.

"I am hot." She tugged at her cloak fastening. But her eyes were closed so she could not see it. Or perhaps her gloves were too tight. She picked at them, but it turned out she wasn't wearing any.

"Where have my gloves gone?"

"You removed them some time ago. They are in your pocket."

"Oh, *good*. Papa gave me to them—*them* to *me* last Christmas. They are quite fine. From London you know. Like you."

"I am not from London, Miss Lucas."

She gripped his lapels and pressed her cheek to his chest. So solid. So warm. So *Mr. Yale*. He smelled very, *very* good, of clean linen and something else that was *deeply* nice.

"*Do* cease calling me Miss Lucas." She squeezed her eyes closed. "I *don't* like it, but I *would* like to remove this cloak. I am positively *sweltering*."

Her back met the wall of the building and then he was unfastening her cloak and she was so happy she nearly wept. She danced free of it.

"Oh, *thank* you. Thank you. A thousand thank you's!"

"One will do." He followed her across the nubby drive farther into the dark.

She spread her arms. "Am I drunk, Mr. Yale?"

"You are, indeed, Miss Lucas."

She whirled around to face him, the cool night air swirling in her skirts and across her neck where it felt positively wonderful. "And are you drunk, Mr. Yale?"

"Relatively speaking, no, Miss Lucas."

"Oh." She pivoted to a halt. The world spun, disappointment smothering her. "Because if you were you *would* put your hands on me again, I daresay."

"Then we must both be very glad that I am not."

There were many thoughts in her head then. Her mouth tasted like paste. She could not bring the lamp-lit tufts of grass poking up from the drive into focus. It was too dark and a big black circle surrounded her tube of vision.

She peered at the building. "Whose carriage are we stealing?"

"Sir Henry's."

"That seems *terribly* rude after we enjoyed his hospitality all afternoon."

"Yet unavoidable. It is the only vehicle remaining at this late hour that accommodates your traveling trunk and the three of us. Unless you wish to make the journey in a hay wagon?"

She laughed. Then she sighed. She could sigh forever if he stood before her. "Four."

"Four?"

"Ramses."

"Ramses?"

She pointed behind him. "Our dog, Mr. Yale!"

"Ah." He nodded.

"It was that name or Spider. He has black eyes, you know. Unlike yours. I *admire* your eyes very much. I will leave my necklace."

"Your necklace?"

"As recompense."

"You wear no necklace, Miss Lucas."

"You told me to remove my valuables from the traveling trunk, and so I *did*. It is in the bandbox. We must leave it in the stable to pay Sir Henry for his carriage and horses. It is very valuable."

"That will not be necessary."

"I insist! I hid it, you see, so when my mother stole my sisters' jewels she did not find it." She wagged a finger. "It is not right to steal, Mr. Yale, whatever you have been accustomed to doing in the past."

Her cloak was folded over his arm and he stood three yards away. The drive tilted this way and that, taking him and the spot of golden-orange lamp with it from side to side. She was excessively uncomfortable.

Her eyes widened. "I think I am going to be ill."

He moved toward her.

She was ill. Violently so.

It was horrid.

Chapter 7

Diantha awoke in a sticky sweat with her mouth lined in gum paper. Wretched tasting gum paper. She swallowed thickly and her tongue felt large. So did her eyelids, and her stomach, and her head. She groaned a little and tried to breathe.

"Awake, then?" Mrs. Polley spoke close by. "Must feel like old Beelzebub himself. Mr. Polley always did when he enjoyed too many pints at the miller's on a Sunday."

Diantha cracked her eyes open. "He drank on Sundays? At a mill?" The room was minuscule, allowing only a small bed, the chair that Mrs. Polley's little round form inhabited, and a rustic dressing table. The fabric over the window was striped and drawn back to allow in gray light. "Isn't that blasphemous?"

"Mr. Polley left the praying to womenfolk, miss, as good men do." She went to the foot of the bed. "*That* man—and I'm not saying he's a good man—will be wanting to speak with you now. But we'll have you dressed before I'll allow him in here."

She blinked to clear the discomfort in her head and

stomach, to no avail. "Whyever would you allow him into my bedchamber at all?"

Her companion held forth stays and petticoat. "We were needing some explanation to these nice folk for you being weak as a chick and none too clear-headed, I told them you were expecting a wee one, and bad off because of it. I've seen ladies worse on account of babes in the womb. Seeing as they believed it, they'd surely wonder if I didn't allow him in here."

Good heavens; they were not at an inn apparently. She dragged her legs over the edge of the bed and pressed her face into her hands. "Who are the nice folk, Mrs. Polley?" she uttered into her palms, her stomach doing thick, nasty flip-flops.

Mrs. Polley strapped the stays around Diantha's ribs. "A farmer and his wife, and a pack of children." She scowled. "He's charmed the lot of them with his pretty London ways."

Diantha cupped her splitting brow in one palm and pressed the other over her rebellious midsection. "Has he?"

"Took the four little ones up the hill to see the sheep this morning, and brought them back smiling and so worn-out they dropped right off after lunch."

The petticoat came over her head. "Is it afternoon already?"

"Near four o'clock, miss." Mrs. Polley guided her hands through the sleeves and tugged Diantha to her feet.

She swayed and grabbed the bedpost. The night was coming back to her in bits. Awful, shameful, truly appalling bits. She sincerely hoped the bits she did not remember were not any worse than those she did. Her throat felt prickly.

"I think I may be ill."

"I don't imagine there's anything left in there to come up, miss."

Her modesty? Her self-respect? Oh, no, of course not. *Those* were already thrown entirely to the wind.

She clutched the bedpost while Mrs. Polley fastened her gown, then pinned her hair with the same swift efficiency with which she did all such tasks. It was remarkable that anyone would release such a servant from service. But of course Mrs. Polley hadn't been of much use to her modesty and self-respect, sleeping the evening away while she drank glass after glass of punch.

"Now there, miss, you go out there and hold your head up." She clucked her tongue. "It wasn't your fault that man led you into debauchery."

"He did not lead me, Mrs. Polley. I drank the punch by my own will."

Her companion's bulgy eyes narrowed. "I know what I know."

Then she knew wrongly. One of Diantha's few pristine memories of the night was of Mr. Yale gently but firmly removing her hands from his person. Repeatedly. The debauchery had been entirely hers.

She faced the door, heartbeats smacking against her protesting stomach. But there was nowhere to hide, and she did not particularly wish to hide now. Last night she had seized life and lived it with abandon—at least the parts she recalled. She would not now cower in a tiny bedchamber of a farmhouse somewhere in Shropshire for another moment, no matter the certain embarrassment she faced beyond.

She grasped the handle and went out.

It was a long, unadorned room boasting a wooden table flanked by benches and an enormous kitchen hearth before which an apron-clad woman and girl stood. Ramses popped up from a spot before the fire and padded over to her, wiggling happily. Standing at the far window, Mr. Yale turned.

He smiled his slight smile, nothing mocking or knowing or any different from before, and a little chord of dread unwound within her. She curtsied and nearly tumbled over. His smile lengthened only a bit. He bowed.

"Good day, ma'am. How are you feeling?"

"Not perfectly well." *Wretched.* She smelled wretched too, her skin radiating a treacly acridness that made her nostrils curl. She probably looked wretched too. But the bedchamber had no mirror, which was for the best. Best not to know what he saw now.

Because what she saw was perfection. Even garbed in his usual black coat, breeches, and boots, a waistcoat of exquisite quality and crisp white shirt and cravat, he made her throat tighten up a bit. But today he looked different. His cheeks carried a glow even in the dimness of the gray day filtering through the windows, and his eyes seemed especially clear.

"Mrs. Dyer, may I make you known to our hostess, Mrs. Bates? And this is her eldest daughter, Miss Elizabeth Bates, whose excellent cooking we enjoyed for dinner today."

"How do you do, ma'am?" The mistress of the house curtsied with a rustle of apron. "We're sorry you've been poorly. I was ill when I carried my first, Tom, and Betsy here too." She nodded confidingly. "It'll be easier with the third."

"Thank you for your hospitality." She went forward, the steam from the pot rising to her nose and catching up her throat again. She swallowed tightly and smiled. "I cannot imagine what you must have thought when we were obliged to stop here in the thick of the night like that. You and your husband are very kind to have taken us in."

"The good Lord says that when we invite in a stranger, we invite Him in, ma'am. And Mr. Dyer being so gentlemanly, we'd no worry."

The girl bounced a curtsy, all coltish slenderness, the exact opposite of Diantha at that age. But exactly *like* her then in another manner: Elizabeth's cheeks and brow were peppered with red spots. Each one seemed to radiate brighter as she blushed.

"I'm only Betsy, miss. And my cooking ain't nearly so fine as the gentleman says." She directed a starry-eyed glance at Mr. Yale.

"I am certain you must deserve the praise, Betsy." Diantha had no doubt she'd directed precisely the same starry look at him last night. Because she was madly curious to see how he liked the flattery of awkward girls still in the schoolroom, she mustered the courage to glance at him. But he was not looking at Betsy, he was looking at her, and her gruesomely uncomfortable stomach did another flip-flop.

"My saints, Betsy," Mrs. Bates said, setting down her cooking spoon and peering out the window. "You run out and close the gate before that goat escapes, and I'll fetch the . . . eggs. Mrs. Dyer, I've set tea for you." With a thoroughly transparent look at her daughter, she ushered Betsy out.

Mr. Yale moved toward a sturdy oaken sideboard against the wall that bore a set of cups and plates decorated with little pink flowers along the rims. "Can you tolerate food?"

"No." She watched him pour from a jug into a cup and cross the room toward her. "But I will eat if you do."

"While you slept away the day, I dined with our hosts." He extended the cup. She accepted it and lifted it to her mouth.

"It seems we are to— *Oh!*" She spit the spirits back into the cup. "What do you think you're doing giving me *that*? Do you want to see me cast up my accounts all over again?"

His brow lifted. "Not in the least." He took her hand and urged it toward her mouth. "But you must trust me on this."

"No." She resisted. Her tongue was crimping at its base

and her stomach turning over, and also his hand was quite firm and warm around hers. Resisting apparently meant that he would touch her, so she gladly resisted. Clearly she had learned nothing from the failure of her adventure into wicked waywardness the previous night.

He pushed back gently. Rather than spill the liquor on her gown, finally she set the rim to her mouth again.

"They call it taking a dose of the hair of the dog that bit you." He stood close, looking down at her as she sipped. Her throat revolted, but she managed to swallow.

"An old superstition?" she managed between clenched teeth.

"It has a restorative effect."

She released the empty cup back into his hand. "I cannot believe you do that all the time. What I mean to say is, it was . . . *uncomfortable.* No wonder you've decreased a stone since last I saw you."

"I've not been sick since I was a boy."

"You haven't?"

"A man learns to hold his drink if he is wise."

"Did you really eat dinner?"

"I did. Would you like to know the measures of portions and each item on the plate?"

She chuckled, and he smiled in return. Beneath the blanket of that smile she did not feel her rebellious stomach or smell her putrid sweat or even mind her somewhat weak knees.

"I *am* hungry. And as we are apparently to have those children after all, I probably should eat to maintain my health."

He laughed. "Unusual young lady, indeed."

"Well, it wasn't my idea to assign to me an interesting condition." Now the whole of her legs felt wobbly. She slipped around him and went to the table where a plate of biscuits sat beside a teapot. "I cannot imagine what Mrs. Polley was thinking to invent that."

"No doubt she thought it would seem to our hosts a more appealing incapacity than drunkenness. Or disease. And I believe she hoped to impose a veneer of domestic responsibility upon her role in the thing." A beat of silence. "And mine."

Her fingers stalled on the teapot handle. "Yours?"

"With each cup of punch you took last evening, her glower at me deepened."

"Whatever for?"

"I am under the impression that she feels I was responsible for your excess."

"Well I know you were not." She poured the tea and drank it and her hands barely even shook, which was remarkable since he was watching her and there were any number of things she and he both could say now that would be highly uncomfortable. For her, at least. "How did we come to be here, and where precisely is here?"

"Imprecisely, somewhere between Shrewsbury and Bishops Castle."

"Bishops Castle? Isn't that—?"

"West? Yes. I thought it best to avoid the main road, for both secrecy and safety's sake."

"I recall you saying something about driving far enough so that no one would recognize Sir Henry's carriage and horses, so I suppose this family does not. They were very kind to take us in." She chewed on a biscuit and took a second. "Oh!" She looked up. "Did you leave my necklace?"

Now his eyes twinkled. "You would have it no other way."

"It was the honorable thing to do."

"It is a shame, really, that upon this quest you cannot yourself play the role of the hero."

"I don't have to. You are playing it. And . . ." She fiddled with a biscuit, crumbling it between the tips of her fingers. "I am grateful to you for being honorable." She was also mortified. And keenly disappointed.

Fortunately, he understood her meaning.

"We shall call it even then, shall we?" He said it quietly, but he sounded perfectly undisturbed.

Then, because she feared that her cheeks were red, she flipped a hand in the air and said with mock insouciance, "Anyway, you must play the role of the hero because we are heading south, and Scotland is north, of course."

"Scotland?"

"Where villains take innocent damsels when eloping."

"Ah. Of course." He moved away from her, returning to the sideboard and pouring another cup of spirits. "I suspect your Mr. H would have something to say to you haring off to Scotland to marry another man."

She nodded.

"Why do you call your intended by an initial only?"

"Because his name is far too silly to say aloud."

He allowed a moment's silence.

She released a thick breath. "Hinkle Highbottom. It's true: his parents should have been drawn and quartered to name him that. But . . ." She sealed her lips.

"I fear I pry, but I cannot withhold my curiosity. *But . . .* ?"

"But . . . it rather suits him. Not that he isn't perfectly amiable. It is only that he is . . ." She turned away from him and went to the stove because she suspected that if she looked at him she would cast him another of Betsy's starry-eyed looks. "He is a good man and I am sure I shall be very happy with him."

"What will he think of this mission of yours?"

She took up the long wooden spoon and stirred the stew. Sometimes she helped with simple tasks when Cook was entertaining Faith with biscuits or bread making. In the midst of this wild adventure, it felt familiar. Like this man. Despite the moments she had of pure awareness that he was not entirely safe, somehow he made her escapade to find her mother seem sane.

"He won't know about this," she replied. "No one will.

Except you. And Mrs. Polley, of course. Will we leave here now?"

"We have escaped Eads's notice for the time. It is already late in the day. I drove through the night and—despite my heroic status—require rest before taking to the road anew. Tomorrow will be soon enough."

"Tomorrow?" Her heart skipped. "But . . ." It did several little jigs about her chest. She lowered her voice and darted a glance at the window. "They believe we are married."

The slightest crease appeared in one lean cheek. Crossing his arms, he propped a broad shoulder against the sideboard. "If you recall, it was your idea."

"To pretend to the *Miss Blevinses* and *Sir Henry*. Not the entire Shropshire countryside." Mr. and Mrs. Bates would expect them to share a bedchamber. Diantha believed that she had the courage of a true heroine in her heart. But this she could not face, not with the pieces of her memories from the night before skittering around in her head. In short: she did not trust herself, even sober. The more she looked at him the more she wanted to feel again that alarming excitement she'd felt when he touched her in the stable.

There was a light in his eyes again that she did not perfectly understand, a bit fierce and not at all familiar.

"You are trying to make me feel uncomfortable," she mumbled.

"Now, why would I do that?"

"Because you think me disobedient and misguided. And immodest."

He came to her. She released the spoon to meet him head on. Inside she quaked, but she would not allow him to see that, not after everything she had allowed him to see the night before.

"I think you are all that is admirable, minx," he said when he stood close. "But you were nearer to the mark before."

Her breaths came fast and she could not resist looking at his mouth. "Nearer to the mark?"

"In believing that I possess sufficient honor not to take advantage of a lady in desperate straits."

She wanted to reach out and touch his waistcoat again to see if she had not imagined the hard muscle beneath it. "I believe that."

"Then, pray, pay me the compliment of knowing that I have your best interests at heart. And, Miss Lucas"—he held her gaze steadily—"I assure you that those best interests do not include me."

Her heart rose in her throat. She nearly choked on it.

"Of course," she managed fairly credibly. "You will sleep on the floor, then?"

The corner of his mouth quirked up. "I will sleep in the hayloft. For the benefit of our hosts we shall put it off to your illness and need for the comfort of a female companion who understands such matters. Mrs. Polley will share your quarters." His voice caressed. He mustn't know it or he would never speak to her in such a manner. It made her entire body hum.

The door opened and Mrs. Bates and Betsy found them like that, standing close together, as though they were truly a newly wedded couple expecting a happy event. Not, rather, that she was a wayward, wicked girl who wanted quite fervidly to kiss a man to whom she was not betrothed, and he had just told her quite clearly that she may not.

But she was a practical-thinking person, not the dreamer her stepsister Serena had always been, nor a meek lamb like her sister Charity. So she asked their hostess if she could assist in preparing supper, and as she moved about the room she tried not to notice that—despite his words—he watched her without ceasing.

Chapter 8

"**H**e's a beauty, sir." The farm boy stroked Galahad's nose.

"Are you fond of horses, Tom?" Wyn affixed the leading line to the inside carriage horse and drew the trace through its ring. Sir Henry's cattle were not in the first flush of youth, but they were far from hacks, and they'd managed the narrow track he had taken southwest handily enough in the moonless night. Wyn regretted the theft. But the necklace would compensate the old squire for the loss until he returned to London and could send money. His funds were slim, but sufficient. Then he would retrieve Miss Lucas's jewelry and restore it to her.

Rather, he would ask Leam or Jinan to do so. Neither would deny him, for by then he would be in no position to do anything of his own volition.

In the meantime he hoped she would not regret the loss of her jewels. But she didn't seem the sort to regret, rather to seize what she wanted without hesitation, as she had tried to seize him.

"These here are the finest I've seen." Thomas hefted a forkful of hay. "Is that one the lady's saddle horse?"

"No. This one was bred to be a hunter and she belongs to a duke." As Miss Lucas belonged to her father and eventually to Mr. Highbottom. It was a damn good thing her father had already arranged a match for her. With her ripe lips and eyes full of a desire as heated as it was innocent, she wouldn't last a season in town with her maidenhood intact. She would offer that sparkling smile and those questing hands to the next man she naïvely trusted, and that man certainly would not refuse her. What fool other than he would?

The boy's eyes rounded. "Well, that's a fine thing, you knowing a duke."

"I know him only by hearsay." By the report of a girl with red, puckered scars across her cheeks and brow.

"What's he like, then?"

"He lives alone in an impregnable fortress."

The lad whistled through his teeth. "A castle?"

"A castle he never leaves and into which he never allows a soul. The duke is a recluse." A recluse who prized his lost filly beyond telling, but who had insisted to the Falcon Club's director that he would not pay for her return unless he first saw her, and that the man who retrieved her bring her directly to him. Into his fortress.

"They do say some of them great lords is nicked in the head."

Wyn settled the pads and collar about the nearside horse's breast. "Not only the great lords."

"The lady seems to be feeling better this morning." Tom split a smile. "My mother and Betsy are crowing to have a real lady helping with the chores."

"I don't believe she minds it. She is an unusual lady." A country girl, reared on the stark coast of Devonshire by a recluse stepfather and an unkind mother. A girl who, when she drank to excess, became as affectionate as a kitten and as lusty as an opera singer.

The eldest Bates daughter appeared in the stable doorway. "Tom, Papa wants you at the cote."

"I'll be up soon."

Her glance flickered to Wyn then back to her brother. "He wants you now."

The lad set the pitchfork against the wall and tugged at his cap. "I'd best see to those sheep, sir." He cast Galahad another appreciative look then left. Betsy gave Wyn a shy smile and followed. Trailing behind them, the dog turned at the door, trotted on its three good legs back to the carriage, and leapt up onto the box. Wyn shook his head.

"Ramses," he said, slipping the bit into a horse's mouth. "A royal name for a scrap of a mongrel." It watched as he ran the breaching strap along the offside horse's flank and buckled it. "You do know that you are not my dog."

It peered back at him with its black eyes set in a mat of brown and gray fur, just as it had when he climbed into the loft the night before.

"I suspect you do not in fact know that." He moved around to affix the straps on the other horse. "But you see, Ramses, I cannot have a dog at this time." As he could not have a girl with lapis eyes and a beautiful smile and the most damnably persistent hands he'd ever had the torturous pleasure of being obliged to remove from his body.

She'd spent the previous evening on a wooden chair far from the hearth, embroidering an apron. Brow creased and luscious lower lip caught between her teeth, she plied the needle with quivering fingers—still suffering from her excess of the night before, he'd no doubt. But she had not complained. Instead, when she finished the work she presented it to the farmer's eldest daughter with a smile. Then she sewed lace to the edges of Mrs. Bates's nightcap.

"Took that lace from one of her own dresses," Mrs.

Polley had muttered to him as she removed his empty glass from the table. He'd taken only cider, and this morning the tremors were worse because of that discipline. "Wants to give these good people something of true value, just like herself." Her bulbous eyes had narrowed. "An angel who doesn't think anything of herself, my mistress. She deserves to be treated right."

Wyn agreed wholeheartedly. He'd kept that notion in the front of his mind the night of Sir Henry's fete as she pressed her curves to him and the whiskey in his blood told him to pull her closer yet.

True value. Though perhaps not an angel, not with her delight in teasing and her determination to succeed on her mission. And her seeking hands and perfect breasts.

Better than an angel.

The dog stared at him from ebony buttons in a curious face.

"Yes, I am aware that a man with intent to murder a duke has no business putting his hands on any woman." He attached the traces, drew the horses one after another to the pole and affixed the coupling reins.

A shadow crossed the square of pale light from the yard. Her knew her shadow. He knew the contour of her neck, and the dimples that flashed in her cheeks, and how her eyes rolled back when she laughed at him. He could describe the shape of each of her fingers and shades of golden brown in her hair, and the precise locations of the tiny scars on her pert nose. These were the sorts of details he had trained himself at an early age to notice and served him well as an agent of the Falcon Club. He was not slipping, it seemed. And knowing her in this manner provided him a decadent sort of agonizing satisfaction.

She came toward him. "Good day, sir."

"Good day, ma'am. How do you do this morning?"

She laid her hand on a horse's neck and stroked, her ungloved fingers slender and comfortable upon the animal.

"Considerably better. Fully recovered, in fact." She wore a plain blue gown cinched with a ribbon beneath her breasts. The night before as he lay in the straw alone he'd spent time imagining those breasts stripped of garments. He had imagined touching her. He had told himself it provided distraction from the pull of the bottle Bates offered him earlier, which he'd declined. No more whiskey while in the company of Diantha Lucas. He didn't trust himself.

Now her breasts were before him, albeit clothed. Still, reality proved greater than imagination. "I am glad for you, then." He turned from her to recheck the reins.

"It's true, I will not be experimenting with spirits again. Will we leave soon?"

"Momentarily."

She glanced toward the stable door. "The Bateses are wonderfully kind people. It is a marvel we were so fortunate to happen upon them." She hovered at his shoulder on the balls of her feet. "Betsy is their eldest, you know. A year older than Tom. She entered the harvest fair baking competition this year with her own entry and won. She is very proud of that accomplishment."

He glanced at her. The slightest stain of pink covered her cheeks.

"She must be." He moved to the rear of the carriage and took up a rope to fasten the traveling trunk in place.

She came again to his side and Wyn felt her move the air. He *felt* it. She was a spring breeze that with the gentlest aggression threatened to send his world spinning.

"She is fifteen. She told me she has a *tendre* for a boy who lives on the next farm, yet she is afraid to reveal to him her interest for fear he will scorn her." She spoke more slowly now. "I think it is more than shyness on her part."

"Do you?" He tightened the rope about the trunk.

"She hides her face when she can."

Ah. Of course. "She will learn confidence in time. She is young yet," he only said.

"I don't think it is her age."

"Perhaps not."

A lengthy pause. "*Do* men notice such things?"

He could not pretend he hadn't any idea what she meant. Naïve regarding man's baser nature or not, Diantha Lucas was much cleverer than she liked others to think.

"Yes. I am afraid most men do."

She was silent a moment. "I knew that, of course. I mostly asked to see how you would . . ." Her voice faltered. "How you would . . ."

He turned. "How I would re—"

Her chin collided with his jaw.

They both jerked back. Her hand flew to her face. A full, rosy flush washed across her lovely features, and tension flooded Wyn precisely where he did not wish it.

Fingers over her mouth, she backed away a step. He crouched and looped the rope above the rear axle, pulling in a slow breath.

"I will not insult either of our dignities, Miss Lucas, by pretending that you did not just attempt to kiss me." He glanced at her over his shoulder.

"I did." She performed the usual damnably taking twist of her lips. "I should very much like to."

He leaned his forearm onto his knee to turn to her. "Did you hear nothing I said to you yesterday afternoon?"

"I wish I had managed it more successfully."

"Apparently not," he answered himself, and stood.

She frowned, her features coming to life again. "Oh, why *not*? The Bateses believe we are wed, and Mrs. Polley has just dropped off to sleep so she will not discover it. I am not proposing marriage to you. It would just be one kiss, and no one would know."

"*I* would know."

"Well then you could simply forget about it right after, couldn't you?"

"No." Never. Dear God, she was unbearably pretty. He

scanned her face aglow with mingled indignation and hope, unable not to take his fill of looking. "Do you even hear yourself now?"

"Yes. Don't be silly. Although I suppose it isn't silliness but rather gentlemanliness. I admire that about you enormously, of course, but it is inconvenient at the present."

He laughed, because the only other alternative was to drag her delectable body against him and kiss her until neither of them could see straight.

A crease slipped across her brow. "You already know that I occasionally have lapses in modesty. But why must you be a gentleman at all times? Except of course in that stable."

He had not been a gentleman when she'd drunkenly clung to him and he'd nearly given her what she wanted. The thoughts he'd had then were not gentlemanlike. Nor was fantasizing about her the night before. Nor was the ready tenor of his body now.

Damn it, where were the rules when a man needed them?

Rule #8!

"A man is only a gentleman if he is never otherwise." He matched her tone, seeking steadiness. "Except perhaps in a stable," he admitted.

Her lashes flickered up. "We are in a stable now."

God help him. "That we are."

"Just one kiss," she whispered. "I promise I shan't bother you about it again."

Bother? Rather, enchant, torment, torture. Her lips and eyes and silken neck and perfect breasts beckoned.

Damn the rules. If only for a moment.

He cupped his hand around the side of her face, his palm reveling in the warmth of satin. Soft skin. Soft hair. Soft woman. He nearly groaned from the pleasure of it. Her eyes were wide as moonlight. He bent to her.

Her lips were infinitely sweeter than he had imagined,

plump and yielding. For the barest moment he allowed himself to breathe her in, to capture her scent of fresh air and sunshine amid the autumn mist, to feel the caress of her against his mouth.

Long enough for his body to stir and a hot thread of panic to dart through him. Good Lord, *he had to have her.*

Intoxicate.

She intoxicated him.

He drew away. She gulped breath, her lashes stuttering open. Then she smiled and the lapis pools shone.

He choked back a groan.

Mistake. Weakness. Enormous mistake. *What had he been thinking?*

"That was a perfect first kiss," she breathed.

"Second." His voice was uneven.

"Second?"

He tapped a fingertip to the place on his jaw that she had first attempted. Her berry lips opened in a grin of pure delight.

He should kill himself now rather than wait to meet his end after murdering the duke. None of the thoughts in his head were gentlemanly. None of the desires. He saw a flash of her pink tongue and wanted it wrapped around every inch of his body—several inches in particular. He wanted her here, beneath him in the straw and damn every scruple, rule, and plan he'd had for the past five years. Ten. Fifteen. The way Diantha Lucas made him feel was far from gentlemanly. He needed to be inside her.

She had no idea. Despite her inebriated advances and innocent insistence, her face wore an expression of complete satisfaction. She hadn't any notion what lay beyond kissing, of what he could do to her now.

The air seemed thin.

He could regain control.

"Are you in the habit of assigning numbers to the kisses you share with gentlemen, Miss Lucas?" Speech.

Inane speech would help. He would imagine himself in a London drawing room trading flirtatious banter with a lady of society. In a manner of weeks she would be just that, after all, safely surrounded by propriety and safely none of his business.

"Numbers?"

"Counting them up on your fingers, as it were, like points in a card game."

"No. Why would you think that?"

" 'First' suggests you anticipate a second."

" 'First' actually means that you are the first man I have ever kissed."

Her first kiss? *Impossible.* Yet he was a scoundrel for even imagining otherwise.

"Your suitors have not—?"

"Oh, well, I didn't have any suitors in Devon—except Mr. H. I was all spots and two stone rounder until last summer, after all. Gentlemen found nothing of interest in me. *You* didn't." She said it so blithely, as though commenting on the shade of the grass.

"I found your quantity of opinion interesting. And before that I found that you danced quite prettily."

"You *remember*?" She drew her chin in, disbelief bright in her wonderful eyes. "You remember at Savege Park two years ago when I told you that you should not drink as you did? Do?"

"I do. Remember, that is."

"Oh." She seemed to consider it. "But you don't really remember dancing with me on the terrace at Lord and Lady Blackwood's wedding. You *were* drunk then."

"I remember everything, Miss Lucas. It is my curse."

She seemed not to hear the last. "Do you . . . ?" Her gaze fluttered past his mouth, then down his chest. "Do you remember what those young men were saying to me?"

"I remember that you wished them to cease teasing you."

Her voice quieted. "You saved me."

He turned back to the carriage. "I merely recalled them to their manners." He affixed the final loop of rope and pulled it tight. "All is ready here. We can leave immed—"

She grasped his arm. His every muscle tensed. She would not make this easy, but Wyn didn't know if he wanted it to be easy. Part of him wished to crave something he could not have, and to suffer accordingly. It was the foolish part of him, the part that had trod that path of craving and suffering so well he knew it by heart, the part he'd thought he left behind when he escaped home, then again when he joined the Falcon Club, but that nevertheless clung tenaciously.

"Can—" She caught her lip in her teeth. "Can you tell me . . . ? How does one breathe?"

Very unsteadily while those eyes gazed up at him. "Breathe?"

"While kissing."

Not easy. He tried to moderate his voice. "In the usual manner, I imagine."

Her slender brows dipped.

"At opportune moments," he suggested.

Her lips twisted up in that manner he both dreaded and longed for.

"Through one's nose, perhaps," he said, because his only refuge was to continue speaking or to walk away.

"Really?" She appeared unconvinced.

And so, because her skepticism suited his need to have her lips beneath his again, he showed her how one breathed while kissing. To her soft gasp of surprise, he took her waist in his hands, bent to her mouth, and kissed her in truth this time. Her lips were warm and still, and then not still as he felt her eager beauty, tasted her, and made her respond.

She held back at first, and then she gave herself up to it. Her mouth opened to him as though by nature, offering him a sweet breath of the temptation within. If he'd gone seeking an innocent with more ready hunger he could not have found her. But he had not wanted an innocent. He'd wanted no one, yet here he was with his hands on a girl he could not release, his tongue tracing the seam of sweet, full lips that she parted for him willingly.

"Now, breathe," he whispered against those lips, then he sought her deeper. She made sounds of surrender in the back of her throat. He wanted to run his hands over her body, to pull her to him and make her know what a real kiss could be.

"Breathe." *God, she smelled so good.* He could press his face against her neck and remain there simply breathing her. But he feared that if he enjoyed much more of Diantha Lucas he would be in a very bad way when it came to giving her over to her stepfather and subsequently her intended. A very bad way indeed. And she didn't deserve it. *Rule #9: A gentleman must always place a lady's welfare before his own.*

She slipped her tongue alongside his, gasped a little whimper of pleasure, and he coaxed her lips open and showed her more than how to breathe. He showed her how he wanted her.

It was a pity for Miss Lucas's welfare that no gentleman could be found here, after all.

She wanted it to go on and on, forever and ever.

His first kiss had not been what she expected. Having a man actually touching her face was a bit odd. It was not soft like when a woman bussed her on the cheek, but firm, and he smelled of leather and horse and a hint of elegant cologne. But after a moment she'd thought it was quite nice. *Quite.* It made her heart beat swiftly and her breathing cease. She'd been glad she arranged for Betsy to play lookout so Mrs. Polley would not discover it.

It did not feel odd any longer, and *glad* seemed an enormous understatement.

She never allowed anyone to touch her waist, not even

her sisters when they embraced. Told so often by her mother and the girls at school that she was as wide as a tree trunk, she'd learned to pleat her gowns to hide her belly. When he grasped her waist she recoiled. But his hands were so large and strong and certain, and anyway his lips on hers made her forget entirely about her waist because she simply could not think. She gripped his arm, which was thrillingly hard, unlike his mouth that was a little bit open over hers and hot and made her hot too. But not just on her mouth. Rather, in other places that he was not even touching with his lips or hands, below her belly especially—deliciously warm and needy in a strange sort of way. It wasn't what she had imagined—not in the least. She had always assumed it would be wet and distasteful, but the only place she felt wet was between her legs and he seemed to be doing the tasting.

She slipped her fingers higher on his coat sleeve to feel more. His muscles contracted beneath them, and the warmth low inside her fluttered.   •

"Breathe," he murmured again, his voice a bit rough, and again she made the attempt, more of a choke than anything before his mouth covered hers anew. And while it was only lips touching, she felt like he was touching quite a bit *more* with each kiss. His hands slipped up over her ribs, so warm and strong and holding her firmly, halting just below her breasts.

Yes. She liked a man's hands so close to her breasts. It made her feel very hot and not at all uncomfortable. A little wild, truth be told, with delicious swirlings in the tips of her breasts. Her fingers clutched him and she let his lips urge hers open farther.

His tongue caressed hers. She gasped.

This—this *perfect* touching—this could not be a typical kiss. She parted her lips, inviting him to touch her like that again. He did, then again, mating their tongues in a hot, slow dance that made her feel a little frantic. She met his advances, welcomed him inside her. It felt *so good*, indescribably good, like he was touching the very center of her. He was making her weak but she wanted more. More of *him*. All the little points of her body, her *skin*, wanted to be closer to him.

She curved her fingers around his shoulder and pressed herself forward. His grip tightened, holding her in place apart from him.

Abruptly he ended the kiss.

She opened her eyes. It took a moment to focus.

"Second," she said in a remarkably thin voice. He was so handsome, his hands were tight around her where no one's hands had ever been, and he made her dizzy. "Or rather, third."

"Did you breathe?" His voice was very deep.

She nodded. By some miracle she *had* breathed while he kissed her, but frankly could not seem to now. "I regret having asked for just one."

He released her and stepped back. His silvery eyes looked like mercury, like the soft throbbing inside her, but his brow creased. "Did you plan that?"

"Of course. I always have a plan f—"

"For everything." He turned and moved toward his horses, and her heart did a few stuttered beats. Her lips were moist, and she still wanted his on them, and much more of his hands on her body.

She darted a glance at the door. No Betsy in sight. Mrs. Polley must still be safe in the house.

"Would you perhaps kiss me once more?"

He turned to face her, but now his silvery eyes were fierce and his jaw looked hard.

"Miss Lucas, do not ask again."

"But, I—"

"If you ask again, I vow I will tie you up, stuff you in that traveling trunk, and haul you back to your stepfather's home at once."

"I would not fit in my traveling trunk. It is too full of other items."

"I would remove those first, of course." He turned to the brown horse and drew it forward. "Was your claim the other night that you can drive an empty boast or truth?"

"I never boast. It's true. I learned when I was quite young." At a ridiculously tender age she had convinced the coachman at Glenhaven Hall to teach her. Her stepfather always complained about how successfully she cozened the servants into agreeing to her wayward plans.

He tethered the brown horse to his mount. "Then you may drive. Only do not overturn the carriage. Mrs. Polley would undoubtedly find some justification for scolding me for it rather than you." It seemed that he teased, but his eyes still glittered sharply.

"I promise not to overturn it." She watched him move through the stable door ahead with his horses. "Thank you."

"You needn't thank me. Galahad prefers to be ridden rather than follow."

She touched her fingertips to her lips to see if they felt different on the outside. They did not. But *she* did. He had just taught her how to breathe, and everything inside her felt different.

"I meant thank you for the kiss."

He did not pause or acknowledge her words. But she thought she heard him mutter "Minx" as he went into the yard.

Chapter 9

Fellow Subjects,

*I have frustrating news. The man I hired to follow
the member of the Falcon Club that I discovered
has lost the trail. I share with you this information
because I have had letters from many of you excited
at my discovery, and I cannot bear to hold you in
suspense. It warms my heart that you are as desir-
ous as I to know the truth of this club.*

—Lady Justice

Dearest Lady,

*I beg of you—mercy! You must cease this teasing
prose. When you write of warmth, your heart, and
desire all in the same sentence, I vow I can barely
hold my seat. I would erect a tent before the office
of your publisher and sleep in it nights in the hopes
of capturing a glimpse of you entering the building
upon the dawn. Indeed, I have attempted it! Alas,*

*the street warden will not allow it. Thus I am forced
to beg of you, my lady, consider my febrile imagination and give it rest.*

Increasingly yours, &c.,
Peregrine
Secretary, The Falcon Club

Sir,

*You needn't concern yourself over Lady Rabble-
Rouser's recent ramblings. Raven's skill at avoiding
danger is unmatched. He will throw off this un-
wanted attention without trouble.*

—Peregrine

Chapter 10

He must get rid of her.

He could not wait on Carlyle's arrival at the rendezvous place he'd indicated in the note sent with young William. He must be rid of her now before she invited him to take greater liberties with her. Before she made further *plans*.

Dear God, she could drive a man mad with her eager hands and ripe lips and the hunger in her mouth. If she offered him herself again, he wouldn't even bother resisting. Nine girls in ten years, and he'd never been truly tempted. But now the bottle called to him more stridently than it ever had before too. Undoubtedly, he was slipping. His desires were not entirely within his control any longer.

But if he could keep temptation distant he could fight it. Riding provided some relief. When she rested from driving, however, and he tethered Galahad behind the carriage and took up the ribbons, she did not retire to the back of the carriage with Mrs. Polley. Instead she sat beside him, her arm brushing his with each bump in the road, and she told him stories obviously intended to amuse that gave him opportunity to watch her supple lips move, her hands that had clutched him gesture. She spoke with warmth and laughter, frequently darting glances at him. Despite her open manner, she was not at ease; her eyes shone in a manner they had not before.

He did not trust her not to come at him again. And so, rid of her he must be.

Opportunity presented itself mid-afternoon as the sun dipped, hovering over the hills of the Welsh marches as it did so often in his dreams. Years ago, smothered in the heat of the East Indies, during fitful nights he'd dreamed of this temperate, emerald land, the land he'd come to know in his youth, moving from farm to farm as he found work, carrying only his strength, a pack full of books, and the anger in his heart. During those years he had occasionally allowed himself rest. Every six months or so he visited the single place he'd ever felt at home. The only place he had ever been safe. The place he hadn't allowed himself to go now in five years and to which he had intended to take Miss Lucas until Carlyle came to retrieve her.

Now he could avoid going there. This was not the opportunity he would have chosen, but he couldn't throw it away. She seemed shy of nothing and her dedication to her mission was high. But when faced with true danger, she would not continue.

Duncan Eads would assist. Unintentionally. The Highlander had found them. Now he trailed them on the road, never approaching close. But soon Wyn would allow him to come close—not close enough to truly threaten her, but enough to frighten her into being eager to return home.

The man in brown pursued too, albeit less subtly, in plain sight throughout the morning. It was frankly a miracle Eads hadn't yet dispatched his competition.

They stopped to eat the lunch Mrs. Bates had prepared, pulling the carriage into the shade of a copse of pine and oak in a shallow valley dominated by a mill. The place was deserted, miller and laborers at home for their midday repast. Nothing stirred now but the wooly denizens on the hills and the wildflowers that carpeted the valley fields in yellow, blown by the autumn breeze.

"The birds sing in every voice imaginable here." She tossed the reins into his hands and hopped off the box. "At home I only ever hear endless crashing waves, and gulls." She opened the carriage door and, as though she were the servant, hooked her arm beneath Mrs. Polley's to support the elder woman. "At the Park it's even worse up on that rock. Mrs. Polley, you must come visit Savege Park someday. It is far too grand for my tastes, but my stepsister is a countess. Truly! I knew you would never believe it, so I didn't mention it before."

Mrs. Polley patted her charge's arm. "I'll believe anything fine of you, miss. You're such a sweet one." She climbed stiffly from the carriage, nevertheless managing to glare at him. "Isn't she, sir?"

"She is, indeed." Sweet to taste. Sweet in his hands.

He glanced down the road. Eads would come along soon.

"The two of you will flatter my head into enormity." She dimpled but her gaze skittered away from him. She did not believe the praise. All the better.

She led her companion to a stone seat devised from a wall of the mill. The building was high-roofed, the wheel turning as the little river snaking through the valley rushed beneath it, washing the place with sound. Within the hour the miller would return and again set to work on the mounds of freshly harvested grain stacked beneath the roof. Wyn knew the rhythm of harvest season in this country as well as he knew the workings of a pistol and precisely how to employ it to his advantage. For now they were alone, appealingly isolated.

He uncorked the bottle Bates had given him that morning and made certain she saw him drink from it. White gin, poorly distilled, it burned his throat and empty stomach.

But it served the purpose. Within minutes the tremors in his hands would cease, and within half an hour she would believe what she must to make this charade a success.

Pretense and lies, masquerades and subterfuge. The stuff of his life. He swallowed another mouthful, peace streaming through his veins at last.

It was a damn good thing his great-aunt had died when she did, before she knew the truth. She would never have believed it. Or she would have, and it would have broken her heart.

Diantha watched him covertly. She was accustomed to covert watching. Discouraged by her mother from putting herself forward among her parents' friends, and perfectly aware that behind her back the other girls her age were poking fun at her, she'd learned how to watch and listen without being seen. With one exception: Serena had always seen her. Her stepsister, the kindest person she had ever known, had eyes in the back of her head. If she'd learned anything good in life, she'd learned it all from Serena. But when she found her eavesdropping, Serena's loving looks always made Diantha feel guilty as sin.

But her mother was a sinner, so she clearly had gotten that in her blood.

She laid out the picnic, serving Mrs. Polley from the loaf of bread and crock of soft cheese, watching out of the corner of her eye as Mr. Yale again eschewed food for drink. She didn't blame him. Her appetite had fled, though undoubtedly for another reason than his.

The butterflies in her stomach would not cease. Even prattling on about thorough inconsequentials while he drove hadn't distracted her. His hands holding the reins looked so strong and *they had been on her*. On her waist. *Nearly touching her breasts*. Recalling it made her short of breath. And recalling his tongue in her mouth made her very hot, especially in her most intimate quarters.

She was a thorough wanton.

He reclined now in the rear seat of the open carriage, a bottle in one hand. Beneath hooded lids, he watched her. With an indolent grin, he lifted the bottle in salute to her.

A strange pulse went through her. It was not his usual smile, not the slight smile that gave the butterflies wing. This one made her feel a little sick.

She glanced about her. The brown horse grazed peacefully in the shade at the edge of the trees. But Galahad's head was up, his ears perked high. Diantha threw her escort another glance. His eyes were closed now, his hand slack about the bottle. Mrs. Polley snored, propped up by Diantha's folded cloak, Ramses curled in a ball at her feet, worn out too.

She slipped off the bench and crossed to Galahad, passing the carriage and the sleeping man. Diantha knew little about horses, but he was certainly alert. Perhaps a rabbit had caught his attention, or the miller had returned. Galahad turned to glance at her approach, his ears flickering, then shifted his attention ahead again.

"What is it?" She changed direction toward the corner of the mill, the ground beneath her feet damp in the shade of the trees abutting the far side of the building. "It must be very—"

She froze.

Her first reaction should have been to scream. Her sisters would have. They would respond appropriately to encountering a villain. But all Diantha could think was how huge the man was. At least a head and a half taller than her, he was not fat but thick in his arms, chest, and neck. Even the pistol he pointed at her looked burly.

"Whisper a breath o' sound," he said in a deep, quiet voice, "an A'll shoot ye."

She locked her lips shut. But they quivered. Her entire body quivered. If Mr. Yale were to glance her way, he would see her standing unnaturally like a statue and come to her rescue. But he was asleep from too much liquor. And if he came running then the man would shoot him, for this must certainly be the Highland Scot who was as strong as a Dover dockworker.

She nodded, pleading instead with her eyes to be allowed speech.

"Ye'll go inta those woods nou." He gestured with the pistol. "Ye'll remain there until A tell ye ta come out."

"I won't," she whispered.

He cocked the pistol.

That it had not been cocked before took some of the edge off the rush of fear that accompanied the clicking sound. But she really should have screamed. She should have run. She was a complete failure as a heroine, and now her hero would be killed. "I won't," she repeated with as much volume as she could muster; fear choked her throat. "You are the man following Mr. Yale, aren't you? Mr. Eads?"

Interest lit his dark eyes. His skin was tanned by the sun, the hair beneath his hat dark and long. He was clean-shaven and well-dressed, and except for his accent spoke like a cultivated Englishman. He must be a gentleman of sorts.

That notion opened her throat a bit. "I won't go," she rasped.

From the edge of the woods came the unmistakable click of another pistol cocking.

"Miss Lucas, do oblige me by removing to the carriage at this time."

Mr. Eads went perfectly still. *"Yale."* The single word conveyed anger and threat at once.

"Good day, Eads. I would bow to you but it would ruin my aim, and in any case if you even flinch, *mein tumhe maar daaloonga.*" He stood in the shadow of trees. "But I should rather not do so in the presence of a lady. Miss Lucas, if you will?"

"No. Was that Scottish? What did you just say?"

"Lass," the giant rumbled, "tell him ta lay down the pistol nou."

"No. You have evil designs upon him and I will not allow you to see them through."

"Evil designs he brought upon himself." He seemed very certain of that. Diantha's heart leaped from a gallop into a career. "Nou, tell him ta lay down the pistol."

She scrambled for words. "Well, who hasn't brought bad fortune upon themselves at one time or another?"

"Eads, lower your weapon and release the hammer. Carefully." Mr. Yale's voice had dropped.

"Ye told her ma name." Mr. Eads studied her with his dark eyes. "Ye willna allow her ta be harmed, A think."

"Ah, the mountain pauses to think. This is something of a surprise, I shall admit."

"Ye imagine the Raven is the only man to think in the midst of action?"

"The *Raven*?"

"Madam, if you would step away from the man pointing a pistol at you, that would uncomplicate matters considerably." His voice was so smooth she knew he could not be inebriated. The breeze fluttered in the tails of his coat and the lock of black hair across his brow, but his hand pointing the pistol at the Highlander did not waver.

She must not allow this.

"Mr. Eads, do you have a Christian name?" she blurted out.

He frowned.

"A first name," she explained. "So that I may speak to you as a friend of sorts."

He didn't look away from her. "What is this, Yale? What trick are ye playing?"

"No trick to speak of. She does this. Befriends people." He sounded perfectly at ease. "It is one of her many charms."

Diantha did not take her eyes off the tower of man. "I suspect Mr. Yale is being sarcastic, but—"

"I am not."

"But I should like to know the Christian name of the man who will murder me. Because you see, Mr. Eads, I shan't allow you to kill him."

His gaze flickered over her gown then back to her hair. "No even ta save yer life?"

"Of course not. What would my life be worth if I allowed another to die so that I could live? But more to the point, I have need of him at present. You see, four years ago my mother ran away from home, abandoning me with my young sister and going off to live in a brothel." A brothel from which, she realized quite abruptly, she did not wish to retrieve Lady Carlyle. "I—I am determined to—to find her." Her heart pounded. That *was* what she wanted, after all, to see her mother and speak with her, *not* however to be thrown back into the daily misery of life with her. Somehow contemplating the potential end of her existence presently, amidst the shimmering glow of an adventure both dangerous and delicious, this became very clear to her.

"Despite my stepfather's objections I have set off on this road to find her," she continued a bit less steadily. "But, being unfamiliar with the route, I require assistance, and Mr. Yale has pledged to render it to me. So, you see"—she could hear her voice growing stronger with each word—"if you kill him I shall be destitute, not to mention rather desperate, for I have only a fortnight to find my mother again before I am discovered by my family and sent home probably to be locked away for the remainder of my life for having done such a scandalous thing. In any case, I simply must go. Therefore, you and Mr. Yale must settle your differences in some manner today that is not killing each other." She glanced at her traveling companion then back at the giant. "Do you both completely understand?"

To her utter astonishment, Mr. Eads lowered his pistol.

The weapon made a soft metallic sound as he released the hammer. Diantha didn't dare breathe.

"Wise man." Mr. Yale walked forward, pistol still pointed at the Scot's chest.

Mr. Eads's square jaw locked and he slewed his gaze aside. "Damn ye, Yale."

"Already taken care of, old chap."

She darted glances between the two. Their eyes looked deadly.

"You may not shoot him," she said hastily.

"Thank you, Miss Lucas. But if you could now—"

A female shriek cut the air, followed by a cracking noise, a massive thud, and a series of yips then a man's shout: "Oh, *God*!"

Then everything seemed to happen at once. Ramses came flying around the corner, barking wildly. Mr. Yale snapped the pistol across Mr. Eads's wrist. The Scot cried out, dropped his weapon, and swung a huge fist at Mr. Yale's jaw. It went wide of the mark while the butt of Mr. Yale's pistol instead found its home upon Mr. Eads's brow. Ramses clamped on the Highlander's boot, snarling. Mr. Eads's hand flew to his head, a string of foreign words flowing from his mouth, and the little dog left off his ankle and retreated warily.

"Don't try it again." Mr. Yale plucked the weapon from the ground. "Are you otherwise armed?"

"O' course A am." The other man scowled, pressing his fingers to a small gash on his forehead. "A won't use them. A only hit ye because ye hit me."

"You should have dropped your weapon when I told you to."

The moaning from the yard beyond took up epic proportions. Mrs. Polley's scolds rang over it. Diantha moved toward the sounds then glanced back. Her breath jerked. Her traveling companion was holding his pistol barrel against Mr. Eads's brow.

"I will have your word on that, Duncan."

Duncan?

The Highlander's massive shoulders heaved. "God damn, Yale." He glared. "Ye have it."

Mr. Yale lowered the pistol. "And I'll know why you've given it too, after I have seen to the trouble that lies beyond." He tossed the other man's weapon onto the ground at his feet again, as though it were nothing at all. "Leave now or assist, as you wish. But do not go far, or your fate will prove much worse than in Calcutta."

Diantha stared. He came to her side and she finally thought to snap her gaping mouth shut.

"You are *giving him back* the pistol? You *know* him? His *Christian name*?"

"And his birthday, as well as his mother's favorite marmalade. Now, Miss Lucas, if you would finally oblige me by following my instructions, I pray you make yourself a shadow behind me and come along. Your lady's companion, it seems, has attacked a man."

She did as he bid, mostly because it seemed foolish to defy a man who had bested a person of Mr. Eads's size with such little to-do, but also because she was rather shaky and following him felt safe. He made her feel safe, despite the hulking Highlander retrieving his pistol behind her and the moaning man in the yard ahead. Yet at the same time it was quite apparent to her that he was the cause of her shaking.

"This may all be somewhat unusual to me," she whispered. "Naturally."

"I imagine so, but it is over now." He paused and looked down at her. "Thank you for your assistance." It was not what he wished to say. She could see this clearly in his silver eyes that seemed to seek within her where she trembled with emotion at once both terrible and wonderful. His gaze only made the trembling worse.

"And?"

His brow drew down. "And you needn't worry again."

"Mr. Eads will not threaten me again, or he will not threaten you?"

"Even were he to, I suspect you could hold your own." It seemed for an instant as though he wished to smile, but now his eyes held no light.

"Why did you pretend to be inebriated?"

"You mistake it. I did not pretend." He turned and followed the wall around the corner.

Mrs. Polley stood over a prone man, little bits of white cheese and crockery spread all about the place like snow. The man's face was contorted with pain. He glanced at Mr. Yale and groaned anew.

"See here, sir," Mrs. Polley directed at Mr. Yale, "if this is that man you're so worried about following us, he's a bag of cowardice."

"Perhaps his courage is merely not as hearty as yours, ma'am." Mr. Yale crouched at the man's shoulder. "It seems your pursuit of me, sir, has landed you in an unhappy place today."

"Who is that harpy?" He gritted his teeth. His left leg was thrust beneath his other at an angle that made Diantha's stomach queasy again.

"Come now, sir. That is no way to speak of a member of the fair sex."

"She—" The man gritted his teeth. "She said you would be a clever son of a—"

"Ladies present, my friend." Mr. Yale clucked his tongue. "Do mind your manners. Now, tell me, who are you and who is 'she'?"

The man closed his eyes, his lips a zigzag.

Mr. Yale nodded. "I see. You are probably wise. I would not tell me who I am and what my purpose is in following me if I were you either."

"What will you do with him?" Diantha asked. "He is in terrible pain."

"From the bump on his head as well as the broken leg, no doubt." He looked at Mrs. Polley. "You have outdone yourself, madam."

"A man's never snuck up on me without suffering for it," she said indignantly, brandishing a crockery handle bereft of crock.

"Have you many men sneaking up on you, then?"

"In my younger days I wasn't a dog to look at. Some of those so-called gentlemen in my lady's house didn't know where their hands shouldn't be." She slanted him a knowing look then turned her orbs meaningfully to Diantha.

Diantha ignored it. "What will you do with him?"

Mr. Yale looked down the road. "I shan't have to do much, in fact. Would you be so kind as to retrieve that bottle of spirits from the carriage and give it to him?"

The man's eyes popped open. "You wouldn't kill me."

Mr. Yale's brows went up. "Of course I wouldn't. What sort of person do you imagine you are pursuing?"

But he had threatened Mr. Eads moments ago with murder. Hadn't he? Diantha's heart would not cease racing. It was quite clear that he was not what he seemed on the surface, but she did not understand which was real and which was not. Within moments her journey had gone from reckless to truly dangerous.

"The miller who is now returning to work after his dinner will set your leg," he said. "You will want to have gin in you before that, I daresay." He glanced at her. "The bottle?"

She went, casting a glance over her shoulder to see him walking toward the miller, an aged man, short, dark and wiry with age, followed by two younger men, all in rough garments. Mr. Eads was nowhere to be seen.

She returned to the prone man as Mr. Yale and the others approached from the road. The miller and Mr. Yale were in quiet conversation but she understood nothing of it. The language met her ears peculiarly, lilting yet at once rough with strange rolls and crunches.

Mr. Yale stopped before the man in brown and crouched again, scratching his fingers through the shaggy fur between Ramses' ears as the dog pressed against his thigh. The muscle was clearly defined by his breeches now. Diantha became warmly aware that she had never stared at a man's thigh before. It was a day, it seemed, for disconcerting realizations.

"This is Mr. Argall," he said to the man in brown, gesturing toward the miller whose wrinkled face was grim. "He and his sons here will set your leg then convey you to their home, where Mrs. Argall will care for you until you are able to be taken in a cart to the nearest public house. You needn't concern yourself with compensating your hosts; I have arranged for that. No—" He raised a palm, though the man's tight lips showed no sign of speech. "You needn't thank me. Only, be a considerate guest, if you will. The Welsh are infinitely generous with their hospitality, but they do not take kindly to ingratitude." He paused and lowered his voice. "As I do not take kindly to being followed. Pray, sir, bear this in mind when you are once again on your feet."

He stood, spoke again with Mr. Argall, then shook the miller's hand and came to her.

"Miss Lucas," he said quietly, grasping her elbow and drawing her away from the scene of broken bones and crockery toward Galahad. "Would you be so kind as to busy Mrs. Polley in preparing for our departure while I converse with our friend for a moment in private? He has gone down the path to avoid notice, which is undoubtedly for the best."

"I will, as long as you do not shoot him and he does not shoot you."

"I shan't. He shan't. Not on this occasion. I promise it." He released her and mounted his horse. "I won't be but a minute and then we will be on our way again."

She stroked Galahad's satin neck. "The miller looked at you as though he knew you. *Do* you know him?"

"The Welsh are a curious folk, Miss Lucas. One must never mind their peculiarities."

"How do you know the language? Have you lived here?"

"For the first eighteen years of my life."

He was Welsh. She didn't know why it should surprise her, except that she had never imagined him living anywhere but London. He had always seemed so elegant, so gentlemanlike and refined in speech and manner. But now she had seen him unshaven, his eyes glittering with anger. And when he had kissed her, she hadn't felt like a lady being kissed by a gentleman. She'd felt like a woman being wanted by a man.

She needed to know more about him. She needed it in some place deep inside her she did not quite understand. "Are you familiar with this region, then? Is your family here?"

"My father's home is considerably north and west, on the coast of Gwynedd."

"Why are we in Wales now, Mr. Yale?"

"Because that is the direction in which the road went, Miss Lucas." He pulled Galahad away and along the path that ran abreast of the wood.

He was not telling the entire truth. Given circumstances, she should not trust him. But the bleak flatness of his gray eyes now pressed all such worries aside. He was not the man she had met thrice at Savege Park, nor even the man in the Mail Coach two days ago. Something was terribly amiss.

Chapter 11

"**Y**er drunk, Wyn."

"That I am, Duncan." He drew Galahad to a halt in shadows beneath the pine boughs and dismounted. The muscular roan tethered to a branch nearby lifted its head. Wyn turned to the Scot sitting with his broad back against a tree trunk. The evergreen looked small in comparison. Pistol or no, Eads could kill a man with his bare hands. But they'd fought hand-to-hand before. Wyn knew Duncan's weaknesses. *Very few.* And he was indeed far drunker than he had intended.

He hadn't intended to be drunk at all. Only to pretend. Allow Eads to come close enough to frighten her but not close enough for danger. But Eads threatened her in truth. History repeating itself. Pride. Arrogance. A bottle. A girl in danger.

"A could take ye nou." Eads's posture was relaxed, his eyes alert. "A'm nae so quick as ye. But yer reflexes must be slower when yer drunk."

"Myles is no doubt paying you a fortune to bring back my heart. Still beating, I suspect."

The hulk's eyes narrowed.

"I did not intend to cross him, you know. I merely needed to retrieve a girl." A girl Myles had borrowed from her family without leave. A girl that the anonymous director of the Falcon Club had assigned him to retrieve. The director hadn't known, of course, that he had once worked for Myles too. For Myles . . . and others.

"Yer lying."

"You've no idea how often." He stared at the spot on Galahad's neck where a girl with lapis eyes had laid her hand minutes earlier while her wide gaze sought more answers than he could give. His vision fogged into the black.

Eads climbed to his feet. He stood only an inch or two taller than Wyn, but his mass gave him impressive size. "A'm short-tempered with liars."

"Ah, but you have given your word." He tipped his brow against the horse's neck. The gin had rendered his body somewhat numb. "And my reflexes are—" He snapped back the cock on the pistol beneath his arm, the barrel pointing dead on the Scot's chest. "—fine."

Eads whistled through his teeth. "How do ye move with such haste, man? What sort of demon are ye?"

"Take care, Duncan. The superstitions of your ancestors are surfacing."

"And yer the man who has no ancestors, aren't ye? Or so ye claim."

"Why did you relinquish your weapon after she told her story?" He tilted the pistol's mouth aside.

"Yer unpredictable with drink in ye. Ye'd never harm me sober, but ye woudna hesitate ta nou if A drew on ye. Or if A'd truly threatened her. She means something ta ye, A think."

"Don't bother thinking, Duncan, old chap. You know how it wearies me."

"Yer a conceited ass, Wyn."

"Possibly." He closed his eyes. The scenery and man

before him were crossing, as they had by the mill—when he'd drawn on the assassin pointing a pistol at a lady with the heart of a hero—when every vein and artery in his body had shook with fear. "Tell me why, or I will in fact shoot you now. I will shoot you in the kneecap and you will spend a month in Mr. Argall's barn whiling away the hours with that chap with the soft skull." He leaned back into his horse, the beast's steadiness the only solid thing in existence. "Poor fellow."

"Who is he?"

Wyn opened his eyes, the lids heavy. His throat and tongue were dry. He needed water, but he wanted brandy. "Haven't the foggiest. Do you?"

"A won't let him have ye. Yer mine, Yale."

"Yes, I am flattered. And so you see I find it remarkably interesting that you promised the lady you would not harm me. Now, do put my rampant curiosity to rest and tell me why you are granting me such a boon." A boon. He was beginning to talk like her. Before long he would be singing songs of knights and maidens cavorting in the glade. Or not.

" 'Twas for ma sister."

"Which sister?" He brought the Highlander's face into focus for an instant. "Ah. A sister who lost her way, much as the lady's mother has lost her way, I am to guess."

The Scot's jaw worked. Within Wyn, so deep he almost did not feel it, some memory of compassion stirred.

"I see." He uncocked the pistol and slid it into his traveling pack. "I wish her to believe that you remain a threat to me."

"A do remain a threat ta ye."

"A threat to me while she is in my company. And a threat to her."

Eads glared. "Yer playing a deep game with this girl, Wyn."

"Unfortunately not as deep as your depraved imagination has taken you, Duncan. But you have given your word and I anticipate your assistance."

"A'll be there at the end."

"I expect you to. Once I have delivered her safely into the hands of her family, you may do with me what you will. But . . ." He turned his head to the man that he had tracked halfway across Bengal, searching for a Highland rebel only to discover a man beaten by grief and angry as a cobra to have been found. "If you would first allow me to take care of an errand, I would be much obliged."

"A don't owe ye anything."

Wyn set his foot in the stirrup. "I haven't the least idea why you are still working for Myles when you have an estate—good Lord, a *title*—to retrieve in Scotland." He hauled himself into the saddle, recognizing even in his muddled state the hypocrisy of these words. "But if you truly cannot wait to kill me, then I ask only one thing."

The Scot's eyes narrowed.

Wyn swallowed over the desert of his throat. "If you must kill me, Duncan," he said slowly so as to get the words just right, "don't make it easy on me. Draw the thing out, will you?" He turned away, pressed his knees into Galahad's sides and guided him out from beneath the trees into the slanting afternoon sunlight, toward the mill in which as a lad more than a decade ago he had worked a harvest season.

Mr. Argall did not in fact recognize him. He no longer resembled that boy who had loaded grain and hauled sacks of flour hour after hour, week after week, gaining strength in his arms, hot meals, and a few coins for his labors. That boy had been angry. Running away. But he'd not yet killed in cold blood.

Diantha had saved them both. Instead of cowering in fear and begging him to return her home, she met danger with passionate sincerity. In baring her heart to the man pointing a pistol at her, she had been braver than he'd ever been. Begging Eads to spare his life so she could save another's. Believing he would help her.

He pinned his gaze between his horse's ears, dead ahead to the carriage waiting on the road. Chestnut curls spilling out of her bonnet caught the light filtering through high clouds and glistened.

Once before a girl had trusted him. Chloe Martin, the Duke of Yarmouth's terrified ward, had told him her horrifying story and he promised to help her. Just like today, he had trusted in his extraordinary abilities—his intelligence and reflexes. And, in a tragic accident, instead of saving Chloe he had killed her.

He would not help Diantha Lucas. She had put her faith in the wrong man.

Another ten miles along the narrow southerly road skirting hills that for centuries the English had called Shropshire and the Welsh theirs, the modest town of Knighton rose along a steep main street. Wyn installed the ladies in a tidy inn, arranged for their dinner to be served in a small private parlor, and saw the horses bedded in stalls with dry straw. When the ladies bid him good-night—the maiden with creased brow, the matron with suspicious eyes—and ascended to their bedchamber, he went to the taproom.

Diantha knew she oughtn't to be standing where she was standing or contemplating what she was contemplating.

In theory, while lying restlessly in bed beside a snoring Mrs. Polley, it had seemed a reasonable enough program: knock on his door, demand that he answer her questions about Mr. Eads and the man in brown, then return to bed and finally sleep. It was not a plan in the truest sense, but it seemed the only solution to calming her nerves. She must understand better what had passed. She must understand *him* better. With knowledge, a woman could plan.

She lifted her fist toward the door panel and took a deep breath. Then a deeper one. Then she closed her eyes and—

"Impressive, Miss Lucas."

She whirled around. He stood across the short corridor, at the top of the stair. A sconce in the stairwell lit him from below, casting shadows into his eyes and carving dark hollows in his cheeks. His arms were crossed loosely over his chest, one black-clad shoulder propped against the wall.

Her lungs released a little whorl of air. "Oh, there you are."

"I wondered how long you would stand there before you mustered the courage to knock. Or the wisdom to return to your own bedchamber without knocking." His voice sounded unfamiliar, slow. *Emotionless*. Without any feeling at all, like his eyes at the mill. "Not as long as I had imagined."

She should walk over to him and make this conversation unremarkable by behaving as she always did. She could not. His unnerving stillness glued her feet to the floorboards.

"I wish to speak with you about what happened today."

"And you could not wait until breakfast to do so, I gather?" No warmth either—the warmth that was always there beneath the teasing.

"Mrs. Polley will be with us at breakfast. I understood that you wished her to remain ignorant of our encounter with Mr. Eads today. Did I understand you incorrectly?"

He moved toward her, his steps very deliberate. A shiver of fear passed up her spine. Why she should fear him, she hadn't any idea, unless it was the lusterless steel of his eyes in the dark corridor or the scent of cigar smoke and whiskey that accompanied him. But she was accustomed enough to the latter from parties during her visits to Savege Park. Her fear must come from the incident with the pistols earlier that day.

No. It was not the pistols. It was his eyes, the absence

of any light in them. It made her at once cold and un-
nervingly hot—cold with that unexpected fear, and hot
with . . . she knew not what.

"You understood me well enough. In that matter." He
halted close. Unbidden, her foot inched back, her heel tap-
ping the door panel, and he watched her. "But it seems,
Miss Lucas, that you understand me very poorly in another." His gaze flickered down her face to her mouth,
black lashes obscuring the gray of his darkened eyes. For
a moment he seemed to study her lips. Then it dipped to
her breasts. "Very poorly indeed." He reached forward
and placed a palm against the wall beside her head.

"I—" She pulled in a tight breath, but it made her
breasts jerk upward. He was still looking at them. *Him.*
Mr. Yale. Her gentlemanlike hero. Her hero who'd had
his tongue in her mouth that morning. "I . . ." Her own
tongue seemed to forget its purpose, lost in the memory
of his caressing it.

He leaned toward her, bending his head, and the scents
of strong liquor and tall, very dark man tumbled over her.

"You should go to your bedchamber now." His voice
was husky.

"I want you to kiss me again." She nearly choked on
the words as they tumbled out. "Or rather *more,* actually."
She had not meant to say this. She had not planned it.
But she did want it. She'd wanted it since he walked out
of the Bates's stable that morning, yet he had told her she
mustn't ask again. But now she might take advantage of
the fact that he had been drinking spirits. A great quantity
of spirits, it seemed. His gaze returned to hers, but it did
not really look at her, rather, it focused elsewhere even as
he stared directly at her from only inches away.

His fingers clamped about her wrist before she even
saw him move. She gasped. His grip dug into her flesh.

"Do you? Now why doesn't that come as a surprise to
me, I wonder?"

"Mr. Yale," she managed in a whisper, her breaths fast in the close space between them. "You are hurting me."

"With every pleasure there is also pain, Miss Lucas." His eyes were dull and distant. "Has no one ever told you that?" He tilted his head down. Half of her wished to flee, the other half to rise onto her toes and press her lips to his hovering so close.

"Just how intoxicated *are* you?"

His gaze traveled over her face, and for an instant she saw a spark of light. "Entirely."

His mouth covered hers.

It was not like the kisses he had given her that morning in the stable. It did not begin gently or slowly. It was complete, his mouth seizing hers thoroughly and demanding of hers reciprocal treatment. And she could not deny that she wanted him to kiss her like this. Her lips would not deny it. They sought his as eagerly as his sought hers. Feeling him made her more eager yet, and hungry for even more with each meeting. His flavor, whiskey and tobacco, was another world, a world of men and pistols and honor and danger, and she was weak with her entrance into that world. *His* world. He was kissing her and she knew he did not wish to but he was doing so anyway. *Because he was foxed?*

She didn't care. She didn't care that she was standing by a man's bedchamber door in the corridor of an inn, letting herself be kissed like no lady should. She *wanted* this.

His hand came around her face, scraping through the hair at her temple and holding her tight, then his other as well. He drew her to him, capturing her mouth again and again in a succession of kisses that grew more intense. The tip of his tongue strafed her lips, slipping along the edges, stalling her breaths in her throat. Then he dipped inside her and she melted.

It was like dying and coming alive at once, so perfect, sublime, and she felt it *everywhere*—in her mouth, in her breasts and belly and in the deliciously hot place between her legs. A sound came from her throat she did not intend, a sigh slipping from her lips to his. "*Oh, yes.*"

He broke away.

One powerful hand went to his face. His breaths came hard, like hers, his fingers pressed into his eyes at the bridge of his nose. He shook his head once.

"No," he uttered. "God, no." He turned and moved to the stair with lurching steps.

She touched her lips, hot and damp now. Her heart raced. "Why did you stop?"

He swiveled around to face her, catching the wall hard with one hand. To *steady* himself? New fear rushed through her, tangling with the pleasure.

He returned to her in three fast strides and she hadn't time to think, to plan, before he was upon her. He grabbed her arm, then the door handle behind her.

"Do you want to know what a man does to a pretty girl who begs him for kisses one too many times, Miss Lucas?" His voice was a growl.

"No." She couldn't breathe. "*Yes,*" the whisper stole from her.

He yanked her into the chamber and seized her about the waist. She fell against him and he grabbed her chin with an ungentle hand, trapping her face tilted up to him. His eyes were dark, no pleasure in them.

He lowered his head and kissed her and she was the wayward wanton her mother had borne, wanting his lips on hers and his tongue in her mouth, and hers in his, dizzy with the feeling of her body pressed to his. He was all muscle and strength she had not imagined—the iron strength in his arms, the power in his hands, his hard chest and thighs. She was far too weak to withstand him, but she didn't want to. She sank her fingers into his arms and met his mouth hungrily, the thrusts of his tongue making her ache deep in her body, making her press her breasts to him more fully. Her skin and crevices seemed to hum for more contact. More kisses. More of *him*.

His hand spread on her waist gripped hard, his other slipping away from her face, fingertips trailing a rough path down her throat, then her neck. She gasped in air through the kisses, his hand spreading over her collarbone.

"This," he whispered against her lips, "is what he does." His hand surrounded her breast. "He touches her as he should not."

She gulped in breaths—swallowed—sought air. She had *not* known this. She had not even imagined this. She had been very naïve. How could his hand on her breast make her feel this way, like laughing and crying and wanting his tongue in her again more than anything? The place between her legs filled with warmth and a strange, urgent hunger. She gripped his arms tight and tilted her head back against the door, her breaths hard and fast as he fondled her, his thumb passing over the fabric beneath which her nipple pressed. She shuddered, a light ripple of every part of her, oddly frantic beneath her skin. It was almost too much. *Almost.* She did not understand the feelings, but they felt so good and she wanted them. But it *must* be wrong to want them.

She reached for his hand. "Mr. Yale," she managed to whisper, "you must not—"

His thumb slipped beneath her bodice. She moaned. He caught her mouth with his and his fingers stroked, and she did not protest. She trembled and told herself that this was all right because she could not stop him. He was too strong and she hadn't the will for it.

He pressed her body against the door with his own, trapping his hand within her garments, against her skin. She felt weak in his arms, the sheer size of him and his touch more than pleasure. She slid her hands to his shoulders, slipping them about his neck, feeling fine linen then skin—his skin, hot and wonderfully male—and into his hair. His mouth left hers to sink to her neck and she twined her fingers through his short, satiny locks.

"Ohh." There was *nothing* like this. Nothing had prepared her for touching a man so, or being touched by him. There could be nothing better than this, nothing more wonderful.

His fingers snagged in her garments, dragged the fabric down, and exposed her breasts, and swiftly Diantha discovered that there could in fact be something better.

She had always hated her breasts, too big and soft drooping over her big belly. But now even without that belly they were still ungainly, and there were the ugly stretch marks along the sides. She'd taken comfort in the notion that no one would ever see any of it.

Now Mr. Yale could see, but he seemed entirely disinterested in looking.

Touching was another matter altogether. He touched, his hips pinning hers to the door, his mouth caressing her neck deliciously, and he stroked her breasts and did remarkable things with the nipples that made Diantha feel she might simply perish of pleasure. She heard herself make little whimpering sounds and could not seem to withhold them. She gripped the back of his neck and struggled to keep his mouth upon her throat where it made her feel *insanely* good. But she also wanted him kissing her again.

Then he did kiss her, but not on her mouth.

He grabbed her hands from about his shoulders in a firm grip, then he dipped to her breast and licked it.

"Mr. Yale." She could barely muster sound, her breaths broken. His jaw was rough against her tender skin.

"This is what men do to girls who beg for kisses, Miss Lucas." His hands trapped her wrists to her sides with such little effort. "These are the kisses they receive." He licked her again, passing across a tight nipple then circling around it, then circling again barely skimming the peak. Then again, still avoiding the center. She squirmed, sunk in the pleasure he was giving her with this scandalous intimacy. Finally he kissed the nipple again. Her knees went to water. How could such a thing *feel this good*? And *how could she be allowing it*?

His grip on her hands was like iron. His teeth slid across the tight peak.

"Oh, *please*," she gasped, not certain whether she pleaded to be released or for more.

He pulled her mouth beneath his again. His hand tangled in her skirts, drawing them up swiftly, so swiftly the heat of his palm slipped along her thigh before she could gather breath to object.

Finally, she panicked.

"Please, no." She pushed her skirts down, against his hand pressing up. "Mr. Yale, you mustn't— *Uh!*"

He touched her, where she was most hot and wet and private, and she ceased struggling. She ceased breathing. She ceased existing except to be touched by him like this.

"But I must." His voice seemed so deep. His fingers stroked across her flesh, certain, meeting the needy ache. He touched her on the surface but she felt it inside and everywhere, her breasts throbbing with hunger, her thighs wanting to close around his wrist.

"Yes," she whispered, quivering, then *"Yes"* again when his fingertips skirted her entrance. Then she felt him enter her.

"Oh-h, Go-od." She closed her eyes, his lips brushing hers, his hand around her neck. "You should not do this." Her words were a mere breath, entirely unconvinced, her body ecstatic in his hands.

"This is more than you wanted?" He pushed his finger in again, fully this time. She gasped into his mouth. She felt him *completely*, so deeply pleasurable inside her it made her want to scream.

"Yes. *No*. I didn't know— *Ohh*." Now she did not

impede his efforts; she aided them. She pressed onto him, the feeling of him inside her making her wild. She wrapped her hands around his shoulders and welcomed him into her mouth and she knew he would have her now as a man had a woman. His kiss was hard, his hand ungentle, driving the need within her higher, tighter, deeper. She felt his desperation. She *wanted* his desperation. He bit at her lips, a groan rumbling in his chest she felt against her breasts, his fingers commanding her.

"*Diantha.*" It was a sound of protest, and anger.

He dragged his hand from beneath her skirts, gripped her head and kissed her over and over, crushing her against the wall, harder, and then brutally. She could not breathe. She ached. Her body burned. Her lungs screamed. She pushed at his shoulders, then shoved, then struggled.

He released her, falling back a step. She gulped in air. His gaze swept over her, black in the moonlit chamber, and perfectly, horribly empty.

She clutched her arms across her chest, trembling.

He reached forward, and she flinched. He blinked, then again, his breaths uneven. He grabbed the door handle and pulled the panel wide. Then he was out in the corridor and gone.

Diantha stood there—she did not know for how long—growing cold and shaking in the dark. He did not return.

After some time, when her heart had nearly regained its regular rhythm and her breathing slowed, she rearranged her garments, smoothed her hair back from her face, and went to her bedchamber, to the snores of Mrs. Polley, to her traveling trunk full of her belongings, to everything that seemed common and simple and safe. Unlike the rawness of her swollen lips, the thrumming readiness in her body, the frustrated coil that promised something much greater, she suspected, than he had allowed her. Unlike the man who had made her feel wanted because he was drunk.

Chapter 12

During the night the rain returned. The ostler muttered about moldy straw and hoof rot while Wyn harnessed Sir Henry's horses to the carriage. With unsteady hands he affixed the tether to Lady Priscilla's halter then to Galahad's saddle and drew them into the alley.

A pair of boys tossed a ball against a wall, Ramses scrambling after it, a cock and his harem scuffled about puddles for seed and corn, and despite the drizzle the town was awake with morning business. Across the street a bakery bustled with early patrons, a farmer's cart laden with bales of grain trundled in the direction of the mill, and laborers and townsmen passed in and out of the inn's taproom for their morning pint. Wyn tied Galahad to the tethering post and tossed a coin to a lad sitting idle beneath the archway.

"Watch the horses," he said in the language of his countrymen, the language he had not employed in years until the previous day. The lad tugged his cap and leaped up.

Wyn drew in a long breath and moved toward the doorway to the inn. She appeared there, dressed in cloak and bonnet, bandbox in hand, shoulders square. She did not disappoint his expectations; she came straight to him.

"Good morning, sir. Mrs. Polley is finishing her tea and will be out directly. But I suspected it would be best for us to address this swiftly rather than await an opportunity for private conversation later, so I am here." She held her chin high, no missishness or shame about her. But her gaze was not without wariness, and a soft flush of pink colored her cheeks.

"Miss Lucas, I am profoundly grieved over the offense I offered you last night." The words he had been practicing to himself silently since he rose were, nevertheless, not easy to speak aloud. "If you wish it, I will give you my name."

She stared, lashes fanned out from eyes as wide as astonishment could fashion, her perfect berry lips a perfect O. Then a small, choked sound came forth: "Oh."

She did not elaborate.

"It is a modest name as carried by my branch of the family, but respectable," he continued. "I must leave it to you to decide whether you require the protection of it now."

Her thick lashes flickered, the swift beat of a hummingbird's wings suspended in the moment above the gaping violation of what he had done to her.

Finally she blinked once and said, "Thank you. That will not be necessary."

He swallowed over the sickening sensation of his deliverance. And hers. "Are you quite certain?"

"Yes. My future lies with Mr. H. It has long been anticipated. And, of course, he did not offer for me at gunpoint."

"No one is pointing a gun at me."

"Only your conscience, I suspect, which is probably more noxious to you than any weapon. Anyway, the relevant fact is that I am already spoken for."

They stood for a moment like that, silent, while it seemed she might speak again. But she did not.

"Then, pray allow me to apologize."

"Apologize?" Her mouth popped open, providing him a glimpse of the temptation within. "But weren't you trying to teach me a lesson?"

Good God. "No."

"No? Then . . . ?"

He could say nothing. She did this to him, robbed him of words, and at the moment he was grateful for it.

"You needn't apologize." Her gaze darted away now, twisting the burning in Wyn's belly. "You know, I think it would be better sometimes to be French. French people seem to toss off uncomfortable incidents without the slightest tickle of conscience."

"Miss Lucas, I beg you will forgive—"

"Truly, it isn't necessary." Her fingers gripped the cord of her bandbox, stretching the leather over her knuckles.

"Please, allow me to—"

"I do not require—"

"Woman, let me apologize."

Her gaze returned to him. "But you *needn't* apologize. You did not intend—" She halted, then: "You were not at fault."

He stared. "Forgive me for disagreeing, but you have a peculiar notion of suitable behavior for a gentleman."

"I don't, really. But while I do not understand the particulars of your acquaintance with Mr. Eads, it is clear to me that your encounter with him was not a simple matter, and I cannot blame you for drinking to excess last night."

"You are too generous. Also misguided not to blame me for a great deal more than that."

Her lips twisted up. "Well, then claim the blame if you must, but allow me a share of it too. I should not have encouraged you. But I have learned my lesson and I shan't do that again."

"You needn't have concern. I will not harass you further."

Her eyes seemed to retreat again. "You will not?"

"I will not." He wanted to now. Even with his head aching and regret fierce, he wanted to take her body in his hands and enjoy what he hadn't been clear-headed enough to enjoy when he'd had the opportunity. "I will not touch you again. Upon my honor."

The graceful column of her throat constricted in a jerky swallow. "You said if I asked you again to kiss me that you would take me home. Do you intend to take me home now?"

He should. He must. "I recall no such request last night."

The wide blue eyes lit again with hope. "You don't?"

He shook his head. In fact he remembered only one thing with piercing clarity, the reason he had released her finally. And it had not been her halfhearted protests.

"I suppose that is for the best," she said with a wrinkle of her brow. "If you tried to take me home, I would be obliged to escape you again."

"You would not succeed."

She took a decisive breath. "We have had this debate before. I think we must agree to disagree. In any case, the point is moot." A twinkle lit her eyes. "Presently." Her spirit was irrepressible.

"Miss Lucas."

"Yes?"

His chest felt tight, his heartbeats fast. "Forgive me."

"If you can forgive yourself, we shall call it even." The corner of her lips twitched. "Again."

Mrs. Polley emerged from the inn. "Rain and more rain. We'll be soaked through." She bustled forth, traveling bag clutched in round fingers.

"Oh, not at all." Miss Lucas flashed her an encouraging smile. "The carriage has a—" Her gaze shifted and her face brightened. "Isn't this a coincidence? We know that boy." She moved toward the lad holding Galahad's lead. "Hello. Do you remember me? We shared a coach a few days ago, the Mail from Manchester. This gentleman was sitting beside you that afternoon. Was this your destination?"

The lad snatched off his cap, cheeks reddening in round spots beneath a layer of soot. "G'day, miss. No, it weren't." His English sufficed, but it came forth from a tongue accustomed to the tones of the Celts. His fingers, stained black, proclaimed him a mine worker.

"It was not my destination either. Or this gentleman's." She chuckled. "But here we all are. And how nice it is to see a familiar face upon a strange road."

The boy's blush brightened.

"Where are you headed now, then? If you are going our way, you might travel with us rather than by coach. We have ever so much space in our carriage."

The lad's face fell into shock. Mrs. Polley beamed.

"Well, there, miss," the lad stuttered. "I can't be doing that, not with my grubs, not in a lady's carriage. But if you'd be having any work for me, well then I'd be much obliged, as I've run though my last coin two days ago."

"Two *days*? But how have you eaten since then?"

"The baker threw me the heel of an old loaf this morning." His teeth showed in a skin-and-bones grimace. Like most mining boys, he was light of flesh.

Brows perked high, she turned to Wyn. "Well, I am certain we have a task or two he can perform, haven't we?"

The boy's dark eyes were hesitantly hopeful now.

Wyn spoke to him in Welsh. "From what are you running, lad?"

"Why do you think I'm running away from somewhat, sir?"

"Because I was once there myself."

The lad seemed to consider a moment. "I was down at Cyfarthfa with my sister till fever took her. Went up to Uncle's in Manchester with my last coin, but he sent me back on the Mail."

The iron mines on the other side of the Black Mountains

had killed the boy's sister—taken by disease no doubt—yet his uncle had insisted he return there. A common enough story, even for children younger than this one.

"I couldn't go back, sir." His brow was small beneath a thatch of black hair, but fixed. "Sold my seat on the Mail for a strip of jerky."

"Can you tend horses, lad?"

"Yes, sir. My brother works the pulleys at Merthyr Tydfil. I helped him with the animals there before my sister came on and we hired at Cyfarthfa."

"I will pay you in coin for your labor, and you will be fed." He turned to Miss Lucas and said in English, "He will come."

Her face lit into a smile. "Splendid. What is your name?"

"Owen, miss."

"It is a pleasure to make your acquaintance, Owen."

Wyn watched the lad squirm, unaccustomed to pretty ladies paying him attention, no doubt. But he could prove useful later in the day. Although he gazed at Miss Lucas with the instant devotion she drew from most she encountered, the boy would not gainsay a fellow countryman. Welshmen were a loyal band. Her generosity, Wyn knew, would serve him well.

He gestured for Owen to take the luggage and turned toward the stable. He paused.

"Oh, good heavens," she whispered at his shoulder.

"Good heavens, indeed," he replied quietly, the rain on the cobbles beyond the archway muting their voices.

"That is the Misses Blevinses' groom, isn't it?"

"It is." The old coachman stood in the shadow of the carriage house, stroking the neck of one of Sir Henry's horses. A thoughtful frown crumpled his wrinkles.

"What an unfortunate coincidence." She bit her lip. "He has recognized the carriage."

"It seems so."

"If he is here, the Misses Blevinses must be too."

"Have you still got your valuables in that bandbox?"

"Yes."

"Good girl. Go inside now. Take Mrs. Polley with you."

"And then?"

"I will come for you in three minutes. Three. Be ready to depart swiftly."

She turned and drew her companion into the inn. Owen's dark gaze shifted to the stable, curious yet aware. Wyn almost smiled, but now was not the time to enjoy having returned to his native land, to appreciate the quick, savvy mind of another Welshman.

"Owen, did you see a large man saddle a roan in that stable earlier, perhaps an hour ago?"

"Yessir."

"Where is that man now?"

He shrugged. "Haven't seen him since."

Eads had remained very close; his horse had been saddled in its stall when Wyn went to prepare Galahad and the filly. The Highlander would not be far now, ready to follow when they departed. But his momentary absence was sheer good luck.

He took Galahad's lead. "Go fetch that horse. Tell the ostler that the gentleman named Eads intends to drive my carriage today. Then meet me below the crossing." He pointed down the main street.

"Yes, sir." With a light step the boy went toward the stable. Ramses followed for a pace, then returned to Wyn.

"It seems we are to amplify our party by two," he murmured to the dog.

Ramses' black eyes peered up at him.

"You are thinking what I am thinking, of course. The more people she has to protect her from me, the better."

She'd thought he was trying to teach her a lesson. And perhaps at the moment he had been. Perhaps he was trying to stop himself from dishonoring her.

But he would prove no further threat to Miss Lucas.

He had set aside the bottle once before. It hadn't been particularly easy, but then he didn't have particular reason for it then, he merely wished to prove to himself that he could stop. Pride: the sin his father and brothers had accused him of so often.

He had exemplary reason now.

He could not frighten her into returning home voluntarily; her spirit of adventure and confidence were far too strong. But now he would use the serendipitous appearance of the Misses Blevinses to finally bring her to the place he'd told her stepfather to retrieve her—a place where the locals would not reveal their presence to any lawmen who might happen to catch up with them. Upon the road the rain would also be his ally, as well as her care for the people in her company. She would agree to stop for a time if it meant their comfort, long enough to allow Carlyle to arrive. If not the baron, then Kitty Blackwood. Kitty and Leam must be in London now, and the note he'd posted an hour earlier would ride the Mail to town swiftly, and Kitty would come.

In the meantime, he would regain control. The girl with the wide lapis eyes deserved it.

Sometimes behind the silvery gray she saw the eyes of a bird, intense and predatory. Or perhaps merely very, very hungry. Perhaps not the eyes of a predator but of a creature that wished to eat but who would not allow himself to kill. Behind the silver hid the famished eyes of a scavenger.

Mr. Eads had called him a raven. *The* Raven.

But his eyes only looked like that in the morning, before he began drinking spirits. He never drank them in the morning, although it seemed that at noon he gave himself leave.

Not today. Perhaps he did not trust himself. Perhaps he did not trust her. And well he should not. She had proven herself untrustworthy.

But as the morning slipped into afternoon and the rain became a steady drone, his eyes took on the hungry look again. Still, his boots trod the puddle-strewn road in steady strides. For hours he had walked thus, not sharing her mount even once. She was sore from riding awkwardly on a man's saddle, but he must be exhausted. Yet his stride did not falter, his hand firm on the lead of the big horse he had stolen from the inn's stable when they left Sir Henry's carriage behind.

"Mrs. Polley is asleep again." She glanced over her shoulder at Galahad bearing her companion and the luggage like a mule. Owen walked beside Lady Priscilla.

Mr. Yale did not respond.

"She does not believe we must travel quite this far west to escape the Miss Blevinses' notice," she tried again.

Still he did not speak, his gaze on the narrow road flanked by rock walls stretching endlessly ahead into the haze of rain. To either side, hills rose steeply in glorious hues of emerald and evergreen, copses of trees cresting the heights and sheep speckling the fields oblivious to the rain in their thin, late summer coats, all of it now veiled in silvery gray.

"I suppose she has less concern than we since she knows nothing of the threat Mr. Eads poses."

No reply.

She had been talking to herself like this all day. And staring at him, his broad shoulders covered by his black overcoat, the damp curl of his hair about his collar. She had touched him there. She still couldn't quite believe it. But she had the memory of sensation within her gloves now, and everywhere else in her body. And, of course, there was his altered mien, not in the least uncivil, only subdued.

He regretted having kissed her, touched her, and he did not remember it. She—brazen, wanton daughter of a wayward, wicked mother—remembered every moment. And she could not stop thinking about it.

"Are you familiar with this part of Wales?"

"I heard many stories of it in my childhood." He did not sound exhausted, or piqued, or unhappy. He sounded . . . normal.

She released a tiny breath. "What sorts of stories?"

"In Knighton, the town we left this morning, there is a clock tower at the top of the main street. Did you notice it?"

"Yes." She hadn't. She'd noticed only the regret on his handsome features and the flicker of relief when she refused his offer of marriage.

"If a man of Knighton wishes to divorce his wife, he may bring her to that clock tower in the center of town and sell her to whomever will take her."

She laughed. "That is positively barbaric!"

"Isn't it?"

"Of course you would never do that."

"Of course not." A pause. "Only if she were very troublesome." For the first time since the Bates's stable, his voice seemed to smile.

Happiness caught at her, simple and warm. She swiped rain off the tip of her nose. "Then it is a good thing we are not to marry after all, because I daresay you would be selling me at the clock tower within days."

He did not immediately respond. Then: "I daresay."

She swallowed over the sudden thickness in her throat. "Are we lost, Mr. Yale?"

"Not precisely, Miss Lucas."

He had called her Diantha the night before. And for a moment, in that moment, he had truly frightened her.

"Slightly lost?"

"Possibly." Another silence, washed by the steady stream of rain about them and punctuated by Mrs. Polley's snores.

"Probably lost?"

"Yes."

"What shall we do about it, then?"

He glanced up and she realized that she missed his eyes when he did not look at her. She drank in the profile of his jaw and the contours of his mouth. Droplets of rain fell from his hat brim onto his coat.

"Mrs. Polley is sodden to the bone," she continued, because speaking was considerably easier than contemplating his mouth and wishing for things she could not have, "and I think Owen is sleeping as he walks."

"It will be best to find a place to hide for a bit."

"To 'hide'?" He did not strike her as the sort of man who hid. From anything.

"To take shelter."

The rain fell heavily now, silencing all but itself. But he also did not seem the sort to shy from bad weather.

"Oh," she said. "For my safety from Mr. Eads."

Back to no reply again.

"But you said he agreed to allow you to assist me on my quest because of a tragedy having to do with his sister and a brothel."

"That was before you rode out of town on his horse."

Her hands jerked on the reins and the big roan snorted.

"You *stole*—" She glanced back at her sleeping companion and lowered her voice. "You stole *his* horse?"

"It was Eads or the law."

"Hm. I see. Given the policy on troublesome wives in that town, one might not hope to meet with justice over the theft of a carriage and pair."

"My thought precisely."

"Probably a good one. You don't think he will turn us in to the authorities?"

"I believe he will wish to avoid the authorities altogether."

She looked over her shoulder. The road behind was swathed in gray. "Perhaps we should pick up our pace a bit?"

"Or take shelter off the road where Eads will not look."

"Perhaps you're right. My available time is already growing short and we have had to make more detours than I like. It would be silly to advance yet farther. How far is Bristol from here?"

"Several days' ride."

"And perhaps the man in brown has confederates too. I would not want to run afoul of any more of your enemies."

"It cannot be wondered at."

"It would further delay us."

Finally the slight smile shaped his mouth. Diantha could not look away, her insides all tangled again.

"Why are you smiling now? You have not smiled at me all day, which cannot be wondered at, of course. But I cannot imagine now that this is a good sign."

He drew the horse to a halt. "The rain is worsening. I will send Owen ahead to scout out a place to rest for the night."

"An inn upon this deserted road? And you did not answer my question."

He glanced at their companions approaching from behind. "An inn may be too much to expect."

"A farm then." She could not ask if they would once again pretend to be married.

He seemed thoughtful. "I would encourage you to come down from there and rest while he goes ahead if it weren't for the mud and the prospect of Eads catching up."

"I would come down if Owen would take the opportunity to ride. Or you."

The smile lingered at one corner of his mouth. "You think infrequently of yourself."

"What on earth do you mean? I've done nothing but think of myself since I left Brennon Manor." Especially with him, begging for kisses when he told her not to.

His regard shifted to Ramses trotting ahead on the narrow road, his coat a matted mass, then again to Owen and Mrs. Polley. "You adopt strays," he said beneath the rattle of the rain.

"They needed our help, and we needed theirs."

"Not precisely." His eyes seemed to glimmer now. "Why do you do it? Do you intend to save the world from its ills, one lost soul at a time?"

He did not tease. She could see this. His voice held a desolate note that burrowed into her and made her feel achy again, but not like the night before. This ache was different.

"Give me your hand, Mr. Yale."

His gaze arrested. He did not move.

"Please," she said more quietly, her voice nearly lost in the rain.

He did as she asked, offering his hand, palm up. She brought hers beneath it and through her sodden gloves felt his heat so that, within, she stirred.

"Your hands are large and strong. You are accustomed to doing with them what you will. With very little effort, I suspect, you have an effect upon others." She could no longer hold his gaze. She laid her other hand upon his, matching palm to palm, fingers to fingers. "My hands are quite small, as you can see. I can do very little of effect. But what little I am able to do, I will always try to do." Wresting her courage from her soaked shoes, she lifted her gaze. He drew a visible breath.

"*Hem.*" Galahad appeared beside them, Mrs. Polley staring pointedly from the saddle.

Mr. Yale's hand slipped from hers.

"Owen, walk a pace with me up the road while I apprise you of our—" He glanced at her. "—plan." He set his hand on the boy's bony shoulder and the two moved away.

Mrs. Polley glared after them. Of course, she would glare much more pointedly if she had any idea that the hand he'd just allowed Diantha to hold had been up her skirts the night before.

She sighed. "I do wish you would cease looking at him as though he were a villain intent on my ruination. He has no such designs." Would that he did. Teresa had told her there were many duties gentlemen expected of their wives, other men's wives, opera singers, and an occasional French maid. Diantha thought she had discovered one of those duties last night while pressed up against his bedchamber wall. She wanted to discover more but that, unfortunately, was not in his program. "He merely wishes to help me, you know."

"I'll not be saying what I think his true intentions are, or not," her companion said with a wag of her head, bonnet spewing water in all directions. "But I'll warn you, miss, gentlemen with a dark look like that one do only what's to their advantage."

"Well don't we all? I think you will soon come to see your mistake."

Mr. Yale came toward them, alone now. "He is looking for a dry refuge ahead."

Mrs. Polley clucked her tongue disapprovingly. "There's nothing dry for miles, sir. You've brought us into Noah's flood."

"I am sorry for your discomfort, ma'am." He stroked down the filly's neck with quiet care. Diantha's insides went wobbly. He looked up and found her staring at him, and his eyes shaded. "No doubt we will find shelter soon."

Three quarters of an hour of green hills and muddy road later, Owen reappeared.

"Found a house ahead, back from the road." He glanced at her with a shy smile. "It's a grand place, miss. Looks like a church. But there's no one about. Knocked on all the doors and the gatehouse." He was speaking English for her sake, and she smiled in return. His cheeks bloomed with red spots beneath his pallor. Even he was tired, all of them weary of the rain, Diantha's teeth chattering and Mrs. Polley's face pale.

"Well, if it has a dry stable we might borrow it for a bit, mightn't we, Mr. Yale?"

"We might." He studied the boy. "Fine work, Owen. Thank you."

The lad took Galahad's lead. "Just up the road a bit, sir." He gestured.

They went. Not more than a quarter mile ahead, where the road bent south, a tiny lane led off north, overhung by a stand of old oaks interspersed with the tall dark pines that seemed so comfortable in this lush world. Vines twined in thick majesty around the gatehouse built of gray stone and the stone fence running along the lane, some still flowering and content in the rain. The drive was pebbled, sprigs of grass poking up here and there.

Hidden behind a copse of ancient trees, the house sat on a rise, a very large structure that did indeed have the look of a church about it—rather, several churches all connected in one grand sprawl. Its roofs sloped steeply to points, turreted towers of gray stone rising over the treetops. But the towers featured chimneys of modern appearance. Windows gleamed dimly, reflecting the black trees and the gray sky above.

A long, low building ran along the drive to another barnlike structure—the stable and carriage house, presumably. Huge rosebushes clustered about the buildings' knees. Beyond, close to the low wall that ran another fifty yards to a fenced sheep field, a wooden rope swing hung from a branch of a solitary grand oak.

"It's perfectly charming," she whispered, although of course that was silly since the horse's hooves were loud enough to be heard by a stable hand if there were one. She glanced at Mr. Yale. He scanned the house, his face sober.

"Owen, go around to the back and make certain there are none here."

Owen disappeared at a jog.

Mrs. Polley accepted Mr. Yale's assistance dismounting. "We're here now, sir. So what would you have us do?" She made a show of stretching her back, her squat round form like a tilting teapot, bonnet and cloak drooping. "It'd best be deserted or the poor souls that live here will have a sorry shock when they discover us soggier than stewed mutton on their doorstep."

"Stewed mutton sounds wonderful right about now," Diantha mumbled.

He smiled his slight smile and came to her. "Wishing for roast and shepherd's pie?" He grasped her by the waist and drew her off the horse. The moment her feet met the earth he released her, but he did not move away and she was obliged to pretend to him up close that his hands on her hadn't felt like heaven. Her knees and behind were wretchedly sore, but a tingle danced inside her now where he had touched her so deeply the night before.

"I don't suppose anyone is cooking stewed mutton for dinner inside?"

"I doubt it. But let us see how matters lie within before we relinquish hope of dinner entirely." He moved toward the front door.

She followed. "I thought we were to rest in the stable. Do you intend to enter the *house*?"

"I do."

Owen came around from the opposite side. "All's clear, sir."

Mr. Yale climbed the two steps to the door, a heavy wooden panel without adornment, and she went behind him. Closer, the stone seemed to be a subtle pink.

"But what if they return without notice?"

"Then we will hope they are gracious hosts. And Owen will keep a watch on the drive from the gatehouse. Owen, how would you like turning your talents to guard duty?"

"It'd be better than the mines, sir."

"You see? All is well." But his eyes gleamed with an odd intensity. Diantha followed as he ascended the stoop. He tried the door latch.

"Locked," Mrs. Polley harrumphed.

He reached into his coat and withdrew a leather case no larger than a billfold.

Diantha peered around his shoulder. "What is that?"

"Why are you whispering?" he replied as quietly. He opened the case with hands slick with rainwater and withdrew two tiny metal tools.

"Because what you are doing there seems remarkably clandestine."

"No doubt it is."

She wished he wore gloves. She wished she could not see his capable hands that made her feel weak all over.

"What are those tools, Mr. Yale?"

"They are a lock pick, Miss Lucas." He fit it into the keyhole.

"I suppose I should be shocked that you carry a lock pick in your topcoat pocket."

"Yet it seems you are not."

"That would be remarkably silly of me by now, wouldn't it?"

"Probably." Two metallic clicks sounded from the door. With the picks still in the keyhole, he lifted the latch. "Push on the door, if you will."

She reached past his shoulder. "What do you do when you haven't a third hand to do this for you?"

"On those occasions I do not break into houses, of course." The door remained fast. "It is bolted from within." He released the handle.

Her teeth clacked and she gripped her sodden cloak tighter about her. "What will we do now?"

"Try the back door. Remain here, if you will." He moved down the steps and around the rosebushes, Ramses trailing after.

In minutes a clunking sound came from within and upon heavy hinges the door swung open. Mr. Yale stepped back and bowed.

"Welcome to Abbaty Fran Ddu, ladies."

She stepped into the foyer, dragging off her sodden bonnet. It was a modest space and well appointed with dark wooden paneling, a graceful iron chandelier, and a tiled floor. The scent of dust was heavy upon the still air, but no mold.

"It is so modern. And wonderfully dry. I feel badly dragging in all our rain."

"As nice a place as I've seen, for all it being hid away in a valley." Mrs. Polley looked shrewdly about.

"How do you know the name of this house, Mr. Yale?"

He took Mrs. Polley's coat and her cloak, and gestured toward a row of servants' bells above an open doorway. Beside the bells hung an embroidered frame with the words ABBATY FRAN DDU picked out delicately in green and blue silk.

"Owen will bring in the luggage then light a fire. I suspect there is a parlor above." He motioned toward a staircase winding up from the foyer.

"Oh, but we cannot possibly go upstairs. We should remain here. The kitchen must be down that corridor. You have not removed your coat."

"I must see to the horses. But the place is empty. Be at your leisure. See to your comforts and your companion's first, then if you will, investigate the kitchen. The lad will not fare well for much longer without dinner."

"And me as well, you mean."

He offered a hint of a smile then bowed and went through the front door again.

Chapter 13

She moved about the house in obvious appreciation. Wyn watched her discovering, drawn to follow her as though he had not trodden these floors thousands of times before. Every opening door drew another smile from her, another murmur of pleasure.

"It is all so lovely, though remarkably dusty." She ran her finger along a windowsill in the East Parlor. "Perhaps the owners have been away for some time."

Five years. "Perhaps."

"We should confine ourselves to only this chamber, and try not to disturb too much. And we must leave compensation for food and fuel."

"There's peat to spare." Owen set a brick of dried earth in the grate and the musky scent twined throughout the chamber. The chimney was blessedly clean. No one had inhabited this house in five years, but it had not been left entirely untended.

She peeked under a Holland cover. "The furniture is in very fine condition. And everything is so neat and tidy and well appointed. I think a woman lives here. A woman of excellent taste. I wonder where she is now? London, perhaps, where I will soon be, and though she has been my hostess I won't even know if I pass her by on the street."

She drew a cover off a chair and folded it, dust swirling in the air. Her nose twitched, and she passed the back of her hand across it unselfconsciously. She hadn't the manners of a town lady; the country girl clung, unspoiled. Yet she was wise in reading others. Except him.

She had changed her clothing and wore now a simple gown of moss green that left her neck and arms bare but for the shawl about her elbows. She had creamy skin, a graceful neck and beautiful shape, and looking upon her Wyn was thirsty. He craved her. His heart beat fast, his breaths short. He wanted to touch her, to explore her satin skin with his hands and mouth, to caress her everywhere.

It was the liquor calling, making him crave.

"How long will we remain here?" She came to his side. "Overnight?"

"Perhaps a day or two." Until young William arrived with the baron, or Kitty came from London. "We must make certain Eads is well away from the road before we turn back east."

"Mrs. Polley was grumbling again about this detour. But she has made herself comfortable in the kitchen. She even found an unspoiled jar of oil and another of flour. It seems she enjoys baking." She smiled, the dimples denting her pale cheeks.

Wyn went to the door. "Owen, come along to the gatehouse with me. We will see you settled in."

The lad walked beside him along the drive. "Sir . . ." He kicked a stone with his toe.

"Owen?"

"You're not telling her, then, about this place?"

"I am not telling her."

"She's a good one, sir."

"She is indeed."

"Mr. Guyther says he can't hold the fold up in the hills many more weeks."

"We shan't be here weeks, Owen. Days only. And Mr. Guyther will do as I say. As will you, I trust." He halted and set his hand on the boy's shoulder. "You must not tell her. If she knows, she will leave here and put herself in danger." But now he questioned whether she would, even if he told her the truth. She was reckless, yes, but perhaps now wiser than when she'd set out upon her quest. Perhaps, in fact, she merely possessed desires beyond her situation in life—desires she could not easily fulfill, like rescuing her mother, and being touched by a man.

"Aye." Owen nodded, frowning. "But I don't like it, sir."

Wyn wanted a brandy. Whiskey. Whatever it would take. "Neither do I."

Mrs. Polley concocted a modest dinner from the pantry that was well stocked with pickled and dried foods, and simple oatcakes she baked on the grate over the peat fire in the kitchen. Miss Lucas ate happily, and the boy filled his mouth and stared at her guiltily, while the matron ran a commentary about the house. Wyn barely attended. As the evening progressed, the prickly jitters in his blood increased to a cry then a roar that he struggled to ignore. But it was of little use. He could think of nothing but brandy and the maiden sitting across the room—both unprofitable desires.

He went to the stable and tended the horses, pulling hay and oats from the supply Owen had brought from the house of Aled Guyther, the abbey's land steward. He walked the perimeters of the estate's wild gardens and walls, and along the sodden, mossy irrigation canal that ran to the stream. He looked into the gatehouse again. Then he saddled Galahad and set out across the hills where no animals grazed now because his orders to

Guyther, conveyed by Owen, specified that the place be emptied of people and livestock. Now he could go speak with Guyther, but instead he avoided the path to the village a mile distant and the tiny pub there, as well as the modest chapel with the cemetery and a five-year-old grave he had not yet seen, had not yet visited.

The hills grew dark beneath steady rain, and finally he returned to the house. The drawing room with its dusty bottles tucked into the sideboard cabinet beckoned. He didn't care what was in those bottles. His very marrow wanted their contents.

She met him at the parlor door, silhouetted in firelight and Mrs. Polley's snores.

"I heard you come in. You must be exhausted. You don't look well." Her eyes were tired but soft. He stepped close to her to feel her warmth and to tease himself for a moment that there could be some satisfaction had this night.

"You know precisely how to bolster a man's confidence."

"In fact I find you remarkably handsome, but you no doubt already know that, and anyway, fine London ladies probably tell you that all the time so it isn't any marvelous surprise that I would too. But I don't know how you manage to maintain it here. I am a soggy, crumpled mess. My mother will be horrified when she sees me. But you appear elegant even soaked with rain." Her blue eyes turned up, wide now and as hungry as the need within him.

"Good night, Miss Lucas." He turned toward the stair.

"Where are you going?

"To sleep. I suggest you find a comfortable spot and do the same."

"Where?"

He gestured along the corridor.

Slender brows shot up. "In a *bedchamber*?"

"That is usually where one sleeps." And did other things that he wanted to do to her now.

"But—"

A sneeze interrupted Mrs. Polley's snores. She coughed then settled back into sleep.

Miss Lucas's brow dipped. "I think she took a chill today. I suggested she make a soothing broth from the dried meat but she scoffed at that. I am an indifferent cook." She shrugged lightly. "It is a very good thing we shan't be here long and that Mrs. Polley likes the kitchen, or else we would certainly starve."

He could not entirely resist her good humor. "No doubt you have other talents."

"Oh, I can embroider up a storm and do a fine watercolor of a garden trellis. Truly useful skills under present circumstances."

He smiled. "Eating is overrated."

"I've no doubt *you* believe so. I, on the other hand, am still famished." She placed a hand beneath her breasts, over her stomach. "Do you really intend for us to remain here more than a night?"

"Through tomorrow night. Longer if Mrs. Polley is ill."

She seemed to study him, her gaze dipping to his mouth. "I have something I must say to you."

He bowed. "As you please."

"Earlier today, when you said I save lost souls, you seemed puzzled, as though speaking of a foreign thing. But I don't think it is as foreign to you as you allow." Her fingertips pressed into her ribs, her gaze steady upon him. "I think—I *know*—you have helped people before this."

They had all been assignments, means to ends. Not like this woman whose touch when she'd taken his hand earlier had nearly sent him to his knees on the muddy road. She looked up at him now not with the eyes of infatuation. Infatuation he recognized; he'd seen it plenty of times. This was different. This he could not entirely fathom and did not want.

"Whether I have or have not is immaterial to our situation now." Their situation in which he lied to her and lusted after her at once. "See to your companion's comfort then find a place yourself to sleep and get some rest." Taking a candle from the foyer table, he went up to the drawing room. In the dark chamber filled with furniture that looked like ghosts beneath their covers, he opened the cabinet. The bottles gleamed dully. His hand shook as he reached for the nearest.

Owen woke him in the rainy depths of the night. Inside the gatehouse, young William slumped against a wall, sleeping. Ramses bathed his narrow face with his tongue and William roused and told Wyn what he feared: Lord Carlyle could not be found in Devon, nor the Earl or Countess of Savege. All were in London already, it seemed. As instructed, William had spoken his secret to no one and come swiftly here.

Wyn cursed himself. He had been a fool to send to Devon first. But he hadn't truly believed she would not be deterred. He had made many mistakes with her and was possibly in the process of making the worst yet.

He bid Owen feed the messenger, gave William a sack of coins, and instructed the youth to be on his way the moment the sun rose. Then he set off again onto the hills of his great-aunt's estate, sleep never farther and thirst dragging at him like the rain that showed no sign of abating. With the dog in his footsteps he walked until dawn when, far up in the sheep fields, he found a hollow of rocks he'd frequented as a child. In those days he had made of it a fort from which he conquered the flocks as though they were dragons set upon destroying his great-aunt's castle.

It was nominally dry. He settled into it, Ramses tucking into a ball beneath the mantle of his coat.

He did not sleep. The cruel humming in his blood would not allow it. Instead he thought of Diantha Lucas, of her need and desires, and for the first time in his life knew not what path to take next.

When the sky lightened and he finally stood to shake off the night, to find his limbs weak, his head light, and hands trembling beyond his ability to still them, every fiber in his body wanted brandy. Then he finally understood the path before him. It suited him well enough. That it was going to be a hellish several days until Kitty Blackwood arrived from London, he had no doubt. But if it kept Diantha Lucas in one place, he would do it. His demons had ruled him long enough.

"**E**ggs!" Mrs. Polley trumpeted her red nose into a rag and upon her opposite palm produced a little brown treasure. The hen from which she had taken it seemed unperturbed.

Diantha's stomach rumbled. She licked her lips—without Mr. Yale anywhere in sight to inspire it. Remarkable.

"Those are some right small eggs," Owen said skeptically.

Diantha shrugged. "They will still taste divine. Perhaps the chickens are small?"

Mrs. Polley tucked her hand beneath another feathered belly and withdrew a second treasure. "It's plain neither of you know a thing about fowl."

"It cannot be wondered at."

Diantha swung around. Mr. Yale stood in the shed's doorway, arms crossed loosely, a shoulder propped against the doorjamb, the hem of his black topcoat brushing the packed dirt ground.

Her breath petered out of her. She didn't care what she told herself—that she'd been very happy today reading, chatting with Owen, and assisting Mrs. Polley with cooking and baking tasks. Seeing him now after so many hours was beyond pleasurable.

She went to him. "Owen discovered this shed and the chickens."

A single black brow rose and he directed a sharp look at the boy. "Did he?"

Owen tugged at his cap. "Afternoon, sir."

"Isn't it wonderful? We will have eggs for dinner shortly, and Mrs. Polley has baked oat bread."

"Not that *that* man will eat a bite of it." Mrs. Polley waddled to another chicken and foraged beneath it. "Hasn't eaten a bit of anything I've cooked."

He bent his head and spoke sotto voice to Diantha. "I see I have descended a rung in your companion's estimation."

"How is that?"

"She is speaking to me in the third person."

"And now you are doing the same of her."

"Yes, but I am actually speaking to you."

Mrs. Polley harrumphed. "Too high and mighty for simple cookery."

"Ah," he said with his slight smile, "we have come to the root of the problem."

"Truly, Mr. Yale." Diantha laughed. "You are far too high and mighty. You must come down from your loft." She leaned in close to him and resisted taking a big breath of his scent of rain and man. "You really should share dinner with us. I think she is honestly insulted."

"I've no need to be begging the gentleman to eat my food. If he doesn't like it, he can go on back to London and his perfumed chefs."

"I would be honored to eschew my perfumed chef's culinary offerings for yours, ma'am." He spoke with that slight smile still, but his voice was not perfectly smooth.

"Isn't this place curious?" Diantha gestured. "It is not a hen house, so it must not be these chickens' regular home, I suspect, but they are laying very contentedly nonetheless."

"Curious, indeed." He cast Owen another glance. "One

wonders what other surprises he may produce." The boy ducked out the door and Mr. Yale followed him for a pace with his gaze then returned his regard to her.

"We found a cow."

His brow rose.

"She was eating clover over on the hedge in the rain and lowing. Quite mournfully. Owen put her in the stable with the horses and now they all seem perfectly happy together eating hay. She must be lost. Someone will no doubt come looking for her and discover us interloping, then we shall be hauled before the magistrate and all will be ruined." She took a big breath and sighed it away theatrically. "So, you see, we have had a very adventuresome day while you were gone."

A glimmer shone in his eyes, but his stance was rigid and he did not unlock his arms.

"Where have you been?" she asked.

"About."

"Where?"

Mrs. Polley bustled past them, apron full of eggs. "Dark gentlemen like to keep secrets. I've said so already."

He looked after her as she wobbled down the path toward the house. "She has?"

"Oh, any number of times. She believes I must be warned repeatedly. I don't know if that is because she thinks my memory is faulty or that she imagines my fear of you will increase with her repetition." She touched his arm, he returned his gaze to her, and then she felt his shaking, a definite vibration of his body. "But—" She struggled to remain light. "But she needn't repeat herself, because I am already terrified of you, of course."

He drew away from her. "Of course." He moved from the shed and to the path toward the house. The rain had slackened, but the sky was still thickly gray, and upon his cheeks rode a thin sheen of moisture.

"Are you ill, Mr. Yale?"

"In fact I am not perfectly well today, Miss Lucas."

"Oh, *no*. You must have taken a chill from the road. Is that why you have stayed away today? You don't wish to share it with us?"

"I am happy to report that this is not an illness any of you can contract." He said this grimly.

"I don't understand."

He stopped, turned to her, and strain showed upon his brow. "It is a temporary state, not one that you need concern yourself over. Do leave it at that, if you will."

"You look very serious."

"There is probably a reason for that."

"I am supposed to take that as a hint, but instead I will now pretend to be remarkably obtuse. I was worried about you, being gone all day."

"I am well able to take care of myself, Miss Lucas."

"We are quite remote here, in the middle of nowhere. I only wondered where you had gone."

This seemed to give him pause. "Were you afraid here? Without me?"

"Not afraid. It's very peaceful here. And frankly after the constant excitement I don't mind a day of rest in such a pleasant place. I was only worried about you."

"Then you needn't worry further. I will not leave again."

"Perhaps you ought to sleep."

"Excellent idea."

But he did not. He attended her to the kitchen where she assisted Mrs. Polley with preparations for dinner while Owen blithely regaled them with stories of the ironworks that made Diantha's hair stand on end.

"When my sister took the fever, they put her in the sick house. She caught the croup. Didn't last two days after that." His shoulders drooped.

"Those places aren't fit for animals." Mrs. Polley scowled. "Best you've found my mistress here to take you in."

Diantha chopped herbs without finesse and cracked

eggs into a bowl and was lucky she did not cut off her fingers with the knife or spill their dinner onto the floor. She had no attention for anything but the gentleman. He also watched her, shadows beneath his eyes and hands in his pockets. But he seemed unusually restless.

They ate picnic style, without ceremony in the kitchen. Owen consumed half the platter of eggs, bread, and jam the moment Mrs. Polley set it on the table. Diantha made a plate for Mr. Yale and, remarkably, he ate. Then, with a "Thank you" to Mrs. Polley and a bow to her, he left.

Diantha gobbled up the remainder of her food and went after him. She found him in the parlor, facing the hearth where the peat simmered, hands thrust deeply into his pockets, his eyes closed. He opened them as she entered and turned to her.

"Forgive my hasty exit, if you will, Miss Lucas."

"You are truly ill." She went toward him and he withdrew from her a step. She halted, her stomach turning over.

"I am less than comfortable, it is true." His jaw seemed very tight.

"Perhaps you have taken Mrs. Polley's chill."

"Now you are repeating yourself."

"Well, I may be, because although I'd thought before that I had a lot of courage, I may not after all, for I cannot possibly allow you to be suffering some more serious, dreadful disease, because I do not wish to sit here helplessly in the wilds of Wales and watch you *die*."

His brow lifted. "You have a fine flare for the dramatic, Miss Lucas. Usually dormant, admittedly. But when it animates it is truly impressive."

She wrung her hands. "You are very frustrating to converse with sometimes. Tell me what is *wrong* with you."

He looked toward the window. "Nothing that a few fingers of brandy would not put to rights. Ah, it has begun again to rain."

"You look like you wish to say 'fitting' or something equally dispiriting."

"Not at all. It is only that when one has spent a night outside in the rain without sleep, a night enjoyed within doors in a fire-heated room seems a vast luxury." He smiled then, but barely, and his eyes held a peculiar look. The look of the predator again.

A shiver skipped up her spine. "You spent last night outside in the rain? After exhorting me to find a bedchamber in which to sleep?"

"I fully admit to being a hypocrite. Throw me in irons and bear me to the hangman's noose, if you wish. I will be there soon in any case." He said this last seemingly as an afterthought.

"Now who's the nonsensical one? You are irrational. You should go to sleep."

"Thank you, I will remain here. But you are welcome to go yourself."

"It is only dusk."

For a moment his eyes flashed bleakly, a shadow of desperation like that night in the hotel corridor in Knighton when he had touched her, that night that he did not remember because he had drunk too many spirits.

Then, abruptly, she understood. Or thought she did.

"But you won't have a few fingers of brandy now," she said slowly. "Or even one. Will you?"

His gaze shifted to her face but he said nothing.

"You have ceased drinking spirits, haven't you? Altogether."

"You—" He paused, and seemed to reconsider, then said only, "I have."

"And it is making you ill."

A moment's silence, then: "Yes."

Another silence stretched during which she was entirely unable to say the many things that rushed to her tongue. Her virtue and his honor were now tangled in a piteous mess.

"Because of what happened between us at the inn in Knighton," she finally said.

"Because of that," he replied.

Her unsteady hands found a chair and she lowered herself into it. "You should sit down."

"I am comfortable standing."

"You look about as comfortable as my sister Charity when my mother tried to marry her to Lord Savege. Before he married Serena, that is."

A smile creased his delicious mouth. "I hadn't heard that story."

"They all keep it very quiet. It was one of the reasons my mother left, I think." She could not look at him directly now. "She was disappointed in her high hopes for Charity."

A pause. "And what of her hopes for you?"

"Oh, she had none to speak of for me. Charity is very beautiful and demure, of course."

"Ah."

He could not possibly understand, not this handsome gentleman, elegant and well mannered even when he was ill and in the impossible situation into which she had gotten him with her reckless quest and her brazen behavior.

"My father always said he would cease drinking spirits," she said. "He did so once, but he didn't last the sennight. I was very young, but I remember it because after several days when he wished to drink his whiskey again he told me to fetch him the bottle."

"And did you?"

"I refused." She shrugged. "I liked him better without the whiskey. He was more enjoyable to talk with. Not that day, of course. He was furious, and when my mother returned home she locked me in my bedchamber. Shortly after that my father became ill. My mother said he drank himself to an early grave."

There was another very long silence then during which nothing stirred but muffled sounds from the kitchen and Ramses' soft snores from the hearth rug.

"This is not the first time."

Her breaths stilled. It seemed he would confide in her after all, this man who owned secrets she feared she could not hope to understand.

"How was it that time?" she asked. "Those times?"

"That time. Better than this. Considerably better."

She took a big breath and stood up. "It goes against my feelings on the matter in general, but you should not do this. Not now, at least. If I promise not to—"

"No. Be still."

"Be *still*?"

"Rather, as still as you are able." It seemed that he wished to smile, but he looked remarkably poorly, for all his elegant cravat and coat and perfectly handsome face. His eyes were the worst, as though the hungry predator searched for something he could not find and the desperation was building even as they spoke.

"You look peculiar." She moved a step toward him and this time he did not retreat. "You are thinking about taking me home again." His mind must have gone where hers had. It would be so much easier for him if she simply weren't his responsibility. Then he could do as he wished, go where he wished, drink whatever he chose without fear of her throwing herself at him. "I would be if I were you."

"Then it is a good thing for you that you are not me."

But she could not be satisfied with this, not when his gaze seemed now to consume her, each feature of her face at a time.

"Then what are you thinking about?"

His attention fixed on her mouth. "The . . ."

She could not breathe properly. "The . . . ?"

"I cannot stop thinking about"—his gaze rose to her eyes—"the cellar."

She must be very stupid. "The cellar?"

He swallowed and she saw the rigid movement of his throat above his neck cloth. "Last night I emptied the bottles in the drawing room and the library, but . . ."

Oh. "But there is a wine cellar belowstairs, isn't there?"

He nodded, a ripple of a shiver crossing his shoulders quite visibly. She had not really understood until this moment.

Now she did.

She set her hands on her hips. "Then we must empty those bottles as well."

"No."

"Do you want to give up on this, then, after all? It would be easier, of course, at least while I am demanding that you—"

"*No.*"

They looked at one another for a long moment.

He took a tight breath. "Down to the cellar it seems we must go."

"I can do it alone," she offered.

"No."

"I really should tally the number of times you say that word to me." Beginning with the moment he had stopped kissing her in the inn at Knighton, then had done so anyway. The moment that had led them here.

Chapter 14

As it happened, he was little help after all, except in keeping her company, and at least this way she could watch him and make certain he did not expire on the spot. The wine cellar was small and dark but remarkably dry and removed from the kitchen where Mrs. Polley had fallen asleep.

He leaned against the doorjamb and seemed more at ease. But he traced the path of liquid from each bottle into the drain with an increasingly feverish stare.

"The clarets must go first," he murmured.

"Why? Are they the strongest?"

"God, no. I simply don't care for claret."

"Then we should empty them last." She took up the nearest bottle of brandy and glanced over the racks stacked with bottles lying on their sides. "Uncorking each is something of a chore. I don't know how butlers do this every day. My fingers are already beginning to blister."

"Break the necks." His voice was tight.

She did not look at him. She would beg him to go upstairs, but she knew he would not. He was a very strong man. He had borne with her for days already, after all, and now he was doing this. For her.

"Break them on what?"

"A rock." He looked grim.

"Outside?"

"Outside."

"In the rain?"

"On the side of the well."

"The well? Then the water will be—"

"It is dry."

"How do you know that?"

He stared at her, his eyes slightly glassy now.

"All right," she mumbled. "But then I shall have to carry them all out there."

"I will help."

She donned her cloak and he his coat, and armful after armful they lugged the contents of the cellar—five score bottles in all—to the well beyond the kitchen door.

He sat on the wall at the edge of the courtyard in the rain and watched her snap each bottle on the rock and pour its contents into the well.

"That one smelled horrid." She wrinkled up her nose.

"It did not."

"You cannot smell them from all the way over there."

"Care to wager on that?"

"I suppose not." She shook another bottle dry then threw it down the well shaft. "We shall have to compensate these poor people for the ruination of their cellar."

"Indeed."

Rain pattered softly now on the glistening gray stone of the well and the grass between them, the dusk advancing into night.

"You can go inside, you know. I can finish here quite well on my own."

"I do not wish to go inside."

She sighed. "You do not wish to leave sight of all these bottles of wine, I suppose."

"I do not wish to leave sight of a pretty girl."

Her pulse did a little uncomfortable leap, which was silly, because although she had thrown off her spots and fat she was by no means pretty. But he was possibly a little delirious.

"If you can smell the wine from such a distance," she said, willing away her swift heartbeats, "what else can you smell?"

"You."

Another leap, quite a bit more forceful. "R-Really? What do I smell like?"

"Fresh air."

If he'd said something silly, like roses, she would have known he was flattering emptily. Instead, warmth invaded her in crucial places that she couldn't like. He made her feel hot and off kilter, but she could do nothing to satisfy that feeling, so she wished he wouldn't.

"You are being metaphorical, aren't you?"

"No. You actually smell like fresh air."

His words pleased her far too much. Perhaps Mrs. Polley was right and he was the devil sent to frustrate her.

The remainder of the wine flowed down the well. She shook out her weary hands and wrists and followed him into the house.

"I am exhausted."

"I am rather exhausted myself, and I only watched." He drew the thick bolt on the front door and it thunked into place.

"How do you feel?"

"Do not ask me that."

"Why not?"

"Because, contrary to expectations, I don't care for you in the role of nursemaid. To me."

Expectations? "Why not?"

He looked down at her and his eyes seemed for a moment at peace, gently silver in the candlelight. "You ask too many questions, minx."

"I like it when you call me minx. No one ever has, you know."

"I confess myself somewhat shocked."

"I am not yet out in society and there is no one around Glenhaven Hall or the Park that would call me such a thing. Except you. But you have so rarely visited." She thought then an astounding thing, that perhaps she had not been entirely honest with herself about her memories of him, that perhaps she had remembered her brief encounters with him too well. "Will you turn in now?" she managed over the sudden hammering of her heart. "You do look tired."

"I am, rather." He bowed. "Good night, minx." He turned and made his way up the stairs.

Diantha went to the kitchen still warm from the fire and draped Mrs. Polley with a blanket. Then she climbed the stairs and found the bed in which she and her companion had slept the night before, the linens still musty but dry. Curling up beneath wool blankets that smelled of camphor balls, she lay there with her uncomfortable thoughts and worried about him.

As day broke she woke with renewed courage and confidence. Sleep healed all ills, and she had thrown off her silly notions. Young girls would have foolish *tendres* for elegant gentlemen and she could not chastise herself for having had one herself, especially since he'd been so gallant that time. Today they would again set off on their journey and once they found her mother he would go his own way and she would no longer constantly think about him.

Snatching a piece of bread from the kitchen, with a

light step she returned to the foyer. He stood at the base of the stair, hollow-eyed and gaunt-cheeked.

"Miss Lucas, if you would be so kind, I require your assistance."

"To stand?"

He seemed to attempt a smile. "To drive me on a short errand."

"An errand?" She felt wholly incapable of forming longer sentences. He had not recovered overnight. Her heart felt atrociously tight.

"Owen informs me that there is a village nearby, including a shop at which I might purchase several items of which I am in need. I fear that I am not up to my best this morning. I would appreciate your help."

She swallowed back her distress and the intense desire to throw her arms about him. "You have it, of course."

He gestured toward the door, his other hand clutching the knob at the bottom of the stair rail so that the knuckles were white. "After you, madam."

"But there is no carriage."

"The carriage house boasts a modest gig."

"There is no carriage *horse*."

"Galahad will suffer it. He has before."

"He has?" She went at his side across the yard toward the stable.

"On occasion. Will you mind it?"

"Of course not. But why didn't you send Owen?"

"He is sleeping, as well he should be. He has worked hard and deserves rest."

"That's very considerate of you."

The gig was modest indeed; upon the box, they sat touching from shoulder to thigh. She could contrive no suitable conversation; the pleasure of this connection was too sharp.

The village was not far along the narrow road that ran beside the stream, tucked into a crevice of the valley. It wasn't much of a village, in truth, only a handful of build-ings and a squat stone church that in comparison to the abbey seemed negligible.

He seemed to know precisely where to go, pointing her to a cottage with a trellis festooned with vines that glistened with rain. He descended from the carriage and offered his hand.

She took it, which was strong but not steady. "I should probably be assisting you down."

"As you are the one wearing skirts this arrangement must suffice."

She squeezed her fingers into his. "You will tell me if I can help you, won't you?"

"You are helping me now."

Two men emerged from the next building and peered at them quite blatantly. Mr. Yale drew her hand onto his arm and nodded to them.

"Good day, sir," one said with a narrowed eye, but he bowed. He was an older man, gruff of face and whisker and neatly dressed like any man of Glen Village back in Devon might be. Her escort nodded then opened the door accompanied by a jingle of bells.

Within, all was fragrant of roses, rosemary, and sage. Little brown bottles lined shelves, candles of many hues were stacked in piles about the place, and jars stuffed with dried herbs and prettily colored dried flowers. A woman with a mass of gray hair snaking around her head topped with an enormous cap stood from a rocking chair in the corner and came forward.

"Well well, sir. A good day to you!" She curtsied. "And to you, miss." But she did not take her eyes off Mr. Yale, for which Diantha couldn't fault her. "What brings a lady and a gentleman such as yourselves to my shop today, I wonder?" Then she did look at Diantha, an up and down assessing regard. But it had nothing of scorn in it, only curiosity.

"Good day, ma'am." Mr. Yale produced a folded paper from his waistcoat pocket. "Will you be so kind as to supply me with these items if you possess them?"

She stared at him while she unfolded the paper, then glanced down. Her brow furrowed.

"St. John's Wort . . . Milk Thistle . . . Powder of Cayenne . . . Laud—" Her eyes snapped up, this time assessing him it seemed. "You are in luck, sir. These I have, and a few other items you might like."

"Ah. I hoped so."

She gave him a close look then hurried to the back of the shop and through a door.

"Whatever is Powder of Cayenne?" Diantha whispered, but the woman appeared again.

"A pepper from the Americas, miss. Dried and ground to a dust."

"A pepper?" She flicked a glance at Mr. Yale, but his attention seemed intent upon the little paper pouches the shop mistress was now preparing at her counter. "For what is it used?"

"Certain complaints," the woman said, her fingers deft as she scooped tiny spoonfuls of red dust into a pouch, then opened a large jar and drew out several sprigs of dried weed with the faintest hint of purple clinging to the shriveled flowers.

Diantha leaned over the herbs, inspecting. "This must be the Milk Thistle. But I don't recognize many of the others here. What a wonderful shop you have! However do you come to have all these plants?"

"There was a young gentleman lived here not too long ago, miss, who taught me about them." She glanced at Mr. Yale. "Now, don't you misunderstand, miss. Molly Cerwydn learned herb craft from her mother and nobody's been better at it in these parts in a hundred years. But this young man, well, he'd been traveling all over the world to places where they've got healing tricks I didn't know about, you see. So, being eager to improve my craft, I sat him down and bid him tell me what he'd learned. The people in this village, farmers, even the animals, they've been glad of it ever since."

"Whatever happened to the young man?" She ran her fingertip down the side of a big glass jar. "Is he still here telling tales of exotic lands?"

"He's gone off to who knows where, miss. Though he's welcome to return when he likes. Everyone here would be glad to see him again."

Mr. Yale cleared his throat softly. "Ladies, if you will excuse me, I'll see that the horse is well." He set a handful of coins on the counter and went out of the shop.

Mrs. Cerwydn wrapped the packets in paper and tied them with a string. "There, miss. Now then." She looked Diantha over carefully. Then she dug into a deep pocket in her skirt and pulled forth a bottle of brown glass the size of her hand.

Diantha stared; she had seen such a bottle before when her father was ill. Before he died.

The herbalist reached for her hand, tucked the bottle into it, and nodded. "You see that your young man there has the caring he needs."

But he was not her young man.

Diantha curtsied, took up the package and went out of the shop. Mr. Yale stood across the street with the whiskered man. He came across to the carriage, Ramses trotting along beside. He took the package and she could see clearly the strain upon his brow.

"Back to the house?" she said quietly.

"Back to the house." His voice was taut.

"What were you talking about with that man?" Mr. Whiskers was still looking at them, and Diantha caught a glimpse of the herbalist peering out the window, and another face in a window in the next building too. "Everybody here is madly curious about us."

"Villagers. Always like that." He took up the reins.

"Don't you want me to drive?"

"If necessary, in a bit." He snapped Galahad into motion.

Mr. Whiskers stared them down the road.

"You don't want that man to see me driving, is that it?"

"I don't care what that man sees." His hands were tight around the ribbons.

"Then, why—"

"The activity is useful, Miss Lucas. It provides me something upon which to concentrate."

She turned her attention from the road onto his handsome face fraught with tension. "Is it that bad?"

A muscle in his jaw contracted. "It is that bad."

Once back at the abbey, with Galahad unharnessed, he took the herbalist's package and bottle, thanked her, and went into the house without awaiting her. She followed, but to the kitchen where she found Mrs. Polley sniffling over a pot of tea and a table spread with biscuit dough.

"It seems you've found sugar." Diantha tucked her companion's shawl tighter about her shoulders.

"The boy found it." Mrs. Polley rolled out the dough. "He's a wily one. I don't like to know whose kitchen's wanting now."

"He *stole* the sugar from someone's *house*?" She sat down beside the round little form of her companion. "Goodness, I've been gone from my friend's home no more than a sennight and I've broken more laws than I can count." And Mrs. Polley didn't know the half of it, certainly not the laws of morality she'd broken. She picked at a corner of the dough, the tawny sugar crystals tempting. "I suppose I always knew I would come to no good end. My mother has."

"Now, miss. You'll find her and make it all right again."

"You will have time to recuperate entirely from your

chill, I think. We will be here longer than anticipated. And if the villagers begin to suspect where their sugar and chickens have gone, or if someone comes for the cow or recognized the gig we took to the village this morning, we will probably be arrested."

"It'll be no more than that man deserves."

"Perhaps. And me. But not you." Diantha took her companion's thick little hands into her own, flour dust swirling about. "I don't wish for you to come to grief because of me. But I cannot leave here without Mr. Yale. I fear, however, that he will not be able to leave for some days yet. He is quite unwell and I am terribly worried about him."

Mrs. Polley pulled her hands away and set them to the pin again. "Elizabeth Polley isn't one to desert her mistress at the drop of a hat."

Diantha looked toward the doorway that went to the foyer and stairs that could take her to wherever in the house he now was. She curled her fingers around the edges of the bench, holding herself in place.

"I'm afraid it may come to be a great deal more uncomfortable than a hat dropping."

Chapter 15

"She's wanting to be milked, miss."

"I seems so." Diantha stood beside Owen, elbows propped on the stall's half door, the cow's mournful lowing filling the stable with misery. The poor creature's udder certainly *looked* heavy. But Diantha didn't know anything about cows. The situation might not be truly dire. "I don't suppose you know how to milk a cow?"

"No, miss. Know a thing or two about tending sheep, though."

"Not, I suppose, how to milk one?"

He cast her a peculiar look.

She folded her arms. The stable was heavy with moisture, the poor weather persisting as though it meant to rain and rain forever. Diantha's gown and undergarments were soggy, her hair a horrid tangle of damp curls, and her slippers a travesty. Likewise, she had only the gown she'd worn when they traveled to the abbey and this one, and after only three nights she was tired of sleeping without a pillow or proper fire. Her entire world felt like it was in a bog.

"I suppose it is beyond hoping that Mrs. Polley knows how to milk a cow," she mumbled.

"I'd suppose that too, miss."

"Though she made those scrumptious biscuits yesterday, and with so few ingredients at hand, so we should be happy enough."

"Should be, miss."

"And the tasty porridge with the dried fruit this morning, even without milk."

"Surely was a fine porridge, miss."

"She says we will have greens for dinner today. Despite her cough, she went foraging and found them in the garden."

"I do like a fine boiled green, miss."

The cow groaned. The horses chomped at their hay. Diantha chewed on the edge of her lips. "Who will milk the cow, Owen?"

He set his hand on his chin like a man of great dignity and stroked as though stroking a beard. Diantha suppressed a giggle. But it felt good to want to giggle. She hadn't seen Mr. Yale all day, though Owen said he'd taken Galahad riding just after dawn and she knew he had returned to the house. But if he wished for her company, he would surely seek it out.

"Miss," the boy said, "we might ask the master."

She chuckled. "Oh, Owen, he is a gentleman. With a London address, no less. Gentlemen with London addresses know how to waltz and play cards shockingly well." And stand perfectly still pointing a pistol at another man, apparently. "They do not know how to do things like milk cows."

Owen shrugged. "Like as not. But someone's got to do it or she'll sicken, and we'll have to haul her into the village and the rig'll be up."

She slapped her hands against her skirts. "She *will* sicken. Though it is perhaps the silliest thing I've ever done, I will go ask him." And see him. She wanted an excuse.

She went to the house and up the winding stairway to the parlor, eager as she hadn't been since breakfast. He was not there. She went to the next door along the corridor. Much larger than the parlor, the drawing room seemed too grand to disturb and she hadn't been in it since the first day. But she knocked and opened the door a crack.

Ramses' shaggy nose appeared sniffing at the aperture. She pulled the panel wide.

Gray light filtered into the chamber, casting the white linens that covered furniture and paintings in a ghostly glow, everything except the man standing in silhouette at a dust-smeared window with his back to her.

"I really must ask Owen to wash these windows," she said into the silence. "Or do it myself, I suppose. It is the least I can do for these people who don't even—"

He turned to her. Diantha's throat closed. Light glinted off the weapon dangling from his fingers.

"Wh-Wha—" she tried, but her words died again as he came toward her, her heartbeats filling her throat now, her gaze locked on the pistol.

He halted before her, so close she could see the dark circles beneath his eyes.

"What are you going to do with that?" she whispered.

He grasped her hand, pressed the pistol against her palm, and curled her fingers around it. The metal was heavy and cold, his large hand around hers scalding.

"Hide this." His voice was very low, laced with tension.

She nodded, little jerks of her head. He reached into his coat pocket and upturned her other hand. Bullets jingled into her cupped palm.

"And these. But not together." He released her. "And do remember where you have hidden them, Miss Lucas. I shall be needing them again."

"Do you think," she said shakily, "that given all, you might call me Diantha?"

"Remember where you have hidden them, Diantha. Now . . ." He drew a hard breath, fever glinting in his darkened eyes. "Leave me. And if by chance I should come for you and am not entirely myself . . . run."

Her heart stopped. "I won't."

His hand flexed into a fist at his side. "Diantha, I pray you."

She left, but she sent Owen to him. Then she went to the stable where the cow lowed a sad soliloquy. Stroking Galahad's ebony and white nose, she leaned into him and allowed all the fear and confusion and strange, pressing need to ripple through her. Then she returned to the house and Mrs. Polley in the kitchen, where she might be of use.

Day was torment, an endless search for activities that would engage his mind sufficient to distract him from the craving and dysfunction of his body. Day offered him light by which to read. Day gave him Owen's prattling company when the boy was not busy elsewhere. Day allowed him to imagine Diantha moving about the house, making it home just as she made every fallen log a throne and every cast-off soul a bosom bow.

Day lasted for many more hours than the sun was high, it seemed, sending him searching through cupboards in the library and drawing room in desperation to find cards, a chessboard, anything that he could pore over, sweating blood with every labored breath, knowing in the frenzied fog that only by keeping his mind engaged would he see this through. As he had conquered pain inflicted by others so many years ago, his mind could conquer this as well.

Day was torture.

But night was hell.

Night never ended. Night came on claws, tearing at his insides and whispering that he could end it, until he was deaf with it. Night persisted, hour after hour of darkness. He went to the stable, but even Galahad's presence did not calm the panic. So he went again into the rain that teased with its scent and natural ease, climbed to the sheepcote and upon a ridge slept. But sleeping was merely another variety of torturous waking, his body shaking and bones burning and the agony in his head making him blind. But worse were the visions of people he had long since abandoned and places he had left behind years ago. In the dark he went to his knees and drank water from the stream, arising with a thirst he could not slake.

At moments he recognized that he was in a fever. Delirium. When Owen came and Wyn forced himself to speak, tried to restrain the trembling of his limbs, he saw himself as though at a distance. But he did not allow the boy to remain long, and the darkness descended again eagerly.

Yet the darkness was not alone. Deep beyond it, in a place he could see only at moments, relief dwelled.

Relief, kind and sweet like the touch of a lady's berry smile.

Relief that—finally—it was over.

By the end of the third day Diantha could bear it no longer.

"I am going up." She wiped her hands on a towel tied around her waist and pulled it off.

Mrs. Polley frowned as she scrubbed a pan. "He told you not to. Seeing as it's the most gentlemanlike thing he's done yet, you should listen to him."

"That is not true, Mrs. Polley." Diantha arranged a tray with a cup, saucer, and pot beside a plate of oat biscuits. She reached for the kettle. "Owen said he ate nothing today."

Mrs. Polley shook her head. "I'll go up with you."

"No. Finish cleaning up then go to bed. Your cough

persists and you need the sleep." She poured boiling water into the pot and affixed the lid.

"And you, a fine miss running about dusting and sweeping."

"I need the activity." Rather, *distraction*. But it was perfectly silly that she was even trying to distract herself from thinking of him. "Now I will take this up and then I will turn in too. Good night, Mrs. Polley."

She climbed the stairs with the stub of a candle on the tray to guide her steps. Dust rose as she went. The house was so large that it would take her weeks to clean it completely. Weeks she did not have. Her fortnight was slipping away and she was no closer to Calais, lost in the wilds of Wales.

At the door to his bedchamber she knocked. No response came. She knocked again, louder.

The door opened and her heart fell over. In shirtsleeves that clung to his arms with sweat, he was drawn, cheekbones prominent, the black centers of his eyes overcoming the gray.

"I told you to stay away."

"Good evening to you too, sir." She pushed past him and he allowed it, falling back a step to lean against the door lintel. She went across the room and set the tray on the dressing table, bending to stroke Ramses' brow. "You didn't tell me to stay away. You told me to run if you approached me. But you don't look well enough to chase a turtle." Taking up the candle, she plucked a taper from the mantel and held it to the flame then bent and lit the peat block in the hearth. "Why is the window open?" She moved to shut it. "You will catch your death."

He tilted his head against the wall and his eyes closed. "Entirely possible I'm already dead."

"Not quite yet."

"Fires of Purgatory and all that, with you, my Beatrice, beckoning from Paradise."

"But you are certainly delirious and will probably be dead soon if you don't eat."

"Rather be at present." The words were barely a whisper.

Diantha's heart beat so hard she could hear it in the silence. "No doubt." She crossed to him, every nerve in her body ridiculously aware that she was alone in a gentleman's bedchamber with him. "I have brought tea and Mrs. Polley's biscuits."

His eyes opened, reflecting the firelight's golden heat. "Leave."

"No."

His hands darted out and his fingers bit into her shoulders. He dragged her close. The planes of his face as he looked down at her were harsh, his eyes glittering with fever and the ravenous intent of the predator.

"Please." The sound came from so deep in his chest she barely understood the word.

She struggled for breath, squaring her shoulders in his hold. "Why did you make me hide the pistol when you were planning to starve yourself to death anyway?"

"You"—his voice grated—"are"—each word was forced—"a difficult girl."

"I am not a girl, and I am trying to help. But you must allow me."

For an instant something she recognized flickered in his eyes. Then, as though it cost him great effort, he released her. With deliberate steps he crossed the chamber and took up the teapot. It clinked against the cup, steam twining in the cold air.

"Take care. It will still be quite h—" Her warning died upon her tongue. He swallowed the scalding tea, then poured another cup and drank it as well.

"The biscuits too," she said.

"Go." He spoke with his back to her.

"No."

"While I still allow you to."

"I thought the remedies we purchased at the herbalist's shop were intended to—"

"They require time to take effect."

Her gaze darted to the brown bottle on the writing table. "You haven't taken the laudanum yet, have you?"

His head bowed. "Makes a man insensible."

"I should think insensibility and life preferable to sharp senses and death."

"Six of one . . ." His fingertips pressed onto the surface of the dressing table, white with strain, and she realized he was holding himself up thus. She had the most powerful urge to go to him, wrap her arms about him and let him use her as a crutch.

"Wyn," she whispered, "I think you should sit down before you topple over."

"Not . . . in the . . . presence of a—"

"Don't be silly. *Oh!*"

He wavered. She flew toward him and threw her arms around him as she'd imagined, *dreamed*, but not quickly enough and she was not strong enough. He went to his knees, and she with him.

"You are the foolish one," she uttered against his shoulder, damp fabric against her cheek covering hard muscle. His body shook. He burned. "Quite a foolish man, Mr. Yale."

His trembling hand clutched hers against his chest. She pressed her mouth to his shoulder, her fingers crushed within his grasp, her body wedged against his, and kissed him. Her lips brushed fine linen and his suffering became part of her.

"You will probably not remember this," she whispered, and kissed his shoulder again. "That is a consolation." She could not stop herself. Need she had never imagined beset her, need to be with him, to touch him and fill her senses with him.

And then she did stop, because it was not about what

she needed now. He needed her. She did not have weeks for this delay, or even days now. But she would give him her days and weeks if necessary.

"You know," she said, resting her cheek against his broad back, the quick, shallow beat of his heart beneath her hand, "you mustn't die, or even continue in this state for much longer."

"I will remember this, Diantha." His words were not strong to the ear, but she felt them vibrate through his body, and hers. "I remember everything."

She squeezed her eyes shut. "Not everything," she whispered.

"Not everything."

"There is a cow desperately needing to be milked. And I don't know what to do about it. So you must get well quickly and solve that little problem so she won't grow sick and die. You see? Now you have two lives for which you are responsible."

She lifted his arm and it was remarkably heavy, but he must have aided her because she got her shoulder beneath his.

"Come now. We will take you to that chair. It is closer than the bed."

"Slept on the ground before. Number of times."

"You have?"

"Not so bad."

"Still, I've an inkling you haven't actually been sleeping at all since we came here. So if you're not to sleep now, you may as well not sleep in a chair rather than on the floor."

Somehow they got him to the chair. It was large, comfortably stuffed leather. He closed his eyes and in another moment seemed to sleep. She watched him, the slight rise of his chest with each shallow breath, the sunken hollows and stark bones of his beautiful cheeks, and felt a tickle of shame that even now staring at him made her warm where she should not be.

"You needn't hover."

She jumped, then twisted her fingers together. "I'm afraid you will slide out of that chair and injure yourself."

"Shan't break." The words were a breath between clicking teeth. "Not made of glass."

Rather, steel. Fired steel. Foundry hot. She glanced at the bed and her cheeks warmed now. It was maidenly idiocy for a woman nursing an ill man. But she'd never looked at a gentleman's bed before.

There was no sign of a blanket through the bed curtains.

"Foolish man," she muttered. She went to the bedchamber she shared with Mrs. Polley, collected blankets, and returned to him.

"Thought you'd gone."

"To fetch this." She draped the coverlet over him. It sagged at one side onto the floor. But shock no longer propelled her actions, and she was—belatedly—shy of touching him, even to tuck it around him. "Now you must eat."

"But do feel free to go at any time," he added in the unexceptionable tone he had used with her a hundred times, albeit a bit unsteady, and she suspected this nonchalance cost him.

"You are wonderfully droll, sir. But I shan't be deterred so easily." She poured another cup, took up several biscuits, and wrapped his hands around both. That operation left her entirely without breath, so she retreated to the writing desk and sat on the wooden chair there. "Now, eat. And drink. And I will read this book while I wait to be certain you don't feed those to Ramses." She took up the volume. "*Blaise Pascal and the Curiously Unsubstantiated Axioms of Euclidean Geometry.* Well, Mr. Yale, you have succeeded in astounding me anew. Unless of course this was Ramses' choice."

"Have we reverted to Mr. Yale and Miss Lucas, then?"

Her pulse tripped. His eyes were closed, the empty cup on his upturned palm resting on his knee.

"No." She set down the book, uncorked the bottle of laudanum and went to him. She poured a spoonful of the syrup into the cup then put it once again against his palm.

His hand came around hers. "Diantha, thank you."

"You can thank me," she whispered, "after you don't die."

The slightest smile tilted up his mouth at one side, but his flesh still burned.

"Drink it." She whispered to disguise the tremble in her throat.

His eyes were dark, seeking as they scanned her face, and vulnerable in a manner she could not have anticipated of this man. Then trusting. Trusting *her*.

He did as she bid. She drew away and set down the empty cup on the tea tray. She stared at the pretty porcelain painted with lavender flowers and tiny green vines and rimmed in silver. A lady's porcelain. The lady in whose house they were now living like a troop of genteel Gypsies. Lost in the wilds of Wales and no one the wiser for it.

Her fortnight would end in three days. Papa would send the carriage to Brennon Manor to collect her, but it would not find her there. She was no closer to Bristol and Calais than she had been a sennight ago.

She cared about this problem, very much. Two peculiar weeks on the road with a man she did not entirely understand, having an adventure she could never have imagined, had not dulled her desire to see her mother. Now she wanted that reunion even more than before. She needed to see her. To *ask* her. She needed to *know*.

But the desperation simmering in her had nothing to do with hurrying back to the road, instead all to do with this man she did not truly know but who at times felt as though she had known her whole life.

He finally seemed to sleep. She set about straightening the chamber, although in truth he'd barely lived in it. His coat, boots, and neck cloth were arranged neatly upon the coat horse. A shallow dish containing a bushy white brush, a bar of soap, and a remarkably lethal-looking blade were certainly his shaving gear and gave her a little frisson of nerves—as much because she had never before seen a man's personal items and it seemed very daring to see his now, as because he clearly didn't need the pistol if he wished to do himself or anybody else damage.

Dragging her gaze away, she neatened the packets of herbs atop the writing desk, sticking her nose into them one at a time to sniff. The Cayenne pepper made her eyes well up and she sneezed, but Wyn did not flinch.

She pulled the Holland cover off a side table, and another from a framed painting on the wall. It showed a black-haired lady settled atop a gray horse. But her eyes, which matched her mount's coat, were somber—too somber for Diantha, and she covered the image again. Finally she steeled herself, went to the bed and drew back the curtain fully. A stack of folded linens sat at the foot of the mattress. With her heart beating fast she made up the bed.

Finished tidying, she went to her knees on the dusty floor. For the first time in four years she folded her hands and bent her head.

"Allow me this," she whispered, the remnants of the pepper filling her eyes with tears again. "I pray you, allow me to do something with my life that matters."

Chapter 16

Fellow Subjects of Britain,

Due to Unanticipated Circumstances my agent in Shropshire is once again detained in pursuing his Falcon Club quarry. In short, I begin to despair of this particular quest.

No—I shan't cease seeking justice! Yes—I shall hound the members of this wasteful club until they are all discovered!

But, as I have fretfully awaited my agent's communications, I have learned a valuable lesson: subterfuge is not my bailiwick. I would rather approach a man directly, accuse him of wrongdoing justifiably and without recourse to secrecy, and hear him defend himself with mine own ears than sit like an Eastern despot upon his throne who waits for his henchmen to perform Despicable Deeds in his name. My methods must remain pristine so that my victory is too.

I have not recalled my agent from the country-side; his troubles are sufficiently noisome to inhibit his progress without my intervention. But when he is again mobile I will inform him of my desire to quit this project. For now. For when this Falcon Club member returns to London, I will confront him and he will be obliged to answer to you, the People of Britain, for his criminal excess.

—Lady Justice

My dearest lady,

I breathe a sigh of profound relief. Quit your pursuit of my fellow club member, indeed. But know this: I am already in London. I entreat you, pursue me instead. If you should find me, I promise you a most satisfying Interrogation.

In eager anticipation,
Peregrine
Secretary, The Falcon Club

Chapter 17

Wyn did not recover that night, nor the following night, nor the day after that. Diantha's fortnight came to a quiet close as she rolled dough in the fading light of evening for yet another batch of Mrs. Polley's ingenious oat biscuits. She glanced at Owen pumping away at the old butter churn they'd found in the chicken shed. Somehow he had managed to milk the cow, lugging in a bucket of milk that tasted like sheer heaven. Her mouth watered anticipating butter. She thought of Glenhaven Hall and Cook's seed biscuits and roast goose with drippings and lemonade and pork jelly and crumbly cheese with crisp apples and shepherd's pie, and then, of course, the man abovestairs.

"The tarts I could make with a dozen apples, if I had them," Mrs. Polley mumbled as though reading her mind.

"There's apples, ma'am." Owen's narrow shoulders leaned into his work. "In the grove a ways past the stile."

"Well, why didn't you say that before, boy?"

Diantha could nearly taste them. "Tomorrow I will see what I can collect."

The following morning she had excellent reason to escape the house and seek out the grove. Entering the kitchen for breakfast she discovered Wyn and Mrs. Polley at the table and her heart flew into her throat. Without a coat, in shirt and waistcoat, breeches and boots, he looked better. No fever darkened his cheeks, and the glimmer in his eyes as he turned to her was familiar.

"You are *better*!"

"To a degree."

She expected him to smile. He did not. He stood up.

She thrust out a palm to stay him. "No! You've been so ill. You mustn't stand merely because I have entered the room."

"In fact I must." He offered her a modest bow. "But I also happen to be leaving."

Already? "Oh."

Silence filled the kitchen. Mrs. Polley muttered beneath her breath and took up the dishes.

Diantha fought to recover her tongue. "To where?"

He paused, then said, "To the drawing room."

It was too awkward. Nothing had ever been awkward between them before, not even those moments outside the inn in Knighton. Then he had been determined to do the right thing by her. Now he seemed cautious.

"Well, then." She moved toward the table and around him as though passing him by so closely did not cause every one of her joints to turn to jelly. "I'm very glad you are feeling well enough to be up and about. We have worried." She flicked a glance at him. "And, naturally, we are anxious to be on our way."

Mrs. Polley harrumphed.

"We shall be soon." A peculiar note in his voice turned her around.

"Not too soon," she said hastily. "Not until you are ready." Her heart beat ridiculously fast.

"Thank you." He left.

She stared at the door. After a minute she could no longer bear the discomfort in her belly and the disapproving silence of her companion.

She set off along the canal toward the stile, carrying only a bucket and her confused thoughts. Her shoes sank deep into the sodden moss along the bank. The abbey was not so different from Glenhaven Hall where she busied herself with small tasks and spent the days with her young sister and servants. Her stepfather was a recluse, his scholarly books claiming most of his attention. When it came to his children, he cared most for his true daughters, Serena and Viola and little Faith. As a stepdaughter, Diantha had long understood that. But the people of Glen Village were always kind, and her weekly visits to Savege Park when Alex and Serena were in residence were happy occasions.

London would be different, she knew. There were museums and historical sites and shops in the hundreds. There would also be grand ladies like those she had sometimes encountered at Savege Park, but in much greater number. Grand, elegant, proper ladies. Slender, with porcelain complexions. Beautiful, like his friend Lady Constance Read.

What he must think of her, in her wrinkled frock and soggy slippers, her hair a mess of unkempt curls and her manners a mess of overfamiliarity. No wonder he wished to keep her at a distance.

She released a long breath, looking up from her toes to see the grove just ahead. Heaps upon heaps of apples lay on the ground, some still hanging on branches, red and green and thoroughly neglected and bursting to be picked. She plucked one off a low branch.

Firm, sweet, juicy. *Heaven.* She ate another, leaning back against a lichen-mottled old trunk and watching the clouds parting above.

Perhaps her stepfather would not banish her to Devon

forever after all. Perhaps she would go to town as planned, and Serena would dress her up like a lady, and she would attend balls and use the dance steps she'd barely had occasion to practice in Devon. The only occasion she really remembered was when she had danced with a handsome Welshman on the terrace at Savege Park.

She wandered through the grove, searching out the choicest apples. When the bucket was three quarters full she hefted the handle over her elbow, picked an apple to eat during the walk, and started out of the grove. And she saw the man.

Her heartbeat stalled. With broad strides he approached from across the slope toward the road above.

Then her heart simply halted.

As before at the mill, Mr. Eads looked enormous. She was too far away to see his face, but she knew him well enough by his size and shape.

The pistol! She must get to Wyn—tell him—warn him. Flinging down the bucket, she ran. But the stile was distant. She lost a slipper and her foot sank into the soft earth. Her lungs pounded, damp skirts tangled about her calves. She threw back a glance. He was running too and had closed the distance between them by half.

She flew, pressing away terror, her footfalls silent on the moss. She threw herself upon the stile, scrabbled for a handhold, then a foothold, and another, dragging her damp garments up, up. Another step—

He grabbed her cloak. She yanked back, hands slippery on the rock, and flailed. She fell. He caught her, banding both arms about her and hauling her against his massive chest. It was hopeless, but she fought, grunting and pounding his arms with her fists until he trapped them too.

"Yer a mettle lass." He sounded unperturbed. "But A'm no wishing ta harm ye, so ye can cease yer struggling nou."

"I shall cease struggling when you unhand me!" She kicked back against his calf and he grunted. His arms were rock. But instead of releasing her, with one big shake he turned her to face him.

"Nou will ye cease struggling?" He looked down at her with a face entirely devoid of menace. His features were strong and good, remarkably attractive really if one liked bulky men that tossed one around like a doll, which Diantha did not. At least not the bulky part. She definitely preferred lean muscle. And Wyn had not precisely tossed her around, rather seized her with purpose. She dearly hoped Mr. Eads's purpose was not similar to Wyn's when he'd held her this close.

She made herself stiff in his arms. "I will cease struggling if you will unhand me."

One dark brow tilted up. "A will if ye'll no run off again."

"I would be a perfect imbecile not to run off, wouldn't I?"

For another moment he studied her like he had at the mill. "A've come for ma horse."

"I suppose you have, but I've no doubt you've also come for Mr. Yale. But, as before, I shall not allow you to harm him. You will have to tie me up, bind my mouth with a gag and throw me into the shed with the chickens and bolt the door first." She bit her tongue belatedly. Silly to give him ideas. But her head was muddled. It did *not* feel good to be hugged to his chest, and she thought she might be ill. It was, she supposed, useful to learn that the embraces of all men were not equally thrilling. "Now unhand me, if you please."

Astoundingly, he did. She took an unsteady step back and glanced at the house in the distance. His eyes narrowed. Then he moved away from her, climbed over the stile and started toward the house.

She scrambled up the stile. "What are you doing? Where are you going?" She ran to meet his long strides. "You promised!"

"A promised nothing except ta unhand ye."

"It's true. But, please, I pray you. I *beg* you." She grabbed his arm and tugged with all her strength. "Please! You *mustn't* harm him."

He halted. She slammed into him. He set her away and his brow came down over fixed blue eyes.

"A wonder, miss, why ye would imagine A could harm a man who's bested me once in yer sight, another out of it, and half a dozen times afore that?"

Her jaw loosened. "I suppose I did not perfectly understand that."

"What's amiss with him then?"

"Amiss?" *Oh, God.* Her foolish tongue. "I don't understand you. There is nothing amiss with Mr. Yale. It is only that I did not wish you to surprise him."

"A reckon he's never been surprised a day in his life." He crossed his massive arms. "A'm nae a dull-witted man, lass. A'll have the truth from ye nou, or A'll be taking more than ma horse with me today." He scanned her from brow to toe. There was no mistaking the threat. "All the way ta the duke, if A must."

"The *duke*?" Could he be speaking of Wyn's duke?

"His Grace'll no take kindly ta ye standing in his way."

Fear clogged her throat; a scream would not come. But even if she were to scream, Wyn could not come and save her. She must save him.

"Mr. Eads," she said, drawing in steadying breaths. "I will tell you what you wish to know."

Satisfaction settled upon his square jaw. "Ye will, nou?"

"I will." She hated to manipulate a man in this manner, but God could not give her a mind that tended toward reckless calculation then fault her for using it for the good of another. "But first I would like to hear about your sister."

"**R**ook to Queen four. Check."

Sunlight streamed across the library onto the chessboard and Owen's face wreathed in cheroot smoke.

Wyn studied the board. The scent of the smoke relieved the thirst that still dragged at him, though it did nothing to ease the hunger. Each time Diantha entered a room, as she'd entered the kitchen that morning, he could not wrest his attention from her. She moved with unselfconscious grace, erect and tempting and apparently unaware that she dazzled him. *Dazzled.* She made him hungry as the devil.

He knew it was the lack his body suffered now that made him want her with such intensity. But he also knew that he'd never before been dazzled by a woman.

"You have forgotten my other knight, young friend." He glanced at the cigar in the dish, the last remaining that he must nurse, as once he'd been able to nurse a glass of brandy. But he had lost that ability. He saw this clearly now. "I urge you to reconsider."

Owen whistled through his teeth. "It's a tricky game, sir."

"You will master it. You possess the natural intelligence." He slid the black knight across the board. "You also possess a tendency toward defiance of authority that can prove useful for a man."

The boy shook his head and reached for his rook. "The old girl didn't mind coming home. But it's true, sir, I didn't know someone would need to be milking her."

"Do you imagine cows drop their milk like one drops a hat?"

"Not now, I don't. Should've learned to milk, I guess." He studied the board. "Uncle always says a man can't earn his keep with his head."

"Mm. I have heard that before." So many times as a boy he'd lost count. "Your uncle is wrong."

"Sir?"

Wyn nodded.

The boy bent again to the game. His hand descended upon the white bishop.

Wyn cleared his throat. "My knight?"

"My knight!" Diantha swept into the library in a cascade of sunshine. "Mr. Yale, you milked the cow."

Owen jumped up and pulled off his cap. "G'day, miss."

"Hello, Owen. And Ramses." She bent and stroked the dog's head, her fingers tender in the beast's matted fur. "Owen, since the sun is finally shining, will you bathe poor Ramses?"

"Yes, miss. Right away." His cheeks sported fiery red spots. "Come on, boy." He hurried out of the library, Ramses alongside.

She set her lapis gaze upon Wyn. "How did you do it? How did you milk that cow?" Ribbons glimmered in her hair, her dimples glowed with life, and he could only stare. She was simply dazzling.

"In the usual manner," he managed.

The pink on her cheeks deepened and he remembered when he'd last used those words with her, when he had taught her how to breathe.

But she recovered swiftly. "There is no usual manner in which a gentleman milks a cow. Mrs. Polley told me just now that it was you and not Owen. I could not believe it. But now here you are saying it is to be believed." Her smile could not be bridled even by embarrassment.

He turned back to the chessboard. He had not stood when she entered, not because of weakness but because of a remarkable strength in one area of his body whenever she came near. "I am variously talented, it seems."

"You truly are. I have never met a gentleman like you, Wyn."

"Under the circumstances, Diantha, I am not quite certain how to take that. Although of course you have admitted that you are acquainted with very few gentlemen."

"It's true: my society has been limited." She ran a finger down the glass panel of a bookcase. "Mrs. Polley dusted in here." She opened the door and drew forth a volume. "She would be a remarkably fine housekeeper. Bess at

Glenhaven Hall does not drop off to sleep unexpectedly, of course, but she's not so clever in the kitchen. Or perhaps Mrs. Polley could open a bakery." She slanted him a quick glance, her lips twisting. "And Owen could open a school for blushing ne'er-do-wells."

Wyn allowed a grin. "He is very taken with you."

"He is a thief."

Not precisely. "He wishes to please you."

"He will get us discovered." She reshelved the book, drew out another, and pursed her lips to blow across its binding. Dust puffed into the air. "But so are we thieves lately, of course," she said, her fingertip turning pages swiftly. "By the by, Mr. Eads has just been by to retrieve his horse." She took the book in both hands before her like a shield. "We spoke then he left with his horse."

Wyn stood and, carefully—because although today he was considerably improved, his pulse ran now with unaccustomed speed—moved toward her.

"About what did you speak, I wonder?" His voice pitched low without any effort.

Her gaze flickered up and down him. "You shouldn't be upsetting yourself. You haven't been well, which of course is an extraordinary understatement."

"Upsetting myself? Isn't that rather inaccurately fixing the blame?" He halted before her, the scent drifting about her not her usual scent yet so familiar. "You are wearing perfume."

"I am." She blinked. "You know, you were just about to chastise me. Are you still delirious, then?"

"Merely easily distracted, it seems. Why did Eads leave without speaking to me?"

"He said it would be far too easy to take advantage of you in your current state. As he prides himself on being a man of his word, he thought it best to depart and return when you are more yourself."

"He said that?"

"Not in so many words. But, yes."

Of course he had. Duncan Eads was not a dishonorable man, only misguided. But Eads's quarry was equally misguided, standing now far too close to a maiden whose berry lips tasted like honey and kissed like sin.

He backed away and returned to the table. She would put it off to his illness. Damn Carlyle for not being home when he should. If Kitty Blackwood didn't arrive within a day he just might tie up Diantha Lucas, sling her across Galahad's flanks, and carry her to London himself.

"Where did you find the perfume?" He knew perfectly well.

"If you are asking if Owen stole it, he didn't. I found it here in the master suite." She tucked the book back into the case and ran her fingertips along the row of gold-embossed bindings then plucked out another volume. "Mrs. Polley made a tasty oatcake with buttermilk contrived with beeswing from a recipe I found in here yesterday." She opened the book and seemed to peruse it, but her body had stilled. "Are you hungry?" Her lashes flickered but she did not lift her gaze. "That is, will you have some of the oatcake concoction?" In the light streaming through the window her hair gleamed like polished oak, her figure picked out in motes of sun.

"I am Welsh, Diantha. A surfeit of oats is the reason I started drinking to excess."

"Really?"

"No."

She tilted her head. "Why *did* you start drinking to excess?"

"To be able to talk to my father and elder brothers."

Her brow dipped.

"They drank every night," he said simply, as though it were simple. "When I did not, they were . . . disinterested in my conversation."

"Why didn't you just tell them to sod off?"

He lifted a brow. She twisted her damnably delectable lips.

"I did not tell them to 'sod off,' " he said, "because if I did not make myself available to them for sport they invariably turned to my mother instead."

"Oh."

"Oh, indeed." He set the white queen in the velvet-lined case and—as always—the black king beside her, just as his great-aunt used to like to arrange them. Remarkable how the gesture could push those other memories back, like the scent of perfume in a dusty room. "But that is ancient history and best forgotten."

She moved toward the window, a book in her hands. "Well, this is marvelous." She drew a loose page from the volume, unfolded it, and read aloud, " 'Rules a Man is Well Advised to Follow in Order to Be a True Gentleman.' "

Breath stalling, Wyn closed the case's lid. She reached for a chair and settled onto it without taking her eyes from the page.

"Oh, I simply must read them to you! You will adore it." She glanced up.

He could only nod her onward. His heart beat slow and hard now, but he could not resist.

"They are in descending order. 'Rule Number Ten,' " she read. " 'A gentleman must always act with honor and honesty toward other men—men of lesser rank, equal rank, and higher rank.' I suppose that is good advice, isn't it?"

"Quite good."

" 'Rule Number Nine: A gentleman must always put a lady's welfare before his own.' Well, I like that one a lot." Her dimples appeared. " 'Rule Number Eight: A man is only a gentleman if he is never otherwise.' " Her brow puckered. "You said something very much like that once, I think."

"Did I?" He should leave. He should walk over to her, take the page from her hand, and distract her with other activity. He should entreat her to play chess. Or promise to eat the oatcakes. Or grab her and kiss her until she forgot about everything but touching him. "Rule Number Seven?"

" 'A gentleman must never blaspheme before a lady.' Oh, very right. Ladies can become offended so easily." But her dimples peeked out again. " 'Rule Number Six: All ladies like to be recognized for their accomplishments, but a virtuous lady is immune to empty praise. Compliment her on that which she excels, but do not seek to flatter.' That one is tremendous, don't you agree?"

"Ladies do not like to be flattered emptily."

"Not only ladies. *All* women. Rule Number Two makes that clear: 'A gentleman must treat a lady with utmost respect, consideration, and reverence, whether she is common or highborn, antidote or beauty, poor as a pauper or wealthy as a princess.' " She dropped her hands to her lap, a smile of pure impenitence shaping her luscious lips. "So you mustn't go flattering Mrs. Polley emptily."

"I shall endeavor not to."

"Of course you will. And she will berate you for it. Now here, I like Rule Number One the best: 'If a lady is kind of heart, generous and virtuous, a gentleman should acquiesce to her every request. He should deny her nothing.' " Her shoulders dipped. "But of course you follow this rule even for ladies who do not possess all these virtues, so you are an even more impressive gentleman than the rules require. Really, these might have been written with you in mind." Her voice had grown softer, less animated. "Down to a one."

The pit of his stomach burned. "What of the rule that requires a gentleman to ravish an innocent girl while he is in his cups?"

"No. That one is not on this list." Her blue eyes turned up, glimmering with hope. "But we could add it."

Wyn stood and left the library.

He did not remember that entire night at the inn in Knighton. He remembered touching her, but not how it felt to have her body in his hands. Amid the black of memory, he only recalled his inability to use her as he had intended in his blind desire. The thought of it now made him sick—the only night of his life of which he did not recall every single moment. That alone had made him suffer through fevered torture over the past sennight without complaint.

Now he found himself on the threshold of his great-aunt's chambers. Dust lay thick on the floor, Diantha's footprints crossing to the dressing table. Ever curious and full of adventure, she had come exploring.

He took up the bottle of perfume, cut crystal of the deepest violet that shone even in the dimness like a jewel. He had purchased it in Vienna. He'd traveled there supposedly in search of another missing noble girl, assigned to it by the director, given his orders by Colin, sent on his way this time without Leam, his partner, who had by then wearied of the work. But he'd known they were preparing him for something more, that this assignment was not like those that had preceded it. The girl was not truly the reason they'd sent him abroad. The real quarry, it turned out, was him.

There in the secret back chambers of the Congress of Vienna, the men who ruled Britain examined him. Impressed, they courted him. His skills were too valuable to waste on runaways, they said. Britain's safety lay in its interests abroad. The director would release him and he would come to work for them. His future was golden. The boy who'd been beaten again and again for the aptitude of his mind was now, as a man, to be rewarded for it.

For three months in Vienna he got drunk on it, drunk on the praise of powerful men, the finest tobacco, aged liquor, women of aristocratic blood that undressed like any other women but seemed more enticing for being forbidden. While they offered their bodies to him, their husbands spoke loftily of ideals, of victories, and of the people around the world that would come to serve Britain. But all the while the Welsh blood in him—the blood that had fought for hundreds of years to remain free of English kings—kept telling him that the promises of these powerful men sparkled like diamonds but tasted like sewage.

He escaped, departing after the New Year and returning to England on the pretext that his great-aunt was ill, only to discover that to be the truth.

He remained with her as she returned to health, and all the while she exhorted him not to fear the pride of which his father and brothers had always accused him. He should be proud; he had accomplished everything he'd ever set out to accomplish by the strength of his arms and his natural intelligence. She told him to make the choice that best suited his heart.

He agreed to work for them. The Duke of Yarmouth gave him his first assignment: find a traitor and assassinate her.

But she hadn't been a traitor after all. She'd been barely more than a girl, begging him to believe her story. Begging him for help.

He unstoppered the bottle and the scent rose to him. Closing his eyes, he saw his great-aunt's sober eyes so like his mother's, gray and wise and kind. But not always serious. She had taught him how to laugh. She had taught him many things, but the laughter he'd nearly forgotten. He had forgotten it until he encountered a determined young lady who was loyal and steadfast and strong, yet who loved to laugh, who knew how to delight, who sought happiness in every nook and crevice of the life she'd been dealt. She had shown him a sort of bravery he'd also forgotten.

He set down the perfume and returned to the library.

She stood by the window looking out onto the dusk, still as a sylph poised upon her toes to spring into the air, but listening for him; she turned immediately.

"When I encountered Mr. Eads, I dropped the bucket of apples I collected," she said. "In the excitement of seeing him off with his horse I forgot about it. But now it is becoming too dark to retrieve it. I spent most of the day looking forward to apple tarts, and I'll admit I am disappointed over this turn of events."

Her blue eyes sparkled in the fading light, quietly wise. She was no more an innocent girl than he was still the boy whose father had punished him out of spite. Rather, she was a determined woman with a goal and, with few words—carefully chosen to deflect the truth of what lay between them—she was telling him that she would not allow him to deter her from that goal, even now.

"Tomorrow we will walk to the grove and you shall make another attempt at it," he said. "One final activity here upon the eve of our departure."

Only the slightest beat of lashes revealed her surprise. She turned her face askance and peered at him from the corner of her eye. "And I would like to learn how to milk the cow."

"Would you?"

Her lips twitched. Then she smiled fully, and he felt that smile in every corner of his body. He was, quite possibly, the greatest fool alive.

Kitty Blackwood could not arrive soon enough. If she did not appear and take Diantha away he would surely do something unwise and not in either of their best interests. Something quite thoroughly ungentlemanlike.

And this time nothing would stop him.

Chapter 18

"My gown is growing mold." She held it up to the morning light peeking through the window.

"All that rain." Mrs. Polley took up Diantha's other gown. "And this one a shambles with no iron to be found."

"Perhaps the mold can be washed out." Diantha scrubbed at the misty smear on the hem of the pin-striped muslin, but it clung. The green gown truly was a shambles, torn at the hem and horrendously crumpled from when she'd followed Mr. Eads over the stile.

She sighed. She'd wanted to look especially like a lady today. Perhaps even as elegant as the lady whose house they camped in now. "We haven't yet looked in the attic!"

"I'll not go prying into other folks' closets."

"Mrs. Polley, you knocked a stranger over the head with a cheese crock yet you will not peek into an attic now in search of an iron?"

"It was a shame to ruin that crockery." Mrs. Polley shook her head. "If I'd had a flatiron I would've used it on him instead."

Diantha stifled a giggle and went into the corridor to

the attic door. Wyn had taken Galahad out for a ride, and Owen was collecting eggs. Her feet were cold, but she could wander about in her shift and petticoat without concern for propriety. Wyn had already seen her naked breasts, of course, but he didn't remember it so he may as well not have.

She climbed stairs to the room at the top of the house, its ceiling narrowing to a point. Like in the attic at Glenhaven Hall, traveling trunks and old furniture were everywhere. She found an unlocked trunk and the pungent scent of camphor balls sprang forth. Then she sighed in sheer pleasure. Drawing out one after another fine gown, tenderly stroking muslin, silk, and wool, she sighed again and missed her own clothing acutely.

Her gaze darted to the next trunk. She reached for it. Slippers, boots, pattens, fichus, petticoats, shifts, stays, ribbons, reticules, garters, stockings, shawls, pelisses, and handkerchiefs with initials embroidered into them— all smelling of camphor—tumbled into her hands. But she didn't care about the odor. She could live with a wrinkled nose for a day if the rest of her weren't wrinkled.

She plucked up a gown and held it before her. It was short by several inches. Her petticoat would show. But not if she wore the lady's petticoat too.

She paused a moment in her head-on rush toward more thievery to consider. But she could not see the crime in it. She would return the garments in neat order before they departed the abbey tomorrow. Also, Wyn wouldn't care if he saw her ankles. He had threatened a man who jeopardized her safety with a pistol, caressed her intimately while foxed, and walked through a torrential downpour leading her horse for an entire day. And she had seen him—*touched him*—in his shirtsleeves, without a cravat. Also, she'd made his bed. They may as well be on ankle-glimpsing terms too.

Before she could delay another moment—because Guilt

was even now poking up its ugly head—she grabbed a gown of figured blue muslin and an armful of undergarments, slammed the trunks shut with her toes, and hurried down the stairs.

She halted abruptly.

As though arrested in mid-stride, Wyn stood in the corridor in coat and breeches and boots, looking remarkably well and directly at her. Then his gaze dropped to her breasts.

At that moment Diantha discovered another useful thing: standing before a gentleman, in stays and petticoat and in the bright light of day, was not in fact the same as being furtively divested of those garments by him in the darkness. It was thrilling, in a ladies-are-taught-not-to-do-precisely-this-unless-they-are-quite-wanton manner, and she felt not merely underdressed but entirely naked beneath his sober regard. Every inch of her body flushed with heat.

His gaze snapped away and she shoved the borrowed garments in front of her breasts.

"Good day, Miss Lucas," he said to a floorboard in the region of her bare feet. "It seems you have visited the attic."

"Yes." Her tongue was a piece of flypaper on the roof of her mouth. "In search of fresh clothing. Mine is somewhat bedraggled."

"Ah." Slowly his gaze traveled from her feet, along her legs, past her hips and the clothing in her arms, to her face. But he said nothing more.

"These smell strongly of camphor," she mumbled. "But I can probably mask the odor with perfume." Nerves made her shrug. His attention shifted to her shoulder, then her bare arm.

"I should say so." He sounded a little hoarse. "Quite a lot of perfume will be necessary, no doubt."

"I suppose so."

"Vast quantities."

"Oh. Yes."

The horrible awkwardness again, like in the kitchen the previous day. It made her feel a little ill. Ducking around him in the narrow corridor, she ran to her bedchamber, threw the door shut and sank against it.

"What's gone and frightened you, miss?" Mrs. Polley hurried forward. "Have you seen a ghost?"

Only a man. "Mrs. Polley, I would like to try to look pretty today."

Her companion crinkled up her brow. But she did as Diantha wished.

In the end it didn't matter that Mrs. Polley spent a quarter hour arranging Diantha's hair, or that her gown while reaching barely to her ankles was only moderately creased from storage and the color nearly matched her eyes, nor that the fringe on her paisley shawl fluttered in the breeze like butterfly wings and her shoes were perfectly unexceptionable footwear for a lady. Wyn barely glanced at her as they left the house.

Owen went with them, tossing a stick for Ramses and chattering about the mines.

"I think losing his sister was terribly hard for him," she said when Owen ran ahead along the canal after the dog. "He speaks so often of the mines."

"It was his life until recently." Wyn walked beside her, hands clasped loosely behind his back, black coat and snowy cravat elegant as always, boots sparkling. The sun shone again, golden like a ripe peach, and the breeze was cool slipping across Diantha's cheeks, which seemed perpetually warm now when he was near.

"She is always in the stories he tells. Perhaps he misses her."

"Perhaps."

"You rarely speak of your life."

He cast her a swift glance. "I haven't any cause to."

"A man threatening us with violence seems sufficient cause, if you ask me."

"Since you cleared away that particular trouble again yesterday without my assistance, the point is moot."

"I realize I am not supposed to ask after your health, but . . . would you have been *able* to assist?"

"I am fairly certain you know the answer to that question."

She did. If he had known she was in danger, he would have done whatever he must to defend her, as he was now defending her even from himself by avoiding drink.

"Then, you are feeling better?"

"As well as can be expected."

"Would you like your pistol and bullets returned?"

"Yes, thank you." At a fence that ran with vines of big white flowers, he plucked one and proffered it to her with a bow. "For saving me from the wrath of Duncan Eads."

She tucked it into her hair. "Well, I could not allow him to kill you."

"Naturally." But now he was not smiling.

For the remainder of the walk to the orchard he was unfailingly polite. He remained by her side and said nothing that he might not say to any lady whose acquaintance he had recently made and who had not seen him suffering because she had driven him to it. He assisted her over the stile with a firm hand but held hers only as long as necessary. When they came upon her lost slipper poking from the grass, he restored it to her without comment, as though gentlemen encountered ladies' footwear along mossy canals every day.

Owen found the bucket and set off for the grove, but he was more interested in eating apples than picking them and soon grew tired of the activity. He waded across the canal flowing swiftly from the rains and threw himself onto the grass on the opposite hill. Ramses followed, settling down with his tongue lolling out.

Then Owen fell asleep, and everything changed, as though the hand of a god who had drawn a curtain now pushed it aside. Approaching her from behind, beneath the boughs of a gnarled old tree, Wyn said, "It seems that you did not don perfume after all." His voice was low and sent tingles through her.

"I did not." She turned. In the dappled sunshine falling through the tree branches his eyes seemed to glitter. "I suppose I give off the most horrid aroma of camphor."

The slightest crease appeared in his cheek. "I would never say so." He drew forth a cigar he'd carried from the house.

"But you are probably thinking it."

"No. That is not what I am thinking now." He moved away. She could not help but follow; it seemed natural to her now, as a bird that did not ponder flying south for the winter but simply did.

"Will you teach me how to smoke?"

He looked over his shoulder, brow raised, the corner of his mouth tilted up. "If you wish."

"I have always wanted to smoke a cigar but I never before had the opportunity. That is, the opportunity to ask a gentleman who would not think I was a hoyden for asking. But with you that cat is already out of the bag, as it were."

"I do not think you are a hoyden." He didn't look at her as he spoke, but at the cigar.

"Now you have twice said what you don't think, but not what you do."

What Wyn thought was that he could quite easily lay this girl down in the grass and make love to her for a week. Her eyes sparkled the truest blue beneath the autumn sky and her cheeks glowed from the walk and he wanted to touch her. He would begin where her slender ankles peeked out from beneath the too-short gown, peeling her stockings away and slipping his hands along the shapeliness of her legs, upward.

"Have I?"

Her brow knit. "You are evasive."

"And you are far too curious, minx."

She curtsied. "Hoyden." Her dimples flashed, and rather predictably his groin tightened.

He proffered the cigar. Perhaps if she were smoking she would not smile so and he would not descend again into the drooling fool who'd discovered her by the attic door with her beautiful bosom spilling from her under-garments. Within moments his imagination had seen her breasts fallen fully from the shift, corset, and petticoat, and their perfect tips in his mouth.

"This is yours." She refused the cigar. "Don't you have another?"

"This is my last." Only decades of practice at deception schooled his voice to its regular cadence. "Learn on this, or learn not at all. As you wish."

"I probably shan't have this opportunity again." She chewed the edge of her berry lips, and quite abruptly Wyn's years of practice went to the devil.

"Probably not." His voice sounded rough even to his own ears. Her gaze shot up, but he could not look away from her lips. Beautiful lips, dark pink and slightly parted and *God, he wanted to taste her again*. He wanted to feel her tongue against his and make her moan.

She closed her lips and they were no less sweet sealed. He imagined what it would take to urge them apart again. If he kissed her now, what she would do . . .

He made himself speak. "The cigar, Miss Lucas?"

"Thank you, Mr. Yale." She took it. "What must I do?"

Press her beautiful body to his and submit to him. "Inhale, but very lightly, and try not to actually breathe."

"How does one inhale without— *Ach! Eh!*" She

wheezed, coughed, and grabbed her mouth, a rush of smoke escaping between her fingers. "I *cannot* have done that right."

"Had enough?"

"No! If making another attempt means you will smile at me again as you have just done, I shall do it."

Dear God, he'd lost every ounce of discipline over himself with this woman. "How did I smile at you?"

"As though you like me." She stated it without any coquetry. So he replied as honestly.

"There is no 'as though' about it, Diantha."

She smiled and poked the cigar back into her mouth. Her lips puckered and the smoke rose between them, and he nearly snatched the thing away and used her lips himself.

Torture. Possibly worse than the fevered nights he'd just survived. At least then he'd had the comfort of imagining he might die.

She coughed again. "I shan't be sick," she said upon a gasp, "if you are worried about that."

"No worries. Not on my account."

"Why on earth do you smoke these things?"

"Because it is what gentlemen do. And at this time in particular, it eases the desire for brandy."

"Oh." She seemed to accept that without trouble, as she had accepted everything about this adventure, with many questions but without distress. Except at one moment, the moment in his bedchamber that stilled his heart to recall.

"I'd like to get it right," she said.

"You are tenacious."

Her mouth tilted into an uncertain smile, the dimples reluctant.

"But I think both of us already knew that," he added, and handed her the cigar once more. She made another attempt. Eventually she conquered it, as she conquered all she wished to conquer, including him. He gazed upon her face gently marked with the mementos of her youth, a naturally lovely face made lovelier by the spirit that shone from within. He had traveled thousands of miles, trekked through jungles and drawing rooms, monsoons and secret chambers, since the age of fifteen rarely pausing for a moment in any one place, and through all of this the road had never troubled him. Yet now within sight of his own house, looking into a pair of blue eyes, he was, quite possibly, lost.

"Congratulations, Miss Lucas." His voice was unsteady. "You may now apply for membership at any one of the gentlemen's clubs of London."

"Splendid." She returned the cigar to him, brushing her fingers against his, and moved away. "At times I have wished fervently to be a gentleman, you know. They have all sorts of adventures—obviously." She gestured to him as she set her foot on the lowest branch of a tree and reached up. "And some gentlemen can even be counted upon to rescue a damsel in distress."

He followed to the base of the tree, the unsteadiness becoming complete, like the tremors that had seized him days ago. But this was new. This was not suffering. "Yet, despite all they have seen of such damsels, some gentlemen are nevertheless somewhat astounded when said damsels take to the sudden climbing of trees."

"Oh, an ordinary gentleman might be. But a hero is never surprised by unexpected turns." She pulled herself onto a thick branch and climbed to the next, providing him a delectable view of the calves he wished to caress. "Especially when the damsel is merely seeking a treasure in said tree." She pointed toward a bird's nest tucked in the crook of a branch, stretching to peer over its edge. "See?"

"I do. Now that you have found your treasure, will you come down before I am obliged to watch you fall and break your neck?"

"I don't suppose you would like it if I died such an undramatic death, after all the trouble I have put you through."

"Especially not given that, it's true."

"Do you think the parents are far?"

"Why? Do you hope to steal the eggs and fetch them up to Mrs. Polley to cook for dinner?"

"No!" Her head cocked to the side. "I think you are speaking from experience."

"You are probably right about that."

She twisted her lips. "How old were you?"

"Young enough to be considered blameless for the misdeed." *Blameless for his misdeed*. His breaths came short. "Now will you come down before I climb up there and retrieve you?"

She dimpled. "You wouldn't."

He moved toward the trunk.

She scrambled down. As she came to the last branch he offered his hand, then his other. Any young lady who could climb a tree with such alacrity could get herself down from it. But he wanted to hold her. He grasped her waist and she allowed him to draw her to the ground.

He knew why he had done this. A sennight ago she would have taken this opportunity to invite him to touch her further. But now her lashes only flickered, her breasts rising on a quick breath, and with a small smile she slipped out of his grasp. He let her go. She knew now of what he was capable, and she would not make the mistake of putting herself in his hands again. Her swift departure from the corridor that morning proved it.

She glanced back up at the nest. "Then, I am to understand you have been a thief since your boyhood, like Owen?"

"No."

She lifted a skeptical brow.

He smiled. "Not continuously, that is. Now, come. Mrs.

Polley will have dinner waiting, and there is a cow to be milked."

"Eggs and bread again. And apples. I will be very glad for a change in menu soon. Will we truly leave tomorrow?"

"Truly." Or he would go mad. Kitty and Leam would have arrived already if they were in London. He may have to take her there himself. But he knew now that she was too clever to deceive. When they reached England he would tell her their destination. She might balk, but he didn't believe she would. She had learned the true nature of men, and she was wary now.

"For a London gentleman, Wyn, you certainly seem very comfortable in a barn."

"This is a stable, Diantha, and I have told you that I am not from London." He drew a stool close to the side of the big brownish red and white cow.

"Not *from* London." She dangled the empty bucket against the knee of her pin-striped skirt. The stained muslin was more suited to farm tasks than the blue gown from the attic, and it didn't smell like camphor. "But you spend a great deal of time there, don't you?"

"There and elsewhere." He took the bucket from her.

"Where elsewhere?"

"I believe this is an occasion when if you persist in prying I may rely upon evasion." He sat on the low stool and placed the bucket beneath the cow's heavy udder, and Diantha stared quite unashamedly. It did not feel wrong to look at him overlong. It felt *right*.

She licked her lips. "Do you believe in Destiny?"

"No." He drew off his coat and deposited it on a bench, his white shirt stretching tight across his shoulders. "But I have absolutely no doubt that you do."

"Why?"

"A Grand Plan . . ." He unbuttoned his cuffs and folded the linen up his forearms.

"Oh." It was difficult to manage more words. If God had invented a sight to set her entire body aquiver, Wyn Yale removing his clothes was it. She gripped the stall door for steadiness. "But I suspect destiny would tend to disturb any plans a person made," she mumbled, "so it is complicated."

"I daresay."

She moved closer to him. He drew her like this, from that first day. It might have something to do with the way his shirt pulled at his shoulders, or the strength in his arms revealed by the cuffed sleeves. She could not breathe properly. Not to be wondered at. He'd put his hands on the cow's teats and they were strong and sinewy too, and although it was perfectly ridiculous and a little peculiar she could not help remembering them on *her* teats. And then for the hundredth time she thought about his mouth there and how he had touched her and what he'd said to her.

"What about Reincarnation? Do you believe in that?"

"Probably not." The muscles in his hands and arms flexed, and jets of milk squirted into the bucket with tinny clangs. "Are we to engage in a discussion of world philosophies today, Miss Lucas?" he said with a slight smile.

She believed in Reincarnation. At this moment she was certain she had been here before, with him. Not milking a cow, of course. But together like this doing mundane tasks. Alone together. Her *heart* felt it, and it was incredibly disconcerting because she didn't believe in any of that heart nonsense. But Reincarnation seemed another thing altogether.

"I've been reading a lot these past few days," she managed. "I always thought my stepfather's collection of archeological journals and scholarly what-have-you peculiar enough. But the library here is very curious. A remarkable selection for a lady, really."

"Perhaps the lady did not live here alone."

"You may be right. Yesterday I came across a book on the religions of the East Indies."

"Thus Reincarnation."

"The day before that I found a book on a man named Buddha who often went about without a shirt, apparently. There were picture plates." She stared at Wyn's muscle-corded arms and thought perhaps Annie could not be blamed for having run off with the farmhand after all. Every time Wyn's hand flexed, a muscle strained the cuff above his elbow. It made her agitated inside. "It seems that Buddha started an entire religion, quite an interesting one with some truly marvelous ideas."

"You read this book?"

"Wouldn't you?"

He smiled. It made her warm, rather low. She wanted him to touch her again. *There.* "I didn't understand the half of it, really." Her voice was foolishly breathy. The milk was making a light splashing sound now. "You are very good at that."

"I have recently had practice. Will you come over here or shall I bring the cow to you?"

He gave up the stool to crouch in the straw beside her. The cow turned its head and stared at her with wide-set eyes.

"Is this any easier than smoking a cigar?"

"About the same level of difficulty, I should say. Like putting on one's shoes or sweeping a stoop. I imagine you will be able to manage it."

"Have you swept *stoops*?"

"In my day, I did it all. Are you actually interested in milking this cow? Because—"

"I am!" She grasped a teat. It was warm and soft. She tugged. "Nothing is happening."

"It is not a bellpull, minx. You cannot summon a maid with it."

"You are very droll, Mr. Yale."

"That is what they say, Miss Lucas."

Her delight deflated. "Who? All the ladies in London?"

"No." He reached forward and surrounded her hand with his, and all the ladies in London simply vanished. His palm was large and wonderfully warm, and she wanted to sit here holding hands with him forever. He repositioned her fingers, but she could barely attend. He was so close now, at her shoulder, as close as he'd been when he assisted her down from the tree and she had almost planted her mouth on his.

"Then who?" she asked a little thinly.

His hand cupped hers. "All the gentlemen in London, of course. Apply pressure in this manner." His voice sounded husky. It *was not* only her, then. He felt this too, this thing that made her heart thud and body weak with anticipation. He must.

If she did not divert her thoughts she would be begging him for kisses in moments. "Do you think it would be naïve for a person to believe in Destiny and Reincarnation at once?" she uttered.

"I have never felt the need to insist upon a man confining his most cherished beliefs to the parameters of a system devised by others."

Her hand, guided by his, caught the rhythm. Then she was sorry she'd learned so swiftly because he released her.

"But you do believe in God." She felt light-headed. "Don't you?"

"I admit that I am not entirely convinced."

"Then what *do* you believe in?"

"Good manners, the faculty of human reason, and hell." The words fell starkly into the straw-scented air.

Diantha's fingers ceased moving of their own accord. The urge to weep beset her.

In a clear, quiet voice he added, "And, lately, hope."

Her hand slipped away from the teat and she swiveled around to face him. There was no bleakness in his face. Desire lit his silvery eyes and something else she did not understand but it dashed away all thought of weeping. A muscle in his jaw flexed and she saw him take a breath, heard it in the stillness surrounded by the soft sounds of animals and the mad chatter of birds in the hedge without.

His gaze dipped to her mouth and there was nothing more she wanted than to be kissed by him. Nothing in the world.

She could not prevent herself; she leaned forward. He leaned forward. Their breaths mingled, an intimacy for which she was thoroughly unprepared.

He closed the space between them. It was a mere brushing of lips, the most innocent caress.

And then it was not. Then it became more.

His hand came around the back of her neck and secured her mouth against his and he kissed her like she'd dreamed every night for endless nights, like there was nothing more *he* wanted than to be kissing her, feeling her like she felt him in every part of her body. He tasted her, used the tip of his tongue to part her lips, and she succumbed. She allowed him into her mouth, to touch her like he had touched her before, but this was not the same. Now the caress of his mouth recalled her to his hands on her body, and to his body when she'd held him in the midst of fever, and she knew it was all different. She wanted even more than kisses. She wanted *him*. She ached with wanting him.

His thumb stroked her cheek, his fingertips slipping into her hair, and it was sublime, the most tender touch, reverent and delectable like the opening up within her that needed him. She lifted her hand and skimmed her fingers along the taut strength of his forearm. It made her hungry. It made her delirious with pleasure. A sound came from his chest and he sought her deeper, capturing her tongue and making her *desperate* for more, for his body against hers, for his hands all over her. She slid forward on the stool.

The cow lowed.

Wyn pulled back and his hand fell.

Diantha sucked in breath and opened her eyes. His looked unfocused. Then something else flickered within the gray, something unsettling that made her stomach plunge.

She leaped up. "D-Don't say 'God, no,'" she stuttered. "Please."

"What?" He seemed confused. "I wasn't going to say—"

"I did not ask for that." She pressed her fingertips to her damp lips. "You cannot stuff me into my traveling trunk and take me home."

He bent his head and ran his hand around the back of his neck. Each motion struck her with agonizing beauty. She couldn't bear it. She *wanted* him so much. Not just in her feminine regions where she was becoming accustomed to feeling her response to his male angularity and elegance. This need spread in her chest and limbs. She felt *moved* and deep down inside her this all felt right, like she was meant to be kissing him and only him.

She backed away. "Don't say something horrid or make threats."

His gaze snapped up, a spark of anger in it. "I won't. Damn it, Diantha—"

"And don't swear at me. It is against the rules. Number Seven." She darted forward and snatched up the bucket. "Thank you for teaching me how to milk a cow. I'm leaving now." Dragging the bucket at her side, she hastened from the stable because she knew she must run away or throw herself at him, and the first seemed a better alternative for eventually reaching Calais.

But at present she did not wish to be in Calais. She wished to be in his arms.

Chapter 19

If Mrs. Polley noticed that her employers were not on speaking terms with each other at supper, she was remarkably discreet about it. Fortunately Owen prattled on—as always—and the meal was consumed until Wyn excused himself courteously—as always.

Mrs. Polley ushered Owen to his gatehouse. "That man will have us at an early start tomorrow and we'll be in the rain and mud and Lord knows what other troubles again, so you'd best have yourself a good sleep, boy."

He snatched up another biscuit, tipped his cap with an "Evening, miss," and whistled for Ramses to follow.

Diantha took her plate to the washbasin. "We must have straightening up to do before departing."

"I saw to that already, miss." Mrs. Polley wiped the table.

"Thank you, Mrs. Polley. You have been a great help this past fortnight and I'm very glad you agreed to come with us."

"Well now, miss, I couldn't let a fine young lady go off on a wild goose chase with that dark man intending no good."

Intending no good. If that meant he had intended for her to develop an enormous partiality for the caress of his mouth and hands, then yes certainly he had intended her no good.

"It is not a wild goose chase, Mrs. Polley. And despite all I have demanded of him, he has tried diligently to behave as a gentleman."

"A gentleman is as a gentleman does," she muttered, packing away the remaining oatcakes.

In their bedchamber, Mrs. Polley unlaced her stays and Diantha laid her stained, wrinkled gown across a chair and could barely remember what it was like to live in her stepfather's house and wear fresh garments and not know a dark, handsome Welshman.

Without conversation, her companion fell asleep. Diantha had become accustomed to this, missing Faith's chatter at night, and occasionally talked herself to sleep because Mrs. Polley never woke anyway. But she could not rest now. Too much had happened to her lips and sensibilities today, and her stomach rumbled.

Finally she arose, slipped into her green gown and tied it about her waist with a sash, then stole on quiet feet down to the kitchen.

The scent of tobacco smoke met her in the foyer. She ought to have anticipated this; the nights when he had touched her he'd been awake late too. But on those nights he had been foxed.

Stomach wild with butterflies, she went along the corridor to the kitchen. He stood by the hearth. A cigar burned atop the simmering remains of the peat fire.

"Good evening." Without seeing, he knew she stood there. He seemed to have an uncanny sense of such things.

"I thought the cigar that you let me smoke today was your last," she said, because what else, after all, could be said?

"This is it."

"But why aren't you smoking it?"

He turned toward her then, and his silvery eyes gleamed unnaturally. *Hot.*

Fear jerked through her. "It hasn't passed entirely, has it? The illness. It has come back."

"No."

"But you have that fevered look in your eyes again. You want a brandy, don't you?"

"Of course I want a brandy." He ran a hand through his hair and gripped the back of his neck. "But I want you rather a great deal more."

Her body flushed with an achy thrill.

"You can have me," she said shakily. "Only for the present, of course," she added, because the flash of panic in his eyes was worse than the feverishness. "I must eventually accept Mr. H since that is the plan. But you can have me first."

"I cannot."

"I am compromised anyway. But I was perfectly aware that would be the case when I set out from Teresa's house. So if anyone were ever to discover—"

"They will not," he said firmly. "It is my job to ensure that they do not."

"My family will." Very soon they would find her absent from Brennon Manor and begin looking for her.

"Certain members of your family have reason to trust me in this." He seemed very serious.

"I knew there was something more to—to everything about you," she said in a hushed tone. "Mr. Eads called you the Raven, and I'm not such a ninny that I don't understand special names like that have some significance. But I don't know why that would mean my family would trust you if they were to discover I've been with you these past weeks. Anyway, they are fully aware that I am prone to inappropriate behavior. My stepfather tells me nearly every day."

He took a tight breath, his shoulders rigid. "Rescuing girls like you is what I do."

"*Rescuing* girls? Like *me*?"

"Lost girls, in particular. Runaways. Though occasionally a child or amnesiac if I am fortunate. Or a horse." He seemed to speak ironically. "But mostly it seems to be the girls they assign me. I am, it seems, adept at encouraging young women to do as I wish."

"*Assign* you? Who are 'they'?"

"There really isn't any more I can say." He turned away. "Now, if you will be so good as to absent yourself from this room and not reappear until the morning, I will be much obliged."

"But I *want* you to kiss me."

"You haven't any idea what you're saying. You are an innocent."

"I am quite ready not to be so any longer. I've been quite ready for an age already. Perhaps it runs in my blood, my mother being what—" She halted, desperation rising in her breast. "I'm not really asking all that much."

"You're not asking . . . ?" He was clearly struggling. "Allow me to put it in terms you may understand better: Heroes do not deflower innocent girls."

"Oh, for pity's sake!" She slapped her hands against her skirt. "I am through with trying to convince you to kiss me and—er—do whatever else."

"Yes, well, it is the 'whatever else' that presents the problem." He ran his hand around to the back of his neck again, tightening linen over muscle. Diantha nearly launched herself at him.

Her hands fisted. "My pride"—and self-control—"cannot take any more of this battering." Against every desire, she pivoted about, but swung back around and burst out, "When you kissed me— The way you— And you look at me so intensely at moments. Like a wolf sizing up his prey."

"It is the drink," he said quietly.

She swallowed hard over her thick heartbeats. "The drink?"

"I crave intoxication. In my blood there is a hunger beyond all else to lose myself in something that is not me. To feel pleasure and satisfaction, and relief, at any cost." He held her gaze steadily. "It would not be you. You would be merely a female body."

"Oh." She had not understood this. "And ouch."

"Diantha." His voice dropped. "You know that I find you beautiful."

"You called me pretty, but with all due respect, gentlemen tend to break Rule Number Six remarkably often." This hurt. Wretchedly. But it *should* not hurt so much. "And actually, it would be mutual, the—the part about simply wanting to feel pleasure and satisfaction. So that is only suitable." She ignored the tight ball of nausea in her midriff.

"No." There was the uncompromising word again. "Allow me to behave as the gentleman you believe me to be."

She wanted to damn him for being a gentleman when she least wanted that. But her throat was closed. Instead she folded her arms over her sick middle, swiveled about again, and tripped over the bucket of milk she left in the corridor earlier when she'd been so distracted by his kiss. She went sprawling with a clang and creamy milk and skirts all jumbling sloppily across the cold stone floor.

He came flying into the corridor and onto his knees before her with a haste she might have liked if she weren't mortified.

"Are you injured?" His quick gaze scanned her from brow to toe.

"Only embarrassed. That was not the grand exit I intended."

"Grand exits are often tiresome anyway." He grasped

her hand, and she could sit in this puddle forever if he would continue looking at her with such intensity.

"Who would have thought that cow could best me after all?" she mumbled. "I suppose I must now be wary of putting on my shoes and sweeping stoops too."

He grinned, drew her up, and released her.

"I'd thought rain, mud, and mold were the only indignities this gown would be obliged to suffer." She laughed a little unevenly because he did not move away. "I was clearly wrong."

"You were wrong." His voice was low.

Her gaze shot up. He set his palm on the wall behind her and leaned in.

Diantha's mouth opened and closed, searching for a response, her throat working to hold back a plea. She *would* not beg again. She squeezed her eyes shut against the temptation, and snapped them open when she felt his breath upon her cheek, then—*oh, God*—his lips. He breathed against her skin and her body quivered at his closeness.

He drew back and his gaze traveled over her face, his eyes sparks of light in the darkness. Slowly he bent to her lips.

"Don't ask for this," he whispered huskily, "because, God help me, I don't want to take you home."

She shook her head. "I w—"

His mouth caught hers not at all gently but with unmistakable possession. He kissed her seriously, deeply. He kissed her weak-kneed and he did it without touching any other part of her body.

Then his hands were cupping her head, sinking into her hair, and he kissed her cheek then her jaw.

"I want you far too much," he whispered into the tender place beneath her ear. It sounded like a prayer, a supplication brought forth from his soul. He kissed her neck, the caress shimmering through her. "I am not a good man."

She allowed him to tilt her face up to kiss her throat, and shivered at the sublime pleasure of it. How could it feel *this good*? "I know you are." She grabbed his waistcoat and pulled him against her and put her mouth beneath his.

He was hard everywhere. She ran her hands down his arms, and touching him only made her need to feel him even more, especially against the hot crux of her legs. She slipped her palms to his chest and moaned softly at the sensation of his taut muscles, so alien and male and exactly what her body wanted now. Her fingers worked at the top button of his waistcoat until it came loose. She sought the next, the delicious ache growing so fierce between her legs she whimpered.

He grabbed her hands.

"No, Diantha." His voice was a growl. "Don't."

"No more *no's*." She pulled a hand free and unfastened another button.

"If you undress me, I will swiftly lose all remnants of self-control."

"Thank heaven." She bit at his lower lip as he had done to her in the inn and slipped the tip of her tongue between her teeth to caress him. He groaned and his hands swept down her back, over her buttocks.

"Where did you learn that?" His breaths were hard. "Don't say from another man."

"From you. I've told you, you were my first. My only." The last button came free. Wild with need, she slid her hands across his chest then closed her eyes just to feel him. "Oh, Wyn." Her entire body seemed wound in a coil of delectable expectancy. "Teach me more. Please." She pressed into him, seeking him with her hips. His hand slipped down the back of her leg, and as he bent and took her mouth completely, he parted her thighs and met her hunger with his very hard and perfect body.

"*Ohh.*" She accepted him in her mouth and between her thighs eagerly, aching, *dying* for whatever came next.

He broke away, grasped her hand and pulled her toward the foyer. She tripped along behind, dripping milk and bleary with pleasure. Halfway up the stairs he halted, snagged her against him and kissed her again.

"I would carry you up," he said urgently, "but I fear I haven't the— *Blast it*." He seized her up in his arms and ascended the stairs. In his borrowed bedchamber he lowered her to her feet and she clung to him while his hands moved over her back and hips. She pressed herself as close as she could and he bent to claim her lips again.

She heard the door close and tore her mouth away. She stared at her surroundings, the writing table stacked with books, the four-poster bed with the dark curtains open.

"I am in a man's bedchamber." His bedchamber.

"You have been here before." He took her earlobe with his teeth and used his tongue, and she nearly collapsed with the pleasure of it.

"To nurse you. Not to—to—"

"To give me your body." He grasped her waist in his strong hands and pressed his brow to hers, his breathing rough. "Say it, Diantha, so there is no mistaking it."

"To give you my body." She was terrified but she wanted it with everything in her.

His hands slipped up her back, working at the sash tying her gown closed. "We will have to marry after this."

Have to? As in *be obliged to*. He could do this to her without actually caring deeply for her. But now that she was in his bedchamber poised to give her virginity to him, it came to her with remarkable clarity that whenever she'd imagined the intimate things men and women did together she had always imagined doing them with him. *Always.*

The circumstances were clearly not reciprocal.

"I cannot marry you, or—or Mr. H, or anybody until I find my mother."

The sash fell away.

"He will not have you after I have."

"I will not tell him you have had me." She shivered as he drew the sleeves of her gown down her arms.

"A man has other ways of knowing a woman is a maiden than her word alone." His voice was hoarse, his gaze upon her breasts. Covered now only by the fine linen of her shift, her tight nipples poked out, dark beneath the thin fabric.

She felt light-headed and she wanted to cover herself again. "Then I will discover a method of making it appear otherwise. Women are cleverer than most men."

"Yet few have your determination and courage."

"You are not referring to my maidenhood now, are you?"

He smiled, but there was fever in his gaze. Hunger for her. She thought that if she were ever to drown, it would be in his eyes. His hand came around her face, strong and purposeful.

She couldn't seem to breathe. "Suddenly I am excessively nervous. Or, perhaps not suddenly, simply again. And don't tell me I do not look excessively nervous like you did that night at Sir Henry's, because I would know this time it was a flat-out lie."

"You look . . ." He swallowed, his gaze dipping to her breasts again, and the movement of his throat made her insides flutter. " . . . perfect."

She felt like butter must when it melted. She probably smelled like it too, covered in milk. But he didn't seem to mind it. Circling an arm about her, he pulled her close. Their bodies brushed. He bent his mouth to her neck again, then nuzzled her earlobe.

"We needn't do this." His hand was drawing her shift up her legs, sliding it over her behind. "We can stop now, if you wish. At any moment."

"If you think I've been throwing myself at you for over a fortnight so that I will demand that we stop now, I will have to reconsider my opinion of your intelligence. And—" Her breaths hitched. "How on earth could you imagine I would want you to stop just when you are doing *that*?" His hand covered her buttock and caressed. Her joints went liquid.

"God, you are so soft."

She went onto her tiptoes and put her lips against his cheek. "Rule Number Five: 'Always respect a lady's wishes.'" She was a wanton. She didn't care, not now in his arms.

"I was thinking about that."

"About what, exactly?"

"About being a gentleman." His hands left her and he drew off his waistcoat. "It would be ungentlemanly to expect a lady to remove her clothing while everyone else remains dressed."

She watched, mesmerized, as he unwound his cravat, revealing taut male perfection.

"E-Everyone?"

"Whoever happens to be around at the time." His eyes sparkled as he drew the tail of his shirt from his trousers and pulled it off.

"Uh." She stared. "I . . ."

His hands came around her face, fingers threading through her hair, and he brought their mouths together. "Now, minx," he murmured against her lips. "As a gentleman, I must beg the lady to precede me."

Her heart was a drumstick beating against the wall of her throat. "Pr-Precede you?" It sounded like a croak. "I cannot seem to stop stuttering. It is very embarrassing."

"Yet, to be expected." He kissed her again, a coaxing caress. "Precede me in touching."

Heat enveloped her, cheeks to toes but especially in her feminine areas. She had never imagined touching his naked body. Clearly she had been tragically naïve.

"*Touching*?"

Golden sparks from the fire illuminated his eyes, and the corner of his delicious mouth tilted up. "Come now. Will Lady Intrepid be timid in this?"

"No!" He was large and beautiful and so very male, all lean muscle in his arms and wide shoulders and gorgeous chest tapering to his waist bathed in amber firelight. The line of dark hair extending from his navel beneath his trousers made her achy again. She lifted a hand and set two fingertips to the depression at the base of his throat that made her mouth water. He drew in a slow breath, his chest rising. She laid all five fingertips down and slid them across his skin.

Her eyelashes fluttered of their own accord, the place between her legs as damp as her mouth now. His skin was hot, firm, and with only her fingertips she could feel the pounding of his heart. She traced her fingers to one flat brown nipple. He closed his eyes, pulled in a hard breath and drew her closer.

"I may have overestimated my gentlemanliness again," he said tightly.

"Overestimated?"

"Diantha, keep touching me." He did not open his eyes. "Your hands . . ." His voice was low and rough. "I pray you."

There was a quality about his request she recognized amidst the delicious danger of this exploration, a need that she'd heard that night when she held him. She obeyed. Flattening her palms on his chest, she felt him, the smoothness of his hot skin, the shape of muscles that made her weak with longing, the hard beat of his heart. Her hands moved as though knowing where to touch him, curving about his shoulders, along the strong line of his collarbone, across the day's whiskers on his jaw, then into his hair. He smelled good, of fire smoke and man. She went onto her toes and followed her fingers with her lips. His hands held her to him, spread upon her back, and she felt held and wanted and protected. She knew he would protect her. She had known it from the beginning.

The fabric of her shift bunched in his grasp.

"A gentleman should not compromise a lady's modesty in order to make love to her," he murmured. "I should allow you to remain gowned. But I want to see you, minx. I want to see all of you."

Alarm leaped in her throat. "You do?"

"When I was fevered, the notion that if I came through it alive I might someday see your body kept me sane."

"But . . ." He *couldn't*. No one had ever seen her like that, not even her sisters or maid. At fourteen she had even turned her mirror toward the wall. Her mother had encouraged it; no need to distress herself daily. "Perhaps if we extinguish the candle first . . . ?"

"Diantha, do not deny me." His eyes held such heat now.

She closed her own eyes so that she would not see his reaction as she drew off her shift and he helped her.

A moment of silence became two. "Dear God." His voice sounded strangled.

She slapped her arms across her belly. "I know I'm not— That is to say, if I could—"

"If you could ask God to fashion a woman of pure beauty, he would deny the request. For he has already created you."

She snapped her eyes open to see his gaze upon her, rapt. He touched her then precisely upon the ugly white stripes across her hips and belly. Nurse had told her that these and the marks flanking her breasts showed where her skin had stretched to accommodate her flesh before, and would always remember that time in scars. Now his fingertips stroked there tenderly.

"Beautiful, unique Diantha."

Her throat choked in a sob she would not allow. This was fantasy. She must not weep now, even for joy. "Do you really mean it? Are you speaking the truth?"

"Yes, I really mean it. Why would I lie? You are already here, willing. I've nothing to gain from you by lying yet all to enjoy simply by looking and speaking my thoughts and waiting for those dimples to appear."

"You are not looking at my dimples."

"Easily distracted." He captured her lips and his warm, strong hands drew her to him and finally they came skin-to-skin. Her breasts flattened against his chest and the throbbing apex of her thighs met with a hardness that showered her with pleasure. "Good God, Diantha." He cupped her behind and pulled her hips tight against him. "If you wish evidence of how enticing I find you, delay another moment in getting on that bed and I will take you down to the floor right here and have you. I can wait no longer."

She pulled out of his arms, relief and desire tumbling through her. "To the bed!"

He dragged off his boots as he went, then grabbed the bedpost as though to steady himself. She didn't know whether to sit or lie down, ending up somehow in between the two, and he was staring.

"What are you waiting for?" Her voice quavered.

"For reality to waken me." He said this quite seriously.

A little sob of elation escaped her after all. "This is reality."

He unfastened his trousers and removed them, and then it was her turn to stare. Indeed she could not prevent herself, frightened and shocked and so achy between her legs she had little doubt what came next; her body was telling her.

He came to her and beneath his hungry gaze she did, for the moment, feel truly beautiful.

"You are damnably kissable," he murmured. "Every inch of you." He stroked her nipple with his thumb, passing over it once then again, gently, deliciously. He bent and took it into his mouth.

"Oh, *yes*," she sighed. "I have been wanting you to do this again since Knighton."

"I mistreated you that night." His tongue flicked over her breast's tender peak. Then again. "I touched you when you did not invite it—"

"I *did* invite it." She arched beneath the stroking of his hand down her waist, lifting her hips, inviting him there. "Why didn't you have me?"

"I could not." His caresses stilled. "The drink had made me incapable."

She blinked.

"Do you understand?" he whispered somewhat unsteadily against her cheek.

"I think so." She glanced downward. "It—It isn't always like this, is it?"

A crease formed at the corner of his mouth. "It is when you are near." Then his smile faded. "Except that night." His grasp tightened on her waist. "Will you withdraw your forgiveness for that offense now—now that you know it was not by my honor but by my failure that I left you a maiden that night?"

"I don't believe it."

"Diantha—"

"I don't believe you would have. Not if I had refused you." She stroked her fingertips along his chest and closed her eyes. "More to the point," she whispered, and slipped her hand down his waist. "You haven't been drinking tonight."

His breaths came hard. She curved her fingers around his man part. It was as solid as it looked, and smooth and as hot as the need that throbbed inside her. "If I refused you now, at this moment, would you truly let me go?"

"You will not refuse me." There was a rawness to his voice, the craving he had spoken of now at the surface.

"No." Her voice shook like her body. But she ached and she needed the ache answered by him. She parted her knees and he moved between them, his body hot, his skin caressing hers so that she could not catch her breath.

"I will not hurt you," he said quietly.

"I know." It was barely a whisper. "You won't?"

He kissed her brow, beside her mouth, her throat, then her lips so beautifully. "Never again."

"But—"

He touched her with his fingers, deftly, intimately. She froze. Then he stroked again, his caress certain, and skillful. Her body seemed to remember him inside her, wanted it, and opened with a shudder. Upon that shudder he entered her.

He went still, his breaths heavy and fast. "My God." His voice sounded strange, at once rough and tight. "Are you all right?"

"Yes. I think so." Oddly stretched, not entirely comfortable, but boggled that her body could do this with his. She let her hand slip across his shoulder, taut male strength beneath her fingertips. He was all around her, his arms holding her even as her body held him. She had never imagined this sort of thorough intimacy. For all she had dreamed of his embraces, she had never imagined *this*. "There is no pain. Not really. Shouldn't there be pain the first time?"

He threaded his fingers through her hair. "We may have taken care of that in Knighton."

"I thought you didn't remember Knighton," she whispered.

He kissed her mouth softly. "I could not forget that."

"There is more to this." She tilted her head back, accepting his kisses on her throat, sliding her toes along the counterpane, feeling him so solid inside her, so *attached*. "Isn't there?"

"Considerably more." His eyes glimmered like diamonds. "Let me show you."

"Yes."

He showed her. Rather—gentleman that he was—in response to her many questions, he taught her.

He was very patient. But he was a very good teacher. She learned quickly. And as he touched her and made her body hunger then fed her hunger with his, she learned most of all that her flesh could be teased, it could be tormented to the point of desperation. But it could not, after all, be divorced from her heart. Because amidst the caresses and kisses, when he whispered her name, that was when she lost all control.

Then the pleasure that she did not expect came, tightly wound, seizing her, tumbling through her so that she groaned quite uncontrollably, then whimpered, then actually shouted.

"Oh, *no*." She dug her fingertips into his waist, pulling him tighter, harder, and wanting it to go on and on. "*Kiss me* so that I will cease making these noises."

He kissed her. With a strong hand he pulled her knee up beside his hip, and she loved this intimacy amidst intimacy, the brush of skin against skin, her thighs cradling him, the heat of their bodies as he moved in her. His thrusts came faster, his muscles like rock beneath her hands. He delved to the very center of her it seemed and everything inside her opened again.

"*Ohh!*"

Eyes closed, abruptly he gripped her hard and did not move except within her. "My God," he growled, then upon a hard breath, "*Diantha*."

She gulped in air, her lips and brow damp and his skin beneath her hands. He lowered himself to his elbows, his chest brushing the tips of her breasts, and kissed her anew. They were kisses of satisfaction and tasted different, salt clinging to her lips and the flavor of him. He passed his thumb across her lower lip, then stroked down her throat and shoulder, her entire body skimming upon the surface of unbearable sensitivity.

He drew away from her, his hand trailing across her waist. Falling onto the mattress at her side, he closed his eyes and released a long breath that sounded no steadier than her erratic heartbeats.

She turned to look at him, at the angle of his cheek and jaw, the strength in his shoulders and arms that had held her. Her lungs felt astoundingly tight. She had tried and succeeded at many remarkable endeavors of late. It was strange how in this most natural endeavor—simple breathing—she now failed.

Chapter 20

Wyn listened to the soft, stuttered breathing of the maiden who had given him her body with generous passion, and a purely foreign sensation paralyzed him. For a minute he remained still, then another, and another, allowing the chill of the chamber to stave off sleep so that he could think, reason, understand. He opened his eyes, stared at the canopy above, seeing the details in the wood with the aid of moonlight.

He could see the imperfections in the wood grain, the knothole in the third board, a dark whorl of a blemish that brought character to the plain adornment. He could focus on those details. He *thought of* focusing on them. His mind was clear. Perfectly clear. And yet he was content.

Considerably more than content. His body was satisfied as it had not been in memory. No thirst lingered close to the surface, no craving simmered in his veins, no anger that the craving could not be assuaged. He craved nothing. It had been so long since he'd felt anything stronger than the sensation of desperate need, peace was foreign to him.

"To be honest," the sweet beauty beside him murmured, "Teresa's stories did not entirely prepare me for that."

He turned his head, beginning to smile, but only stared. She had shifted onto her side, her knees tucked up, rounding the curve of her hip. Her hands were folded beneath her cheek, and soft chestnut curls tumbled about. Thick lashes shaded rich, sleepy eyes.

He still craved. Dear God, did he crave.

"Miss Finch-Freeworth seems a knowledgeable lady."

"Not as knowledgeable as I'd thought." She spoke as though falling asleep, but her berry lips twitched. Then her eyes shot open fully. "I only mentioned Teresa's surname that first day, before I realized belatedly that I was not a friend for bandying it about in such a fashion. How is it that you remember it?"

He reached for a blanket and drew it over her, allowing himself to caress again her silken skin. It had been so long since he had allowed himself to touch a woman in this manner. For too long he had not believed he deserved such simple, honest pleasure.

"I've told you, minx." He stroked the back of his fingers across her cheek, soft as dew and mobile as rain. "I have an uncanny memory."

"Wyn," she whispered, tilting her face into his touch. "Will you tell me now about rescuing girls?"

"It is not my tale to tell. It belongs to those whom I serve."

She looked up at him. "Are you a spy?"

"No."

She pushed up to sit, the coverlet spilling onto her lap and leaving bare her generous breasts, the tips lushly pink and soft now. "But if you were a spy you would not be permitted to tell anyone. You would simply go about doing secret deeds that if anyone else did them would be considered nefarious." Her eyes twinkled and he tried to concentrate on them, but the cold of the bedchamber was turning the soft tips of her breasts into peaks he wanted in his mouth.

"More stories from Miss Finch-Freeworth?" he managed.

She dimpled and lifted a playful brow. "Her brothers."

"Ah. There are brothers with whom you spent your sojourn at Brennon Manor?" The dimples held his gaze above her neck, but they only spiked his craving. He would explore each with his tongue, then elsewhere. Everywhere. He would know all of her. "Have I reason to be jealous?"

"Of Teresa's horrid bro—" Her lips snapped shut. "Would you be?"

He snared her around the waist and looked down into her sparkling eyes. "Yes." She deserved more than scandal and a widow's veil. For five years he'd had one goal: the duke must die. At present he could not remember why.

He pressed his face into the curve of her shoulder and breathed in her scent. It intoxicated him, thoroughly fresh air and her. But it more than intoxicated. It made him whole. She made him whole.

"You are mine, minx," he whispered against her skin. "Mine, for good or ill."

Diantha had no experience in such things, but she suspected this was only lovers' talk. Trembling upon her own tongue now, after all, were words she had absolutely no intention of saying because she believed them only insofar as the pleasure he had just brought her body was indescribably wonderful. And the "for good or ill" part seemed remarkably begrudging, despite being murmured seductively at her throat. So she said what she knew to be true.

"I liked what we just did."

"Did you?" His mouth against her neck smiled.

"Can we do it again? Now?"

He kissed her chin, then either side of her mouth, slowly, warmly, then finally her lips, and she pressed herself to him.

"Please?" she whispered. "If I admit that I liked it *very much*, can we?"

"Not quite yet, minx. A man requires time to—"

Her graceful hand wrapped around his cock and proceeded to demonstrate to them both that he required a lot less time than he had previously believed.

Wyn awoke at dawn wanting her again.

Rumpled and glowing with gentle vulnerability in sleep, Diantha breathed evenly, her slumber deep. He could not rouse her, not even to sheer the edge off the scratching thirst that again attended him.

He dressed and went to the stable where Galahad and Lady Priscilla greeted him with soft whickers. Perched on the stool beside the cow, Owen tugged his cap.

"Morning, sir."

"We depart today. If you prefer to remain here, I will leave the filly in your charge and instruct Mr. Guyther to allow you authority with her."

The boy gaped. "I'd like that, sir."

"She is a valuable animal." Owen was a natural with horses. Wyn's absence would not be long, and Guyther would oversee. "Are you certain you wish the responsibility?"

"Yes, sir!"

He threw the blanket and saddle over Galahad's back. "When you have finished milking, go to the village and ask Mrs. Cerwydn for a repetition of the herbs she recently prepared for me. Wait for them, then return here."

Wyn rode to Guyther's house. The land steward met him with an improved air from their encounter in the village. The Welsh were a wary, wise folk, and the people of Abbaty Fran Ddu did not understand why he had not returned when his great aunt fell ill that final time, then for her funeral. They'd known he was in London. They hadn't known, of course, that between the time they had seen him last and his aunt's swift decline he'd killed a girl—a girl he was trying to help—killed her because he had acted hastily, too proud of his abilities, too confident, and drunk. They hadn't known that he could not bear to tell this to the woman who had taught him everything about being a good man.

They also did not understand why it had taken him five years to return. But in ten days they had become accustomed to his presence, curious at the circumstances of it and of the lady accompanying him. Guyther made that clear.

He spoke with the steward about the estate then rode back to the house through the mists lifting into the silvery morning. Owen had gone, and Wyn saw to Galahad's needs then went along the stable to the far end. A stack of new hay beckoned, the sunlight warm. As though he were a boy again he removed his coat, lay down on his back, crooked his arms behind his head and listened to the sounds of the animals and the stream in the distance, the birds in the hedges, the day rising.

He heard her approach before he saw her, her footsteps light on the floor.

"I saw you return with Galahad. No—don't get up!" She plopped down onto her knees beside him, sunlight spilling through her hair. "I was surprised you went riding when we are to travel today."

"I imagined you still asleep." He took her hand and brought it to his lips. She set her other palm on his chest and pressed him back onto the hay.

"I couldn't sleep." The bright blue showed pure intention, the dimples full blown. She crawled over him. "My dreams were all about what we did last night and they simply woke me up."

He laughed. "Have you breakfasted yet, minx?"

She straddled his hips, her skirts a froth about her thighs. "I don't want to eat."

"This is unprecedented."

"I want you to make love to me again. Now. In a stable, the first place I was ever kissed." Her smile dazzled.

"Your companion—"

"Mrs. Polley is not awake and I haven't yet seen Owen." She found his cock through his breeches with the soft core of her femininity. He settled his hands on her hips and groaned as her hand sought him. Then placing her palms on his shoulders, she tilted forward and rocked against him. Her eyelids fluttered. "You make this feel so good," she whispered almost shyly now, her lashes low.

He slipped his hand up to the back of her head and drew her down. Her lips were no less sweet this morning than the night before. More so.

"It is designed to feel good, minx," he murmured, twining his fingers through her curls.

Her lapis eyes opened wide. "Do you never claim the credit for anything good?"

"Claiming the credit for the pleasure in sex would be an act of hubris of which even I am not capable."

"You are not an overly proud man, though I think you imagine you are. And if sex is naturally pleasurable, why are there so many married ladies who go about with their faces pinched in dissatisfaction?"

He laughed and kissed her, and for some time there was no haste, only the warmth of her lips and her body in his hands, her fingers pressing into his shoulders. When she began to make soft sounds of want in the back of her throat, her thighs clasping his hips as she moved herself against him, seeking pleasure, he saw no need to delay further what they both wanted. He slipped his tongue into her mouth to taste her. Her fingers plucked at his shirt and waistcoat impatiently.

"Oh, please remove these," she said upon a hard exhale, pressing to him. "I want to touch you."

"There is a bedchamber not twenty yards distant."

"I am rewriting Rule Number One." She unbuttoned his waistcoat and pushed it over his shoulders. " 'Deny her nothing, even if she is not particularly virtuous.' "

"I am obliged to submit, for kind of heart and generous you are in spades, Diantha Lucas." She slipped from his lap and he drew off his waistcoat, but the twinkle in his gray eyes stole her attention from even the sight of him undressing. "And, of course, I am complicit in your loss of virtue," he added.

"Only because I forced you." She touched him and the thrill of it shivered through her. Touching him was *not* a dream. It was beyond sublime.

"No one forces me to do anything I do not wish to do." He took up his shirttail.

"Allow that I badgered, at least." She helped him with the linen, wanting the excuse to run her hands over his back, to feel the strength beneath his skin and revel in the eagerness of her own body. "It's true that if others don't initially accede to my wishes, I usually convince them in one manner or—" Her fingertips arrested on his spine. "What—"

"Don't"—he whipped around and clamped her wrist in a brutal grip—"touch."

Circular scars ascended in a line from the base of his spine, each the size of a man's thumbprint, their texture hard and rough.

"Why not?" Her voice was a rasp.

Wyn's iron grasp loosened. "Diantha, I beg your pardon." He took a deep breath.

"They are very old. Do they still pain you?"

"No."

"They look like burns." Vicious marks. "Intentionally inflicted."

"Indeed."

"Was it a fireplace iron?"

"Nothing so dramatic. Merely cigars, my father and eldest brother's fondest tools of chastisement."

"Why did they do that to you?"

He stared at the ground. "Because I read books that they did not." He released a rough laugh. "Because I read books, full stop."

"Because you *read books*? Why, that is *evil*."

"Diantha." His voice was quiet. "It is ancient history. Twenty years."

"If it is truly ancient history, then why can't I touch you there?"

His silvery gaze swung to her, searching her face. He reached forward, wrapped an arm around her and pulled her to him. He kissed her, and it was not a kiss intended to distract, but something else, something more. After a moment he simply held her, their hearts beating against each other's, and she vowed to herself that she would ask for no more than this in life.

"Let me touch," she whispered.

He set his lips to her brow and remained still while she slipped her hand around his back and beneath his shirt.

"One. Two. Three." Her fingertips explored the damaged skin over bone, where the pain must have been agony. "Four. Five. Six."

"Seven." He brushed his cheek to hers. "The first time, I was reading a book about the seven wonders of the ancient world. After that, it amused them to try to confine their efforts to trodden paths. Proving their marksmanship despite the whiskey they'd consumed, you see."

"What are the seven wonders of the ancient world?"

"Were, mostly. Magnificent structures wrought by man. I told my father and brother that I aimed to visit the great pyramid at Giza someday." He was silent a moment. "I believe I was six at the time."

"You were precocious." She slid her hand up his broad back beneath the shirt fabric. "Too clever for them."

"Too clever for my own good." His thumbs skirted the undersides of her unbound breasts.

"I like you clever, Mr. Yale."

"And I like you sitting in my lap, minx."

She kissed his shoulder, pulling the linen back to place her lips against his skin. "Will you make love to me now?"

"Will you allow me to do so in a bed rather than on a pile of musty hay?"

"I like musty hay." She nibbled his unshaven jaw. To touch him and see him like this, less than perfectly groomed, made her heart do deliciously uncomfortable tumbles. "Though I suppose I should acquiesce to the superior experience of the elegant London gentleman."

"The elegant London gentleman napping on a haystack." His thumb passed over her nipple. She shivered and tilted her head back. The sun shone brilliantly through the stable's half door. Somewhere not far away a dog's bark mingled with birdsong.

"Have you experience in making love on haystacks, Mr. Yale?"

"If I reply in the negative will you be vastly disappointed, Miss Lucas?"

"That was evasive."

"Old habit." He slipped his thumb beneath her bodice. "Must see to that." He caressed and her breaths caught and she needed to be kissing him.

Ramses' barking grew frantic. Wyn's hands stilled.

"Diantha."

She pressed another kiss onto his lips. "Must we leave here this morning?" She ran her hands down his chest. "I am determined to be in Calais as soon as possible. But I like this place. It will be difficult to leave, especially now that the sun is shining." She smiled against his jaw. "I'm glad we got lost here."

"Diantha." He gripped her waist and held her off him. "Get up. Straighten your hair and gown."

"What?"

"Please. Now. Someone is arriving."

"Someone— *Here?*"

He grasped her hand and she stood, and he helped her brush the straw from her skirts then took up his waistcoat and coat. Now she heard the rumble of hooves and clatter of carriage wheels on the pebbly drive.

"Oh, no. Do you think the owners have returned? If only we'd left an hour ago . . ."

His gaze scanned her. "Go around the path from the shed to the back of the house, and bid Mrs. Polley dress you properly."

She nodded but went to the door. "I want to peek first."

"You needn't." He remained where he stood.

"But I cannot wait another moment to see if she is very grand or—"

The carriage drew to a halt on the drive before the house, an enormous, black, shining traveling chaise drawn by four beautifully matched horses. The servant sitting beside the driver atop wore blue livery.

"There is a crest on the door," she whispered. "Our hostess is noble!"

He hadn't moved, his face sober, and disquiet tickled in Diantha's belly. She glanced back at the carriage. "And . . . it has blue-rimmed wheels. It's the strangest thing, but I . . . I think I recognize that carriage."

"I suspect you have seen it at Savege Park before." He came to her side finally. "It belongs to the Earl and Countess of Blackwood."

Descending from the carriage onto the drive with the assistance of her servant, as beautifully regal as ever, was Lady Katherine Blackwood—Serena's sister-in-law and the wife of Wyn's closest friend.

It required very few moments of confusion for Diantha's

nervous delight to transform into cold shock. A gasp escaped her, then a whimper of sheer, gut-deep hurt. When she finally looked at Wyn, his face revealed nothing.

"Go to the house, Diantha. I will see Lady Blackwood to the parlor. Please join us there when you are able."

Though she understood little, only suspected, she went without speaking, because nothing she wished to say could be said without shouting. Or crying. And, just as with all of those who had hurt her in the past—the neighborhood children, her schoolmates, her mother—she would not cry in front of him.

Chapter 21

Wyn buttoned his coat and went onto the drive as Leam descended from the carriage after his wife. The Earl of Blackwood was a tall, loose-limbed man of considerable strength, the furrow in his brow forbidding.

"My lady." Wyn accepted the countess's outstretched hand. "How lovely you appear even after the discomforts of the road."

"Not a terrible discomfort, as it happened. The carriage is delightfully well sprung." She smiled, her dark gray eyes scanning him then darting to the house. "Where is she? Have we come in vain or have you managed to hold onto her for this long?"

Not long enough. "She is within. We were to depart today."

"Then we have arrived just in time." Kitty's smile took him in entirely. "You look well, Wyn, and your house is sublime all tucked away in this valley like a monastery. What does Abbaty Fran Ddu mean?"

"Abbey of the Black Crows."

The earl coughed.

Kitty knew about the Falcon Club, but she did not know all, like the code names the director had assigned the five agents years earlier. At the time, Wyn shared the information only with his great-aunt, and they laughed over the coincidence. It had seemed fitting. A destiny fulfilled.

He gestured to the front door. "Come inside and we will find you refreshment, albeit modest. The abbey is presently operating on a rather short staff."

"Of course, the charade," Kitty said. "You gentlemen spies will do what you must to pull the wool over a lady's eyes."

"Not spies," her husband said. "Yale, what sort of trouble is this?"

"Pleasure to see you too, Blackwood. How I've missed your glowering. The white streak in your hair is wider than last we met. It must be all of that churlish indignation."

"Constance said Gray sent you off for a horse over a month ago." A hint of Scots colored his voice, marking his temper. "A damned *horse*?"

"Really, Leam, must you?" Kitty slipped her hand through her husband's arm. "But truly, Wyn, I am as curious as a cat. Leam is too, or else he would not be here. You said so little in your note, which we received by the way the moment we opened the house in town. We only arrived there Wednesday."

"Thank you for coming in such haste, my lady." He glanced at Leam. "My lord."

"Don't you be giving me that arched brow—"

"If you call me 'lad,' I will draw on you, Leam."

"You're not carrying, Wyn."

"Concealed. All about me. Knives. Pistols. What have you."

"It is the what-have-you's I am most concerned about." Kitty's eyes gleamed. "Of course we came in haste for Diantha's sake, as you wished. Now do take us inside this lovely place. Fall blooming roses! Positively delightful. Why have you never invited us here before?"

Because since he'd known Kitty he hadn't been here. And before that, during the years he worked with Leam for the Falcon Club, the house belonged to his great-aunt, the woman who had saved him, gave him a haven, a home, and taught him everything he cherished and valued. The woman who had taught him how to be the opposite of that which he despised in his father and brothers.

Mrs. Polley met them in the foyer.

"Lord and Lady Blackwood, may I introduce you to Mrs. Polley, currently in Miss Lucas's service. She bakes an excellent oat biscuit. Mrs. Polley, would you be so kind as to bring refreshments to the parlor for his lord and ladyship?"

Mrs. Polley's eyes bulged, but she curtsied and bustled away.

Leam glanced about as he entered the parlor. "I don't think Mrs. Polley cares for you, Yale."

"You don't know the half of it."

"I suspected as much." The Scots burr was gone now, the Cambridge-and Edinburgh-educated lord again at the fore.

"What *is* the half of it, Wyn?" Kitty crossed to the window and glanced out.

Leam settled in a chair. "How long shall I wait before I must go searching out whiskey myself?"

"Indefinitely," Wyn said. "I'm afraid there is none about the place. And, by the by, it's only nine o'clock in the morning. Joints troubling you, old man?"

"Drink it all before I got here, Yale?"

Wyn turned to Kitty. "Couldn't you have left him in London?"

She laughed. "He refused. He said that a maiden and a matron mustn't be left to travel with only a Welsh spy all the way from the wilds of the west to London."

"Many thanks for the vote of confidence, old friend."

A gleam lit Leam's eye. "No whiskey, hm?"

Kitty tilted her head. "Is she still a maiden, Wyn? Is it that sort of trouble from which you are wresting her, the sort that impetuous girls get themselves into upon occasion?"

Leam tapped his fingertips on the arm of his chair, his dark gaze thoughtful upon his wife.

"No," Diantha said from the doorway. "It was not that sort of trouble." She entered the room, went to Kitty and curtsied. "Good day, Lady Blackwood. My lord."

"How many times must I entreat you to call me Kitty?" Kitty grasped Diantha's hand. "We are family. But of course that is why Mr. Yale called on us for assistance."

"I am sorry you have had to come all this distance on my account." She spoke to Kitty, her shoulder to Wyn. The color had gone from her cheeks. "I have little luggage and am prepared to depart at any moment you wish, although I suppose you may like to rest from your journey."

"In fact last night we stopped at an inn not three miles down the road and I slept wonderfully well." Kitty's gaze shifted to Wyn, then back to Diantha. "Why don't we take some tea first?"

"As you wish, Kitty." Her voice was subdued, but with a flicker of her lashes she darted him the swiftest glance then again lowered her eyes.

The countess took Diantha's hand and slipped it through her arm. "But before that, you know, I would very much enjoy a stroll, if you will accompany me."

"I will be happy to. The gardens have not been tended lately, but the path is largely free of debris." She had entirely disappeared, the girl who had sat on her traveling trunk on the side of the road in the rain and defied him. In her place was a proper, ghostly lady.

"Gentlemen," Kitty said, "we will return shortly." They departed.

Leam scrubbed a hand across his jaw. "You've done it again, haven't you?"

Wyn stared at the doorway. "Done what again?"

"Taken a girl's heart and twined it around your little finger to achieve your goal."

Slowly Wyn pivoted to him. "It astounds me that a man who spent years pretending to be a tragic widower—when he was nothing of the sort—in order to cozen females into trusting him, now seeks to criticize my actions with regard to the fairer sex."

Leam's brow creased, the white streak through his auburn hair more pronounced in the sunlight filtering through the windows.

"Wyn—"

"Leam, call me by my Christian name again and I will force-feed to you Mrs. Polley's oats and buttermilk stew."

The earl grinned but his dark eyes studied, years of companionship and familiarity behind the regard. "Did you mislay your razor somewhere along the road?"

"Did you mislay your wisdom to ask me such a question?"

"A stranger stands before me, unshaven, without a neck cloth in sight or a bottle of whiskey in the house, and he speaks of wisdom." His brow sat high. "What have you done?"

Wyn folded his hands behind his back. "Wish me happy, Blackwood."

Leam's gaze arrested. He did not immediately respond. "Interesting that she does not look happy about it."

"She did not expect you here today, of course. She is disappointed in her plans." He went toward the door. "Thank you for coming. She won't evade Kitty."

"Remarkable that she evaded you. Unprecedented, rather."

"Isn't it? She is resourceful and I was not at my best." Now he could see this quite clearly. His friends had been right to worry; drink had gotten the best of him. That he had gone as long as he did without making more mistakes like Chloe Martin was a miracle. "I would not have sent for you otherwise."

"How are you so certain she won't evade us?"

It had been Wyn's expertise to study others for years in order to anticipate their actions. He'd made mistakes with Diantha he had never made with a quarry before. But the bottle had muddled his reason, and he knew her now. She cared too much for the welfare of her family to distress them in the manner she would if she resisted.

He went to the window and looked out onto the garden. "I suspect you devised a story to explain to Lord Carlyle why you and Kitty will arrive in town with his stepdaughter?"

"Before we left town, Kitty sent a note to Lady Savege. Serena will tell Carlyle that she requested we make a detour on our journey to London to gather Miss Lucas at Brennon Manor and convey her with us, to save her father's servants the journey."

"Ah."

"Kitty thought it best to tell Serena about her stepsister's escapade, although apparently not her purpose for it. Serena's history with Lady Carlyle is an unhappy one."

"And the baron?" he asked.

"Carlyle is unlikely to notice anything odd," Leam replied. "He is a negligent parent."

"As soon as I have seen to matters here I will follow you to town." Wyn left the house and went to the garden, where the ladies walked amid wandering vines, arms linked.

Diantha saw him and drew her hand away from Kitty's. "I would like to speak privately with you, Mr. Yale."

He bowed. "At your command."

"I am eager to taste Mrs. Polley's biscuits," Kitty said, looking swiftly between them, assessing. "I will leave you two to chat." She glided away.

"Kitty said that you sent for her more than a sennight ago." Diantha's voice was tight, her stance rigid in the dappled shadow of the great oak bowing over the yard.

"I posted a message to London the morning we left Knighton."

"Knighton?" Her lashes beat. "All right. I understand."

"Probably not entirely."

"I know that Mr. Eads was truly following us. But it was no accident that we came here in particular, was it?"

"I needed to take you to someplace from which you would be unlikely to seek to escape and where we would not be recognized by other travelers. This seemed best."

"You were never lost."

"Five years ago before her death, my great-aunt bequeathed this estate to me. The abbey is mine."

"Yours?" Her gaze seemed to seek purchase. "When Kitty and Lord Blackwood arrived, I guessed that you were familiar with this place. But . . ." She took a quick, hard breath, turning away from him upon the balls of her feet. "The villagers we encountered, they must know you."

"Some, you might say, raised me. This house was my home for four months each summer from the time I was seven years old."

"But they were all—"

"Instructed not to reveal to you the truth."

The lapis pools swam. "Then everything I—" Her pale brow crinkled up. "The library . . . All those books I thought a lady wouldn't read. And the Gentlemen's Rules . . . ?"

"Dictated by my great-aunt and scribed by my boyish hand, for my benefit when I should someday grow to be a man. So, you see, my great-aunt was not as successful as she had hoped. I choose to apply them rather at whim."

"Stop! You are twisting it."

"Diantha, I told you I am not a good man."

"Do you know what I think?" Her eyes flashed, sparkling. "I think you like to pretend the rules mean a lot to you so that you can justify living with dishonesty and secrets. But that is simply duplicitous. Those rules are about kindness and decency, but you don't want to live with any rules—no more than I do—so you throw everything they mean to the wind and then feel justified calling yourself a bad man." She shook her head. "My mother used to do that to my sisters and my brother, Tracy, and to *me*, taking good things and manipulating them until they were wrong."

"Then why are you trying to rescue her?"

For an instant her face went blank. "Because she is in trouble." Behind her blue eyes glimmered something Wyn had not seen before when she'd spoken to him, only to others. Dishonesty.

His thoughts came jerkily. She hid something from him. That this struck him only now proved his insanity with her. He had watched her invent stories to carefully dictate the actions of others, yet in his arrogance and desire for her he had not imagined she would do the same with him, not after that first day.

She hid something from him.

"Diantha, you—"

"I feel like such a fool." She backed away. "All this time you *knew* I was a fool."

"No. I did not think that."

"To where were you going to take me today? Devon?"

Calais. "London." *Calais.* He had lost all sense, all reason with her. Despite everything he knew about finding lost persons, he'd been about to take her to Calais to search for her mother upon her claim of evidence in an old letter. To Calais, because all he truly wished now was to be lost with her, to leave behind the life he'd led and begin afresh. Only the arrival of a carriage from London had jarred him back into reality, to the responsibility that had weighed upon him forever it seemed. "Your stepsister and Lord Savege are in town already, awaiting your arrival from Brennon Manor. Your stepfather as well."

"How do you know that?"

"I sent a messenger to Devon."

Her face paled entirely. "When?"

"Just after Mrs. Polley joined us."

She seemed to struggle for breath. "And the fool just keeps feeling more foolish. Why didn't you *tell* me?"

"When I told you I intended to escort you home, you ran away from me and stranded yourself upon the road with none but a dog to protect you. I could not allow that to happen again. But I came to suspect that you would not allow your family to suffer from your absence."

"I understand." Then her voice dipped to a whisper. "You should have told me when—" She looked away. "Days ago."

He should have. He'd no clear idea why he hadn't, except that perhaps he had feared to lose her when he was not well enough to pursue her. But it could not be undone now. She felt betrayed, and justifiably so.

"I have been absent from the abbey for some time and must see to several matters. I will follow you to London and call upon you as soon as I have spoken with your stepfather."

"I suppose you haven't any choice in the matter now," she said with quiet firmness. "A gentleman would never renege on such a thing, no matter what the circumstances. You are rather more bound by your great-aunt's rules than you seem to believe."

"Rules have little to do with it now. On your part as well."

"My part?" Her eyes flared. "Well, yes. If lust were all there was to marriage I would be glad to wed you because I do have that for you. But after years of watching both my fathers with my mother I learned that marriage is a travesty without honesty and consideration." Her voice broke. "How could you have lied to me for so many *days*? After—" She pivoted toward the house. Then she halted. "Why did you make love to me last night, after putting me off for so long?"

Because he wished to hold her and to breathe in her fresh beauty every day. "You know."

She sucked in a hard breath. "Do you wish to know where I hid your pistol and bullets? In the drawer of the writing table in your bedchamber. You see? I trusted you more than you trusted yourself." Shoulders back, she went quickly to the house.

Chapter 22

My dearest Lady Justice,

My admiration for you has grown such that I cannot hide the news: I have lost another member of the Falcon Club. Since you have become so adept at hounding down my fellow club members, I wonder if I could prevail upon you to search out this one and bring her back into the fold. She is difficult to miss: walks with a stoop, carries a cane, suffers from myopia. I haven't an idea as to where she has gone. Perhaps your sleuthing skills will save the day.

*With all my gratitude and
ever increasing affection,
Peregrine
Secretary, The Falcon Club*

To Peregrine, at large:

You are a cabbage head. I hadn't any idea that one of your members was a lady. I am not a nitwit, Mr. Bird Man. You chose to describe a woman of ill appearance to make my quest seem ridiculous. But your attempt at cleverness reveals you; you would not have mentioned a lady at all if there weren't one in your club. No gentleman would have even paused to consider it.

Point goes to Lady Justice.

You are arrogant and bored, and thus seek to taunt me to amuse yourself. Idle wealth corrupts as swiftly as absolute power. You, Mr. Peregrine, are corrupted.

— Lady Justice

My dearest lady,

To be corrupted with you would be to live heaven upon earth. Name the day, the hour, the location. I will bring a single red rose and my ardor.

Yours entirely,
Peregrine

Dear Peregrine,

I am not lost. I am here in London. You have not seen me because I am still cross with you for abusing Raven with that insulting assignment. I will come see you, but unhappily, as I do not Like you now.

Fondly,
Sparrow

P.S. What on earth has happened to you? You have become very silly in this public correspondence with Lady Justice. I think you are infatuated. I daresay that will prove most inconvenient if she turns out to be a seventy-year-old man.

Chapter 23

To the gold-and-black liveried maids and footmen in the Earl of Savege's town house, the gathering of three ladies appeared to be a cozy tea shared between fond sisters.

In fact it was a conclave of thorough liars.

"My father needn't be told the truth." Lady Savege's voice was hushed. "We will tell him that Diantha and Wyn renewed their acquaintance here in town as soon as she arrived and he offered for her immediately."

"That will be best," the Countess of Blackwood replied in subdued tones.

Diantha swung around from the window through which she was staring onto the street. Kitty sat across the tea tray from Serena, shining brunette head bent close to honey blond in conference.

"You will lie to Papa about where I have been?" She stared at both titled ladies, her momentary shock dulling into resignation. She had already learned, after all, that an elegant London gentleman could lie quite well without a qualm. Why not elegant ladies too? "But I always intended to tell him the truth of it afterward. I only withheld the truth before I did it so that I would *be able* to do it."

"Yes, darling," Serena tilted her head. "But now that the deed is done, we must devise an alternate plan."

The deed had not been done. Not the *intended* deed. She was no closer to speaking with her mother than she'd been before leaving Devon. But Kitty had not told Serena the entire truth about her errant sojourn. Instead she'd said that Diantha had run away from Brennon Manor for merely an adventure. Perhaps that had been a prudent lie. Serena and her mother had never gotten along when they both lived at Glenhaven Hall.

"I thought I was the only one that lied to Papa in order to embark upon reckless escapades," she finally said.

Kitty took up the teapot. "No one else need know of your journey than we three, Alex and Leam. Wyn assured me that Mrs. Polley can be trusted as well." She offered Diantha an interested look. They had not spoken of him on the trip to London, but Kitty must be curious of the details of their time at the abbey.

Diantha turned back to the window and tried to focus on the trees and not the street where she kept expecting to see a black thoroughbred with a rider wearing a black greatcoat. The parlor window overlooked an enormous green square in the middle of London. They had only arrived the previous night and she had seen little of town as yet, but her heart wasn't in it anyway. She felt peculiarly battered and not at all as though she were embarking upon her debut in society, and certainly not as though she were betrothed to be married.

The soft swish of Serena's skirts sounded beside her, then her stepsister's hand slipped through her elbow.

"He is one of my favorite people in the world, Diantha. Kitty's and our sister Viola's as well." She spoke with the gentle grace Diantha always admired. "I cannot pretend to understand why you wished to escape Teresa's home when you and she are such close friends, nor why you seem so reticent regarding Mr. Yale's suit. But it cannot be undone now."

"I am as fond of Teresa as ever." Her friend would be amazed to learn what had come of her plan. "And I am sensible of the honor Mr. Yale does me. I understand that I am fortunate. But I cannot like it that he offered for me because he feels it is his duty." She would not admit to them to quite what extent.

"Many a gentleman has offered for a lady upon much less honorable grounds." Kitty sipped her tea. "And Wyn is not the sort of man to enter into such an alliance lightly."

Serena's brow furrowed. "Are you afraid that others will imagine you trapped him into offering? No one else need know how it came about. Even our brother, Tracy." Diantha's stepsister did not possess classical beauty; she was far too tall, her shoulders too square, and her blond locks did not approach the sparkling gold of Charity's and Tracy's. Their mother had always said Serena would never make a good match—or a match at all—but she had, an exceptionally good match that had plucked her out of spinsterhood and made her a countess. And Serena was happy with it. Alex treated her with remarkable solicitude, and when he looked at her, his eyes shone with pride and something else that Diantha had never seen in either of her fathers' eyes when they looked at her mother. Genuine affection, and desire.

It occurred to her that she'd never known before what to make of that look in a man's eyes. Now she did. Wyn had said he liked her. He'd said he desired her. But he had also lied to her about the most important matter between them.

"Thank you." What else could she say? That she didn't care if everyone in society knew she had trapped him into it? That although at the time it had all seemed so adventurous and natural, in fact she manipulated him and he lied to her and now they must marry? She drew a fortifying breath.

Serena squeezed her hand. "Now we must visit the modiste so that when Mr. Yale arrives you will be adorned to enter society as elegantly disposed as he."

"I don't think that will ever be possible." And if it were, he would not recognize her. She was confused and hurt, and no amount of fine garments or invitations gathering on the foyer table would cure that.

The following day while Serena napped with the baby, Tracy arrived from the country and came to the house. Diantha dressed in a walking gown with a single delicate flounce and a smart velvet pelisse, and her brother took her up in his phaeton to drive to the shops. London seemed all streets and buildings, horses and carts and carriages and vendors and urchins darting about. It might have been enjoyable if on every corner she didn't wonder whether a certain Welshman had ever walked along the same block and looked into the windows of the same shops that she did now.

"You're very pretty, Di," Tracy said, with a handsome smile beneath his golden curls as she walked on his arm. "Much prettier than you were before with all those spots. Not like Chare, of course . . ."

"Charity is beautiful." She glanced into a shop window from which a display of cigars seemed to jeer at her. "I have only my eyes to recommend me. That's what Mama always said."

"Well, she ain't seen you lately, and she never did like your spirit." He winked, but his blue eyes, light and clear like Charity's, showed the discomfort that always attended mention of their mother.

"I want to speak with her, Tracy." And there it was again, the pain of dishonesty that lingered in her belly. When they'd been on the road it seemed so easy to withhold from Wyn the truth she had come to recognize at the mill. She thought now, in light of the things he had confided to her of his father and brothers, that if she had told him the truth about why she needed to find her mother he might even have sympathized.

Tracy looked grim. "That's a tough prospect, you know. Don't think that'll be possible, seeing as we still don't know where she is." He patted her hand then nodded to a pair of gentlemen coming in the opposite direction. One of them touched the brim of his high-crown hat and winked at her as he passed.

"Tracy, are gentlemen in town at liberty to smile like that at any lady they pass by?"

"Not any lady. I've just told you that you're a taking thing these days. You'll like it in time. All the young ladies do," he assured with a grin.

Diantha had seen plenty of those young ladies on their stroll. Beautiful ladies, elegant ladies, young misses dressed gorgeously and whose faces shone with purity, in town with one purpose: to secure a husband. A husband like Wyn. That was the sort of lady he should wed, not a hoyden.

"She did not like my spirit, it's true," she murmured. "She always said I was hopeless. 'Unbiddable.'"

Tracy darted his gaze to her then back to the road. He cleared his throat. "There now, Di. There's no cause to be dredging up—"

"Charity was biddable."

"Now I've just as much affection for Chare as I have for you, but she's had her own troubles, mark my words."

"I suppose Mama leaving as she did before her wedding must have been hurtful to her."

"Speaking of weddings." Tracy's good humor seemed to rally. "While I wouldn't want some of these rum goers nearer to you than a ten-foot pole, a few of my friends are decent. It'd be a fine thing for you to marry a man I could get along with." For a moment he seemed thoughtful.

"What I'm saying is that whatever our mother used to say, I like you, Di. Always have, even when you were a little sprite running around our father's feet and keeping him out of that chair he liked so much and chasing you around when you shouldn't have even been out of the nursery."

"Did I do that?"

"That time you hid his brandy." He chuckled. "You couldn't have been more than five or six. He flew into the boughs when he discovered it missing. Thought it was that old pilfering footman again. But when he discovered it was you, he laughed and took you to the lake for a boat ride."

She had always been a hoyden. "I hadn't remembered that."

"You were always up to larks, even with Carlyle from the day our mother took you and Charity to Glenhaven Hall. Never shy of letting a man know what you wanted." He looked down at her, a crease in his brow. "Di, I'm determined to fix a good match for you. That's why Carlyle and I brought you to town, of course, and it's why Serena's taking you about to meet all the matrons. Those ladies know which fellows are the decent ones, the sort that wouldn't ever think of hurting a girl's feelings."

She must tell him of Wyn's offer, but her tongue would not function.

"It's just that you've been through plenty, with our mother leaving as she did." His voice was sober now. "You deserve to be happy now. We're settling a pretty dowry on you that'll attract all the regular fortune hunters, but I'll be damned if I'll give you to a man who'll have anything but your best interests at heart."

At the Bates's farm, Wyn had said that he was not in her best interests. But perhaps he had been trying to tell her—carefully, considerately—that she was not in his.

An hour later Tracy stood white-faced in the middle of the drawing room and stared at Diantha.

"I will not allow it." His voice was uncharacteristically firm.

"Come now, Lucas," the Earl of Savege said from his position at the sideboard. "Yale is a suitable candidate for your sister's hand and they are already agreed upon it." He poured from a carafe and walked toward Tracy. He stood several inches taller than her brother, an attractive, large man with an air of confident command that Tracy's usual blithe mode of camaraderie could not match. Alex proffered the glass. "No need to jam a spoke in the thing now."

Serena frowned. "Tracy, have you good reason for withholding your approval?"

Tracy set the glass down on the table. "I needn't have a reason," he said firmly, his brow creased. "I want what's best for my sister and Yale isn't it. I'm afraid that's my final word on the matter. And see here, Savege, you've your way in most matters regarding my family, and it's worked out best for the most part. But this time it's my decision and you'll not tell me my business." He turned to Diantha. "I'm sorry, Di. Until you're five-and-twenty you can't marry without my approval, but I won't give it to Yale." He bowed curtly, went to the door and out.

She stared, her insides a tangle.

"I haven't seen him so agitated in years," Serena said. "What on earth can he hold against Wyn?"

"Nothing I can imagine," Alex said. "Diantha?"

She shook her head.

"We must tell Tracy the truth," Serena said upon a breath.

"No." Diantha gripped her hands in her lap. Tracy was handing Wyn an escape from his responsibility to her.

"Your brother blusters," Alex said, "but I can make him see reason if you wish it."

"I don't wish it. Rather, let this be an end to it."

Serena stood. "Then it is all to be forgotten? I cannot like it. Diantha, you are making a mistake."

"Why hasn't Yale arrived in town yet?" Alex again directed his question at Diantha. She could only answer with the truth.

"Perhaps he wishes to delay the inevitable."

Serena shook her head. "That isn't like him. Didn't you hear anything Kitty or I said to you the other day?"

"I did. But I fancy that after a fortnight traveling with him perhaps I know more of his wishes on the matter than either of you." She stood up on unsteady legs. "He did his best to convince me to return to Brennon Manor. Frankly, he did everything short of tying me up and bringing me home by force. He helped me because he felt obligated and he offered for me because it was the honorable thing to do, but he doesn't want this marriage and I don't wish to hold him to it. Tracy may be nonsensical, but forcing him to change his mind on the matter would be even more nonsensical." She took a tight breath. "I hope you will both understand that. I am quite certain Mr. Yale will be content with the outcome." She strode from the room and to her bedchamber, where she stood at the window looking out at the street and wondering why, in fact, he had not yet come to town.

He did not come the day after, or indeed that sennight. Serena ferried Diantha about to drawing rooms where she became acquainted with other young ladies as well as gentlemen whose flatteries made it clear that none of them had ever considered the merits of a rule like Number Six.

Kitty and her close friend, Lady Emily Vale, made her familiar with London's marginally less social venues.

"I do not understand gentlemen," Diantha said to a painting suspended from the museum wall depicting a grizzled old Venetian glass blower.

"Men are irrational." Standing beside her, Lady Emily pronounced this statement as though it were the natural truth.

"C'est vrai!" Lady Emily's companion, Madame Roche, sighed, swooping her black lace shawl about her shoulders and pursing red lips in a powdered face. "The gentlemen, they are not always speaking of the truth. It is *tragique*, some of the times." She wandered away toward a painting of a winter landscape nearby that seemed to have interested Kitty.

Diantha studied Lady Emily, the clean edge of her profile, the clarity of her skin, the silvery gold locks contained haphazardly in plain pins. A self-proclaimed bluestocking and spinster at no more than three-and-twenty, Emily dressed with economy despite her parents' dedication to high fashion, she required that others call her Cleopatra, and she went about with the most glamorous lady's companion Diantha had ever seen.

"Do you really think men are irrational, Cleopatra?"

"I do. Most men are merely little boys in big bodies, prone to foolish games, overindulgence, and occasional cruelties toward friends and strangers alike."

"Little boys . . ." Diantha drew in a long breath. "Do you recall the wedding of Lady Katherine and Lord Blackwood at Savege Park?"

Emily turned her emerald eyes from the painting. "Yes." She had a way of looking at a person like she was thinking hard, always a small crease between her brows above the brim of her gold spectacles.

"The night of the wedding my stepsister held a ball. I wasn't yet sixteen, but I dressed in my prettiest gown and went to the party. It was splendid, the music and ladies and gentleman all from town dancing so beautifully. No one took notice of me, of course, and eventually I went out onto the terrace."

"I wish I had joined you. I don't care for dancing, but Kitty is a particular friend, so I must have danced that night."

"That night I wanted to dance more than I wanted to breathe."

"Intriguing."

Diantha smiled slightly. "The terrace was empty, so I danced by myself. Then a group of young men came outside and saw me. I'd known most of them for years—they were all local boys—so I asked if any of them would like to dance. I knew a lady mustn't do such a forward thing, but I was so filled up with the music and thrill of the wedding day I didn't care about the . . . rules."

"Did any of them oblige you?"

"They said they would never wish to dance with me, even if there weren't other girls around for miles. They said I looked like a sheep all white and spotty and round, and they made rude gestures. I shouldn't have minded it, really." Except that shortly before her mother left home, she'd called her round as a sheep. "But I cried, right there as they were laughing at me."

"They were disgusting. I am astonished they were guests in Lady Savege's home."

Diantha shrugged. "They were normally all right. But that night they were quite drunk."

"Miss Lucas, a man whose tongue goes astray when he is drunk is not a worthy man when he is sober. But it is true, strong spirits make idiots and cads of men."

"All men?"

Lady Emily lifted her slender brows. "Know you an exception?"

"That night, when those boys said those horrible things . . ." Diantha twisted her fingers in the string of her reticule. "Mr. Yale rescued me. You are acquainted with him, I think."

"Somewhat."

"He was drunk that night too. But he helped me." From the shadow of a tree beside the terrace where she hadn't known he stood, he'd heard it all and come forward. "He told them to go away, and they did. Then he behaved with great gentlemanliness toward me." He asked her to dance and became, irrevocably, her hero.

Lady Emily seemed to consider. "Perhaps a man must be cruel in his heart to be cruel when he has been drinking spirits."

"Have you seen him?" She shouldn't care. With Tracy's pronouncement it didn't matter anyway. But fear had begun to niggle at her, the specter of Mr. Eads never far from her thoughts. "Lately, that is. Here in town?"

"No. Have you?"

"I saw him several weeks ago. He assisted me with some trouble I was having. I had lost my maid on the road, and he helped me. He saw to the hiring of a traveling companion for me and escorted me to"—a magical place where she wished she were still, despite all—"my family."

Lady Emily turned her attention to the painting. "I haven't the least doubt of it, Miss Lucas. You see, several years ago he assisted me in a difficult situation as well. I was having trouble convincing my parents that I did not wish to marry where they chose. Mr. Yale pretended to court me so that the direction of their hopes would shift away from the other gentleman."

"He *did*? And did you— Did you . . . ?"

"Did I what?"

Diantha could not ask what she wished. Emily was a noblewoman, four years her senior, and a bluestocking, after all. There was no telling if she still retained her virtue. Diantha certainly hadn't been able to spend a handful of days with him without eagerly abandoning hers.

"What I mean to say is," she managed, "you must have been pleased with the courtship—pretended or not—of such a gentleman."

Emily's emerald eyes took on a studying look. "My parents ceased insisting I marry their crony."

"But didn't they then want you to marry Mr. Yale?"

"Yes. But he charmed them so thoroughly they barely blamed him when his suit came to naught."

"Oh. They blamed you."

She smiled, but her gaze still seemed to consider Diantha carefully. Her hair sparkled in the sunlight streaming through the window. Lady Emily was wealthy, but she was not a sophisticate like her friend Kitty, nor a beauty. She nearly always had a book in hand, and even now carried a catalogue of the gallery exhibit. And Diantha had never heard her gossip, except now.

"Did he—" she ventured. "That is, I expect that he admired you greatly."

"He was remarkably kind to me. But no, I do not believe he admired me in the manner you suggest. I think he felt responsible for me, although I never understood why, which of course brings us full circle to my original comment concerning the irrationality of the male sex." She opened the catalogue. "Now, Miss Lucas, I have exhausted my patience for speaking about men today. I hope you won't mind if we turn our conversation to a more edifying topic."

Diantha knew already that she had been a responsibility to him. But here was proof. *He rescued girls.* As he had tried to tell her, it was simply what he did.

Wyn went to Yarmouth, traveling north and east as swiftly as the filly could bear. It was madness; he was remarkably unwell. Molly Cerwyden's medicines continued to relieve some of his illness, but without the remedy of Diantha's body there was only craving again. If Duncan Eads appeared on the road, he was done for.

But Duncan would not appear, he knew. For all Diantha's talk of the Highlander's honor, if Duncan truly wanted him he would have taken advantage of his weakness at the abbey. Men of action did not wait upon the convenience of girls.

He rode until he reached the coast and the castle sitting upon its cliff high above the ocean, all sandstone and turrets and imposing medieval majesty. The porter swiftly ushered him into the central courtyard and bid him to His Grace's withdrawing room to wait.

Wyn declined, handed over the filly into the groom's hands, and without looking back rode from the place and put miles between him and the duke before nightfall. He could not fulfill his promise to a living woman if he held to his promise to the girl he had killed. Regret for his misdeed must finally be put aside. With her determination and compassion, Diantha had shown him this. She had turned his life upside down. But now that he was not to be hanged for killing royalty, he would do what he could with that life, beginning with his estate. The abbey was a lucrative property. It had only been his guilt that prevented him from living on its income. It deserved his attention, and he must prepare it for a new mistress.

During his absence Mrs. Polley had gone to the village and harangued the locals into thorough mutual dislike. But the meals she cooked compensated for alienating the people he'd known since childhood, and she managed the returning household staff with grumbling efficiency.

"I am grateful you remained, Mrs. Polley."

"A grand gentleman shouldn't be in the kitchen, now, sir."

"You did not think I was so grand a fortnight ago."

She scowled and waved him out of her realm. As he was packing his bag for the journey to London, two letters arrived.

Dear Mr. Yale,

I received your letter and read it with great interest, alongside the two other similar offers for my stepdaughter's hand put before me in the past sennight. Unfortunately I can promise you nothing. Thrice before I attempted to engineer my daughters' marital prospects, without the smallest degree of success; each of the three are now wed to men I did not choose. Fortunately I like these husbands well enough, and so will leave it to Diantha to determine her future marital bliss. In the end the Female Will shall always prevail anyway.

I wish you the best of luck. Do be aware that her brother, Sir Tracy Lucas, is her legal guardian and must be applied to for approval rather than I.

Sincerely &c.
Charles Carlyle, Baron
London

The other letter, penned on unadorned stationery, came from the unlikeliest of quarters: Lady Emily Vale. Within minutes Wyn saddled Galahad and set off on the road to London.

Chapter 24

"Ah. Beauty and wit in one small chamber. It's good to be back in London."

Standing before a filing cabinet, Lady Constance Read whirled about, her vibrant blue eyes wide.

"Wyn! You have returned." She thrust out her hand and he bowed over it. Her smile that turned intelligent men to blithering idiots glowed.

"If I had known you would be the first lady I saw when I returned to town, I would have returned quicker." He'd been disappointed in the first call he paid. At Savege's house the butler informed him that Diantha was expected to be out for some hours yet. So he had come here to the Secret Office to find what he could.

Constance squeezed his hand and laughed. "You are a rogue, but you hide it well behind lovely flattery, as always." Her gaze flickered up and down him. "You look remarkably good. Where have you been?"

He bowed. "I am honored, madam."

"And . . . ?" She turned back to the filing cabinet. Daughter of a duke, Constance was received everywhere.

She used this popularity in her work for the Falcon Club. "Where . . . ?"

"I went to see a man about a horse. But I suspect you know that already."

"I am still jealous Colin assigned the task to you. Is Lady Priscilla as beautiful as they say?"

"More so. Our august *secretaire* would have sent you, I suspect, if he thought you enjoyed cards, brandy, and scantily clad working girls."

"I see. But you retrieved her successfully, it seems, without too much distraction." She threw him a glance of mild interest.

Wyn wasn't fooled. Golden-haired, voluptuous, and an heiress, she was any man's fantasy. But years ago he had learned that Constance Read's reasons for joining the Falcon Club—and remaining in it after her cousin, Leam, quit—were none he wished to explore.

"Were you that jealous of me, Con?" He wandered to the desk in the modest whitewashed chamber. Sparely furnished, with a single portrait of the old king on the wall and one barred window, the Secret Office looked nothing out of the ordinary. But within filing drawers that lined the walls were stored every letter from every informant in the British Empire that had ever reached London successfully. Most of that correspondence had never been read. "Would you have liked the assignment yourself, or are you busy here with more interesting business?"

"Oh, this is nothing." She shuffled through the file before her. "It was only that you were absent for so long. It should not have taken you over a month to retrieve a horse and deliver her to the duke." Her gaze passed over the papers, but unfocused. "Really, Wyn—"

"Dear Constance, why don't you put that down and ask me what you wish to ask me? Then we might move past it and speak of more pleasant matters."

She pursed her full lips and peered at him closely. "You did not go directly from the house party to Yarmouth."

"Do you know, you are especially beautiful when you are piqued. Would that I could pique you more often."

"How do you imagine I learned of this most unusual detour of yours?"

He sat back against the desk. "I am as ignorant as the next man. Unless, of course, the next man is Colin Gray." He crossed his arms. "What have you two been up to?"

She met his gaze for a long moment. Then she sat down in the office's single chair and draped a hand airily over her brow. "I cannot tell you. If I did, then I would have to kill you and that would ruin my gown, bloodstains being what they are."

He tsked. "It is far too lovely a gown for such abuse, s'truth."

She dropped her hand, her face now devoid of play. "Wyn, I was concerned about you. I am still concerned. You have been so little in touch with us for too long, even when you are here in town. And even with Leam. Will you remain in London for a time?"

His friends imagined him hell-bent on self-destruction, and perhaps he had been when last he'd seen them. But no longer.

"Colin is about to dismiss me from the club, you know."

"I don't think so. When you did not return immediately he would not send anyone to find you. He said you would appear when you wished and that I should trust you. He has great faith in you."

"He did not send anyone after me because he wishes to discover whether Lady Justice truly knows my identity."

"You heard about that already?"

"I have been back in town at least three hours, my dear."

She shrugged. "Believe what you will about Colin's motives. But I know you will believe that this past fortnight since Leam came to town he has been in a perfect stew. I think it's about you, but he won't say."

"The poet is all dramatic anguish when he wishes to impose his notions of rectitude upon another."

Her laughter filled the little room with music. Then abruptly her amusement faded.

"Why were you gone so long, Wyn? Is Leam displeased with you for a particular reason?"

"If you wish to know your cousin's feelings on the matter, I recommend you apply to him, my dear. Now, as much as I am delighted to again be in your company, I have a task to accomplish this afternoon and few hours in which to do so."

She stood and came to his side, bringing with her the scent of white roses. Her bosom brushed his sleeve. "I am happy to see you," she said softly.

"Constance, your sweet seduction will not stir me into unwarranted disclosures," he said without looking at her. "I am better at this game than you." With all but one dimpled girl. His friends did not recognize him because he had become, in fact, unrecognizable, guided by his mind as always but now no longer ruled by it. And . . . he liked it this way.

"You are heartless." Constance leaned her cheek upon his shoulder. "I adore you."

"I am eternally yours."

"You never were," she said sweetly. "And now I think you never shall be."

He swiveled to her. "What precisely am I intended to gather from that?" he drawled while the heart he supposedly lacked beat a quick tempo.

"Only that Colin has a letter for you to read. But I shall leave that to him." She went to the door. "If you depart from London again without telling me, I vow I will send someone after you. Or perhaps I will simply follow you myself. Colin has confined my work to town, but if you cross me again in this manner I will become a wandering hunter like you, and like my cousin and Jin used to be. I vow it."

"Your vow is my bond. Now, leave, dearest lady."

The door clicked shut. He drew the bolt and returned to the file resting atop the drawer. At the top a clerk had scrawled *Davina Lucas Carlyle, Baroness*. He opened the file and read.

"You made it all up?" Diantha sat behind a potted plant in a corner of an enormous ballroom bursting with guests from its cascading entry stairs to its beveled terrace doors. An orchestra's bright notes leaped into the air, the murmurs and laughter of conversation mingling with the wafting aromas of perfumes and colognes, champagne and melting beeswax.

Teresa sat beside her on another embroidered gilt chair, her short, flaming curls sparkling with tiny pearls laced into a white net that matched her snowy white gown. She nodded somberly.

Diantha shook her head. "I imagined *some* of it embellishment." And she had discovered that some of it was enormous understatement. "But . . . *everything*?"

Teresa's eyes were pretty round lily pads. "Not everything," she allowed. "Annie told me stories of her amorous escapades with footmen and stable hands." Her fingers tangled together on her lap. "I merely told those escapades to you as though they had happened to me."

Diantha felt astoundingly ill. Regret had nothing to do with it. "But why would you do such a thing?"

"Why didn't you write and tell me where you were?" Teresa retorted. "After Annie returned to Brennon Manor, I suffered an agony of guilt for having assisted you in leaving. I would have sent my brothers searching for you but they went off hunting with Papa. I could not tell Mama, of course. She would have gone into an instant decline. But more importantly, I knew you would never speak to me again if I revealed you. You'd made me promise not to!"

Diantha peered at her friend.

"I would not have easily forgiven you for betraying me, it's true." She reached for Teresa's hand. "I'm sorry I did not write. I was . . . busy." Busy throwing herself at a man who had lied to her all along, as her mother had for years, and as Teresa had too. But perhaps she was overly primed to see such lies as betrayal.

Teresa's eyes welled with tears. "I think I may weep with relief. Di, I am so very glad you are well."

"Dear T, don't cry here. And forgive me, please," she whispered, knowing she should be begging forgiveness of another person as well, a man who had worried over her just as Teresa had.

"You are here, safe and sound. You are forgiven." Teresa's lips wobbled into a smile. "Now will you tell me of your adventure? You did not go to Calais, I must assume, for your mother is not restored to your family."

"I did not go to Calais. I went . . . Oh, it's too long a story to tell now. Let's save it for later." Or never. How could she tell Teresa *this*? "Now you must tell me about your time in town so far. Has it been wonderful?"

"All my mother speaks of night and day is finding me a husband as quickly as may be." Her brow pleated. "But in the three days since she and Aunt Hortensia have been taking me about, I have yet to be introduced to even one gentleman with whom I should be inspired to do the sorts of things Annie does with the blacksmith's son."

Diantha's cheeks warmed. They never had before when Teresa told stories. But now she knew what it was to share that sort of intimacy with a man. Everything had changed.

"Actually," Teresa whispered, "I kissed one gentleman."

"You did? After I left Brennon Manor?"

Teresa nodded. "He came to visit my brothers before they went off hunting and I felt so guilty that I'd lied to you about all that, so I let him kiss me."

"How did you find it?" Thrilling. *Delicious.*

"Unpleasant." Teresa's brow creased beneath her coppery locks. "His mouth was wet and he said I had a very large bosom."

"You do have a very large bosom."

"He said he liked that about me the best and that he wanted to touch it."

"He sounds like a nincompoop." The sensation of Wyn's touch was indelibly fixed on Diantha's skin. She could not forget it, no matter how tangled her feelings about him. "But now you know he is no gentleman and you should not allow him to court you." She was a thorough hypocrite. But Wyn *was* a gentleman. He was also a man, and he had said he needed her body.

Teresa sighed.

"There now." Diantha patted her hand. "We will arrange an introduction to the most handsome gentleman here tonight and your bosom will charm him instead."

Teresa's sigh became a giggle, which was Diantha's intent. She glanced beyond thick palm fronds to the ballroom bubbling with elegant ladies and gentlemen. "There must be any number of eligible bachelors here."

"It is the ball of the season. Aunt Hortensia says that Lady Beaufetheringstone decorated everything with gold to celebrate the new king, and black since we are still mourning the old. But rumor has it that the black swags are not really for the old king but for the travesty of a trial that our new king has imposed upon the queen for infidelity. Of course everybody says Her Majesty is innocent."

"Oh. Yes." She hadn't heard. Or if she had, she hadn't paid attention. Every day it grew increasingly difficult to attend to gossip. A fortnight had passed and still Wyn did not come to London. Either he had lied to her about intending to marry her, or Mr. Eads had gotten him. Her stomach churned.

"Di, you don't look well." Teresa tugged her to her feet. "Let's find a glass of lemonade for you." She stepped out from behind the plant and Diantha slammed into her back.

"Oh!" Diantha caught her balance. "I beg your—" She looked over Teresa's shoulder and her lungs folded up and placed themselves before her windpipe like a door. She choked.

Teresa's eyes were round. "It is *him*." This said in a weak tone that suggested awe for a deity.

But the man standing alone by the French windows, gaze fixed on Teresa, was not a deity. He was a bulky Highlander with suspicious blue eyes and a penchant for tossing ladies about when he wished them to do his bidding.

Diantha hadn't imagined Mr. Eads could clean up so well. His long dark hair was pulled back in a queue, and he wore evening finery atop with a plaid kilt, stockings, and shining shoes below. But he was still very large, he was still an assassin, and . . . *if he was in London, Wyn might be too*. The notion was a combined joy and agony.

"T, come away," she whispered, but the music drowned her voice and Teresa wasn't listening. She and Mr. Eads stared at one another as though there were not four hundred other people in the place. But his gaze was not now suspicious. It was as wondering as Teresa's. Then with the neatest movement, as though he were indeed a gentleman, he bowed. Teresa swayed forward.

Diantha grabbed her arm and propelled her through clusters of guests into the depths of the crowd.

"What on earth do you mean, 'It is *him*'?" She drew her friend to a halt at the edge of the dance floor.

"What?" Teresa blinked ginger lashes.

"You said, 'It is *him*,' Are you acquainted with that man?"

"He bowed to me." She looked dazed. "He must like my bosom."

"Don't be silly. All men like bosoms."

The sense came back into Teresa's face. "Now wait just a moment. You said that I would meet a handsome gentleman tonight who admired *my* bosom." She craned her neck to look back toward the terrace doors. Mr. Eads was still staring at her. She released a little breath of pleasure.

"A *gentleman*." Not an *assassin*. Diantha twisted her fingers in her skirt. "You see— Oh, good heavens." Her heart raced. She could not lie again, especially not in these circumstances. Never again. "T, I must warn you—"

"Di, if you seek to turn me away from him, you will fail." Teresa's face looked perfectly calm now.

"Turn you *away from him*? But, you have only just *seen* him. You've looked at him *once*."

"Now wait another moment. *You* go off on an epic adventure to save your mother but *I* am not permitted to like a gentleman that catches my eye?" Teresa folded her gloved hands before her. "You are a thorough hypocrite, Diantha Lucas."

"I am."

"You admit it?"

"Of course I admit it. But, T, you really mustn't consider that gentleman. You see, I am acquainted with him. Slightly. And I don't think—"

"Oh!" Teresa's eyes grew filmy again. "Do introduce me to him!"

"Introduce you to whom, dear gel?" Much like the ceiling and walls, the lady who approached wore cascading yards of tulle. Upon her head perched a turban topped with a gilded ostrich feather and a large bejeweled pin, and between a thumb and forefinger encased in peacock-colored gloves she wielded an Oriental fan painted with a gentleman's portrait.

"Now, to whom do you wish an introduction, child?

That lanky pole over there isn't worth your shortened breaths—my fourth cousin thrice removed and an inveterate gambler. But any other gentleman present tonight would be worth the adoration of a girl of such ample charms."

Teresa peered around Lady B. "He is standing by those doors, my lady. A very"—her breath hitched—"tall, large man with long hair."

Their hostess clucked her tongue. "That, dear gel, is the Earl of Eads and a penniless heathen. He's barely been in society since he returned from the East Indies some seven years ago. I wonder that he's here tonight unless it is to scout out husbands for his countless sisters. Half sisters. Must be at least seven of them, the poor man. But he does have remarkably fine legs."

Teresa and Lady Beaufetheringstone nodded in sober agreement.

"I shan't introduce you, Miss Finch-Freeworth." Lady Beaufetheringstone pursed her lips. "You are far too young and innocent to be thrown into the mouth of the lion . . . just yet." She took Teresa's arm. "Now come, child. I will make you acquainted with more suitable gentlemen. That addlepated ninny Hortensia Piffle will succeed in finding you a satisfactory husband when pigs fly. Like two peas in a pod, she and your mother . . ."

Diantha watched them move away. She didn't worry for Teresa. If one of society's greatest hostesses took her friend under her wing, it could be only to Teresa's benefit. And her mind and heart were filled with someone else entirely.

What had Wyn known about Mr. Eads—*Lord* Eads— that he hadn't told her? It hurt. And she did not want to hurt, not because of a man who had apparently abandoned her to her fate.

Why hadn't he come?

She turned about and blindly walked toward the French

windows. She must speak with Lord Eads. She must make certain Wyn was safe, even if he did not want her. She realized this now rather belatedly. And hopelessly. She would have forgiven him if he had come to London. She would have forgiven him everything. And begged his forgiveness in return.

Her brother stepped in front of her, his smile broad. "There you are, sis. You look very pretty this evening. Musgrove and Halstead here have been begging me all night to make introductions."

She greeted Tracy's friends, smiled at their flatteries, and promised them sets, but she barely attended. Weak inside with a strange sort of tragic longing, she allowed her gaze to wander and, through a break in a cluster of guests, met Lady Emily Vale's stare. She forced her lips into another smile she did not feel.

Emily's green eyes remained sober as she turned them directly across the dance floor toward the door to the ballroom. Diantha shifted her attention there and the bottom fell out of her heart.

For it was most certainly her heart that Mr. Wyn Yale commanded. And whether he sat on a stool in his shirtsleeves milking a cow or stood in a ballroom dressed in formal attire and so breathtakingly handsome that she could not breathe, she knew whatever he chose to do with that tangled organ, it would be thoroughly at his mercy.

Chapter 25

Beneath hundreds of chandelier candles she sparkled, dressed not in maidenly white but gold like the firelight sparkling in her hair. The layers of her skirts glittered by some seamstress's skill, fluttering about her toes in the breeze from the dancers passing by. She seemed unaware of the other guests, and that she was staring at him, her berry lips parted and the pink stain on her cheeks flushing down her neck and across the soft mounds of her breasts.

He went to her, regretting that he had not come directly to London, and abruptly understanding the truth of why he hadn't. Because he could not think when he saw her, and he greatly feared that—not thinking—he might do something precipitous for her. *To* her.

She moved toward him, her brow pleating. "Lord Eads is here."

"Good evening, Miss Lucas." He bowed and could not withhold his smile. Even cloaked in displeasure she dazzled him.

"Did you hear what I said? *Lord* Eads?"

"Naturally I heard. I am standing right in front of you."

Yet not close enough. Her scent of wild sunshine twined about him, her slender hands that had been so confident upon his body now clenching in her skirts.

"I knew you did. I was simply emphasizing my point to say *Lord* Eads twice. Now thrice."

"I understood that."

"I am emphasizing in this ridiculous manner, you see, because I am endeavoring to employ irritation to distract myself from alarm caused by the fact that he is *in the same place as you.* What are you doing here?"

"Watching you dazzle those gentlemen you just walked away from without a backward glance. No, don't look. They may not like you to see them licking their wounds."

She expelled a hard breath. "And you say I am nonsensical."

"Who are they, Diantha? Your brother I know, but the others I don't recognize. Is one of them Mr. H?"

"Tracy only now introduced us." A spark of intention lit her eyes then. "But I am surrounded by scores of suitors every day, so it is difficult to keep their names straight in any case." She gestured with an airy hand. "So I simply call them all George."

"And does this system suffice?"

"Suffice?"

"To put them all in their places as you are attempting to put me in mine?"

"You did hear me say thrice that Lord Eads is *here*?"

"I believe I recall you mentioning that, yes."

She twisted her dance card with fraught fingers. "And why don't you seem as concerned about it as I?" Her tone had altered, her distress quite real now. Wyn's smile faded.

"I've known Duncan Eads for years, Diantha. If he truly wished to harm me, he would have in Wales."

She blinked rapidly, quick, short breaths lifting her breasts to press against the bodice of her gown. Her dimples were invisible. "You are a dishonest person."

"I have been so."

"I should not have trusted you."

"You should not have. But you did, and we must both now live with that."

Her cheeks paled, her gaze seeking, but a spark in it dared him to contravene her again. And Wyn knew he wanted that—*her*—tenderness and need matched with strength and determination. He wanted to pick her up and carry her from the ballroom and sink himself into her and remain there, lost together until he discovered every secret she held close and until she knew every truth of his life, every villainous deed and heroic desire.

Her eyes shuttered. "I have something to tell you."

"I am listening. Always."

"It seems that Mr. H does not care about my virtue, or lack of it. He thinks that a lady of spirit is bound to have had some adventures of the amorous sort, just as he has."

Jealousy, hot and fierce, gripped him, which she intended, the minx. Carlyle had not mentioned Highbottom in his letter, but perhaps her suitor had applied to Tracy Lucas. But this game of coquetry was new and he would know why she played it.

"A free-thinker, is he?" he said between clenched teeth.

"I'm not entirely certain. I should have asked him, but it's been a remarkably busy fortnight since I came to town."

He tried to read her eyes. "I arrived only today."

"How nice for you." She smiled politely, as though it meant nothing to her, but there was a brittleness about her raillery that caught at his chest.

"I went to Yarmouth, Diantha."

"*Yarmouth?*" She visibly controlled her surprise. "And how is the duke?"

"I did not see him. I delivered Lady Priscilla and came here as swiftly as I could."

"Oh." Her brow tightened, then her luscious lips, and

her facade collapsed. "Don't imagine you can saunter in here looking outrageously handsome in all of your London elegance and I will forget everything. I think I am still angry with you."

"Diantha—"

"I wish you would not address me in that manner. I am Miss Lucas to these gentlemen, and no doubt it would have been better if I had remained that to you too."

"These gentlemen, I suspect, have never seen you three sheets to the wind."

"Of course they haven't."

"Or on your knees on a dusty floor in prayer."

Her gaze snapped to his. "You saw that? I did not mean for you to see that."

"What were you praying for, minx? That I would die swiftly and you could continue on with your mission?"

She did not reply at once, and about them music swirled and dancers cavorted. "I prayed that I would stay strong for you. That I would be what you needed."

Wyn's heart stumbled, the most disconcerting sensation. But he'd been disconcerted since the moment he encountered Diantha Lucas in a Mail Coach. "I daresay the fruits of your prayer merely gilded the lily."

Her eyes shone. With the return of that light, she was again the woman he had watched climb a tree, the woman who had finagled her first kiss in a stable, the woman who had changed his life though he'd fought every moment of it.

"You seem well," she said.

"I am. Now." Better than he'd ever been.

"I mean, you look well. You look . . ." Her gaze slipped over his shoulders and chest and her cheeks flushed again. " . . . *well*."

"I intend to call on you tomorrow. I have a question to ask you."

"A question?"

"Yes. But now is not the best moment for it. Your brother is looking daggers at me." And if he had to endure her eager perusal much longer he would be hard pressed not to take her off to a secluded alcove so that perusal might turn into something much more satisfying.

Her brow dipped. "I don't know what is wrong with him."

"Perhaps he does not like it that I have distracted you from his friends. I will retire and leave the field to your eager suitors. For the moment."

"But—" She laid her hand on his arm, and his body flooded with heat. "What of Lord Eads? *Are* you telling me the truth?"

Wyn grasped her fingers, blessedly gloved, bowed over them and whispered, "Minx, if you touch me again inappropriately in a crowded ballroom—if you touch me in any manner at all in this ballroom—I will not hold myself accountable for what I do to you before the watching eyes of hundreds of people."

Her throat jerked delicately. She withdrew her hand. "Please tell me the truth about him. I want to help if I can."

"I have told you the truth. I don't believe he poses a threat to me."

"But you don't know that for certain."

"That I am now alive is excellent evidence."

"Perhaps he has only been waiting for opportunity."

"He would have had it at countless moments upon the road to and from Yarmouth." Despite her brother's glare, Wyn stepped closer to speak quietly below the music and voices. "Diantha, be at ease about this."

"I'm afraid I cannot be. My nerves are rather high on the matter. When you did not come to London immediately, I imagined all manner of—all manner . . ." She turned her face from him.

Wyn's chest tightened. He did not want her confusion or distress. He wanted her exuberant smile, her open laughter, and her hot, generous body in his possession at the earliest convenience.

Then her lips opened in a little O and she whispered, "Good heavens!"

He should follow her attention to the source of her surprise, but he could not look away from that perfectly round, soft, berry-pink opening. Her parted lips released a soft breath; he imagined it brushing his skin. He could taste her already, feel her body in his hands, her hands upon him. The memory of those fantastically capable hands blotted out all but the urgent need to have her beneath him.

"The Misses Blevinses!" she uttered.

He wrenched his gaze aside. Two ghostly ladies from a bygone era tottered into the place in draping yellowed lace and dull jewels.

"I never would have thought to see them *here*." Diantha laid her palm impetuously upon his chest, and Wyn saw but one solution to both of his pressing needs.

"Mrs. Dyer, would you care to dance?" He grasped her hand, wrapped his other about her waist, and swept her onto the floor. Diantha might have laughed except for the persistent prick of worry inside her. But the thrill of happiness welling up proved stronger. He had come, he was not in danger, and he was dancing with her.

His arms were strong and his direction, she soon realized, purposeful. With effortless grace he maneuvered them around other couples across the floor toward the crowd opposite—away from the Misses Blevinses. This was not really a dance; it was an escape.

"Mr. Dyer, we will draw attention." She could not resist her joy. "The patronesses of Almack's have not yet given me permission to waltz."

"Lady B is a far more liberal hostess." He guided her off the dance floor and swiftly between clusters of guests, tucking her hand beneath his arm. "Case in point." A French window was propped open, cool air streaming in. He tugged her through, grasped her hand, and she tripped along behind him into a garden. The half-moon was bright, the night air shedding gooseflesh across her bare arms as they skirted a fountain flanking a row of tall rosebushes. It seemed a remarkably ornate place, crowded with robust statues and high hedges and deep shadows everywhere.

"What are we doing?"

"It's a dark garden." He spoke low. "Guess."

She could not think, only feel his hand surrounding hers. "*Tell* me."

"Making a start on those children the Misses Blevinses encouraged us to have." He pulled her around the corner of a trellis and to an abrupt halt. But he released her.

Diantha swallowed her cry of disappointment. "You are not serious."

"A stable is one thing. A ball with half of society in attendance is quite another." But he stood very close and his eyes glimmered in the crisscrossing shadows of twining vines. "We need a plan."

She gulped. "A plan for finding a stable?"

"A plan to deal with the Misses Blevinses," he said patiently, but she could barely hear for the raucous pounding of her heart. His gaze slipped over her neck and shoulders, coming to rest upon her mouth quite as though he did in fact intend to kiss her. Her breaths petered. He wanted her. Still, surrounded by all the elegant ladies of London, he truly wanted *her*.

"I shall plead a megrim and ask Serena to take me home," she barely managed.

"That will suffice until I devise a more lasting solution."

"We are not in a ballroom now." She could not help herself. "If I touch you inappropriately here will you do things to me for which you will not be held accountable?"

"I misspoke." His voice was rough. "I must remain accountable. Always with you."

She laid her palm on his chest and the swift, hard beat of his heart shot heat through her. She slid her fingers down fine fabric to his waist and he remained very still. "Always the gentleman," she murmured.

"Not a gentleman at present."

Her hand dipped lower. "Because you have dragged me into a dark garden to hide?"

"Because I am not going to stop you from doing what you are about to do."

She slipped her palm over the fall of his trousers. He was hard already, from only looking at her, dancing with her, and it made her hot inside. Her eyelids fluttered down as she settled her hand around him. He grasped her arms, his cheek bent to hers. She stroked and his body responded, a sound coming from his chest of pure masculine pleasure. She could not contain her own soft moan. It was *so good* to touch him.

"Oh, Wyn," she breathed, "do you think we might get to work on those children right now after all?"

His mouth was so close to hers, his body thoroughly rigid. He grasped her hand and trapped it to his erection for a moment that seemed wonderfully to last forever. Then, with a harsh breath, he detached her and took a step back. His eyes were heavy with desire. "I will call on you tomorrow, Miss Lucas."

"Wyn—"

"Diantha, if you do not return to that ballroom this moment, find your stepsister, and depart—"

"You will ravish me here and leave me to be discovered by half of society, like a proper villain would?" She flashed a hopeful smile.

"Something like that, except for the leaving part. Go. Now." Tension locked his jaw and shoulders, but his heated gaze was laughing.

Diantha's heart did a series of delicious little trills. She grabbed the lapels of his coat, pressed herself fully to him and tilted her face up to whisper against his neck.

"I like you like this. I like you . . ." she whispered, "without the brandy." The darkness was gone, the desperation of the hunter that had haunted his eyes through Shropshire no longer behind the silver. Before Knighton, the glimpses she'd seen of this man, the man who could laugh with his eyes, had made her long for him. Now he was entirely that man, and she was mad with wanting him. *Needing* him. He made her feel desired. He made her feel treasured, not because of liquor or responsibility but simply because of *her*. She feathered soft kisses along his jaw, her hands delving beneath his coat, reclaiming the hard contours of his body.

"Dear God, Diantha," he groaned, his palms sliding over her behind and pulling her flush against his arousal. "I was serious. I cannot take this." He pressed fervent kisses against her brow, cheeks, and eyes. "Now *go*." He put her abruptly away from him.

She couldn't move. Her heartbeats raced, her skin was overheated, thoroughly alive.

He looked like stone. Fevered stone. *"Go."*

She swallowed hard. "Good night, then, Mr. Yale. I look forward to seeing you tomorrow. Perhaps in the morning?"

"I await the hour."

She went. She fairly ran. She feared that if she did not run, she would hurl herself back into his arms and force him to make love to her beneath the shining half-moon. But she didn't want to make him act contrary to his character ever again. He had suffered for her and she would respect the honor that commanded him by behaving as a real lady, albeit somewhat belatedly.

She met her brother at the terrace doors.

"Tracy, I have a horrid megrim. Will you take me home?"

He cast a frowning glance at the garden, then obliged.

Chapter 26

Duncan stepped out from behind a carriage at the end of the long line of vehicles parked along the block. Nearby a trio of footmen threw dice against the curb, lights blazed from the Beaufetheringstone mansion, and coachmen tended to horses jangling harnesses along the row of carriages. It was a typical Mayfair night except for the Highlander assassin approaching Wyn and the lightness of his own step, which even a tricky departure from a ballroom filled with acquaintances had done nothing to disturb.

"Rather spruced up to be skulking about in the shadows, aren't you, Eads?"

"Playing it cool for a marked man, aren't ye, Yale?"

"Marked? Quite certain you're not thinking of some other chap you've been hounding, old boy?"

In the dim light cast by the gas lamp above, the curve of the Highlander's grin was barely discernable. "Damn, but yer nerves are steady as steel. Yer no even wondering why A'm here."

"Thank you." He reached into his coat pocket, drew out

a cigar case, and proffered it to the earl. Duncan shook his head and Wyn returned the case to his coat. He no longer wanted it. He only wanted the woman with sparkling eyes that he'd had in his hands far too briefly after assuring her that this man posed him no threat. "But I am in fact wondering. Why are you still following me?"

"Because Yarmouth's still paying me for it."

At moments such as these, Wyn felt the scars on his spine and the knife tucked into his sleeve rather more acutely than he imagined was physically possible.

"You are not working for Myles?" That he hadn't managed to learn this weeks ago proved the depths that he had fallen to before encountering Diantha on the road, depths from which he was only now arising.

Duncan's eyes narrowed. "She didna tell ye A was working for the duke?"

"She?"

"The lass."

"If you are referring to Miss Lucas," Wyn managed with credible nonchalance, "she did not. But I am somewhat astounded that you told *her* that bit of information. Tonight?"

"At yer house when A fetched ma horse." Duncan studied him. Wyn didn't like the scrutiny, or the discovery that Diantha had kept yet another secret from him. No doubt she had been trying to protect him, and no wonder her worry over his delayed arrival to town.

"I will dispense with the unnecessary," he said, "and ask only why Yarmouth is still having you follow me when I have delivered him of his prize."

"He daena care about the horse, ye damn fool. He wants ye."

Wyn pinched the bridge of his nose between his fingers. "Do not tell me, Duncan, that you intend to kill me on this street corner now. Not tonight." Not until he told Diantha what he'd learned in his afternoon's research. Not until he apprised her of her mother's situation and of the state of his heart.

Or, perhaps if he were to die shortly after all, it would be best to spare her the latter.

His hands did not shake, no longer after so many months of unsteadiness. But they were cold. He could not have finally come to this place in life only to now have life snatched from him.

"He daena wish me ta kill ye," Duncan rumbled. "Anly ta give ye a message."

"Ah." Wyn pulled in an indiscernible breath. "That is good news. What is the message?"

Duncan's look grew sober. "He wants ye ta call on him."

"To meet with him personally, I presume."

The Highlander nodded.

"And if I do not choose to oblige His Grace?"

Duncan's face was grim. "He'll have the girl."

Now all went icy save his burning gut. He did not need to ask which girl or how the duke would have her. At the mill Duncan had guessed that Diantha meant something more to him than a job, and Wyn had long ago seen how the Duke of Yarmouth treated young females.

He stood breathless, paralyzed. "Goddamn you, Eads, you son of a bitch."

Duncan shook his head. "A told him A woudna hurt her."

"You shouldn't have told him anything at all about her. She isn't part of this." *It could not come to this.*

"He refused me the gold he'd promised. He demanded ta know the reason A didna haul yer Welsh arse to Yarmouth a month ago."

"Then he's hired someone else to threaten her." His mind sped. "You've come here now not because he sent you, but to warn me of that. The least you could do, damn you. Who?"

"He's put a man in Savege's household."

"A servant. A sweep, perhaps, or a tradesman's delivery

boy if necessary." Wyn would do the same if he wished to gain access to a lord's house. "Easy enough to ferret out if he's new to the staff."

Duncan shook his head. "He's determined. Yale, the man hates ye."

"Then why doesn't he simply have me killed? Why insist on seeing me?" Wyn gathered air into his compressed lungs. He turned and started toward the stables where he'd left Galahad. But he paused and looked over his shoulder. A halo of light surrounded Duncan's massive frame.

"Duncan, the next time we meet, it had better be in hell, and you'd better run when you see me."

Wyn went to Brooks's. Viscount Gray could be found at the gentleman's club most nights. Unmarried, with a wide circle of political friends and acquaintances, Colin cultivated his appearance as a gentleman of leisure, all the while watching, studying, and strategizing his next Falcon Club project.

It was yet early, and men lounged about the general chamber enjoying conversation, cards, dinner, and drink. The scent of tobacco smoke twined with cologne in the air, but to Wyn the brandy smelled stronger.

The viscount was nowhere to be seen. Perhaps he was among the crush at the Beaufetheringstone ball. But even Gray could not truly help him. She must not remain in this danger. Going to Yarmouth, offering himself up to the duke, seemed only a partial solution. He could not trust that, suspecting her importance to him, the duke would not harm her even so. Wyn had displeased plenty of men in his years as an agent of the crown. But only one man had he ever threatened with murder.

He turned toward the exit. Tracy Lucas stood there, his companions from the ball at his back.

"Mr. Yale."

"Sir Tracy. A pleasure." Wyn bowed, impatience prickling. But this was the one man in London he could not dismiss swiftly. "Gentlemen." He nodded to the others.

"I'd like a private word with you, sir." Lucas gestured him aside.

"Of course." He hadn't time for this. But desperation ran in his veins, and insane thoughts that if Lucas were a reasonable sort he might enlist his aid, tell him to sneak Diantha out of the house under cover of night, to take her into the countryside. The duke would not expect it. It might buy him time to find a more lasting solution to the danger in which he had put her, a solution that did not require him to travel to Yarmouth and hasten the end of his life.

Lucas went only a few paces before speaking. "I understand you've been out of town."

"Yes. At my estate until today."

"Then perhaps you don't know this, but Carlyle told me you've offered for my sister, and by the way you were looking at her tonight I think you'd better know: she isn't—well, there isn't any other way to say it—she isn't looking for a fellow like you."

Wyn went perfectly still. The scent of a newly uncorked bottle of wine on an adjacent table, the sound of its splash into glasses, were so familiar.

"Sir, I must ask you to explain yourself, if you will."

"And see there." The scowl on her brother's face deepened. "That's precisely why I've got to have my say. If you sincerely wanted her, what I just said should have you throwing down your gauntlet. But you didn't even blink. You're an awfully cool character, Yale, like that night of Blackwood's wedding when you left my sister crying on the terrace at Savege Park."

At *Savege Park*?

Lucas nodded, confidence suffusing his features. "I saw how you had her alone out there in the dark, with her face all blotched and wet. She wasn't even sixteen, for God's sake. Lucky you stopped teasing her when you did. I nearly went out there and corked you, but I'd a lady I couldn't leave in the middle of the set. But my sister's eyes were red all night after that, you scoundrel."

Finally Wyn found his tongue. "Lucas—"

"I won't spare words, sir, no matter how you're welcome in Savege's house. I don't trust you. Haven't since that night. And I saw how she looked tonight when the two of you were talking, like she wanted to blubber again. Then I lost the pair of you only to find her running in from Lady B's garden looking as agitated as I've ever seen her. Damn you, Yale, it ain't right to treat a lady like that."

"You mistake matters, sir."

Lucas puffed out his chest. "I don't think I do, and I won't have you teasing her again. She's had a hard time of it, what with my—our mother—" He stuttered to a halt. "Thing is, she needs my consent to wed, and I won't give her to you."

"Do her wishes have no relevance?"

"She's an impetuous girl. But she's a good sort who'd do anything for someone she likes. Loyal as a hound, don't you know." His words came thickly now; he cared for her greatly, Wyn could see. "She deserves a better fellow than one who'd press his attentions on an awkward, unattractive girl those years ago. Now that she's looking better I still won't have it."

Apparently Lucas had not seen the boys on the terrace the night of that ball. But it didn't matter. Now she was in far greater danger than anything that had come before, and this time he was in fact the cause of it.

"I see," he said, his thoughts sliding together with a peculiarly cool clarity, a solution tugging at him, aligning the pieces. "She has a mind of her own. But no doubt you already know that."

"Don't I! She's headstrong and reckless and she's never

been any different. But that don't mean she's got to settle for a fellow like you."

"Lucas." Wyn lowered his voice. "Your sister has one wish, and you, I believe, are the only man able to fulfill it."

Sir Tracy's bright blue eyes widened. "What are you—"

"You know where Lady Carlyle is now. Do you not?"

Lucas gaped, then spluttered. "Well I don't rightly—"

"I believe you do. I have reason to believe that your mother is in London for a short while and that she sent word to you recently requesting financial assistance in a business venture." In the Secret Office that afternoon he'd read dozens upon dozens of letters before he'd come across the note at the end of one informant's report, identifying the baroness as one of several persons seeking investors to fund a ring of high-end prostitution. The informant had noted that the baroness seemed to be an avid opium smoker, allied to her partner—a City man— to feed her addiction but otherwise living modestly, and of little concern to government now. It was suspected that she and her partner intended to return their business to France. "Have you seen her?"

"I have. Only the once," Lucas admitted roughly. "But how would you know about her unless you had something to do with that all?"

"I don't. I don't even know where she is in London, which is why I need your help."

"*My* help? Of all the—"

"Be quiet, Lucas. And listen to me now."

Lucas's brows shot up beneath his thatch of gold curls.

"Your sister wishes to see her mother. It is her most cherished desire."

Sir Tracy frowned. "She told me that the other day. Told me a few times before too," he added reluctantly. "But she don't understand."

"She does understand. And you must allow it. You must arrange a meeting between them in a secure location so that your sister's safety will not be in jeopardy. Can you do that before your mother departs for the Continent?"

"No." His jaw turned mulish. "If you know what my mother is now you'll know that a girl like my sister shouldn't be exposed to that sort of business."

"Your sister is not a girl. She is a woman. And she already knows your mother's business."

Lucas's shoulders fell. "She—"

"She is headstrong and reckless, but she is also resourceful and uncannily wise." And beautiful and generous-hearted and she drove him insane with wanting her, and with his next words he was giving her away. "Tomorrow I will call upon her and ask for her hand, and she will accept me—"

Lucas's mouth shot open. "Y—"

"—unless you promise me that you will take her to see Lady Carlyle before she leaves London."

Sir Tracy's brow furrowed. "And if I make that promise?"

"I will make certain that after I call on her tomorrow she will be as convinced as you are that I am not the man for her. Quite soundly convinced." His gut was hollow, his pulse erratic, and his lungs seemed to have relinquished their will to function. If this was how it finally felt to be a real hero, heroism could go to the dogs.

Lucas peered at him with wary eyes. "And I suppose you expect to attend this interview too. To make certain I don't renege."

"I am a man of my word, Lucas. I will pay you the compliment of believing you are as well."

"Pretty phrases, Yale. But I'm no blushing virgin to be bamboozled."

Wyn had never imagined that learning his great-aunt's lessons so well would bring him to this. "Then believe this: I could not remain for the interview even if I wished it. I must leave town early tomorrow and haven't an idea of when I will return." But after the morning, Yarmouth's man in Savege's house would have no doubt that Diantha meant more to him than mere sport. Even before Wyn reached Yarmouth, she would be safe.

"No." Lucas shook his head. "She's tenacious. Why, just look at her with my mother! If she wants you she'll stick, whether you like it or not."

"Not after this. I assure you."

Lucas seemed to consider. His eyes narrowed. "Permanently? No making it up to her the day after?"

"Nor next week, nor next month. I give you my word. As a gentleman."

It was with a sick sort of relief sliding through him that he watched Lucas nod, at first tentatively, then with greater conviction.

"All right," he finally said. "Do I have your word, Yale?"

"You have it." Just as a lady with lapis eyes had the rest of him.

Wyn left behind Lucas and the scents of wine and righteous indignation, but the sensation of profound loss he could not throw off. He went to Dover Street. It seemed likely he would die upon reaching the duke's castle, and he wished all his business settled first.

The gold numbers and falcon-shaped knocker on the door of 14½ glittered in the lamplight. Wyn rang the bell and the panel opened, revealing a giant ape of a man with a baby's face.

"Evening, sir."

"Is anyone in, or am I the lone bird in the roost tonight, Grimm?"

"Milord is within."

"Grimm, I've an assignment for you. Are you available for the next several days?"

The Falcon Club's hulking henchman nodded heavily. Wyn gave him the Savege's house number, instructed him to keep watch until he arrived the following day and to learn from the morning tradesmen and servants what he could concerning newcomers in the household.

Grimm planted a hat atop his head. "You can count on Joseph Grimm, sir. None will harm her tonight."

When Wyn turned from the closing door, the Falcon Club's secretary stood in the parlor entrance.

"Welcome home, Yale."

Wyn took Viscount Colin Gray's extended hand. The nobleman's clasp was like everything about him: powerful, steady, confident. Ten years ago Colin had found him at Cambridge, surpassing his masters in every subject, frustrated and restless like a caged animal fed on butchered meat while hungering for the hunt. Colin had brought him here, to help found an agency and do work for which he would rarely be thanked and never feted. Eager to make something of himself through the use of his intelligence, to prove his father and brothers wrong, Wyn had jumped at the chance.

"I have commandeered Grimm." He released the viscount's grasp and moved into the parlor, a modest, paneled chamber of quiet elegance that accommodated only five people. Five original members of the club, of which only he and Constance now remained along with Gray. But not for long.

The viscount moved to the sideboard. "What can I pour you?"

"Nothing, thank you."

Gray's steely blue eyes barely acknowledged the unprecedented moment. He poured and settled into a chair, glass in hand.

"What brings you here tonight, Yale? The need for Grimm only?"

"Alex Savege's sister-in-law, Diantha Lucas, is being watched by a hireling of a nasty fellow. I need Grimm to keep her in sight until I can send you word that she is clear of danger."

Gray nodded. "It was Diantha Lucas, then?"

"What was?"

The viscount stood and opened a small casket set on the mantel. From it he withdrew a folded sheet of foolscap and extended it to Wyn.

The hand crossing the paper was firm and feminine.

Attn: Secretary, The Falcon Club
14½ Dover Street, London

Sir,

Despite the difficulties that my assistant faced on the road in following the member of your club that you call Raven, I do know the identity of this man. I will not disclose it here lest prying eyes intercept this message.

I am telling you this—rather than making it public to the people of England who deserve to know—because with Raven in Shropshire traveled a young lady of Quality. I am not interested in exposing innocent persons to the censure of society, only in uncovering injustice. I do not wish to bring Ignominy down upon the lady, yet I fear that if I reveal the identity of your fellow club member this lady will not escape unscathed. Thus, my hands are tied.

I felt it necessary to bring this to your attention, not only to inform you that I still wish to see your establishment exposed to the public for scrutiny, and its ledgers inspected, but also so that you will know I am quite sincere in my intentions. You, I think, know little of honor and less of gentility. But perhaps your friend, Raven, is another sort of man. I will rely upon it.

—LJ

Wyn folded the paper. "Then you and I needn't dally in pleasantries any further. Clearly I am finished here, but I still need Grimm to watch her."

Gray set the letter in the box and returned to his chair. "It will be his sole task until you say otherwise." He took up his glass again. "But you needn't be finished here."

"I am to be dismissed from the club. I know this as well as you. Cut my jesses and set me free, finally, as you have intended these past several months." The urgency pressing beneath his skin needed this finished now.

"The director has no wish to release you from service. You are valuable to this organization."

"Come now, my lord. The Duke of Yarmouth is a pustule on the face of this kingdom and Lady Priscilla was a reprimand." His heart raced. "Although really I didn't mind it, as it provided me occasion to spend a delightful sojourn in a cramped hunting box in Manchester with a number of whoring gentlemen of little fashion and intelligence and no taste whatsoever in women." And occasion to encounter a determined lady on a Mail Coach in the rain.

"Whether you wish to leave the club by your own volition is, of course, another matter," Gray said as though he hadn't spoken.

Wyn stared at the glass in the viscount's hand. "You never jest, do you?"

"Rarely." Gray's face remained passive, his square jaw, proud nose, and serious regard the portrait of British power. "Do you truly wish to be jesting now?"

The fire crackled low on the grate, and on the street without, beyond the lead-reinforced windows of the Falcon Club's headquarters, the muffled clatter of a carriage passed.

"The director did not choose this assignment for you as chastisement, Wyn. Yarmouth requested you specifically."

Wyn sucked in his breath. He might have guessed it, but it made no sense.

"You have done admirable service for England. More than admirable. And you've made precious few mistakes."

"Colin, you know precisely how many mistakes I have made."

"One." The viscount's dark eyes snapped. "For this with Lady Justice cannot truly be accounted a mistake. That woman has had a watch on this building for nearly three years. Blackwood and Seton have not crossed the threshold in that time, and Constance comes cloaked and hooded in an unmarked carriage. I've little doubt Lady Justice knows my identity too and is merely awaiting the opportune moment to reveal it to the entire kingdom. But until that day I will continue our work. As you should."

Gray knew. Not all, but he knew about Chloe's death. The director knew much more, yet still he wanted him. But now it meant nothing to Wyn, not their praise or their grand designs for his future. Only the safety of a girl with lapis eyes mattered now.

"Colin, I thank you." He bowed and left the club for the last time.

His flat was as he had left it earlier except in two details. Before his manservant departed for the night, as always he'd neatly prepared Wyn's boots. And on the table by the hearth rested, as always, a full carafe of brandy and a single glass.

Wyn removed his coat and loosened his neck cloth as he walked to the table. The crystal decanter sparkled in the soft glow from the lamp. With hands steadier now than in months, he lifted the heavy stopper, and the rich aroma of the distilled wine lifted to him. It smelled remarkably good. But not as good as her. Not even close.

He took up the bottle and poured brandy into the glass. Swirling it, he appreciated the familiar weight in his hand, the comforting warmth of expectation, the knowledge that this glass, this decanter, would give him peace.

He lifted the tumbler to his lips and tilted the brandy back. It tasted like lamp oil and some distant memory of salvation. But he knew now what salvation truly tasted of, and the contents of this glass were not it.

The hope in her eyes tonight, even amidst her consternation and worry, told him that she would not be easily deterred. She believed him a good man, a man worthy of her steadfast heart. And so, although it would be the most difficult task he had ever set himself to, in the morning he would prove to her that he was not.

Chapter 27

Too excited to sleep properly, Diantha awoke to gray splotches beneath her eyes. The maid insisted on cucumber slices, and she submitted, though since Wyn had seen her looking far worse, she hardly thought it mattered.

Still, when the maid arranged her hair carefully and fastened her into a pale yellow muslin gown with rosebuds across the skirt, she smiled. In the glass she looked almost like a London lady, except for the bright anticipation in her eyes, which after nearly three weeks in town she knew wasn't the least bit sophisticated.

Sophistication could go rot! He would come, he would make her a formal offer, and somehow they would convince Tracy not to be such a horse's ass.

Serena and Alex had returned home close to dawn and did not appear for breakfast. Diantha poked at her food, but she had no appetite except for the man she was about to see.

The clock was striking half past ten and she was picking out yet another botched stitch from her embroidery frame and endeavoring to ignore the snoring of the maid in the corner when the door opened and a footman announced, "Mr. Yale," sending her heart into her slippers and stomach into her throat.

He entered, hat and riding crop in hand and glancing about the parlor offered her an elegant bow. "Good day, ma'am."

She could not wait for him to cross the room. She sprang up and went to him.

"I forgot to ask you last night, how are Mrs. Polley, and Owen, and Ramses? How I miss them. It seems an age since I have seen them."

"Softhearted minx." He smiled, but the smile did not reach his eyes. The silver seemed dimmed this morning. Rather, shrouded. "They are fine as can be in the wilds of nowhere." He tossed his hat and crop onto a chair and sat down in the chair beside it, crossing his legs loosely and hanging an arm over his knee. Despite the casual pose, he was beautiful in the angular, masculine way that made her heartbeats falter. He wore a carefully tailored black coat and trousers and snowy white linens, but his waistcoat was of burgundy silk.

"You do look very well," she said when he didn't speak and his gaze traveled about the room again with mild interest, passing over the maid then the open door at which the footman lingered. "The wilds of nowhere seem to have been beneficial to you these past weeks."

"Bucolic rustication does wonders for the constitution," he mumbled, his attention finally coming to her. Then it dropped to her bodice. "Town life is much to be preferred, however."

She tried to laugh. "I don't know that I agree with you. London is interesting, but it is always so busy. I think I prefer the country." In the country he hadn't looked at her like this, staring and yet seeming to look right through her. She glanced at the maid, then back at him, and lowered her voice. "Stop staring at my bosom. It is unnerving me."

"Your nerves are my fondest friends, Diantha. I have been obliged to conquer them any number of times in order to get on with business."

Her throat thickened. "Wyn?"

He looked back toward the door. "Is the family awake?"

"Not yet. But—"

He patted the arm of his chair. "Then I recommend you make haste to this chair, Miss Lucas."

"*That* chair? The chair you are sitting in?" She wanted him to kiss her. She wanted to twine herself about him and let him take her to heaven like he had at the abbey. But this was wrong. Now his eyes were hooded, his gaze again on her body.

"Come now. Will you turn missish after all? I hadn't imagined it of you, minx. But some girls will hold out until the ring is on the finger, whatever's come before, I suppose." He looked away, this time to the window, and gestured languidly with a hand.

Diantha's knees felt weak and she was obliged to grip the back of a chair. "Wyn, what is going on?"

His attention slewed back to her, abruptly focused and—like in Knighton—predatory. He stood up and, with a slight sway, bowed.

"You required my attendance this morning, Miss Lucas. I am here." A wolfish grin crooked his mouth. "I'll admit that after your eagerness last night I was supposing you would make it worth my while."

She backed away, stomach tight, imagining perhaps that she dreamed and would at any moment waken. But her dreams last night had been gorgeous, and this was ugly. In the corner the maid, fully awake now, stared with saucer eyes.

"Did—" Diantha pressed words past the knot in her throat. "Did you come here this morning to offer for me?"

He laughed. "I said I would. And why not?" Now his eyes did not seem to focus, dipping again to her breasts.

"You're a remarkably pretty girl, Diantha Lucas. A man would be fortunate to have you in his bed every night."

She pressed her hands to her belly, her face flaming hot. "You are drunk."

"I may be." He lifted his brows and nodded. "Probably am, in fact."

"I—I thought you meant to . . ." It hurt, in the pit of her stomach, but so much greater even than the hurt of his lies before. She tried to press it in, to be the lady she knew she must. She should ask him to leave and to return when he was sober. She should ask him to leave and never return. But she could not. She loved him. Oh, God, *she loved him.* "It—It isn't even noon yet," she uttered.

"Just saying to the fellows at the club last night that you're a clever girl. A lady who can tell time is to be admired." He nodded in mock admiration.

"You were speaking about *me*? At your club? When you had been drinking, after—" A sob clogged her throat. But she could not cry. *Would* not.

"Not precisely my club, if you'll have the truth of it," he mumbled. Another grin ticked up his lips. "More of a French convent. As it were." He winked.

A choke of misery escaped her.

"There now, my girl. Can't get a man all worked up then expect him to whistle his way to sleep without satisfaction, can you?" He shrugged.

She pressed her fingertips to her eyes and found that, despite her resolve, tears had already come. "This cannot be happening." She had berated herself for her infatuation. She had worried she was not enough of an elegant lady to hold his interest. She had suffered over his lies, and hers. But she'd spent her days wondering and anguishing over all the wrong things. She saw this now. Too late.

"Now, don't cry, minx," she heard him say from across the room. "A man's bound to drink a bit too much when he's with his friends. If you like, I won't once the vows are said. Only on Sundays, that is. Now there, how's that for a promise?" His voice seemed oddly hoarse but her tears were coming too heavily for her to see him clearly.

"I will cry if I must." She searched for her handkerchief. "And you will stand there and watch me cry, Mr. Wyn Yale. You owe that much to me."

"Don't owe you anything but a ring, really."

Her head shot up and she dashed away the cold wetness upon her cheeks. "You owed me your promise that you will fulfill the honor that is in you. But clearly you have failed in that."

He stood without expression now, watching her. "Easy for a girl to speak of honor."

"It is not. Do you know what I thought of you once? I thought that there could be no other man as gallant and honorable. But I was wrong." Valiantly she swallowed back a sob, and it was like torture to Wyn. "You owe me yourself, but that is not what you are offering me now. I don't wish to marry you. Not now. Not any longer."

He had succeeded. With the clarity born of a sleepless night spent convincing himself that this must be done, Wyn watched her fight to contain her tears and ached to tell her the truth. But that was not what he had come here to do. He had come to sever the ties that had so swiftly and unwisely been made between them upon the road, to convince the duke's man that there was nothing between them, nothing that would encourage Yarmouth to use her in order to hurt him. He could not allow another girl to be harmed because of him—especially not this precious girl.

But he must be certain of one matter before he carried this charade to its end.

"Come now, minx. Don't make a fuss over it." He pressed the words through his lips, allowing a slight slur, each syllable an effort. "It's not as though you're in the family way, after all." He gestured flippantly to her waist, then blinked hard and peered more closely. "Are you?"

"No." She crushed her fist to her breast and her beautiful eyes flared. "You know, I don't believe in love—at least not the kind between a man and a woman. So you haven't broken my heart. But if I did believe in it, I think you would have been the man I fell in love with. But I can see I am justified in my skepticism, because instead all you are is—is u-unworthy. Of both of us."

She was wrong. If he knew nothing else at this moment, he knew this, because his need to wrest the unhappiness from her eyes could not be more violent. He believed in the sort of love she now decried because he was, quite simply, hers.

He nearly spoke, the words upon his tongue desperately seeking escape, aching to take it all back and tell her the truth. But he clamped his jaw shut and watched her, with her hand over her mouth, swiftly move to the door.

Sir Tracy stood in the aperture. Behind him hovered three servants not bothering to hide their interest. Wyn would have applauded his own wildly successful plan if he had the spirit to do so. Within minutes of his departure the entire household would know of this scene. Within hours the duke in Yarmouth would have word of it. And she would be safe.

"Yale," Lucas growled, his face blotched with red. "You've done it again."

"Tracy!" Diantha's lashes fanned wide. "What did you hear?"

"I don't need to have heard anything." He scowled. "Your tears speak for themselves. Can you see now why I didn't want this for you? This fine gentleman? Go upstairs. I will speak with you after I have escorted him from the house."

"No need to banish her to the belfry, old chap." Wyn

retrieved his hat and crop and sauntered toward the doorway. "On my way out anyway."

"You won't be welcome here again," Lucas snarled. "I'll thank you to remember that."

"Your servant, sir. Ma'am." He executed a sloppy bow, donned his hat at a foppish angle, and went onto the street to claim his horse, and after that, his future without her. A future he began to hope would be brief after all.

Diantha wrapped her arms around her waist, numb everywhere. She was vaguely aware of Tracy dismissing the servants and shutting the parlor door.

"Sis, don't let that blackguard—"

"The things he said . . ." Hurtful things. If he were any other person, she might imagine he had *intended* to hurt her.

"Here. Sit down." Tracy guided her to the sofa. "Have a cuppa."

She gripped his wrist, sloshing tea across her skirt. "Tracy, how do men usually behave when they are badly foxed?"

"Like cads. Beasts, some of them. Fools, at the very least. Then there are the quiet ones like our father."

"Like our father." Like with her father, the lure of the bottle had proven too much for Wyn. Because of her? Because she had driven him to it by touching him in the garden, like that night at the inn, begging him for touches when he was trying to be a gentleman?

No. *It couldn't be.* He had left behind the bottle in Knighton because of her. *For* her. He had given it up to ensure her safety. Her father had been a loving man but weak, dispirited by his wife's criticism and disapproval. But Wyn was strong.

Why had he done this?

Perhaps . . . because she was unworthy?

But that was not true. Her mother's voice no longer rang in her head, reminding her of her deficiencies. And for pity's sake, why had she wished to hear that voice again? Had she imagined speaking to her mother would change anything? But *she* had changed. She was no longer that girl from four years ago.

"Di?" Tracy pressed the tea forward again.

She sprang up and hurried to the window. In front of the house a stable boy held Galahad's reins. The big horse's attention was turned toward his master standing several paces away beside a closed carriage pulled by four magnificent grays. Marked with a crest, the carriage door was open, revealing only shadows within.

"Diantha." Tracy's footsteps came behind her. "If you're thinking Yale's like our father, then you're thinking wrongly. Our father did his best for all of us before the end."

Sir Reginald Lucas had been a quiet inebriate, not howling and debauched but exhausted and sad. Wyn had been, rather, contained. Disciplined. On the road he'd never shouted or railed, and he had not handed her cruelties. Only that night at the inn the darkness in his eyes and the desperation of his touch had frightened her. But he'd told her afterward that he hadn't been trying to frighten her. He had only wanted her.

An arm extended from the carriage and a heavy hand grasped Wyn's shoulder. He dislodged it then climbed into the vehicle, and the carriage started away. Diantha's gaze followed it around the corner.

"Don't tell me you're hoping he'll return," Tracy said behind her. "Because even if he does I won't allow it."

Out on the street, the boy reached up to stroke Galahad's ebony neck and the thoroughbred dipped his head for the caress.

"Sis, I've news that will take your mind off that bounder." Tracy shifted from one foot to another and shot a glance toward the window. "It's about our mother. You see, she's here in London."

During the moment then in which she could not quite draw breath, Diantha considered the vicious irony of discovering she loved a man and then losing him within minutes of rediscovering the mother who had never loved her. It was, frankly, nearly too much to bear.

"London?" she said weakly. "But I thought her in France. That is to say, Papa said something to that effect."

"Well, there's the thing. I don't know that our stepfather knows she's here." Tracy scrubbed a palm across his jaw. "If she'd told him, he might have alerted the authorities."

"*Authorities?* What do you mean? Is she not supposed to be in England?"

Tracy's eyes widened. "I thought you knew."

"Knew what?"

"About that trouble with the law four years back."

"The law?" She gaped. "Tracy, is Mama in *exile*? Is that why she left?"

"That, and Carlyle wouldn't keep her any longer," he said tightly. "Not after the smuggling."

"Smuggling? *Mama?* Why didn't you tell me this before?"

He shook his head. "Everybody knows it."

"Only I didn't because you never told me!"

"I supposed Serena did, or that you'd read it in the paper, and you didn't wish to speak of it."

Diantha sank into the chair Wyn had vacated minutes earlier. "I didn't," she whispered. "I did not wish to know." It was, it seemed, a day for painful understandings.

The baroness had often said Diantha was not biddable enough, not demure enough, not beautiful enough. But the greatest cruelty her mother had perpetrated on her— the cruelty that only the housekeeper Bess and Teresa knew about—that she had not been brave enough to tell Wyn about even after all he had shown her of himself— *that* cruelty she had only learned of two years ago. In seeking out her mother in Calais, she had wanted to confront her with it, to tell her that she knew about the lie and that she had overcome it. But she could not have pursued that interview if she'd known her family might be hurt by renewing the connection with her mother. So she had never asked them why the baroness left. Not once.

Wyn was not the only one who had told untruths. She had lied to herself. Over and over again.

"Oh, Tracy." She covered her face with her hands. "None of this has gone the way I planned."

"Well, that ain't here nor there. But she's leaving for France again tonight and I don't think she'll be back. So do you wish to see her or not?"

Mouth dry, Diantha nodded.

"All right then," he said stiffly. "I'd better go arrange that. I'll be back for you before dinner. But listen, don't tell Serena. This will be between the two of us, all right?"

Diantha looked into her brother's face and saw uncertainty and weakness. He was Sir Reginald's son, after all. Nothing like Wyn, no matter how she tried to understand it.

"I won't tell her."

Wyn would never know that she'd found her mother either. He hadn't wanted her to go to Calais; perhaps he had known about her mother's exile, as everyone else seemed to. So this was for the best. That he knew nothing further of her at all was for the best, and that she knew nothing more of him.

But not one iota of her aching heart believed that.

Chapter 28

The carriage with the noble crest on the door preyed upon Diantha for the remainder of the day. In the parlor after a walk in the park with the children, Diantha wandered, pretending to herself that she did not intend to go toward the window, then when she went there pressing her nose against the glass and peering down the street. The stable boy sat on a stoop two houses down.

"Serena, I think I left my gloves in the carriage just now."

Serena's head was bent to letter writing. "Ask John to fetch them for you."

"Oh, he's probably busy polishing the silver or some such thing." She hurried to the door. "I'll go myself." She sprinted across the hall. The footman stood in the foyer. She gave him a bright smile then put a silencing finger to her lips. "I won't go far, John," she whispered and slipped out the door. He stood on the stoop and watched after her as she ran along the sidewalk.

The boy looked up, a shiny coin suspended between two fingers. He jumped to his feet and tugged his cap.

"G'day, miss." He wasn't but eight or nine, trim and neat as all the servants in Serena's household.

She smiled. "What are you playing there with your coin?"

His face twisted into an anxious grimace.

"Oh," she said, "I don't intend to take it from you. Only, I saw you playing and wondered what game it is. I am very fond of clever games." And lies, like the lie she'd told Serena about going to Lady Emily's this evening so that she could instead pay a secret call on her wicked mother.

His shoulders relaxed and he flipped the coin between his fingers again. "You see, miss, this here game is good for what you call 'agilities.'" He nodded knowingly.

She drew up her skirts and settled on the stoop. "Will you show me?"

He extended his hand and the coin jumped back and forth between his fingers like a living creature, passing across his knuckles thrice before it fell with a clink to the step. The boy frowned. "Hain't yet got the whole hang of it."

"I am certain you will soon. Have you just learned it?"

"The gentleman what came calling at milord's house this morning taught it me 'fore I held his horse." He peered at the coin with unrest again.

"You don't seem happy with it. Isn't it enough for holding a horse?"

His brows made two upside down U's. "Oh, no, miss, it's plenty. It's just that when the gentleman went, he left his horse behind. It's a fine horse, miss, or I wouldn't a wondered at it."

"Did he ever return to retrieve it?" Despite herself, her fingers twisted in her lap.

"No, miss. I took it to the stable and let old Pomley have it. Too good an animal for me to keep that long waiting, 'specially when the gentleman said it'd only be a quarter hour."

A quarter hour. Enough time to make her an offer she refused before he got into a crested carriage and drove away. Without his horse.

Panic twined in her belly. "You know, I had a glimpse of the horse earlier. It *is* beautiful."

"Strong too. A racer by blood, though he don't have the temperament for the track, the gentleman says." The boy shook his head regretfully.

"Will you show him to me?"

He leaped up. Diantha followed through the carriage passage to the mews, her nerves too high to bother to step gingerly around puddles to the stall in which the head groom had stabled Galahad. Munching on a bucket of oats, the animal turned its head to glance at her.

A wash of helplessness rushed through her. Wyn would never usually leave Galahad behind like this. But perhaps he'd been too drunk to care. Or perhaps the men in that carriage had been friends and they'd taken him off somewhere to drink even more, or to another "French convent" to enjoy themselves.

She pressed her hands to the sides of her face. *No.* Even then, this negligence simply was not *him.* She could not believe it. But she must. She'd no reason not to, except the naïve hope she had harbored in her heart since the moment she saw him on that Mail Coach. She was a perfect fool.

Wyn would eventually be sober again, he would retrieve Galahad, and she would have to resign herself to encountering him in society upon occasion. But after tonight's interview with her mother, the future needn't hold any more reckless plans. That part of her life must end. A new woman must arise from it, sadder but wiser for what she had learned of herself and a man.

By the time Tracy came for her at half past seven Diantha was stretched with nerves. They drove in silence through the lamp-lit streets cluttered with vehicles. Finally he let down the steps onto a narrow byway. Not a hundred yards distant the mast tips of ships rose in a cluster, and heavily laden carts were all about, all swirling with the mists rising as the night cooled.

"The docks," he explained. "Our mother's ship sets sail in an hour from just over there."

"It sails at night?"

He shrugged as though to deny that their mother was a criminal escaping under cover of dark. From doors along the street came the sounds of laughter and music. Men passed in and out, rough-looking people with weathered faces and worn clothing. Sailors, she supposed. One woman drew off the hood of her cloak as she entered a pub, her brassy hair and rouged cheeks garish in the torchlight. This was a different world by far than Devon or even the road through Shropshire and Wales. She hadn't felt the prickly discomfort of walking into an alien world, a dangerous world, since the Mail Coach, before the moment she'd wished for a hero and a dark Welshman appeared.

Glancing left and right, Tracy drew her toward a door. It opened on a bald-pated man of middling years, his chest encompassed in a red waistcoat into which he hooked his thumbs.

"Well well," he said with a grin. "Look who's a pretty thing."

"My sister ain't any of your business, Baker," Tracy said shortly. "Now if you'll bring my mother out here, I'll be much obliged not to inform Savege of her presence in town."

Mr. Baker set a thoughtful hand on his chin. "Well now, sir, your mother might not be up to accepting callers at present."

"She'd better be. I told her this afternoon that we'd come."

Mr. Baker gestured to the stair. "Be my guest." His

gaze shifted to Diantha. "But I don't know that this little lady will appreciate her mother's delicate sensibilities."

Tracy's face reddened. He turned to her. "I'll go up and tell her we're here." She nodded and he ascended.

Mr. Baker's gaze slowly slid from Diantha's crown to her hem. His grin widened. She tugged her cloak firmly about her and went to the narrow window beside the door. Out on the misty street a cart passed by, then an old hackney coach, a few riders, and other traffic, and her hands grew colder and damper. She closed her eyes and the image of a carriage with a crested door and a riderless black horse arose before her.

She popped her eyes open. She needed a plan, anything to distract her from constantly thinking of Wyn.

Her throat caught. Not twenty feet away a man passed through a circle of lamplight, a very large man wearing an overcoat and hat but whose long hair, square jaw, and sheer mass were unmistakable.

She grabbed the door handle.

"Now there, miss," Mr. Baker said. "Where do you think you're going?"

"There's no time." Her heartbeats flew, her hands slippery on the knob.

"Your brother will come down in a minute with your mother."

"Tell him—tell him I will return shortly." She pulled the door open.

He grasped her arm. "Now, wait there, miss."

Lord Eads disappeared behind a cluster of people up the street. She whirled around. "No. Tell my brother that I cannot see her. That I changed my mind. There is a hackney coach just letting off passengers there. I will hire it to drive to my friend's house where I was intended tonight. I cannot see my mother now." Her heart thudded.

"You'll not have this opportunity again. Your mother and I sail on the hour."

"I—I know. I *know*." She yanked her arm free and swung open the door.

Dashing through traffic, she breathed in foul odors of fish and animal refuse, but she didn't care; her senses were alive again after hours of numbness. Her skirts hampered her and the Highlander's broad back moved quickly away.

A pair of men jeered at her from a doorway. "Here, pretty girl! Scamper our way. We'll give you a fine romp." One of them sprang up and grabbed her arm.

"No!" She struggled. "Release me!"

Lord Eads halted, turned about, and Diantha's heart nearly exploded.

Momentarily he was upon them, shoving her accoster aside. "Didna yer mother teach ye how ta treat a leddy, ye ruffian?" He turned his glower upon her as the ruffian retreated. "And didna anybody teach ye no ta run about the streets alone a'nicht, lass?"

"No. I've been in the dark my entire life. But you must rectify that now." Shaking fiercely, she grabbed his thick arm. "Where is he? Have you hurt him? You must tell me or I think I will die. Truly. I am not being dramatic. This feeling in my breast is beyond describable. It's the worst thing I have ever felt. All day I have been trying to pretend I don't feel it, but it's of no use. Have you harmed him? And if not—oh, God, please not—*where is he*?"

His brow lowered. "A haena harmed him, lass. But A dinna ken where he be."

"I need the *truth*," she pleaded. "If you know that he is simply off somewhere with his friends debauching, then I will have to accept that. But this morning he departed strangely, in a carriage with a noble crest on the door pulled by the most spectacular foursome of gray horses, and he left his own horse behind. That isn't like him, and I realize—"

"A team o' fine grays, ye say?"

Diantha's heart did two enormous turnabouts. "Do you know them?"

"Aye, lass." His brow was dark.

"Are . . . ?" She couldn't breathe. "The duke?"

He nodded.

Her fingers dug into his sleeve. "I pray you, *tell* me where to find him."

"I canna." He shook his head. "He'd cut ma throat."

"The duke?"

He peered at her like she was daft.

"Tell me where the duke has taken him! I beg of you."

For a moment he said nothing, the raucous sounds of the street all about them in the torch-lit dark. Finally, he nodded. "A'll go and see what can be done, then send ye word."

"No." She gripped his arm. "You must take me."

"No, lass."

"There's no 'no' about it. I will not leave your side."

He looked about the street. "What're ye doing here all alone?"

"Seeking the truth. Again. Now, you must take me to him. I want to help him. I *need* to help him. If I were one of your sisters, you would understand, wouldn't you?"

The Highlander stared down at her from his vast height. For the second time in years, Diantha prayed.

Despite his long work for the government, and briefly for the underlord Myles, Wyn found himself surprised to discover that a great lord possessed a dungeon—*in town*—a dark basement of some medieval house in which he was now bound to a wall with shackles about his wrists. Given his present state, it was also somewhat difficult to convince himself that he had made the right decision to mount the duke's carriage voluntarily. They had taken his knife. Indeed, he had surrendered it without fuss; mind numbed and heart thrashed from that little charade with Diantha, he hadn't been thinking entirely straight when the carriage door opened and the duke's minion uttered,

"Get in or I'll shoot you in the heart." Since he hadn't wished to die in a bloody mess on the sidewalk before her house, he had acquiesced. A man must have some pride, after all, and the tenderhearted minx deserved better.

A guard dozed in the corner, his lips jiggling with snores, keys to the irons dangling from his belt. Wyn had tried cajoling, even bribery, to win those keys, including an abrupt contortion of his arms when the big fellow came close that had gained him bruises on his wrists and a gash the length of Piccadilly along the side of his face. Perhaps not quite such a long gash, but it bled heartily enough. He felt a bit dizzy and his mouth was a desert. But it seemed clear now that if he'd gone to Yarmouth he would be likewise chained up. At least he'd spared Galahad the journey.

He cleared his throat. "Had you been following me long before you picked me up?"

The guard started awake and rubbed his eyes. "Yester'eve."

"Since yesterday evening only?"

Grunt.

"Ah. The duke must trust you only with brute tasks. How lowering for you."

Disgruntled mumble.

"What was that?"

"Rufus was chasing shadows," the big fellow grumbled. "Told Chopper she weren't nothing. Not to a flash cove like you."

Wyn's heartbeat spiked. "I'll admit I am not entirely following you. Your colleague Rufus failed you, Chopper, and perhaps the duke in some task having to do with apprehending me?"

Nod of righteous indignation. "But now who's already gone off bottle-knocked on a tuppence and left me here?" Scowl.

"Rufus, I suppose?"

Head jerk. Relapse into silence.

From which Wyn deduced with no little satisfaction that Rufus, the duke's employee who had been watching Savege's household from within, had been paid and furloughed by the duke hours ago. Rufus had believed Wyn's ruse and Yarmouth had no more use for him. Diantha was safe.

Footsteps came on the step and another man entered.

"Ah, back so soon," Wyn said. "Since you disappeared swiftly after that lovely carriage ride, I had begun to miss you."

This fellow was not as large as the other guard, though plenty scarred; he'd been the winner in some nasty bouts. But if Wyn had the free use of his arms, he might be able to best him alone. Both, if he had his knife.

"He wants to see you."

They took him up the stair, passing a single landing before the smaller guard opened the door at the top. The odor of decay ushered forth. Lit dimly, the chamber was a fortress, all bricked windows, Flemish tapestries, and a massive bed hung with curtains scrolled with gold cord and tassels. Upon a table by the bed a silver tray laden with porcelain bore testimony to an uneaten meal. In a chair beside the table huddled a narrow woman of indeterminate age tucked into a black cloak and dust veil. She did not lift her eyes as the guards brought Wyn toward the foot of the bed, but she stood and drew the curtain open.

The stench of death rocked him. From the shadows a wraith of a man with long, incongruously thick white hair stared back at him, his eyes cavernous in the darkness. His face was pocked with wet red sores the size of sixpence, and moisture stained the nightshirt pink beneath his velvet dressing gown.

At Yarmouth's castle Wyn had seen a portrait of the duke—a picture of a man in the middle of his life, tall, aristocratically slender and weak-chinned, with round eyes and tapered shoulders exaggerated by an indolent pose, his elbow propped upon a bust of a long-deceased emperor. Caligula, probably.

The monstrosity before Wyn bore little resemblance to the nobleman in that portrait.

"Your Grace, I would bow but these fellows have me trussed too tightly. Or— Wait . . ." He tilted his head thoughtfully. "No, I wouldn't bow anyway." He shrugged, the shackles digging into his wrists.

The duke nodded and the gray woman pulled the curtain back farther. A pair of dueling pistols rested upon the foot of the bed, perfectly presented atop the satin coverlet as though still in their case.

Wyn's throat constricted. "Ah," he said conversationally, "you aim to finish this in a gentlemanly manner." *Curious.* Yarmouth looked barely capable of lifting his hand, let alone of gripping a weapon.

"The s-second . . ." The old man's voice rasped, unused, but diseased too. Syphilis, perhaps, by the look of the sores. If so, this creature sunk upon the mattress had been suffering for some time.

Wyn lifted his brow. "The second?"

"The second . . . is . . ." Yarmouth's cravat pulsed. " . . . if you miss the first."

This, Wyn had not anticipated. In the duke's eyes now he saw the madness. Madness, yes, that may have been there when he had raped and tortured his young ward, Chloe Martin, a girl of no more than sixteen when Wyn found her, fleeing her guardian after finally escaping him. Madness caused by the disease, or merely exacerbated by it.

"Given the hospitality I have been offered today, I don't suppose you intend to pay me for this assassination, as you did for the last," he said laconically. "Do apprise me, then, Your Grace, of your purpose. If you are able."

"Kill . . . me."

"If I am given one of those pistols, I will shoot the large man to my left in the kneecap. If I am then given the other, I will shoot this scarred chap likewise. It would be foolish of me to do otherwise, of course."

A wild gleam lit Yarmouth's eyes. "I hired you . . . to assassinate . . . a French—"

"Spy. That you did. And, imagining myself immensely clever, I gladly accepted your offer, before, that is, I learned that the so-called spy was no more French than you or I, merely a girl upon whom you had practiced your depraved fantasies until she was so scarred she could barely run. Yet still she found the courage to escape you. Remarkable, the human will, isn't it?"

Fingers thick with lesions scrabbled the bed linens. *"Kill me."*

"And satisfy you? Two birds with one stone? End the wretched misery of your existence while damning me to execution for defying you five years ago? *Attempting* to defy you, that is."

"Your letter . . . You-ou vowed . . ." His head shook, uncontrolled tremors.

"I vowed to kill you the next time I saw you," Wyn agreed. "For setting me up to kill her. For lying to me. For—" He could no longer withhold the anger. "She was under your protection. A *girl*. Given to you to protect after her parents died. Instead you hurt her." His hands were fists, the shackles cutting his flesh.

"Vanity . . . got the better of you." The mouth contorted into a grin. "You killed her."

By accident. A message sent to the duke—Chloe the willing bait to lure Yarmouth to his death—Wyn crouching in an alley after midnight—a steady hand yet a head full of brandy—Chloe stepping through the door first— *not the plan.*

How the duke had laughed, his mirth bubbling down that dark corridor of hell as he'd strolled away unharmed.

Weeks later, arising from the trough of forgetfulness into which he'd sunk himself that night after Jin helped him find a proper grave for the body, Wyn had written the duke a letter. Then after five years awaiting opportunity to breach the duke's impregnable fortress, Lady Priscilla had provided that chance, to fulfill the promise he'd made Chloe Martin as she'd lain dying in his arms.

"The horse was another lie, wasn't it? Lady Priscilla was your ploy to lure me once again to do your bidding. You want to die and end your suffering, but you haven't the courage to do it alone. For my attempt at defying you five years ago, I am to have the honor of once again pulling the trigger, aren't I?"

He stared into Yarmouth's dessicated face and, with a clarity born perhaps of equal parts fury and satisfaction, he recognized at this moment his own misdeed. He should not have hurt Diantha. Ready—*eager*—to trust him that morning, she might have done what he wished had he explained the danger. She might have listened for once, and helped him keep her safe.

He said quietly, "There is no greater honor than to be entrusted with a woman's safety and happiness."

The slightest, smallest gasp like a sigh came from the veiled woman in the chair. But Wyn did not remove his attention from the duke.

"You are a twisted man, Your Grace. You deserve to linger in this misery until your madness takes you entirely. For I will not assist you." Not now that he had discovered the tragedy in deception. Not now that he had tasted life.

"She fought me." The words were softly spoken, barely a damp breath from Yarmouth's lips. "Dear Chloe . . . fought . . . every time." The mouth shaped into a grimace of pleasure, the eyes bright.

Wyn turned his face away. "Take me from here," he said to the guard.

Chopper glanced at the cavern of the bed.

Wyn did not know if the duke assented or if his guards could no longer bear their employer's presence either. They pushed him toward the stairwell, and as he went to his uncertain fate below he thought of Diantha . . . safe. He even smiled.

She would not have listened to him. If he'd told her all, she would not have allowed him to hide her away to ensure her safety—not again, not after the abbey. She would have insisted on helping him and by now she would be here, the duke's prisoner, just as he. Instead she was safe in Savege's house, with Grimm keeping watch for surety.

They came to the landing above the basement the moment the door there opened, revealing the Highlander who had promised Wyn the night before that he no longer worked for the Duke of Yarmouth.

And, behind Duncan, Diantha.

Wide-eyed, hair tumbling from a bonnet askew, spots of pink where her dimples ought to be, her mouth tied with cloth and wrists bound with rope, she looked at him and her body went slack.

Duncan caught her up against his side.

"What's this?" Chopper scowled. "Bringing your fancy piece here, Donnan?"

"Does she look like a fancy piece, ye dolt?"

The big guard slavered. "Share a bit of the fun with us, mate?"

Duncan's gaze came straight to Wyn. "No, lads. This lass here be for the pleasure o' His Grace."

Chapter 29

Diantha gagged. She knew the lie was to throw the duke's ruffians off their guard, but even the notion revolted. Swallowing down bile as well as the strip of her shift stuffed between her lips allowed, she recovered from the false swoon and struggled to right herself against Lord Eads, fighting not to look at Wyn. If she looked—truly looked—she might actually swoon.

Iron shackles. *Blood*. Everything inside her screamed to tear out the ruffians' eyes with her fingernails.

She closed her eyes to slits and groaned then shook her head in weak protest, playing the part as Lord Eads had instructed her in the hired hackney coach while they'd bolted through the streets to this house.

"Goddamn you, Eads." Wyn's voice sounded barely human.

The big ruffian looked her up and down like she was dinner.

But the other seemed skeptical. "Listen here, Donnan." He shook his head. "The duke ain't—"

And then the tiny landing between two sets of narrow

stone steps erupted into a melee of male aggression. Wyn slammed his body against the guard to his left, knocking him off balance to teeter on the edge of the steps. Arms flailing, he scrabbled to stay upright. Lord Eads thrust her behind him, blocking the big guard lunging toward Wyn. She struggled not to fall, unwinding the ropes from her wrists and tugging the gag from her mouth. Lord Eads threw himself at his opponent, and the other guard regained his footing and grabbed for Wyn. She screamed. Iron links clanged. In one graceful movement Wyn leaped over the chain and hauled it high to swing around the ruffian's shoulders. Lord Eads's opponent bellowed and fell against the wall clutching his neck, blood oozing through his fingers. The big body thumped to the floor. The other ruffian shouted, then gasped, chains rattling *not* around his shoulders—his *head*.

"Don't kill him!"

"I am not"—grating voice—"going to"—the ruffian slumped—"kill him." Wyn released his captive, iron links clanking as the guard collapsed onto the stairs. He swung around, fire blazing in his silver eyes fixing on Lord Eads. "But I am going to kill *him*."

Diantha pushed away from the door. "He didn't—"

In the darkness above, a door knocked open against the wall. Both men's eyes snapped upward. Then they met, blue challenging gray.

"Allou me."

Wyn nodded and dropped to his knees beside the bleeding guard. The irons jangled. Lord Eads started up the steps.

Diantha surged forward. "But what is he—"

Wyn grabbed her wrist and dragged her through the door. Behind them on the landing the shackles were clamped about the smaller ruffian's wrists.

The misty night air had turned to fog, the alley behind the duke's house hazy and sparkling now like a haunted fairyland. Wyn pulled her, his grip digging into her flesh, and she struggled to keep up. She did not protest the brutality. She had never seen such fury in his eyes as a moment ago. She had also never seen a man murdered.

Their swift footsteps were eerily quiet in the alley that ran along the mews. This neighborhood was not like the street near the docks where Tracy took her, rather more respectable from the glimpse she'd had upon hastily disembarking from the hackney coach. She hadn't known then what they would find inside the duke's house, if they would find Wyn alive or—or—

She stumbled. He caught her shoulders, steadied her, and in the ghostly dark their breaths swirled mist between them. Somewhere far off, the clatter of hooves and carriage wheels echoed.

"Did you bring a horse? A carriage?"

She shook her head. "Lord Eads dismissed the hackney—"

He grasped her wrist again and jarred her into motion. The fog wavered ahead, showing glimpses of a stone building with a sizable wooden door. Wyn jolted her to a halt, a door rattled as it slid in a track, and he pulled her inside.

It was dark and warm, the scents of horses and straw wonderfully clean. Simple and like home.

He released her to close the door and Diantha sank against the wall, trembling. Wyn's boot steps receded into the blackness. But he would not leave her—she knew this—no matter how furious. And finally, as she gulped in air, her lungs filled and her body shed its shock, her anger and hurt rose anew.

He returned, the white of his shirt and neck cloth visible first, then all of him, and she saw again the blood on his face. Her anger deflated. She reached out. "What did they—"

He gripped her wrist, flattened it to the wall, and he covered her mouth with his.

She drank him in, needing his anger, fueling hers with the pain inside her and such profound relief.

This was wrong. She loved him, but she could not be hurt by him again. Years of blind trust in her mother had taught her when to relinquish love so that she would not suffer. She wrenched her face away, struggling to breathe between the wall and his hard body.

"Defend yourself," he growled, biting at her lower lip, and a moan escaped her. "Defend your actions tonight, your willful, reckless involvement in a matter that was none of your affair."

"We saved you." His hands moved along her arms and she offered no resistance. Everything in her was alive, feeling him, wanting him. His hands on her, rough and purposeful, were a dream. "You were in *shackles*."

His palms came around her face, his fingers sinking into her hair, discarding the bonnet, jarring her jaw upward. Red marks circled his wrists. She gasped and he caught her mouth anew. He kissed her, long, deep, not allowing her breath and she clung to his shoulders until her legs got wobbly. She broke free to drag in air. He trailed kisses along her jaw, his hand moving along her neck, drawing her cloak open. She pushed at him with a feeble palm.

"Wyn, I—"

"You are mine, Diantha," he uttered against her throat. "Mine." No softly whispered words of affection or even relief, but gravelly possession like that night at the inn. His palm slid from her shoulder, around her breast, and their groans met in the darkness. He pressed his thigh between hers; she allowed it. Her body wanted this, but her heart was weeping.

"*No.* I cannot do this. Not after you were with a—a woman of ill repute last night."

His hands swept into her hair, casting pins loose, holding her immobile. "I wasn't with anyone last night, except you, in my dreams."

"You *weren't*?"

"How could I be with any other woman when I want only you?"

"But you said—"

"I lied. I lied." He punctuated each utterance with kisses that fused her to him further. "I lied to make you refuse me, and I got what I wanted, but now I want you." He tugged hard at her sleeve. Her breast bulged in the straining bodice. He touched her, sweeping his thumb beneath the fabric and over the nipple, and she felt his pleasure rumble in his chest beneath her palms. "And I will have you." In one powerful move he swept her up into his arms. "Now. In a stable where, I think, you need to be had." He took three strides, the stall door swung shut behind them, and he pinned her to the wall before her feet again met the floor.

She gasped for air. "I don't *want* this." But his hands were everywhere on her, and she was whimpering in need, pushing his coat off his shoulders. She had to feel him, to touch him one last time, anger tangling thickly with desire and desperation. "I don't." She spread her hands over the muscles of his chest and was weak inside with longing.

He pulled her hips hard against his. "I need you, Diantha." His hands moved up her waist, curving around her breasts. "I crave you."

"I suppose I should be flattered you consider me in the same category as brandy." She tore at his waistcoat, tasting his jaw with her lips, pulling his shirttail from his trousers, seeking his skin, the taut, hot perfection of this man. "I won't marry you. If you ask me again I will—"

"Have me." He took her to the ground, pressing her into the sweet, fresh straw with the weight of his body. She rose to him, to feel him. Her skirts skipped up her calves then her thighs, gathered in his hands.

"You make me insane." His voice was husky. Beneath the layers of fabric his hands surrounded her behind.

"Ohh, *God.*"

His mouth covered the soft part of her breast as his hand sought her below. He groaned touching her. She thrust herself to him, the hunger twining fast and desperate this time, the ecstasy of relief and need tumbling through her. He was not gentle; it gave him pleasure to caress her so, she thought, and she wanted that. She wanted to please him. She wanted to love him entirely.

"More," she pleaded upon a whisper. "But I don't— I don't want you inside me. I don't—*uh*—" Her body undulated beneath his touch. She threw her hand out to the wall, her eyes half closed and the beauty of her face exquisite as her pleasure grew. "We are not to marry," she gasped, "and I don't want you to get me with child. So, *don't*—" The remainder of her protest was lost in a moan of pure feminine acquiescence as he slid his finger into her.

"Don't put my hands on you?" Driven by her hot, primed beauty, his other hand moved to his breeches fastenings. "Don't give you this?" Upon every thrust of his finger the creamy swells of her breasts above her bodice jerked upward, a luscious pink aureole peeking out. Wyn bent and drew it into his mouth. "My Diantha." He sucked the peak, bit, and she moaned, meeting his hand faster, and he had to be inside her.

He grabbed her hips and dragged her under him, pressing her to his needy cock, kissing her neck, her throat, feasting upon her silken skin, the luxury of her breasts. She pushed at his chest with one palm, grabbing him closer with her other, her hand sliding down his arm.

"I said—"

"You said more." He must have her. Hands beneath her skirts, kissing her breasts then the curve of her waist, he descended, pushing quantities of silk and lace out of the way.

"What are you doing?"

"Having you in a stable." He pressed her thighs open.

She struggled to push her skirts down. "I told you I don't want you to make love to me."

He grabbed her wrists. "Because you fear me getting you with child only?"

Her breaths were fast, eyes wide and bleary with passion. "Y-Yes."

"Now tell me the truth." He stroked across her femininity, her eyes closed upon a moan, and then he did what he'd wanted to do since he spent a night in a stable loft fantasizing about her.

She was sweet, her scent, her texture, and exquisitely wet. He tasted her, drew her pleasure with his tongue and she gasped. But she allowed it, gripping straw in her slender hands. He used his lips, his teeth, until she called his name, but he wanted more. He could not take his fill. He sank his finger into her.

"Oh, *stop*." Her back arched, her knuckles white against the wall, eyes closed and head thrown back. "I want you to— I want— *Unh!*" She contracted against his tongue to a stuttering series of soft cries. Then again, harder, her groans deeper and breaths short until she was whimpering her pleasure like sobs. "I *need you*."

He moved up between her legs and brought himself against her. He bent and breathed her in, the satin of her curls brushing his cheek. "Ask me."

"Please!" She moved against him, her thighs clutching him close. "I will beg if you like."

"A lady need only ask once." He thrust into her, again, and again, until he was fully embedded. She moaned, gripping his back with her hands, and, desperate for relief, he took her. The mattress of straw was a bed for the tight gift of her body she gave him. He lifted her hips and gave her pleasure until he could only thrust blindly, be inside her as deeply as she could take him, her decadent thighs spread, all of her open to him.

"Wyn." As she shuddered around him, he came.

Beyond reason and control he filled her so deep that no one could ever again deny she belonged to him—not he, not she. And he uttered a curse, perhaps a prayer, that he could be a man worthy of this woman's heart.

Hauling air into his lungs, he bent his mouth to her neck, her breasts, the damp contour of her throat. She pressed her body to his, and he could not leave her yet. He was exhausted, and he was exactly where he wished to be.

Eyes closed, she allowed him to caress her. "I did not know it could be done quite like that. With a man's mouth," she said between slowing breaths.

"I bloody well hope you didn't."

"A gentleman should never swear in the presence of a lady," she murmured. "Rule Number Seven."

"When you speak of 'a man's' mouth rather than mine in particular, naturally it concerns me."

Her lapis eyes opened. "No other man has touched me like you have. You know that."

"I do." He brushed her lips, which were tender from his enjoyment of her, and her hand came up and around his jaw tentatively, then into his hair. Gently she explored the wound on his temple with light fingertips. There was no pain there now, only the pleasure of her caress.

She drew away first. He stroked a damp curl back from her brow and her lashes dipped. But this quiet, sated woman was not all of her. Given her fight, their affinity would not last for long, and he must see her to a safe place now.

He pulled back and fastened his breeches as she pushed her skirts over her legs and tucked her beautiful breasts back into her gown. The darkness surrounded them, the muffled silence of horses in a nearby stall, and the distant Watch calling the hour through the muting fog.

Wyn watched her. "How did you make him do it?"

Her lashes flickered, but her fingers continued picking straw from her wrinkled skirts.

"How did you convince Eads to take you there?"

She pushed to her feet on the uneven ground and shook out her skirts. "Thank you."

"Thank you?"

Her head shot up, eyes alight. "Thank you, Diantha, for saving my life. For caring enough about my brandy-swilling hide that you risked yours despite—*despite* the fact that I lied to you. *Again*." Her voice cracked.

"Thank you." He grabbed her shoulders. "Goddamn it, thank you. Is that what you wish to hear?"

She pulled out of his hold and went from the stall. He followed, her every motion in the dark so natural, so unconsciously beautiful even in her haste, that it stole his anger. She bent to retrieve her cloak and bonnet from the floor and the shape of her body made him breathless. He could not watch her enough.

"What did Lord Eads intend to do to the duke?" Her voice quavered, but he could hear the purpose in it, her bravery.

"I don't know." He touched her shoulder.

She whirled around, eyes glittering, a tear staining her cheek. "Don't touch me. I don't *want* this." She backed away, clutching her cloak before her. "Why didn't you simply tell me you did not wish to marry me? Why did you have to take to the bottle again? Were you afraid that I would not release you from your obligation? That I would beg for your attention?" Pain clouded her eyes. "Well then, Mr. Yale, you don't know me well after all. So I suppose you won't know this unless I tell you: *I don't need you*. Mr. H is still eager for my hand. Even if I do come to be with child from this—this—"

"Truth?" He stepped close again and Diantha's throat caught, cutting off her words. He was very tall, his wide shoulders and chest in clinging linen intimidating, and the line of his delicious mouth severe. His arm wrapped about her waist and he trapped her jaw in his palm so that she was forced to look up at him. "This truth?" He was beautiful, anger sparking in his silver gaze that moved across her features as though he meant to memorize her.

"This is not truth," she whispered. She forced her arms to hang at her sides, not to cling to him as she wished. "I hate the feelings inside me now." Inadequacy. Hurt. Need so profound it made her ache.

"You will marry me, Diantha." His throat constricted in a rough swallow. "Marry me."

She pushed against his chest, her insides swimming in confusion. "You pretended you had been with a prostitute so I would refuse your offer *only this morning*, and now you are insisting that I marry you?" She broke free of his embrace. "You *are* insane."

His fingers scraped through his hair around to the back of his neck. "Yes, I am insane when it comes to you. I nearly did take to the bottle again last night in a desperate attempt to put you off."

"Nearly?"

"Do you know what would have happened to you if we had not bested the duke's guards? Did Eads warn you, or did you go off half-cocked on a rescue mission once again, heedless of the consequences?"

"I have never been heedless of any consequences," she shot back. "*Ever*. And I did this to help you!"

"I don't need that kind of help from you!"

She couldn't breathe. "You were not drunk last night or this morning? You pretended it so that I would refuse you?"

"Yes."

She hadn't thought she could hurt more, but she had been wrong. "You are a beast."

"I did it to protect you from Yarmouth, who threatened to harm you because of his grudge against me."

Diantha's heart slammed over.

Wyn's voice lowered. "I knew that if I told you of his

threats you would invent some reckless plan to save me, which you did anyway despite my charade, because you are tenacious beyond reason. But my pretense was a mistake far beyond that. And part of me hoped, I think, that you would see through it. But you are not to blame, and for it I beg your forgiveness."

He had done it all to protect *her*? He had thrown himself into the hands of a villain so that she would be safe? And now he was begging for her forgiveness?

Diantha's heart pounded, her thoughts staggering. She had forced him into rescuing her time and again. He had never failed her and still would not, even if it continued hurting him, over and over. He would insist upon wedding her though she only caused him trouble. Wayward, foolish, *unbiddable*. Everything she had tried to do for him had bound him more tightly to her though he had never wanted it.

"It is over now, Diantha, and you must marry me."

She could not bear to do this to him. "But don't you see why I cannot? Don't you see *anything*?"

"No, apparently." His chest rose on a hard breath. "I barely even know the words I'm speaking. When I am with you, thinking of you, I don't actually think. For God's sake, I just made love to you three hundred yards from the house in which I was held prisoner today—in a stable, with my boots on. Fifteen years of perfecting every move I make thrown to the dogs the instant I see you. It is like nothing I have known before."

"Do you think I don't regret that it has gone this way as well? That I ever asked you to help me?" She strapped her arms about her middle. "And it is worse even than you know, because it was all for nothing. My mother is not in Calais but London. Tracy took me to see her tonight, but . . . I didn't *care*." The truth of it spiraled through her. The old cruelty no longer imprisoned her. "I didn't want to see her any longer. I didn't need to." *She only needed him.*

"Diantha." He came forward and pulled her into his arms. He kissed her and she loved his kisses and his embrace and him. She loved him so much it hurt. She loved everything about him except how she forced him to be a man he was not. But she lifted her lips to him and allowed him to kiss her because this would be the last time. The last kiss. It astounded her that—even briefly—she had ever dreamed another ending to this story. He was her hero and he always would be, but she was not the heroine he deserved.

"Forgive my anger," he whispered huskily against the corner of her lips. His silvery eyes sought hers, a crease between them. "I have no regrets. None."

The stable door creaked open. Wyn pressed her into shadow and touched his fingertips to her lips.

A shuffling gait accompanied lamplight wobbling through the doorway, and a wrinkled face came into view, a bridle slung over a shoulder. He lifted the lamp and his brows went up.

Wyn bowed. "Our thanks for the use of the stall, my good man." He tipped an imaginary hat, grasped Diantha's hand and pulled her outside. But behind them she left her heart in pieces on the soft-scented straw.

Chapter 30

"**W**here does your family believe you are tonight?"

"Lady Emily Vale's house."

He said nothing more, but clasped her hand tightly in his as they walked. In the muted hush of fog they found a street and, by sound alone it seemed, he identified a passing hackney coach. He bundled her inside, then jumped onto the box with the driver. The ride was long and slow and when he opened the door and offered his hand to assist her, she climbed stiffly out onto the street before Lady Emily's house.

A footman ushered them to a parlor and Lady Emily appeared.

"Miss Lucas." She came forward with a smile, candlelight glinting off her gold-rimmed spectacles and silvery-blond hair, but otherwise a study in sobriety from her dark blue gown to the ubiquitous book in her hand. "And Mr. Yale." She nodded without any show of pleasure.

"Good evening, Lady Cleopatra." He bowed.

"No 'Lady.' Only Cleopatra. She was a queen, you cretin."

"As ever, I stand humbled in the light of your brilliance."

Diantha couldn't bear it. "Cleopatra—"

Emily touched her on the arm. "No, Miss Lucas. You shan't be required to explain to me why the two of you have appeared in my house in the middle of the night looking like you have walked across half of London. I want Mr. Yale to have the honor."

"I am certain you do," he replied. "But you will be denied that pleasure." He moved toward the door. Then he turned, his slight smile quirked to one side. "You understand this brings us even."

"Finally." Lady Emily's smile was barely discernable. "I do wonder, though, that after nearly four years making me wait to repay you, you expect so little of me."

"You mistake it, my lady." His gaze came to Diantha. He bowed. "Good night, Miss Lucas." He departed.

Diantha stared at the door, remembering Emily's story about how years ago Wyn had helped her in a difficult situation, not because of gain for himself but because it was in his nature to do so.

But she knew it was more than that. She knew about his mother, and she had read his great-aunt's rules.

"You mustn't think ill of him," she said softly. "He did not wish me to return home in this unkempt state. He does not wish my family to know the trouble I have been in." She turned to her hostess. "I should write to my brother now, if I may."

"In fact Sir Tracy sent a message to you here not a quarter hour ago. I was only now composing a note to accompany it to Lady Savege's house." Emily drew Diantha's arm through her own. "Come. Let us acquire you a bath and a fresh nightrail. While Clarice brushes out your curls you will read your brother's letter and reply to him if you wish."

"I beg your pardon, and am grateful for your help. I had told Serena that I was coming here tonight."

"How wonderfully convenient. My note will indicate

that we are so enamored of each other's company that neither of us could bear for you to leave before morning." She drew Diantha toward the door. "But, Miss Lucas, regardless of the adventure you have had this evening, I must insist on one matter."

"Of course."

"If you speak a word about that vainglorious quiz in my house, I will be obliged to make you sleep in the coal scuttle."

Diantha could not help but smile. "Vainglorious? He wears black coats, and I have only once seen him in a colored waistcoat."

"Alas, the coal scuttle it will be for you." They ascended the stair. "I admit to being disappointed, as I had gotten used to thinking you somewhat sensible. But some ladies, I understand, will lodge their affections in the most astounding quarters."

Upon returning home in the morning, Diantha had no desire to hear more of her brother's chastisements; his letter the previous night had been full of them and he indicated he would call upon her early. Instead she requested the company of a footman and walked to Teresa's house.

"Have you seen Lord Eads again since the ball, T?"

"No." Teresa drew silk thread through a square of linen, her movements precise. "But when I do, I shall do what I must to make him marry me."

Diantha doubted Lord Eads would return to society. He had only been at the ball because of Wyn. She stared dully at the rainy day, then took a breath and turned back to her friend.

"I called this morning, T, because I have something I must tell you."

Teresa set down her work. "I knew it the moment you entered. Something is amiss." She moved to the sofa beside Diantha.

"I love a gentleman. Mr. Yale. Perhaps you saw him at the ball, so gorgeously elegant except when I have caused him not to be. But even then—tousled, fevered, unshaven, even furious—he is perfect."

"Furious?" Teresa's eyes were wide. "*Unshaven*?" Her pretty red lips gaped. "Diantha!"

"He has compromised me and believes he must now marry me. But I am ruining his life and cannot accept him because I want what is best for him. That is what love should be, and I wish to love like that now."

"I . . . I . . ." Teresa surrounded Diantha's hands warmly. "I daresay."

They sat like that for a moment while Teresa leaned into her shoulder in comfort. Finally she said, "Di, could you perhaps explain that part about him compromising you?"

Diantha laughed, and it felt wretched. "He was my last willful transgression. I must now cease behaving recklessly and instead be a lady of whom my family can be proud."

"Don't you think they would be proud if you married a fine gentleman like Mr. Yale, especially given that . . ."

"Given that I gave my maidenhood to him? No. Tracy has forbidden me to marry him. In any case, it doesn't matter that I am ruined."

"You always said it wouldn't matter," Teresa said very quietly.

"T, could you try to be happy for me, at least for turning over a new leaf?"

Teresa sighed. "I rather liked the old you. This new Diantha may not be to my tastes." She squeezed her hand. "But I daresay I will love you no matter how tiresomely proper you become." She stroked the back of Diantha's hand. "You know, Mr. Yale is likely to be unhappy with your decision not to allow him to be honorable to you. He is bound to call on you."

"That is the trouble. He is bound to." She stared at her hands. "I mustn't be at home when he calls."

"He may call again until he sees you."

"Then I must leave London." Diantha stood, within her heart new purpose seeking to push aside the heavy grief. "I will make a new plan."

"A new plan? Oh, no, Di—"

"You are brilliant, T." She squeezed her friend's hands. "This plan will take me far from London and if he calls on me and tries to convince me to marry him again, I will not be here to succumb."

"This sounds like a remarkably bad plan to me."

Diantha gripped her teeth together, pasted on a smile, and went to the door. "Will you help me pack? I will have a lot to do to prepare. John, the footman, will help me find the closest Mail Coach inn, I've no doubt. He is the sweetest man. And I will ask Cook to prepare a picnic lunch. She is always so kind." She reached for the doorknob. "I should write a letter to Serena explaining that she needn't worry about me. And I must—"

Teresa bolted up from the sofa. "Diantha, you cannot go!"

Diantha swiveled around. "You *must* help me, T." Her voice shook. "I cannot bear to be a burden on him again, to allow him to be hurt because of me. If I stay, I know I will. I always do."

Teresa's lower lip quivered, her eyes entreating. But she nodded. Diantha drew open the door, then paused.

"And . . . T?"

"Di?" The single syllable was thick.

"It will have to be Mr. H for me after all."

"Oh!" She sprang forward and wrapped her arms around Diantha and held her close.

Chapter 31

Raven,

When the trial of the Queen's alleged infidelity comes to a close shortly (in failure of the proposed bill, as all hope it will), she intends to remove from England. She has discreetly inquired as to whom she can depend upon to protect her from the King if he seeks to harm her further in this manner. Since you charmed the Ministers in Vienna, you have remained in their thoughts; those loyal to her recommend you. The King discovered this and—desiring you to remain in his service rather than hers—wishes to reward you for your long tenure in the Club. Our director recommends knighthood.

Congratulations, Sir Raven. Do join me for dinner this evening at the club.

Peregrine

Yale,

 *The duke is dead, suffocation in his bed by the
old servant woman.*

D.E.

Chapter 32

Shuffling into his drawing room with the weary tread of a much older man, the Baron of Carlyle peered at Wyn's calling card. "To what do I owe this visit, sir?"

Wyn bowed. "I regret that it is not a social call, my lord."

Carlyle looked more carefully at him now. "You wrote me a letter offering for my daughter. Now I recall." He nodded. "Excellent property, yours. Enviable income. But as I replied, where I wish Diantha to marry has no bearing on where she will actually do so, much to my regret, but there it is. I'm afraid I cannot help you convince her. She has a mind of her own, as do all my daughters." He shook his head with a regretful air.

"I am not here to ask assistance in convincing your daughter to accept my suit, my lord." He was more than happy to accomplish that task himself. Given time, and encouragement that left her begging and breathless, she would have him. And if Tracy Lucas even so much as peeped in protest, Wyn would favor him with a meaningful stare down the barrel of his pistol. He was through doing the bidding of other men. His future, and Diantha's, was his alone to command.

The baron shook his head. "Don't break your heart over her, Mr. Yale. For all she looks very pretty in a ball gown now, my fourth daughter is still a rambunctious girl. A spruced up fellow like you will be much better off with a wife who knows how to go about like a lady."

"Thank you for that advice, sir." He couldn't disagree more. Diantha it was and Diantha it would be forever for him. She rendered the mere idea of control laughable, and he wanted that. He didn't want her subdued, her spirit cowed as when he left her at Lady Emily's. He wanted her plunging into danger head first, making him shout and rescue her and make love to her in stables as often as possible. He'd been a fool to push her away and an even greater fool in his anger and fear for her not to have told her the entire truth last night. He would not make that mistake again. "I have come to speak with you on another matter. Your wife."

Carlyle's brow pleated.

"Lady Carlyle has been in London and has contacted your stepson. She requested of him funds to finance a high-end brothel."

The baron's face went ashen. "In London?"

"France. It gives me no pleasure to bring you these tidings, my lord. But for your stepdaughter's sake, I thought you should know."

Carlyle passed a distracted hand over his face then moved to the sideboard. "Claret, Mr. Yale?"

"No, thank you. I must be going." To find a lady with lapis eyes and make her the most convincing offer of marriage a man could manage. Only the smallest sliver of doubt bothered him. "But first, my lord, might you share with me a word about Mr. Highbottom? I understand that he has hopes for Miss Lucas's hand."

"Who?" Carlyle's brow twisted.

"Mr. Hinkle Highbottom."

"Hinkle and Highbottom? What hopes would they have concerning my daughter's marriage?"

"They?"

"Alfred Hinkle and Oswald Highbottom." Carlyle moved to a table laden with books and took up a pair of thick volumes. "Two of the finest archeological minds this century, although I don't suppose young fellows like you bother with such things."

Wyn's heart beat unevenly. "If you will, my lord, is this Mr. Highbottom—"

"Professor Highbottom. Master at Christ Church for over forty years now."

Wyn could not help but stare rather blankly. "Is Miss Lucas acquainted with the professor?"

"Since she was a sprig of a girl. Highbottom was dedicated to his scholarship. Never had a family of his own, of course. But he took a quick liking to Diantha when she first came to live at Glenhaven Hall." A ghost of a smile crossed his lips. "Used to dandle her on his knee until rheumatism got the best of him."

"Then, Professor Highbottom has no claim upon your daughter's hand, nor she an interest in wedding him?"

"I said I don't have control over whom my daughter chooses to wed." Carlyle frowned. "But if she were to betroth herself to a man sixty years her senior I would make it my business to halt the alliance at once. Now, sir, I haven't any idea how—"

"Milord!" A footman stood in the doorway.

"What is it, Bernard? Can't you see I am occupied here?"

"Lady Savege's footman insisted I give this to you without delay, milord." He hurried forward, extending an envelope.

Carlyle waved the servant from the room and opened the letter, reaching into his pocket and pulling out a pair of spectacles. "Forgive me, Mr. Yale, but if my—" His eyes widened. He scrabbled with the spectacles and got them hooked over his ears.

"My lord." Wyn bowed, a little dizzy and with a pressing desire to find a blue-eyed lady and kiss her until she admitted every lie she'd ever uttered to him. "I will leave you to your business."

"Good Lord," Carlyle whispered. "You see, sir," he said more forcefully, yanking off his spectacles and jabbing them at the letter. "You are better off without the girl. Troublesome, foolish . . ." He sputtered, but his eyes were watery and he allowed Wyn to take the page from his fingers. Carlyle lowered his brow into his palm. "I told Tracy and Serena that if they brought her to town this would happen. I advised leaving her in Devon where everyone knows her and she cannot throw herself into serious scrapes. Now . . ." He shook his head, his shoulders drooping. "Heedless chit. She'll come to grief upon the road. Then she'll end up just like . . . just like her mother."

Wyn strode for the door. "Not as long as I'm alive."

Chapter 33

"Miss Finch-Freeworth, I have little doubt that you know my purpose in calling upon you today."

The young lady sitting across the tea table from him blinked expressive hazel eyes, cast a quick glance at the maid sitting on the other side of the parlor and shook her head.

Wyn quieted his voice. "You must tell me. Where has Miss Lucas gone this time?"

Again, the silent shake of the head.

Wyn tried to unclench his teeth sufficient to speak. "You do not know, or you will not tell me?"

She dropped her gaze to her lap.

"I know that you were in her confidence before she embarked upon her last journey," he said. "I know all about her last journey, in fact. Everything about it."

Her head snapped up and her eyes widened. "She did not tell me that. She . . . She—"

"She is very fond of withholding truths, but you needn't mimic that inconvenient vice, Miss Finch-Freeworth. Were you with her before she left Lord Savege's house today?"

"Yes," she said hesitantly. "And her maid."

"Tell me where she went, I pray you."

"I cannot," she said upon a hard breath. "I vowed I would tell no one, upon pain of the end of our friendship. And I very much wish to cherish her as my dearest friend for the remainder of my life."

"Madam, forgive me for bluntness, but if you do not divulge to me her whereabouts you may soon no longer have a friend to cherish. The road is dangerous for a gently bred female alone, and I cannot search every Mail Coach that departed London today in order to protect her from that danger, can I? You must tell me which direction she took."

"Mr. Yale, if you know her character as you are suggesting, then you know that wherever she goes, Diantha makes friends. She will find people to help her on this journey. No doubt she already has."

Journey? *Dear God.* He leaned forward and gripped his knees to prevent himself from grabbing the girl and shaking sense into her. "Tell me only her destination, then."

"I cannot. But I can tell you that she did not go unattended."

"Another of your loyal maids?" he ground out.

She had sufficient modesty to blush. "Diantha's own maid from the country arrived in town today. She is a very peculiar woman, really. But she bustled about, muttering about having to wait too long stranded in the country to see how matters proceeded because 'that man' had not sent her a single word in days. I suppose she meant Lord Carlyle. In any case, she knew precisely what was best for Diantha, packing her traveling garments and what have you. So you needn't worry. I believe Mrs. Polley will care for Diantha perfectly well."

For the first time in an hour Wyn could draw more than half a breath. As long as the old girl remained awake, Diantha would be safe. But when Mrs. Polley dropped off to sleep . . .

"Miss Finch-Freeworth, I know not how to further encourage you to share with me Miss Lucas's plan. If harm should come to her, I would not forgive myself."

She shifted uncomfortably. "She said you feel responsible for her, and she doesn't wish you to. That is why she left. She does not want to ruin your life."

God, no. He'd been ten times a fool, mistake after mistake after mistake with her. But he would find her and never make another mistake as long as he lived, so help him God. He would be perfect again, but only for her. Every day, every moment.

"Miss Lucas is a remarkable person, from her kindness to others to her reckless plans . . ." He leaned forward. " . . . to her determination to marry Mr. H."

Miss Finch-Freeworth gaped. "She told you about Mr. H?"

"Yes. But until today I was unaware of a crucial facet of his existence that now I cannot but conclude makes him ineligible for her as a husband."

She drew several long breaths. She was a pretty girl, made prettier still by the gleam of intelligence in her eyes, precisely what he depended upon now.

She nodded decisively. "Yes."

His heart thumped hard. "Yes?"

"Yes, Mr. H is imaginary." She nodded again as though casting off some inner struggle. "Her mother— Do you know about her mother?"

"Some."

"Lady Carlyle was very cruel to Diantha, always telling her she would not attract a husband due to her open spirits and unbiddable nature. She had my friend thoroughly convinced that she was deficient in character and therefore unmarriageable, so much so that when Miss Yarley at the Bailey Academy for Young Ladies—who knows about these matters—tried to assure Diantha she would indeed someday marry a fine man, Diantha laughed at her. Laughed! Then she invented Mr. H."

"She invented him."

"Mr. Yale, you are staring. But you know, Mr. H is really much better than many real men. He has excellent manners and is well dressed but not too fashionable. He possesses a comfortable competence, enough to support a wife and several children, and his house is spacious and nicely furnished though not ostentatious. He drives a well-matched pair, hunts only occasionally, and he likes to read aloud at night by the fire. So he is quite the ideal husband."

Wyn's chest was remarkably tight. He should be convincing her to divulge Diantha's plan, but he could not resist. "How—How does he treat her?"

"He is very gentlemanlike and enormously kind to her. But honestly, I've always thought him something of a dullard, and I think Diantha does too. Also, he is not handsome."

Wyn's brows went up.

She nodded. "You would think if a girl invented a suitor she would make him marvelously handsome, wouldn't you? Mr. H is tall, and he still has all of his hair. But you see, he has this mole problem."

"He has a mole?"

"Rather, moles. Big dark knobby brown ones, all about his neck and a few on his face." She touched a fingertip beside her lips, then by her brow and the side of her nose. Her voice quieted. "You see?"

Throat closed, Wyn could only nod.

"It was her mother who . . ."

He gestured her on.

Her lips were tight but she did not look up now. "Her mother did not only tell her that she was lacking in character." She paused. "She told her—often—that if she were beautiful she might be able to manipulate a man into accepting her, despite her troublesome ways. And . . ."

"And?"

"Every day Lady Carlyle applied a lotion to my friend's skin, as though begrudgingly, suggesting that perhaps it could improve Diantha's appearance sufficient to entrap a man in marriage before he came to know her well enough to avoid such a thing." Her jaw seemed to lock. "Nearly two years ago this pot of lotion emptied, and Diantha asked the housekeeper where she might purchase another. But do you know what? It turned out that Lady Carlyle had made the lotion herself. It was pig fat laced with perfume." Her eyes glistened with tears. "*Grease*, Mr. Yale. Her own *mother* did this to her, because . . . because . . ."

He struggled to steady his breath. "Because she could not control her."

Miss Finch-Freeworth folded her hands in her lap. "Diantha is not a ninnyhammer, Mr. Yale."

"No."

"Mr. H is a code name."

"I understand."

"For her long-held conviction that she will never be good enough for any man to wish to marry her."

"Miss Finch-Freeworth, I do not want to control her." *Never again.* "I want only the best for her. I want everything for her."

Her ginger lashes flickered. "Do you?"

"If Miss Lucas wishes to pursue her journey, I promise not to hinder her. But you must allow me to give her the opportunity to choose otherwise."

She seemed to study him carefully. Then she nodded.

Chapter 34

Peregrine,

I regret that I am occupied with another Matter at present and must unfortunately decline your invitation to dine. However, due to that pressing Matter, I am obliged to address the substance of your message immediately. In short, although grateful for His Majesty's magnanimity, I don't want it. If he and the director truly wish to thank me, I beg of them one thing only: Clemency for a single Act of Villainy that I will shortly commit.

In Service to King & Kingdom,
Raven

Raven,

His Majesty promises Clemency. The director guarantees it.

—Peregrine

P.S. Try not to get yourself killed.

Chapter 35

The Mail Coach to Cardiff via Swindon was more cramped than the vehicles Diantha had ridden in from Manchester to Shrewsbury, and much more rickety. But the London driver—who could by all rights be surly due to traffic and rain—was wonderfully friendly.

Naturally, Mrs. Polley didn't care anything about this as she napped. But the couple sharing the seat with Diantha were full of stories about other journeys they'd taken, with which they regaled her while munching on tasty-looking pies that unfortunately they did not offer to share.

Diantha's stomach rumbled. It was nearly dusk and she'd long since finished the lunch Cook had prepared under duress. None of Serena's servants had been happy about her leaving. But they promised silence until the footman who took her and Mrs. Polley to the Mail Coach inn returned home. Then, if asked, they would tell their master and bear the consequences of it.

She stared at the rain-streaked window, thick sadness in her throat overcoming the hunger in her belly. Despite her vow not to trouble others, she had put Serena and

Alex's servants in a difficult position. Mrs. Polley was a dear to come along, and insisted that she didn't need the position at the abbey, but Diantha suspected that was nonsense too.

She swiped a tear from her cheek. She had purpose now, a new plan with which she could help others without requiring anyone's lives to change for her, and that would take her out of her family's hair for a time. Owen's stories about the horrid accommodations for children at the mines in Monmouthshire had preyed upon her for weeks. With her pin money—which must be a fortune to such children—she could help some of them, especially the sick ones like Owen's sister. When she spent it all, she would return to Glenhaven Hall. Her stepfather had, after all, tolerated her mother for years. He would tolerate a wayward stepdaughter if she promised to be very quiet and good.

Another tear fell and she was quite certain she was lying to herself now. But she saw no other solution.

The coach swerved, tilting violently, and Diantha's shoulder slammed against the woman beside her.

"Good gracious!" The woman clutched her bag.

"What in the devil's going on up there?" her husband demanded.

Mrs. Polley started awake, the other passengers jarring to attention as well. The coach jolted again, and the crack of pistol shot sounded outside. The coach swung to the other side, throwing them against one another anew.

The woman screamed. "Highwaymen!"

Diantha pressed her face to the window. Through the rain obscuring the glass she saw only the dim outline of trees, but the coach was slowing.

"We are to be robbed!" came from behind her.

"Mildred, keep your head about you or we will all be murdered!"

Heart jumping, Diantha patted Mildred's arm and returned Mrs. Polley's worried stare with a shake of her head. Muffled shouts came from above, then from the road ahead. Mildred's bosom rose in preparation for another scream.

"Do not panic," Diantha said in the calmest tone she could muster. "They will want our money and other valuables. If we give them those quickly, they will go away." She didn't know where her words came from. But the others seemed to relax.

Mildred gripped her husband's hand and he said, "Listen to the young lady, dear." The man beside Mrs. Polley nodded. Even Mrs. Polley's round fingers loosened their grip on her bag.

A strange, soft certainty passed through Diantha. This was what she did well. She comforted people. She might be a wretched hash of a lady, a disappointing daughter, and a troublesome sister. But she could give comfort to people that needed comfort, and that was something. It might fill the empty place in her heart, at least a little.

The trouble with that plan, of course, was that her heart was not empty. It was too full, but without the object of her affections with which to share that fullness.

The coach shuddered to a halt. Her stomach clenched. "Remember, don't panic," she said quietly.

The door of the carriage swung open and there stood a man pointing a pistol at them all.

Mildred screamed. Her husband made a choking sound. Mrs. Polley's brow beetled and she crossed her arms with a hearty harrumph.

The highwayman bowed elegantly. Rain pattered on the capes of his black greatcoat and his black hat, and his silvery eyes glimmered.

"Ladies and gentlemen, I have not come for your jewels or billfolds," he said in the most wonderfully deep and menacing voice Diantha had ever heard. His gaze fixed on her. "I only want the girl."

Everything in her smiled—her mouth, her heart, her soul. He offered his hand and she reached for it.

Mildred grabbed her. "You cannot go with him! He will ravish you!"

Mrs. Polley beset Mildred with her bag. "Let a man do his ravishing if he likes."

Diantha tugged free of the woman's grasp, placed her hand in Wyn's, and at his touch everything in her did more than smile; it laughed in joy. He drew her down the steps and a pace away from the carriage into the soft rain. She traced the strong line of his jaw and the beautiful curve of his mouth with her famished gaze then looked into his eyes, and what she saw there turned her knees to jelly.

"You have terrified all those people," she managed to murmur. "One woman fainted."

"She did not." His voice was warm. "I saw her peeking."

"Some ladies admire dangerous villains, I suppose." She tilted up her nose. "I, of course, prefer gentlemen-heroes."

"You have certainly said so."

"All right, I will ask: why have you come when I have made it very clear I did not wish you to?"

"I came to tell you that I have decided to change my name to Highbottom." The corner of his mouth tilted up. "Hinkle Highbottom. It has a fine ring to it, don't you think?"

Diantha sucked in her breath. She was caught. She was rescued. And she was trembling quite uncontrollably. "I—I always have."

He dipped his head and his gaze was wonderful. "Why did you invent him?"

"Because I did not think anyone else would ever have me."

With everyone in the coach looking on, he pulled her to him and kissed her. He kissed her tenderly and then deeply, and she leaned into him and let herself be wrapped in his embrace.

He drew back. "I will have you. Not only that, I will

have you without further foolish delay. I allowed you your way before—"

"No, you did not. You took me to your hideaway and held me there against my will."

A gasp sounded from the carriage.

"I did," he admitted. "But this time, minx, you will do as I wish, without trickery on either of our parts."

She smiled and his gaze went to her cheeks, one then the other. But she had to be clear.

"You know, I am not precisely running away. I am going to Monmouthshire to care for children who work in the mines."

"An admirable goal. But not today's. Today you are riding north with me over the border."

"North? To—To *Scotland?"*

He nodded, his slight smile turning her inside out.

But she frowned. "We will not arrive there in one day."

"We will make stops along the way."

"Does my family know of this plan? It is a plan, isn't it? It isn't simply a quick solution to me escaping you today?"

"They do not. Yes, it is. And, no, it is not, but that last should be obvious after the number of times I have begged your hand."

"My family doesn't *know*?"

"I aim to marry you, Diantha Lucas, whether anybody else approves of it or not. Over the border I need only the sanction of a blacksmith and the insurance of an anvil. And, of course, your consent." He touched her chin and his gaze scanned her face. "Will you give it?"

Disbelieving happiness swept through her. "Yes. Yes. Yes." She flattened her palm upon his chest, the sensation of his heart beating swift and strong lifting hers. "And then what?"

"And then I am taking you to Monmouthshire to save children, if that is what you wish."

She could not speak, only gaze into his beautiful eyes and try to convince herself it was real.

But one thing was certainly real. She glanced at her fellow passengers, then up at the coachman on the box, who seemed remarkably sanguine about having been halted by a gunman. The coach boy appeared to be flipping through a stack of bank notes.

"You won't be in terrible trouble for doing this?"

"I have friends in high places. Very high places. And I intend to tell you all about them as soon as we have a moment's privacy."

"All?"

"Every last sordid detail."

"Sordid? *Really*?"

"Not for the most part." He smiled. "But I know how you like drama on occasion and I wanted this day to be special for you."

"Wyn," she whispered. "I must ask you something."

"Anything, minx."

"Why did you stop drinking spirits after Knighton? It wasn't entirely so you wouldn't touch me, because you did of course, even after that."

"I stopped because I did not want to spend another moment in your company less than thoroughly aware of every detail of you. I wanted to wake up from the nightmare and find you there. I wanted you and I wanted to be worthy of you."

She caught her breath. "I already thought you were worthy."

"And that is one of the many reasons—" He halted and his eyes grew especially silvery, like a stream at midday. "Diantha, I am in love with you. Beyond reason. Beyond anything I have known."

"*Ohh.*"

"I loved you at the abbey. Days before that. And I loved

you even more greatly yesterday morning when you refused me because you believed me unworthy of myself.
I should have told you earlier. I should have told you immediately. I love you."

"Even though I make you insane?"

"Because you make me insane."

She could not manage words. She could not manage to
make her lips cease trembling.

He circled his arm around her waist, drew her to him
and stroked his hand along her cheek. "And you love me."

She released a soft sigh, and Wyn wanted nothing but
to hear her sigh like this in his arms for the remainder of
his days.

"I suppose I shall have to admit to that," she said.

"At your convenience."

"What if my convenience does not come until we have
been married thirty years?" Her dimples peeked out
again. "Can you wait until then?"

"I shan't have to." He tightened his arms about her. "I
shall simply refuse to marry you until you satisfy me in
this."

"That is singularly unchivalric of you."

"I am the villain of this piece, pray recall." He nodded
toward the coach.

"Oh, well." She rolled her blue, blue eyes up and sighed
again, this time with a show of reluctant tolerance. "I suppose I do love you after all."

"You suppose?"

"I suppose." But her cheeks were pink and she ducked
her head and began to fiddle with a button on his coat. "I
suppose I may have loved you since you asked me to dance
on that terrace, actually. I suppose I always dreamed of
you loving me but I never thought love was real until I
could not bear the notion of not spending every day with
you. I suppose I love you more than I ever imagined a
person could love another person, and that love inside fills

me up and bubbles over and makes me want to share it with the world, which is really why I was going to Monmouthshire, because I simply could not contain it and you didn't want it after all."

"Diantha?" He whispered, and there was something in his voice that grabbed at her overflowing heart. She looked up and his face was so handsome, his eyes glittering, but not with cleverness, instead with tears. "I do not deserve you."

"Oh, well, there you are wrong. Because I am quite certain you do. I am very troublesome, you know."

"I have heard that."

"And somewhat wayward."

"Somewhat?"

"And I occasionally invent astoundingly reckless plans."

"Never."

She screwed up her brow. "You cannot mean it."

"Your reckless plan brought you to me."

"I had another plan."

The corner of his mouth tilted up. "What was that?"

"I was going to Monmouthshire because it was the closest I could think to go to the abbey. I thought perhaps from there I could visit you and—well—throw myself upon your doorstep until you agreed to take me in."

"You knew I would."

"I only knew that when I was there I was the happiest I have ever been in my life."

"Happy? You had a surly servant, a limited menu, and an irascible, ill man to care for."

"I had you. All to myself." Beneath his greatcoat she twined her arms about his waist and tucked her face against his chest. "It was like a dream, never mind the evil-smelling well." She couldn't stop smiling. "Will you really abduct me now and carry me across the border to marry me?"

"Yes."

"Perhaps along the way you could ravish me so that I am unfit for any other man? Repeatedly?"

"Yes, although technically that is already taken care of. And most certainly yes."

"Even if I protest, like a proper damsel in distress?"

"Even if you protest, if you wish it."

"You *are* a villain." She went onto her tiptoes and kissed his delicious mouth, and like every time she'd done so, he kissed her back. She whispered, "My one true villain."

Epilogue

Sunshine painted the path along the canal and the hills rising to either side in glorious golds and greens. Sheep dappled the slopes and the breeze blew mild in the valley. A dog galloped toward them and dropped a stick beside the water, and Diantha slipped her hand from Wyn's and ran over to it.

"Silly Ramses. You should bring it all the way to me." She bent to pick up the stick, the grace of her movements stirring Wyn as everything about her always did. He had dreamed once of taking her down in the grass here and making love to her, with only the cloudless sky and birdsong to accompany their pleasure. The servants were on holiday today, and Owen off to the village to practice his new apprenticeship at the smithy.

Wyn watched his wife and his appetite grew. The prospect of fulfilling his dream was looking good.

One matter must be addressed first. He drew the letter from his pocket and snapped open the seal.

Raven,

> *The royal battle has come to its anticipated conclusion and I have had communication from the captain of the Queen's entourage that she wishes your attendance upon her immediately. If you refuse her, His Majesty promises a baronetcy. The director awaits a reply.*
>
> —*Peregrine*

> *P.S. Sparrow bids me convey to you her deepest affection, but between you and me she is furious to have been denied the planning and hosting of your wedding. Beware of a sentimental siren with the intelligence of a man; she is never fully honest.*

Diantha snatched the letter from his grasp.

"From Lord Gray?" She read, her curling locks twining about her wrist and across her eyes. Tenderly Wyn brushed them aside, stealthily reaching for the paper. She whisked it away, reading as she glided along the path ahead. She halted abruptly and turned to him again, her eyes popping wide.

"A baronetcy! You did not tell me about that."

"I was not certain of it until today." He picked up the stick and threw it, Ramses racing after.

"And the queen too. How exciting!" She looked up as he neared. "Which do you want? The queen's retinue and great responsibility, or knighthood and great prestige?"

He seized her about the waist and pulled her against him, plucking the paper from her fingers. "I have but one desire, minx."

Her eyes sparkled. "What is that?"

He released the letter and it floated upon a gust of wind, rising high then dipping and falling into the canal to be carried away by the water. He tightened his arms about her. "This one." He took her mouth beneath his and drank in the intoxicating beauty of her flavor, her scent, and her passion for him. When he drew away, her cheeks were rosy, her lips bruised.

"I have a plan," she murmured, twining her arms about his neck, her dimples deep.

He brushed his lips across hers, feeling her full breasts against his chest, her hips and thighs cradling him, and swiftly assessing the distance to the ground. "You do, hm?"

"This is it: you decline both, and we remain here for the rest of our lives, just humble Mr. and Mrs. Yale and a dog named after a pharaoh. And whoever else comes along, of course."

He kissed her again; he could never kiss her enough. "An excellent plan."

"Really?" Her lips curved into a smile beneath his.

"Yes." He spread his hands on her back. "It suits my wishes entirely. Especially at this moment."

"Why this moment?"

"Because it takes care of that uninteresting business so that we can advance to other matters. You see, I have a plan too." He cupped her behind and drew her against him.

"I *like* your plan." She slipped her hands beneath his waistcoat. "But I didn't know you were in the habit of making plans."

"I am indeed." He set his mouth to the curve of her shoulder. "Many plans." He drew her thigh around his hip, her skirts fluttering in the breeze.

"Show me your plans, Mr. Yale." She leaned into him, her eyes a wonder of desire and love. "And I'll show you mine."

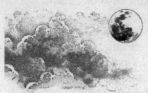

Author's Note

My research for this book took me into the minds and hearts of people dependent or once dependent upon alcohol, and also—as is the case with all my books—into my own life experiences and memories. Theories abound about alcohol dependency today, and an equal abundance of treatments is available. But one fact is certain: detoxification from an alcohol binge can be life threatening. Multiple factors contribute to the severity of an individual's withdrawal symptoms, and the seriousness of these symptoms is not predictable. The laudanum (an opiate) that Wyn used lowered his blood pressure and ultimately saved him. But compared to many, Wyn's detoxification symptoms are mild. Alcohol detoxification should always be undertaken under the supervision of a physician.

For their assistance with my research into alcohol dependency and withdrawal, I thank Marcia Abercrombie, Sarah Avery, Laurie LaBean, Mary Brophy Marcus, and Dr. Ashwan Patkar of the Duke University Medical Center Duke Addictions program, who gave their time and counsel so generously. I thank also those with whom I spoke who prefer to remain anonymous.

My gratitude also goes to Mandakini Dubey for her translation into easily readable Hindi of Wyn's threat to Duncan (which Diantha guessed correctly to be "I will kill you"), to Laura Florand, without whose assistance my foray into chess would be even briefer and not nearly so accurate, and to Gina Lamm and Catherine Gayle for their gracious (and fabulously speedy) research help. Thanks also to wonderful Teresa Kleeman. And big hugs to my sister authoresses of The Ballroom Blog, who make it wildly fun to invent characters that have gardens conveniently packed full of statuary and hedges, and who are in general a great joy to work with.

I offer fulsome thanks to my loving team of manuscript readers, who give their time and care to make my books better (often under outrageous pressures from yours truly); for Marcia Abercrombie, Georgann T. Brophy, Georgie C. Brophy, Dr. Diane Liepzig, and Marquita Valentine I am ever grateful. I also call blessings upon Cathy Maxwell for her kindness and generosity of spirit. To Pam Jaffee, Jessie Edwards, and Meredith Burns of Avon PR I give a grateful shout-out for the wonderfully fun book tour with which I opened my Falcon Club series, as well as to Gail Dubov for yet another gorgeous cover. Many thanks to Esi Sogah, Associate Editor at Avon Books, whose feedback helped me enormously, and always fulsome thanks to my wonderful editor, Lucia Macro.

Special thanks go to my agent, Kimberly Whalen, without whose clear head, keen sense of character and story, and direct approach to publishing I would be at a great loss.

To my husband, Laurent, whose support, love, and encouragement buoy me and give me courage and inspiration, I owe the greatest thanks. I love *all* our dates, not only the ones during which we work out my plots.

Finally, I offer warm, heartfelt thank yous to my readers. Your letters, messages, posts, and tweets, and your visits to me at book events, make writing love stories that much more wonderfully fun. I am grateful for your hearts that are so beautifully and joyfully open to love. I am grateful for you.

For the latest news and gossip about the dashing heroes and daring heroines of my Falcon Club series, I hope you will visit my website at *www.KatharineAshe.com*.

One last literary note: Wyn's feverish reference to purgatory, paradise, and Beatrice is from the *Divine Comedy* of Dante Alighieri. The medieval Florentine poet's love for the unattainable Beatrice was immortalized in his *Purgatorio, Paradiso,* and other poems.

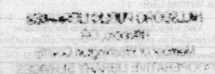

Avail[...] [...]s. [...]to order.